Covidian Tales

Covidian Tales

JOE KANGAU

Book design by Publishing Push

978-1-80541-463-6 (hardback)
978-1-80541-462-9 (paperback)
978-1-80541-464-3 (eBook)

Acknowledgements

There are many people I will be forever grateful to for their encouragement, support and numerous ideas. I am grateful to Smriti, a fantastic lady who out of the blue, one day sent me a text and suggested I should write a book. It was unexpected, so random, so profound, that I seriously began considering it. And thank you to the mystery lady who had some time before, also very randomly, made the same suggestion. And then my sister mentioned it! That's three people who knew nothing of each other all suggesting the same thing. I am glad that they did!

I am also grateful to all my brothers and sisters who were incredibly supportive, especially my two sisters, Cynthia and Sylvia, who persistently lied and told me I was a good writer—until I felt brave enough to work on publishing the book. My father too was a great inspiration, a wonderful man, and my greatest regret is not spending more time with him. He is sorely missed by all.

Many thanks to scores of others for your support and feedback, and to Mark Fay who, after later drafts were complete, provided valuable insights. Some of the stories changed slightly because of his ideas.

Thank you to Fiona (you know who you are) and Albert, Megan and Charlie, who were incredibly supportive. Fiona is one of the few, key individuals whose support enabled the whole project to go ahead.

I would like to acknowledge a lady called Alyssa Matesic. I've never met her, but on my journey learning how to write, among the countless forms of resources and different material I inevitably had to have a look at, technological witchcraft crowbarred her online efforts into my recommended viewings, and I am glad I clicked on it. Her regular content provided a wealth of tips, suggestions and guidance that added to the many other things I had to absorb, and helped in shaping my eventual approach to writing.

Don't tell her though, if she learns of this book, she will immediately faint with horror at my (forced) decision to publish without any professional editing—especially because this is my first book ever!

Lastly, I would like to acknowledge Mr. Adam Patten (and Tracy) for extensive support when we worked together. He had my back and whenever I could, I had his, and the days ground by as we grappled with issues. His invaluable support enabled me to keep going and I sincerely look forward to an opportunity to work with him again in the future.

Preface

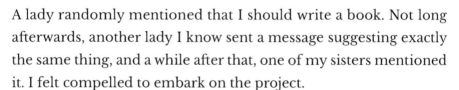

A lady randomly mentioned that I should write a book. Not long afterwards, another lady I know sent a message suggesting exactly the same thing, and a while after that, one of my sisters mentioned it. I felt compelled to embark on the project.

I wrote all eight stories using no assistive software (but with extensive assistance from a useful thesaurus). The title came to me near instantly and seemed the most obvious choice—at the time, most families were cooped up indoors during the COVID-19 lock-down, which was when I earnestly began to work on writing. As my first ever book and an attempt at being an author, it formed and grew upon a very steep learning curve which I am, very humbly, still climbing every day.

I would like to profusely apologize to every wise individual whose good advice I ignored. I found out that after putting in good writing time, a day comes when it appears that you have ironed out the flaws. That's when you hand in your work to a professional who will take one look, ponder jumping out the window, cry out to all the gods asking what past sins invited such torment, sigh in resignation, and then pull up their sleeves, down half a case of energy drinks and bravely attempt to sculpt the cataclysmic train crash you just presented to them into a thing that a human being would willingly, vaguely describe as something resembling a book.

That was the point where I came up against an obstacle! Professionals won't work for free, no matter how much you beg, or offer to clean their car, or offer to mow their lawn every week for the rest of the summer. Considering my entire bank balance consists of a chicken feather, some moths, and an old single sock... and believe me, I offered the entire lot as payment—one editor was tempted... You know, now I think of it, I doubt he was a real editor... his clothes were dirty... and he smelled of alcohol... and he asked if I had any spare change I could give him... But what do I know! I've never hired an editor so I don't know what they look like. Maybe he is the genuine one and all the others are the frauds! I must go and see where he plugs in his computer...

I have digressed a little, haven't I... You see! These are the kinds of things an editor would have spotted!

So, with every human even remotely clued up on the industry clinging to my legs, screaming for me not to do it without professional editing, I dragged them along the ground and grunted my way to a self publishing company (very nice people) and began the process of getting my writings brought to you.

A famous author said that he often begins to write a story and the characters take on a life of their own. They do things he never expected and he goes along with it and allows them to guide events until, eventually, the whole adventure plays out. I understood what he meant when I wrote the last story—Mr. Magatti! The characters insisted on doing their own thing and a new character I hadn't even planned (Marko) made a grand appearance and elbowed himself right into the draft! I didn't mind going along! It was the third easiest of the stories to write.

Nearly everyone who read the initial drafts suggested Alexia Saga, Rachel's Dog, Kiibe's Tales and Mr. Magatti should all have been separate and full books on their own. But the stories all came to me as meant for one book. It shaped what they are. I feared losing the core essence if I tried to separate them.

The most fun section to write was when the three messengers turn up in a field in Moine Together. The scene came to me in a flash and was all typed on to the screen within a few minutes.

The most intense scene for me was when writing Rachel's Dog— when Philip wakes up. Incredibly vivid in my mind, I barely did it justice transforming it into words. Some say I succeeded. I have to be satisfied with that.

The most difficult section was in Kiibe's Tales when I tried to describe what Muume immediately saw after the longest journey to a certain, rocky land.

I enjoyed writing this book—even though on many days, I had to wear a hat filled with ice cubes to cool my brain! It was difficult, it was long but in the end, it was worth it, and I truly hope that you, the reader who chooses to immerse yourself, will forgive any errors or any lack of refinement, and that you will have the sort of experience I intended.

Contents

Tontoii's Entity

He looked again at the big thing in the distance. It was getting bigger. He wondered if he could touch it. Reaching out his little hand, he stretched his tiny fingers towards it. It looked out of place with its dull grey colour and yet soft and fluffy to his innocent gazing eyes. He watched as a flash of light cracked and rippled through it, quickly followed by another, and then jumped when a loud noise drummed a moment later—the sort of noise he heard sometimes when rain was falling. Captivated by the entity, he stared as it appeared to drag its swelling belly towards him, moving without any arms or legs on its body.

The frenzy around him startled the toddler back to reality and he glanced around, nervous and increasingly apprehensive. It was odd seeing so many people scurrying in the dusty streets. He stood still, trying not to get caught in the commotion.

Most days, he played outside with neighbourhood children and they ran around, skipped, jumped, climbed and laughed happily. It was mostly fun for young ones in a world with no burdens, where parents and all the neighbours made sure to look after them.

In his eyes, the grown ups rarely played and almost never ran. They trudged about with a purpose and with never ending errands, sometimes carrying strange bundles and sometimes carrying things that looked like what his mother cut and cooked for him for dinner.

They always appeared busy and always had important things to do, but they kept an eye out and thoughtfully minded the children. He could play and rest and eat and sleep whenever he felt he needed to in mostly safe times where many days were a wonder.

The day looked different because the grown ups were running, many carrying odd things—more things than they usually did—but they sometimes dropped them and oddly, when it happened, they kept on going and did not stop to pick them up. He turned to stare as yet another bag with mystery contents tumbled to the ground and lay sprawled and abandoned. The grown up that dropped it just carried on running with the merest of glances, and with no attempt to stop. The toddler helpfully pointed but the woman took no notice.

Expressions on all faces and the noises they were making made the toddler feel wary and very uneasy. They were not playing; the way they ran did not look like fun. Instinctively, his own expression mirrored their intense looks and he felt the apprehension and the overwhelming panic.

Some children were still outside but parents were rushing to get to them: they scooped them up, held them tight and carried them while running. He stared around, trying to see where they were going. They were running in all directions, some nearly knocking him over, and others scampering away like nothing else mattered.

He turned again to look at the big, giant thing in the distance. The mountain far beyond was broken, and something very big was quickly emerging from it. His head lowered to stare at his bare, dusty feet. A movement had rippled through and gently shook as the warm ground came alive and trembled for a few moments beneath them. In his short life, he had never known the street could do that and wiggling his toes, he marvelled at the sensation. After a while, with the trembling gone, he looked back at the giant thing.

Spellbound by the entity, he tried to understand the texture. Enormous and puffy, it looked soft and fascinating; like a giant, tall ball of ever expanding fluffiness that kept swelling wider and growing even bigger. He watched transfixed, as it got so big, the top reached the clouds and its peak nudged them out of the way. He wondered again if he could touch it. As another flash of light rippled, he reached out his little hand and stretched forward towards it.

The toddler suddenly heard his mother's voice screaming out his name. He looked away long enough to see her running towards him with arms outstretched and a look on her face that, in his short life, he had never seen before. He enjoyed it when she carried him and there was no hesitation to stretch his arms towards her—just as a man ran past almost knocking him over. Stumbling sideways, he regained his balance, raised both arms again and as she picked him up, he pointed at the strange thing to show her.

He wanted to go and play with it. His mother usually stopped to see anything he appeared to like and always played together with him whenever she was not busy. But she did not stop. She held him close and ran towards the house—something she had never done before—and he was mystified by why she also seemed in a hurry. It made him feel uneasy. He clung to her shoulders.

The toddler's mother ran straight back to their house, slammed the door shut behind them and stood staring around in panic. He looked at her face unsure of what she was thinking. She did not look happy and she did not glance towards him to see if he was happy. She was not smiling and did not look like she was having fun. It was not an enjoyable game. It all looked very different. An ominous feeling began to grow with every action.

She ran into the inner room, turned over some furniture, threw down some big cloths and then spilled a lot of water. She placed him in the corner and then pulled a big chair to it, as though building some sort of playful shelter or a fort. She scattered large cloths over the chair and all around the floor and then poured generous amounts of water over them. The toddler watched, perplexed by his mother's strange behaviour and mesmerized by glistening pools spreading right against the wall.

Whenever he dropped some clothes or any garments on the floor, she would pick them up, fold them and carefully put them away. Sometimes, she put them on the long string hanging in the room they all used for sleeping and for dressing, and sometimes, she put them in the big box with all the others. Her soft voice would scold him in a way that he knew that it was where they were meant to go, and though he was yet to learn many of the words she used, he always understood what she was trying to say to him.

His mother and father also changed to look very upset when he spilled any water from any of the containers. The last time he accidentally toppled a freshly filled jug, both of them looked angry and they scolded him so fiercely, he cried for a long time thinking they no longer loved him. His father was not there to see the water being spilled because he carefully dressed up and left every morning. He usually came back just before everywhere went dark—and after the little fire had carefully been placed where it stayed inside the lantern to light up the room.

The toddler always liked it when his father came back home because sometimes he carried a tasty snack or some purple berries and sometimes he reached, with a smile, into his shoulder sack and when his hand came back out, it was holding a new toy. They would all sit together as his parents talked about the day, and they both watched him eat the snack, or play with the new toy. Sometimes he sat on his father's lap and he always felt so comfortable, he would quickly fall asleep.

He worried that his father might scold them when he came back and saw the water spilled over the cloths and on the floor in the corner. But some distance away, beyond the other side of the town, his father and all the people around him, and even those who worked with him, were all also running with fearful faces.

Everywhere in the dusty land, as far as any eye could see, were figures in a stampede; frantically fleeing. One figure was not fleeing with them; a lone man, against the tide, ran the opposite way, consumed by desperation to see his wife and young son.

After using all the water, the toddler's mother knelt in the corner behind the big chair, visibly making an attempt to hide. She made him stand close, facing her, and stared into his eyes. He did not like the look on her face. She was frightened and it made him feel anxious and unsure.

Her eyes were wide and panicked, but a mother's love was plain to see as tears welled up and two torrents flowed down her face. She called his name, stroked his cheek, kissed him on the forehead and then mumbled words and pulled him close, then held him very tightly. With a burst and a stuttering judder, she shuddered in a powerful sob. His bottom lip quivered as he hugged her back and started to cry. He did not understand why his mother was so frightened but he knew well and understood she loved him very deeply.

His father loved him deeply too. Still some distance away, getting closer every moment, he was running as fast as his legs could carry him. His open mouth, rather than shouting in fear, was wildly screaming out their names—even though still too far out for them to hear him.

As they huddled in the corner, a low, rumbling noise became audible outside. It was faint and distant but grew louder and louder, growing rapidly in intensity until it was unbearable. The walls, and then the floor began to shake and tremble. The toddler's mother snatched up handfuls of the wet cloths and covered them both, placing an extra layer over him.

Shivering with sobs, she hugged him and desperately mumbled more words into his ear. She called out his name again then called the name of his father.

The house shook harder. The toddler's mother screamed out. She kissed him on the side of the head and held him closer and tighter.

And then the bad thing came.

It was very, very hot...

And he couldn't even breath...

And peace.

The End

Dreamy Picnic

———∞———

What a fabulous late morning, she was thinking to herself, as she settled on the grass, trying to bury vivid memories of breathlessness and panic. Two years had already gone by since her body ravaged itself in overreaction to the sting from a single wasp. Cathy glanced around again before immersing into the moment to enjoy the deliciously dreamy and breezy day.

They were going to spend some rare time alone with each other and they eagerly decided on an outdoor picnic. With her mother looking after the two children and the baby, there was no need to worry about how long they stayed out. Fond memories lingered from childhood days and Cathy knew why her children loved their grandmother so much. It was easy to luxuriate and indulge in the moment knowing they were safe and happy spending time with their granny. Feeling happier and more in love than she could ever remember, she leaned back on her elbows and stared into the distance.

As a first time visitor to the sprawling, sunny corner of the English Regional County, the field was much larger than she had imagined, stretching out far beyond into rolling wild plain densely covered with meadow grass and bristling with life. Oak, Birch and clumps of tall, dark green conifer trees towered in the landscape— like a dreamy, snazzy, incurably sentimental goddess, knowing

Cathy would be visiting, had gone about placing them where they would look just right.

She gazed at the endless, rolling swathes of wild grass, her eyes darting instinctively to clumps of bright colours where the sight of wild flowers ominously stoked her unease. Flowers attracted wasps! She hoped there would be no wasps. Knowing they had to be there she prayed they would stay away from her. Squashing down stirrings of fear and panic, she perked up, determined to enjoy the dreamy afternoon.

Sitting up a little higher, Cathy looked over to her left. In the distance, the land sloped upwards and peaked, before abruptly disappearing over a green hill. As if plucked out of a nostalgic, childhood, story book, a small yellow cottage sat half way up the incline with light smoke drifting from a white-topped chimney. She stared for a long while wondering who lived there and if hovering in the fireplace was a simmering, midday meal.

She had always wanted a fireplace; often daydreaming of the ambience and romance of a soft, crackling fire. Fond memories surfaced of visiting her grandparents back when she was a little girl still only in kindergarten. They would all huddle near the crackling, flickering, soft glow late in the evening, drinking freshly made lemonade and prattling animatedly about places they visited, and where they would all like to go and visit the following day.

Admiring the cottage on the hill, Cathy cast a silent promise that when the new wood flooring for the hallway was complete, she would casually toss in the suggestion of a fireplace. There was an absolute, perfect spot for it in the sitting room along the east facing wall where there was no window. Even the exterior would be enhanced by a chimney snaking up and rising majestically above the clay tiled roof. She closed her eyes and plunged into the romance of it all.

Looking over to the right after emerging from the reverie, Cathy admired the scenery, as the land sloped gently downwards for nearly a mile. In the distance, she could see the quaint village where her aunt lived, and the ancient trees of the small forest covering the land beyond it. She exhaled slightly, mildly stunned by the beauty. There were cottages, historic structures, a stone church and a market, all beautifully maintained by the loyal, homely villagers. The market was thriving and from her vantage point, she could see the tamed, frantic and purposeful jostling, as miniature figures snapped up myriads of mystery wares.

She scanned around again just to be sure there were no wasps and then leaned back, ran a hand through her light brown hair and soaked in the deliciously prickly, late morning sun rays. The weather had held and the sky remained mostly bright blue with the occasional stray cloud in a slow-motion frolic. Cathy stared at one of them and followed its leisurely trajectory across the vast, blue expanse. Gathering up its stray edges, it slowly formed, and then held, the vaguely distinct, hunched shape of a hedgehog. She watched as it went on to gradually transform into the cloudy inter-pretation of a hovering horse's head.

She wondered where the small cloud was drifting on along to and then stared, mystified by where all clouds went. Lost and carried away by the thought, she grew more curious about the lofty horse's head as it somnolently glided to a mystery destination. How far would it go? Maybe they drifted on, way up high and circled the whole world to appear again from the other side. She giggled to herself at the zany, silliness of the thought. The beautiful day was to blame. She tended to do that when laid back and happy and today was exceptionally, lusciously dreamy.

After scanning around once more to be sure there were no wasps, Cathy wished the horse's head a safe journey and happy adventures. Giggling inwardly, and after yet another glance around to check for wasps, she looked down at the soft, bright green coloured mat they had laid out on the grass to set their food and to sit on. Only the fourth time they had used it, she suddenly wished they used it more. Vowing to make time for more picnics in the future, she made another silent promise to have one every month. They could bring the children next time—she was sure they would love it! And once in a while, they could invite other family and friends. Cathy made up her mind: they would have monthly picnics as a family with the children and occasional romantic ones together as a couple!

She looked down at the traditional, hand woven basket they had eagerly packed with food for the day. Proud in the middle of the mat, it sat enticing and brimming, filled with delicacies and condiments infused with passion. They had settled on making snacks with fresh ingredients and apart from small mishaps, the food prepared mostly turned out close to perfection. The bread they baked the night before was rich, soft and fluffy, the sweet potato crisps they fried were crispy and savoury and the avocado dip they made was seasoned just right. Even the home-made marmalade, flavoured with fresh purple berries had churned, then set and turned out sublime.

Suddenly wishing they had brought the children, she smiled nostalgically then giggled to herself while imagining their deliriously entranced expressions at the sight of the rolling, vibrant scenery. She thought of them gleefully chasing each other all across the open fields, then glaring animatedly and pointing, sparkly eyed, at the painstakingly prepared, home-made food.

They would have played all day long and inquisitively gone exploring in the waving clumps of trees. They would have picked brushy bunches of colourful flowers and asked for crayons and some paper to draw the yellow cottage. They would have gnawed hungrily on fresh banana scones and stuck fingers in the marmalade—even though she asked them not to. And they would have found a toad. They always found a toad. Whenever they spent time outdoors, they would find a toad and catch it, then merrily run to mummy and daddy to show off the pretty "toadie".

She giggled to herself again, sighed contentedly, and then leaned back, wallowing in the soothing magic of the wonderful, glorious day. Only one thing could ruin it! Wasps! The scoundrels! She prayed none would be nearby. They would ruin the afternoon. Allergic to their stings and though she did not fear the pain, Cathy could remember frantic breathlessness and panic of three days and nights spent very unwell in hospital. The mere thought was petrifying! She reached for her bag again to check on the allergy pen.

She looked across at Patch and he gave the smile that always melted her heart. They met in final teenage years and were each others first love. His real name was Colin, but a conspicuous birth mark around his right eye drew jesting comments from childhood friends about a real, living eye patch and myths of pirates. At some point—nobody could really remember when—the name "Patch" floated about, was adopted by everyone, and endured as he grew older into present day life.

Colin never minded the nick-name. All who knew him liked it. And Cathy always liked it too—the default in introductions with new acquaintances. With friends, workmates and family also calling him Patch, it was difficult to think of him by any other name.

Patch enjoyed studying Industrial Engineering at university and rather than a salaried job after graduation, decided to work on a machine of his own design. Cathy stepped up, toiling at two jobs to support them, instinctively feeling it would all work out. After four years of effort and increasingly large debts, the day came when he popped open a bottle of champagne and, sizzling with excitement, announced his creation was finally completed.

Turning down offers to buy the rights to his machine, Patch decided to borrow more and start his own business. Cathy openly struggled to understand the decision but, trusting him once again, she offered her full support. The following months were tough times, rendered more arduous by an unexpected pregnancy with their very first child. A few weeks after giving birth, she went back to the two jobs to help with supporting him and their new baby boy.

Patch borrowed even more for a fledgling workshop. Cathy marvelled at his fierce attention to detail as he crafted an array of bright, creative visuals, artistic logos, unique, branded symbols and giant signs ordered up to hung aloft in businesses. She gazed in astonishment at stunning printed graphics splashed on company vehicles and emblazoned on race cars, and she dressed to look the part and accompany him to meetings where eager suits enquired about billboards for premises. His younger brother and Cathy's sister joined in to help and as more orders rolled in, he employed three staff to handle an avalanche of work.

Physical orders for the machine trickled in from around the world. He could build a reliable, compact version and despatch it half assembled, along with the components, to any eager buyers within weeks of request. The company steadily grew and more people were taken on to help with new premises and the ever swelling workload.

Staring in relief and in gleeful vindication, she had watched, five years later, shortly after Christmas, when he made the final payment to clear off their debts.

It was the first debt free summer since the risky venture began.

They had recently employed three more staff at the workshop—making a total of eleven—and Cathy was enjoying spending time with the children while helping part time with administering the company.

It felt good to be in full control of one's destiny.

She stretched out her arm and gently touched his hand. He smiled in his usual way and squeezed her fingers. Enjoying every moment of the quiet, romantic day, she wished it would go on and never come to an end. After scanning around once again for wandering wasps, she reached into the basket, then carefully removed and laid out all the food. Cutting off two slices of the soft, home-made bread, she began making him a sandwich, with a generous dollop of the home-made marmalade.

She was lovingly engrossed in spreading the chunky jelly to each corner of the slice when the eerie, powdery buzzing droned close to her left ear. From the corner of her eye, Cathy saw the large wasp as it swooped in a half spiral and landed on the mat. It startled her and made her jump. She gasped and woke up. It was the same, detailed dream for six nights in a row about their last picnic together.

In real life on the day, Patch had quickly leaned over and flicked the wasp away to save her. Robbed of re-living that treasured, special moment, for the sixth time, her dream had been cruelly interrupted. With eyes half open, she glanced lethargically at the chic, chrome alarm clock on the bedside cabinet. The bright orange numbers lit up 4:22am. Stirring slowly in the bed, she lazily stretched her legs, took a deep breath and slowly let her eyelids close again.

Moments of bliss lingered as her head sank back into the sensuously soft, cotton, feather stuffed pillows. Her mind floated back from the day out in the grassy fields and drifted to the real world until she was fully awake. Her legs and belly tightened. Reality kicked in and the crushing pain returned.

On the way back home from the picnic, Cathy had decided to drive while Patch sat in the passenger seat, talking with childlike enthusiasm about buying a house in the village. She mostly liked the idea of it but she also liked where they lived. Immense effort had gone into decorating all the rooms and planting the new garden and the thought of abandoning it was very unappealing. The children would also be upset to leave it all behind, especially with three new trees planted—one for each of them. An impossible decision to attempt in that moment, they settled on making it his task to convince her.

They were less than a mile from home when a car jumped a red light and collided into the passenger side where he was sitting. Cathy was shaken about but not seriously injured.

Patch's funeral was today.

The End

Winston away

---◦∞◦---

Life Unease

Winston's jaw dropped. Wide eyed and dumbfounded, he stood, staring in disbelief, unable to comprehend the reality before him. With eyes glued to the screen of his small, second hand television, the rest of the world slunk away from existence.

Nearly a minute went by before he blinked, regained his senses and re-emerged into the middle of his cramped bedsit; a meagre, one room living space containing all his worldly belongings, located in the brown, concrete outskirts of South London. There was a bed on one side and a kitchenette a few feet away—whose space was nearly all taken by the well used microwave—and a clunky old fridge that had lived there forever, or probably as long as the chunky, 70's style sink.

The small, boxy television perched precariously on a miniature, cheap, second hand, self assembly stand that, for lack of any room, stood next to the creaky wardrobe, solemnly leaning against the wall opposite the bed. There was no room for solid chairs; two foldable stand-ins were stored away in the corner in a one-foot gap between the wardrobe and the end of the room. A dining area was also not an option in the bedsit—in four healthy strides, Winston could cover the entire length of the space that, for more than eight years, he had called his home.

He had jumped up from the bed, where he sat to have his meagre dinner and knocked over the microwave meal in the process. With no space for a table, a small, foldable, wooden one made do for all occasions, seeing frequent use in times involving plates and cutlery. He had only just begun to eat his budget chicken dinner which at that moment, lay scattered across the cheaply carpeted floor. The small foldable table lay lonely, on its side, with one leg partly detached from the factory installed fastening.

Earlier that day after the end of his shift, Winston had sat in the changing room buried deep in thought. A standard factory worker, he was tasked with packing away wrapped, fresh chocolates as they trundled out on a belt in final stages of production.

One of a group of six, huddled together, frantically working the section, he had to grab chocolates and lay them into pre-sized boxes, over and over again as the relentless belt spat them out. It had to be done quickly and they had to fit just right; any delays and the whole line could shudder to a creaking halt. After carefully but hastily folding over the marked lids, he sent each box further along to where another zealous worker taped it down, spun it in the ballet dance of moving cargo, and skilfully slid it to a shorter, running belt for stacking.

Sometimes the roles changed and he was one of two workers stacking newly sealed boxes on to pre-sized pallets. He would lay them out neatly, four lengthways and four widthways and then start on a second row, following the counter-layout pattern, stacked tight on top of the other until they were twelve rows high. He was careful to maintain a staggered, neatly packed layout—like an accomplished bricklayer artistically laying out a wall—or the whole thing would topple before he was half way done. The neat stack was snugly wrapped in a tough, plastic film and then wheeled away to be loaded up ready for road transport and as quick as it was gone, a new empty, specialized pallet would appear out of thin air, so he could start the stacking process all over again.

It was physical, monotonous work and though he did not dislike it, he did not enjoy spending so many days there. The wages for the job were enough to cover most bills and to buy food to keep him going for a handful of days. With not much left over after settling monthly payments, Winston had become adept at hunting for bargains. What little there was could be stretched a little further by shopping cheap and having a meal only when he needed to. Most days, in his pockets, was a light blue handkerchief, a rarely used, cheap phone and nothing else apart from dry dusty fluff that lodged there.

Sitting on a bench in the air-conditioned changing room at work, Winston stared into space, pondering his existence. Massaging his temples and then drumming his fingers on his knees, questions about his purpose plagued his weary mind. Nothing in his life seemed to make sense anymore.

More worldly questions stoked his worry and unease; like coping if his monthly rent happened to go up, or if the factory he was working in was suddenly closed down. A raw, unsettled sense of dread haunted his senses, making ordinary objects appear menacing and spiteful—like sentient decoys sent to draw a sense of calm before a lurking force let loose a tumultuous storm.

A way out eluded him and he stumbled on, day by day, spending all his monthly wages barely covering all the bills. No light shone in the end of his menial job tunnel and good things scampered away from any part of his future. For the first time in memory, Winston felt an overwhelming, profound lack of meaning—an experience so new, he possessed no memory or the mentally acquired tools to navigate and cope with it. His pulse and breathing quickened and he was oddly mixed headed—like the wiring in is brain was tangled and shorting out. Shaky and unsteady, he struggled to remain upright as the room and everything in it began to tilt and tremble.

Winston was experiencing his first ever panic attack.

Winston frequently dreamed of seeking out a better job but hirers were doubtful of the value of his skills; an uncanny knack for quick repairs and an analytical mind were apparently, not convincing in his situation. Employers were infatuated with institutional skills. They loved applications gushing recognitions of talents. They wanted documents dripping with guided expertise and formal wads of fancy paper saying you can do big things. Without sought after records and the paper shaped gold dust, ingrained opinions cast doubts, questioning his talents. Lacking embossed papers to unlock worthwhile doors, Winston had to live with what confidence could get him—and that wasn't very much.

He occasionally allowed himself to wallow in alluring dreams of money to equip, open and run his own workshop, or enough to be a big-time, lone-wolf inventor quietly tinkering away at unseen contraptions. Ground down by reality and shift work for a meagre wage, all thoughts of bravely setting out to be his own boss lingered as fantasy.

Guiding Nuggets

Over three decades had gone by since Winston was four years old, when his neglectful, abusive and unpredictable mother unexpectedly and violently took her own life, leaving him on his own with his two year old sister with whom he shared one room in the two bedroom apartment. He never learned what substance his mother decided to swallow, or what parts of herself she sliced with a box cutter blade. Five days went by before a concerned neighbour, incensed by her absence and the overwhelming smell, finally raised the alarm and called in the authorities.

When police turned up and broke down the front door, they found the two emaciated, hopelessly frightened children cowering under the unkempt, charity donated bunk bed, and their mother's decomposing body lying in her bedroom sending putrefying vapours leeching out into the property.

Too frightened and apprehensive to knock on his mother's bedroom door, four year old Winston had crept in to the kitchen each day when his sister complained she was hungry. Using a small, wooden chair to climb on to for elevation, he mixed up two small bowls of cereal with tap water, added extra sugar for taste and then crept back to his wide eyed and fearful, little sibling. His sister hadn't liked it, but he sang to her softly while she scooped up each watery, well sweetened, soggy bite. The only songs he knew were from television programmes, but they worked and she usually ate every last spoonful, even though he sang softly, deathly afraid that he might wake their mother. It was always much safer when his mother was asleep; she was unpredictable and vicious when up and stomping about, making a terrifying existence for two little children.

After their mother's suicide, they went to live with their violent, unstable, alcohol and drug addicted father, who suddenly disappeared without a trace one year later, leaving Winston and his little sister abandoned and homeless when he was five years old and she was barely only three.

With no relatives capable or willing to adopt them, they were taken into care and separated from each other. He never saw her again, but many long years later, someone said that she might have been placed with a couple who lived in London at the time of the adoption, but had later moved to Canada and decided to settle there. No additional useful details were forthcoming and though he desperately wanted to, Winston lacked the resources with which to mount a search.

As the only other being he had ever felt close to, Winston frequently thought of his sister, often pausing to wistfully stare into nothing as his mind scampered away back to the days he had cared for her—when they both clung edgily on—trapped in a hazy void of pain and juvenile hope, and after wading in memories, his mind tumbled forward to nearer days when she was older, ever curious about how she was and whether she even remembered him. And when his mind emerged, blinking, back into his own world, it would make a sincere promise to one day set out to look for and find her— if only he could make the time and afford to pay the travel.

As a child, he never knew what it felt like to be loved, or to have any stability or to live in a caring family. Many like him grew up to be violent individuals and Winston was prime for fast-tracking to a similar fate. Intervention took the form of a local shopkeeper; friendly with all people, he unwittingly became a much needed role model, acting as the beacon that kept Winston tethered with an endless flow-spring of calming advice. A much welcomed source of true sympathy and guidance, he stood in as a lightening rod, helping to keep teenage Winston well grounded.

In later years, Winston chose a quieter, less aggressive life, but the demons of his past had dug in, commandeering his existence and dictating every life path. Callous to all turmoil, the demons made a one-way pact with no clause to relinquish their stranglehold on a being. Rejecting every plea to leave, they burrowed in and hunkered down, cementing themselves as co-authors of his fate.

Unable to maintain or nurture any close relationships, he settled on plain kindness to all he encountered—a fruitful approach to daily functions and manoeuvres that kept each day ticking uneventfully by. The easy, friendly atmosphere, the calm, wandering eyes and relaxed conversations with no confrontation made him popular with colleagues and a valued member of the team. If pressed, they would describe him as pleasant and helpful and a genuine human being who wished every creature well.

Winston had secretly fallen head over heels in love, even though the object of his affection had no knowledge of it. Residing two streets away from where he rented the bedsit, every once in a while, he would bump into her shopping at the local town market, and twice only—he vividly remembered both occasions—walking down the high street in opposite directions.

The first time he saw her, he was leaning forward, reaching for a multi-pack of crinkly crisps—a well deserved treat the following day after payday—when he turned to glance ever so casually, to the right.

The medium sized store he was scouring for groceries in faded into greyness and went from the universe. His hand, barely an inch from the flavoured, fried snacks, hovered motionless, with all craving immediately abandoned, as lifeless and still as his momentarily silenced heart.

Maybe it was the way she stood, or her long yellow skirt, or the sleeveless blouse screaming sleek style and feminine class. She bludgeoned and massaged his visual senses with her aura and every movement, even the way she raised her palm to brush aside a hair with her little finger, wrenched his gaze sideways, and focussed it on to her brown, bottomless, dainty eyes.

He was mesmerized! And in her peripheral vision, she saw him, but she carried on, angelic, browsing through invisible knick-knacks. Non-discerning eyes would be convinced she didn't mind. People who looked like her tend to be accustomed to the stares.

She turned and smiled in a way portraying only politeness, and the mouth from a realm made entirely out of heavens twinned with burgundy coated, tender lips to voice the words "Good afternoon".

Four infernal seconds screamed by before his mind would work and she had almost moved along before he voiced a strained reply which, when it emerged, sounded too polite and formal—and crackled as though coming from a short-wave radio.

She smiled again while walking away—gliding like a seraph—leaving Winston feeling a great mountain squelching down his aching heart. Every time since then and far rarer than he prayed for, he said hello to her, and with a sweet smile, she would raise her hand in a girly wave and say hello back.

Gathering just about sufficient courage to tame his nerves, he spoke to her a few times, and though it was not for very long, and nothing much came out of it, he discovered, among other things—and to his great astonishment—that she had been living alone and single for eight months. She walked out on her husband of only six months after catching him with her cousin—a curvy, intense, naturally pretty twenty-five year old—who lived in a mortgaged flat on the other side of the borough.

It turned out the affair was a year and a half long and he had gone through with their wedding while seeing the other woman. Her cousin, unbelievably, attended the ceremony, but thankfully—and Winston cringed at the mere thought—she had narrowly missed being picked as one of the four bridesmaids.

While speaking of the incident, Winston was taken aback by the rage in her eyes that reminded him of the saying about a woman who was scorned. But in genuine sympathy and a torrent of blind love, he made it well known that he was firmly on her side: and besides, such angelic souls rarely sought vengeance.

Later in the evening, remembering her lips, and the tender way she reached up to adjust her hair, he struggled to imagine betraying such a woman. What a tiny-minded fool her ex husband must be! The utter raving lunatic! The half-brained idiot! Winston shook his head in frustration at the false luck and misplaced, deceptive fortune of some people. Despondently, he sighed and slowly let his head hang, inconsolably disillusioned with his own unhappy life.

Barely able to afford feeding and housing himself, let alone attempt to date her, he abandoned all notions of a romantic escapade and with aching, restrained sorrow, fought the urge to ask her out: how would he buy the new clothes to go and spend time with her! How would he pay for the transport, or the tickets, or the meals!

How would he settle with the barber so his hair was presentable! And he still owned the same pair of shoes for ten months; the soles looked like a race car had worn them on the track!

Wishing he had a better job, and drifting into fantasies about his dream workshop, he indulged in a make-believe world of what could have been and wallowed in thoughts of great credence and splendour. Then he would have pursued her to the ends of the earth. Then he would possess the unwavering boldness to march up, face her, look into her eyes and speak of his desires with open intention. At the age of thirty seven, Winston was single, hopelessly broke and living on his own with his whole world stashed into one tiny bedsit. As each day trudged uneventfully past, he could think of no way of getting himself out of it.

Reflective Jump

Sitting in the changing room pondering his life, he finally reached down, removed his steel-toed work boots and slipped on his ten month old, worn down walking shoes. Having maxed out on the weekly overtime limit—only ten hours permitted—and while the rest of the group stayed, he alone was going home at the end of the standard shift. After some procrastination, he stood up off the bench, put on his usual shirt and vest, and then leaned into his locker to pull out the cheap jacket.

Standing still and staring at the garment for a long while, he slowly raised his left arm and pushed it into the sleeve. He paused for a moment, engrossed in thought, then swung the jacket and slowly pushed his right hand into the other sleeve. Pulling it over his shoulders, he shrugged for adjustment; it fit about the same as always for all the days of wearing, since ten months before when acquired brand new from the same shop, at the same time he bought his trusty walking shoes. The ends of the sleeves were discernibly fraying and every edge, more so the material around the collar, was noticeably faded and softened with use. But it did the job well and would have to keep going. He could not afford a new one for a long while yet.

Standing still for some moments, he wondered how many times he had gone through those precise and predictable motions and for how many more years he was stuck with the routine. Was this what was called life? Was this destined to be his life? Did everyone else love their jobs, making him the odd one out? They seemed to scuttle about on daily chores like they were precious, but for him, nothing felt right or held true any more.

Something about the day was inexplicably out of phase. Every encounter seemed scripted; the simplest, most common tasks occurred as though inside a dream with every object poised like a disguised imposter. His eyes slowly and deliberately scanned around the room, hoping to catch a stray item out of place or unawares, wanting to spot a partly hidden, divine sign or a clue to the fiendish plans fate was cunningly brewing for him.

After a few moments, he reached up, adjusted the collar, and ran flattened palms on the jacket to even out the creases. With one swift movement, he swung an arm to shut the locker then turned to look in the large mirror a few feet away on the opposite wall across the room.

All appeared to be normal no matter how long he stared. He looked down at the cheap, well laundered trousers and his gaze lowered to the tired, leather walking shoes. With sombre reflection and a sprinkling of self pity, his gaze shifted higher to the lightly creased jacket and after lingering, shifted higher still to the resigned eyes. The mirror image paused, bold and tall, obediently staring back and they both stood silent with blunted expressions, gazing blankly at each other... until his reflection flinched—or at least he thought it did.

Jumping half out of his skin, Winston turned to run away. His reflection duly copied him, except in the opposite direction—in exactly the same way a real reflection should do. He closed his eyes, shook his head and paused before reopening them. Glancing back towards the creased jacket in the mirror, he took a breath then raised his gaze to the weary, squinting eyes. Poised, halfway turned in the aborted flee towards the door, he faced the mirror again and took a small, tentative step forward. The image in the mirror faithfully copied every move.

He stopped, blinked hard, shook his head and then turned away. It was a reflection after all. What else could it possibly be! Alone in the changing room, he was beginning to spook himself. He started to step away then turned for one last look to check his jacket, shirt and trousers were tidy and respectable.

Satisfied they looked fine, he reached into his left pocket and lifted out his metal framed, laminated, clocking card. He stared, wondering how many times he had used it. It was the same routine, just like any other day. Nothing looked amiss or out of place and nothing looked wrong and yet somehow, all day, everything felt different.

A few days earlier, Winston was strolling on his way home after the 2 till 10pm shift. In one pocket was the usual, cotton, light blue handkerchief and in the other was his trusty, bargain, under-used phone. There was nothing else inside but the stitching and the fibres and the mystery, dusty fluff that keeps pocket contents company.

Trudging along, he wondered what to eat when he got home. There were three, basic, frozen meals nestling in the freezer and half a loaf of wholemeal bread left from the day before. That food would have to last the whole week, until payday, and he had already lined up some bargains for stocking up. Maybe just the bread would have to do for that night and the frozen meals could be saved and rationed for later. He wished he had some money to buy a little milk or butter, or some cooking oil, and maybe even a small jar of pickled eggs. That would be a glorious luxury he hadn't enjoyed for a while. Eggs or butter rarely made an appearance in his bedsit.

A little after ten-thirty as he ambled along, all alone on one side of the mostly deserted street, a glint on the ground near the wall of a building flashed for a brief, near inconsequential instant, catching the corner of his bored, unstimulated eye. Instinctively stopping to stoop low and investigate, he leaned to get closer, and the object transformed into a shiny £2 coin.

To penniless Winston, this was close to manna from heaven. He snatched it up and breathed a small thank you to the gods of luck—and a silent prayer of sympathy for the person who had lost it. His mind began racing, scanning through a mental shopping list. Butter? Or milk? Or two, cheap, frozen, ready meals; the chicken curry one and a tasty, savoury cheesy pasta one? The cheesy pasta meal was bigger and generous for the price. How about a bag of purple berries with surprising portions? The berries were his favourite and he hadn't had them for weeks!

With a new sparkle brightening his tired, weary eyes, every stride grew longer and the steps sprung higher. His walking pace hastened and his chin tilted upwards, pulled by the allure of a cheese topped concoction. Hurtling along the nearly deserted walkway, the two item shopping list jostled in his mind. He would soon reach the 24hr store he always walked past on his way going to work and again when coming back home. As he turned left after racing to the end of the street, the familiar lit up logo appeared, jutting out from the wall in the usual conspicuous spot a short distance away.

Maybe more bread? Or eggs? But eggs needed cooking oil or at least a little butter... no wait! Unless you boiled them! It was simple and fuss-free! He could just boil the eggs and have them in between the bread, sliced up, spread across in a sandwich with a little salt... even without butter, they should still taste good enough. He wondered if somewhere in the cupboard lurked some pepper. His belly began rumbling. Unconsciously, he licked his lips. The stride stretched longer and the steps bounced higher.

Approaching the store, with his pace grown nearly to a jog, something strange and profoundly unusual diverted his gaze. The sign that always stood outside, rod straight and upright, teetered halfway in the process of toppling over: tilted and leaning, with one corner unintentionally propped up against the full height, shop window. A rogue gust of wind, or maybe some errant yob, had likely made the mostly failed attempt to knock it off balance. The sign defied the action and wisely perched itself at a halfway angle between standing and falling.

It was odd, bewildering and fascinating to look at, as though the frame had reached to steady itself against the window and defiantly placed the other hand upon its narrow hip, mocking the unsuccessful effort to tip it on to its side.

It seemed a freak occurrence, inexplicable and unlikely—the equivalent of tossing a coin which flipped and landed on its edge; a slapstick sight that made you want to stand and watch and take running bets on which way the sign was going to go down. It awkwardly stayed there, not standing and not falling, teetering in a spellbinding, anti-gravity balancing act. He paused for a few moments, mesmerized by the show, curious as to how nature would solve the anomaly.

Only three or so steps from the sliding door entrance and squinting thoughtfully at the angled advertisement, he wondered about its logo and the visual significance. The three foot high, portable, heavy base, lottery sign that always stood outside and lonely near the entrance to the store, appeared to be calling to all inquisitive eyes and in that precise moment, Winston made up his mind. Walking in and up to the counter, he asked for a ticket and after a little hesitation, handed over the £2 coin. Back outside, he made sure to carefully straighten the sign before making his way home, with the ticket safely tucked away inside his jacket pocket.

An hour later in his bedsit, after a shower and some pondering, he settled down to enjoy only the plain bread for dinner, saving the three frozen meals for the following three days.

Sparkling Sequence

Two days later, at home after the jump-scare with the mirror in the changing room, Winston had heated one of the last two frozen meals and settled with the portable table to enjoy his dinner. As he glanced at the chicken and sauce strewn across the carpet, the wasted meal and creamy mess were insignificant issues. His gaze returned to the television, eyes wide and heart pounding, entranced by the spectacle beaming into the room. After a few moments, the screen fell into darkness before lighting up again to show a cheery commercial.

A stunning young woman who was clearly an actress, was pretending to be in what was meant to be her real home. Her hair was swishing and her dress flowed enchantingly, and in between springy, energetic, girly twirls and seductively playful, slight angling of her head, she flashed a wide toothy smile—dazzling and alluring— aimed at the camera for everyone watching to see.

Her eyes twinkled as she flawlessly began to utter what, to any discerning ear, were carefully scripted words. Her entire beauty, from head to toe—the narrative made it seem—came by using the brand of toothpaste on the screen; and didn't you know, you could easily acquire it too... but only if you dedicated your custom and loyalty! You could go to any store now and buy the same brand and if you faithfully used it, for just enough times, and if you brushed just right and never used any another, then you, would in no time, look equally as gorgeous and your hair and wide smile would glow just as brightly.

Winston was no longer listening. Trembling on his feet, eyes still firmly on the screen, his mind was dragged to a fantastical dream world. Reality transformed into a lighter existence; a domain so divergent from his mediocre grind, that he may as well have teleported to another galaxy.

The delightful, smiling woman with the sparkling teeth was sliding gracefully to a climactic finishing pose and with maximum flirtation and the widest, toothy grin, gushing straight at the camera from a flawless face, she swooped behind a padded chair, softly caressed its chic headrest and then skipped on while playfully swishing her hair.

Winston missed the entire performance. Holding up the ticket, trying to steady both his shaking hands, he strained to stay focussed and to see all the numbers. Time stalled while he stared, allowing each printed digit to lay claim to itself and cement its position in the row on the pink paper. Shaky digit by digit, he hoped and verified, painstakingly studying to confirm the full sequence. The sparkly tooth model sprung daintily to the climax as Winston saw the last number trembling in his wary hands.

Every ear in the neighbourhood, on the walkways or milling about winding up the evening activities in their cosy homes heard the mighty bellow roaring into the night sky. Beyond the thin walls and through the small open window thundered rapturous waves of unhindered celebration.

As the sparkly toothed model floated into her final pose, Winston came to terms with the item in his fingers—the valid and the sole winning ticket for the lottery, granting him the full jackpot of £6.5 million!

The End

Alexia saga

———✦———

Chapter one

A lexia stood in front of the full length bathroom mirror and nodded imperceptibly while inspecting herself. She almost liked the way she looked. Regular exercise and dieting were tedious and grinding but the near flawless result softened the pain of all the effort. She smiled slightly at the faint hint of muscle nestled tautly on either side of her almost perfect belly button. Everything looked good enough — though there was always more to do. It was not easy, but strong will to put in the work persisted.

Flicking back her long, natural, dark brown hair, she spent a few moments scrutinising the rest of her body. Satisfied there was no flab, she pulled back the splash screen and stepped into the bath where the shower was already running.

Shuddering ecstatically from the stinging sensation as jets of hot water streamed on to her skin, she closed her eyes and spent precious time savouring the moment: it was one of little joys in life never to take for granted. After soaping, scrubbing and rinsing, she reached for the pink razor to begin shaving her legs.

Lathering generously once again, she reached down and begun drawing the razor in long strokes gliding over the skin. After some years, the ritual had become second nature and with the hand no longer requiring conscious guidance, instinct took over with an effortless ease.

Her mind wandered as thoughts about her new car crept into it. It was love at first sight when she saw the little motor, standing lonely but proud, parked at a convenient angle in an open and conspicuous corner at the dealers. The creamy, off white colour, the shiny silver alloy wheels, the matching logo front grill and classy, subtly grey interior were so delightfully cute, she could barely stop her face deliriously lighting up with glee. It took all of her willpower not to giggle in excitement when, with a chirpy bleep that came from everywhere inside the car, the interior powered up and a built-in, visual display embedded next to the steering wheel, sprung to life with a cascade of minimalist graphics and then coyly flashed and spoke a warm, friendly, cheery greeting.

She tried, but failed miserably, to pretend she wasn't interested. The dealer was merciless. The easiest of sales, he charged near full ticket price. Having just about saved up for a deposit, the little motor would be arriving, brand new, in seven days. It was a small car, but then she lived alone in her brother's first floor apartment in South East England, and didn't really want or need a big car yet.

Straying away from the car, her mind toyed with a diet slimmers swore conjured wizardry, before filing a mental note to acquire the ingredients by the end of the following day. With a blender and food chopper already stashed in the kitchen, it would be an easy start with lots of fun preparation. Then her mind found itself nudging issues of work as it set about pondering an ongoing problem.

As the razor glided up the inside of her right thigh, a thought crashed through the images, startling her and making her unguided hand slip. She cursed softly as a red colour swelled up and bubbled out, then tumbled in a crimson trickle making its way down her leg. Running some water over it, she winced at the sight of a clean, diagonal cut, nearly an inch long, tainting her unmarked skin. She prayed it would not scar, but it would have to wait for a while. Snatching the towel, she stepped out and hastily dried herself whilst half running out, first to apply a peel-plaster over the seeping, fresh wound and then to get to the faux-oak bookshelf, half stocked and standing against the wall in the sitting room.

Grasping at the section reserved only for sciences, Alexia frantically snatched up one book after another. One by one, she flipped through the sizeable volumes, stacking each one on the floor until only four books remained standing on the shelf. With clenched teeth, she fought the urge to scream in frustration.

Reaching out, she grabbed a hard covered, Engineering book. Excitement grew with each detailed, glossy, printed page as "Component Theory" sections laid out their applications. Furrowing her brow at the technical jargon, she tried to remember the odd name she was looking for.

"Barry on!" she commanded, while reaching out to pick up her browsing device before remembering she always left the voice command feature off after an embarrassing incident a few days earlier. Grabbing the device, she pushed the standby button and waited for the dark screen to flicker into life.

Growing more frantic, she browsed through searches until a new word leapt from one of the articles describing complexities of plasma particle stream mechanics. Her eyes greedily gobbled up the twelve page section. There were useful attachments and links to information and Alexia tapped on the device with growing excitement.

"YEEEESSS!!!" she screamed while clapping her hands so close to her mouth, that her fingers fanned and lightly brushed the broad, toothy grin.

A droning noise in the background began to grow louder and became more vivid, drawing Alexia's attention to the phone that was buzzing. Her workmate, Kevin's picture was flashing on the screen. She quickly triple-tapped to answer and his real face appeared but instead of speaking, his smile contorted into a curious expression and he turned to look away. Puzzled, Alexia leaned forward and squinted in curiosity.

"Hi. You okay?"

Kevin did not turn back to the screen. "I think so," crackled out the sheepish reply. "But I'm guessing you're definitely not on your way to work."

She gasped and dropped the phone. She had completely forgotten she was still mostly naked. Searching around for something suitable to wrap up in, she found the discarded towel, crumpled in a crescent shaped heap in the hallway.

Kevin was still waiting when she got back and his face lit up in a wide, cheeky and exaggerated smile.

"Now that's a great outfit!" he humorously declared. "I have one just like it! But mine is not as clean." He shrugged. "Maybe a little bit skimpy for work though?"

She was about to cut back with a stinging reply when he raised and thrust the palm of his hand to the camera.

"But stop!" he commanded. "Stay exactly as you are! You must! I insist... No! Infact... I'm begging! I'll warn everyone you're dressed a little different today!"

Alexia burst into a chuckle. "Oh pardon me, sir!" she scoffed in mock vexation. "What if I add on a necklace, and a pair of high heels?"

Kevin swooned away backwards, slid down the chair and disappeared from view as he pretended to faint. A moment later, his face reappeared from the right. "You'd proper be a murderer!" He gestured towards the office. "Every man over here will have a proper serious heart attack! And that includes me! Are you trying to murder us!?"

Alexia's head snapped back and Kevin smiled as high pitched, musical laughter rang out from his speakers.

When she was able to speak again, Alexia leaned closer and pointed into the camera. "Don't you dare even think of telling anybody what you saw!"

Kevin made a zip gesture across tightly sealed lips and held a flat, open palm pressed over his heart.

Alexia glanced at the sharp edged, dull-blue numbers of the virtual clock hovering next to a painting on her living room wall. Her eyes and mouth flew open in a drawn out gasp; four hours had flown by since she left the shower! The entire morning had all vanished away in an instant!

Alexia made no attempt to go to work on that day — there was far too much to do. Kevin covered for her by telling everyone she was unwell and the hours were spent immersed in studying and research. Some books on her shelf contained lengthy, useful chapters but a trip to the library was necessary to get more.

After three more days buried in reams of information, she sighed deeply, leaned back and nervously surveyed the scattered sheets of A4 paper, generous pile of borrowed books and the used coffee mug resting solemnly on a coaster. It would take more than another day to polish up a short draft setting what she had in mind into a presentation.

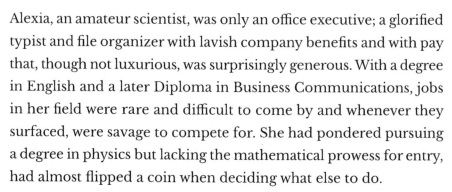

Alexia, an amateur scientist, was only an office executive; a glorified typist and file organizer with lavish company benefits and with pay that, though not luxurious, was surprisingly generous. With a degree in English and a later Diploma in Business Communications, jobs in her field were rare and difficult to come by and whenever they surfaced, were savage to compete for. She had pondered pursuing a degree in physics but lacking the mathematical prowess for entry, had almost flipped a coin when deciding what else to do.

Oscar, her older and over protective brother, repeatedly urged and cajoled her to pack her things, rent out the flat and go to work with him in Spain. Frantically keeping afloat a moderate, eight-room hotel which he had the great fortune to own outright, fourteen hour work days were frequent as the entrepreneur. After recently launching a small catering business as an upcoming venture and a gig on the side, his workload teetered on the verge of unbearable and spurred on a yearning for someone he could trust. It was early days but trade was growing and he gently encouraged her to relocate and work with him so they could nurture them as a family business.

Regular phone calls fed a therapeutic desire after losing both parents and their fourteen year old sister, when the small six-seater plane they were travelling to Scotland in came down in stormy weather in the north of the country.

"I miss Tayleen so much!" Alexia pined over the phone. "And mum and dad... we really did have the best parents ever!" She cleared her throat and paused to allow her choking voice to settle. "I wonder how she would have been as a nineteen year old? What do you think she would have been like? Can you believe it's already five years, just next week!"

Oscar backed up every word and as frequently occurred unplanned in many of their phone calls, they spent the best of half an hour wishing and reminiscing.

Alexia was close to deciding to relocate when she heard about an office job at the facility. If she could just get her foot in — she reasoned zealously — there was every possibility of eventually transferring to a technical role, and with fifty minutes commuting time, she wanted it badly enough to beat and to outmanoeuvre all other applicants.

From the very first day when she walked into the building with head held high and flashing a beaming smile, Alexia relished the moment and tumbled into the culture. On the cutting edge of science, the gadgets and the gizmos created were so new, that some of them had not been officially named yet. She marvelled at bizarre materials so freshly invented, that scientists still used temporary nick-names like "Soft-metallium", "Stretch-bandy" or "Unbreaka-thread", to avoid using the lengthy scientific denotations.

Not being a full scientist made it trickier to grapple with technical aspects of the work, but she thrived among colleagues and found herself the proud owner of a gradually growing collection of advanced books, keenly acquired to help feed her long time hobby.

Alexia felt that everyone was friendly and endearing and though she was fair skinned and described by most as magnetic and attractive, two other girls, Olivia and Jessica, were physically more stunning. Olivia, a mixed race, mid-twenties, mid-height, painfully stylish example of popular modern culture, had curly, natural, light brown hair, impossibly clear features and a lean, subtle posture borne of countless gym visits.

Jessica's captivating and overtly innocent look stared out from under unrealistically impeccable, dyed brown hair, through pale-green, sparkly eyes that gazed with fascination at anything and anybody they happened to stray on to. With tailored, girly dresses and a supply of classy shoes, a glowing, silky energy shimmered, powering a high-pitched, musical laugh that erupted into the office at the slightest provocation.

Jessica, currently single, was an object of obsession for the men in the office and all around the facility. Falling over each other to carry out errands and favours for her, they scuttled about, bound by invisible strings. In one incident, when she mumbled about a migraine and wished for some water to take pain relievers, Alexia watched with envy as three men within earshot shot off, each in a race to be the first to fetch it for her. Sweet and polite as she was, Jessica diplomatically accepted all three glasses and drank from each over an hour and a half which, astonishingly, kept all three men happy.

And there was another time when four men who happened to be in the vicinity, wrestled one another in the printing corner when Jessica's softly sweet, sing-song, girly voice mellifluously announced that the "awful machine" was being all rotten to her. After tinkering and puzzled-finger stabbing of buttons, the men eventually coaxed it into churning out copies and then boisterously celebrated the supposedly mighty feat for which, in a tidal wave of testosterone, each one separately claimed the full credit, as though they alone had offered up the gifted solution. Alexia watched with barely concealed disgust as Jessica unwittingly spurred on the tidal wave by chirping out the most sickeningly sweet and girly "Theeenkyouuuuuu!" she had ever heard.

Alexia was careful never to allow her concealed exasperation over Olivia and Jessica to become openly known. In ever covert effort to compete with the two girls, she plunged into diets and exercise regimes and indulged in pampering skin and beauty treatments.

Walking back in to work with the presentation tucked away in a narrow, leather holder held firmly under her arm, Alexia felt more stunning and confident than ever. Hours had been well spent preparing not just the papers, but carefully pampering and preening to perfection. Everyone glanced as she strode along with chin held high and all the men stared even though some pretended not to. She thought she caught a brief flash of jealousy on Olivia's face but couldn't tell for sure because she was pretending not to look.

Fighting back a looming, smug smile of satisfaction, she walked to Kevin's work space, pulled up a chair and deftly sat next to him.

"I have to show you something!" She leaned forward and gently placed the precious holder onto his desk.

Kevin stared for a moment before reaching to pick it up and after another glance at her enthusiastic expression, carefully began to peruse its contents.

His eyes eventually widened and his expression changed to one of unrestrained astonishment. "Do you know what this could mean?" He flipped back a few pages. "This is super unreal stuff! Do you know if it will work? I mean, it looks like it proper will but I'm not an expert."

"I don't see why not!" Alexia said with certainty. "The concept holds up. And we have great backup." She gestured candidly towards the facility.

"You have to take it to them!" Kevin was insistent. "Take it to Bernard! I bet he's proper going to love it!"

"I was thinking the same," she immediately agreed. "Melissa will just shoot me down!"

Kevin nodded, and then glanced around to be sure Melissa was not in the room.

"You should have heard some stuff she said about you." he whispered conspiratorially. "She likes you even less as each day goes by."

"Does she like me at all?"

"Phhrr! As if! Like a turd in soup! It's like it's all your fault she couldn't get a job in the labs. I don't blame her. She's stuck managing us lowly office types."

"What will she make of this?" Alexia wondered out aloud.

"We both know the answer to that." Kevin answered simply. "You're about to show her up. You don't even actually have formal qualifications and you've come up with something that might save the company! She's going to strangle you... or run you over with her car! If I were you, I wouldn't go anywhere near the car park."

Alexia chuckled then glanced around to see where Melissa was. She was nowhere in the room.

"Go straight to Bernard, I'll back you up." Kevin encouraged. "Melissa might not hand it in. She might pretend she forgot then kill it first opportunity."

Alexia nodded eagerly.

"So this is why you were undressed?" Kevin asked with feigned calmness.

"Shut up!" Alexia's mouth flew open. "Somebody's going to hear you!" She slapped him sharply on the side of his arm.

"Ouch!" he winced mockingly. "So this is what you've been up to for five days, huh? I'm proper impressed! And they proper will be too." He stabbed his thumb towards the management offices.

Alexia tilted her head and flashed a wide, girly smile.

"By the way," Kevin added "I was totally at your place with you day before yesterday and we had a cup of tea and..." he paused "Wait, what even is your actual house number?"

"You forgot?"

"You've never told me."

"Huh... it's thirty three."

"Ah! It's a good thing nobody asked; would have been very awkward! So I had a chocolate muffin and five chocolate biscuits. You told me you were feeling better and you thought there's a good chance you would be coming in today."

Alexia smiled sweetly. "Thanks for covering for me! You're absolutely the awesomest!" She cast her eyes upwards, held up an index finger and pretended to make a vastly important mental note. "Muffins and biscuits. Okay. After work, I'll go and stock up... you know... just in case anybody comes over to check."

He appreciated the humour. "That's *chocolate* muffins and *chocolate* biscuits, I'll have you know!" Then he sighed and shrugged his shoulders. "But when you hand this in, they'll proper know I lied for you. You better tell them I knew about it but had been sworn to secrecy."

Alexia smiled. "Whatever do you mean?" she asked with an exaggerated expression. "Have we met before? I don't even know your name!"

She scooped up the holder, stood up, whirled around and with a last glance to be sure Melissa was nowhere in sight, deftly began to make her way towards the main office. Kevin vigorously signed a mock hangman's noose at her, teasing out more chuckling as she gleefully skipped away.

Chapter two

She always thought Bernard would have suited a different name; in Alexia's mind, he looked more like a 'Jason'. Tall, athletic, focussed, and with jet black hair, she had never seen him wear anything but a dark coloured suit. As the knowledgeable head of all on-site operations, his plush office was the last one at the end of a long corridor above the main wing of the assembling facility. She never considered him particularly handsome — nobody she knew did. But a palpable presence cascaded into consciousness and followed wherever his purposeful strides marched. Radiating an inexplicably tangible aura, and calmness that held when all else was faltering, a cosmic confidence flowed so profound he seemed privy to boundless secrets of the universe. Whenever he was nearby, her eyes disobeyed orders to look away from him. She slyly watched the other girls and knew they all felt the same.

Never known to smile, he was still friendly and approachable, making unquestioned time for anyone grappling with unyielding circumstances. Advice to "go ask Bernard" was frequently bounced around between all levels of staff at the facility. A never-ending wellspring of stockpiled mastery, everyone with tough problems went to him for answers. Alexia often wondered how one brain could hold so much, but then Bernard was a genuine, certified genius with boundless curiosity and an endless thirst for learning.

He was also, to a great fault, too dedicated to his work, eventually driving his wife to take their young son and move away to live with her parents in another part of the country. A raging workaholic, he was an unwitting member of a club of the breed who, possessed with endless passion and a natural born talent, spend far too many hours in service to their calling.

His wife had eventually grown tired of the absences and the long lonely evenings bringing up their baby alone. Friends were no substitution for her missing partner and when the ultimatum was reluctantly handed down, he was unwilling to forgo his thriving career. With heavy hearts all round and endless rivers of tears, she made the painful decision, packed up her belongings and finally moved away back with her family.

Alexia knocked on the office door then pushed down the brass handle to open it slightly and peek her head in. He was sat at his desk, leaning back in the designer chair, deep in what was clearly an important conversation on the landline phone pressed firmly to his ear. He looked up and motioned for her to come in and to have a seat. Shutting the door behind her, she walked across the large office and gingerly settled into one of two padded grey with copper frame chairs placed across from him.

Having been there twice before, she was stunned by how taste-fully decorated the space was. With a mix of bizarre styles among rich earthy browns and vibrant, warm greys, there was uniqueness of class and a depth of honest quality, tethered to reality by a down to earth, deliberate and quirky professionalism.

The wall to the left was panelled in genuine mahogany, two thirds of which lay behind well stocked book shelves that stood far enough away that Alexia was barely able to make out the titles on the vertical stems. A handful of the book colours looked vaguely familiar and two were physics books she thought she already owned. The rest were a population of whispers and curiosity she had no doubt Bernard had personally perused.

Beyond the shelf along the same span of pristine wall was an oak door she knew led in to the plush bathroom and as Bernard rocked in his chair, consumed by the phone call, she fought the urge to run over and have a quick peek.

Looking over to the right — to avoid gazing into his eyes — she could see a wider space dedicated to technology. Mostly done in a light, subtly rich, grey colour, it was teeming with gadgets and models of equipment and machines inventors in the facility had created. Mesmerized by the objects, half of which she had never seen, it took all of her willpower to wrestle down the urge to go over and touch and examine every one of them. Great efforts had gone into showing every piece in elaborate displays, each creatively mounted on machined metal plinths, or suspended in mid-air, using impossibly thin, grey strands of unbreaka-thread attached with non-existent fastenings, straight to the ceiling.

She squinted at a shoe box sized contraption she had never seen anywhere else in the building and fought the urge to walk over to investigate it. With several sharp ridges jutting out along its upper surface and three large protrusions along the side she could see, she pondered its function and why it was worthy of dangling impressively in a prominent position in the mini hall of fame.

Stealing a glance at Bernard, she admired the cheekbones and the way his mouth moved, before averting her gaze to inspect more of his domain. Her roving eyes drifted enviously across the room, stopping entirely, to hover and admire a magnificently thriving weeping fig in a purposed alcove only a few feet away behind his left shoulder. Another inch or so and the peaks of its vibrant, cascading foliage would be brushing the ceiling. She stared at the clay pot it felt so at home in and tried to resist getting up to walk over and run her fingers on the hand-carved patterns; they invoked memories of pottery classes in school. Making a mental note to start shopping for houseplants, she glanced again at Bernard and decided to ask him for recommendations — anything to start a more personal conversation.

Trying to keep her eyes occupied, they wandered once again, from one wall to another and then back to the gadgets. Allowing herself to sink further into the chair, she began feeling more relaxed than she knew she ought to be.

Bernard momentarily glanced from the phone call and pointed to a glass bowl of fresh purple berries standing on one side of the large, carbon fibre and mahogany desk. With a quick motion during another pause in speaking, he indicated she could have as many as she liked. Smiling politely, she grabbed a generous handful then sat back and absently popped one into her mouth.

A cool blast of tangy sweetness bathed her tongue and she popped two more into her mouth in quick succession. Bernard clearly did not scrimp on the cost of his fruit; they were superior in quality to any she could remember. Biting down on yet another, she made a mental note to stop and buy some on the way home at the end of the day.

As she sat, silent, waiting in the calmness of the office, her mind began to wander. There were recent suspicions that he may be attracted to her. Kevin frequently joked of it but she couldn't know for sure and Bernard gave no signs to reveal that he was. If he had, it might have worked; he was currently the only man she would consider dating and came close to the fantasy of a man she could marry.

Her eyes glazed over as her mind floated away leaving her body unattended in the cosy office chair. She was strolling down a dusky, lit up high street, with classy signs, strategic lights, and a warm breeze even though it was winter, and polite smiles with distant eyes from other coupled amblers and a warm, thrilling touch, with his firm hand grasping hers. Then they were pulling up to park in the compound of their lavish home, and she heard fine gravel stones crunching underfoot as they strolled from the car together, after a long day at work, a sideways glance, a flirty smile and a tender arm around the waist and her tired head tilting to find his solid shoulder. Then she was in the kitchen pouring two glasses of wine as he reached to touch her hair mumbling softly about her beauty.

The journey her mind abandoned her and sailed away to felt pleasant and real and insouciantly exciting, but in every image visualized, he was wearing a suit. Having never seen him away from work or out of the facility, there were no clues of his fashion sense or of his personal life. She began to wonder if he preferred boxers or briefs and what sort of casual clothes he picked to wear outside of work. Did he own a pair of jeans? Did he ever un-tuck his shirt? Did he always wear leather shoes and an expensive looking tie? And what did he sleep in? Pyjamas or a t-shirt?

Her face flushed red as she suddenly re-emerged into a room that was eerily and dubiously quiet. Bernard, long finished, was staring with a mildly bemused expression.

"Um... I... I've been working on something," she quickly blurted out, entirely forgetting the rehearsed presentation.

He nodded politely, sat back, and then eloquently invited her to go ahead and speak.

Her face grew warmer and if he had turned off the lights, she was certain her cheeks would have glowed in the dark. Her treacherous brain ran off, dragging confidence and knowledge with it and her body, wracked with nerves and a sudden bout of shyness, forgot its lean muscles and turned into jelly.

Each arm and leg, in a fevered panic, disobeyed all orders and as she began to elaborate, oddly gestured by themselves. Fumbling and stuttering through the "great idea", she haphazardly outlined most of what she had in mind. His undeviating gaze left her flushed and flustered and she mumbled and stumbled, forgot several things, got one detail wrong and then spoke for far too long about others.

When Alexia was done, Bernard stared for a few moments, carrying the expression of a man puzzling over a very rare and valuable gem he had just discovered was lurking hidden inside a badly wrapped package. He appeared to be waiting for something. After a short while, he glanced down towards the leather holder and expressively, with genuine politeness, cleared his throat.

"Maybe I better take a look at that?" he candidly suggested.

She kicked herself inwardly. She had completely forgotten the information that took so much effort to gather. Quickly handing it over, her attempt at confidence appeared convincing. "I've been working very hard on it for five days straight!" The declaration, when she spoke it, sounded more like a report.

For some following minutes, the only sounds in the office were the dull, persistent humming of an invisible air conditioner and occasional slurping sound of paper as he flipped through the pages.

After reading for a while and without looking up, his crystalline, composed tenor resonated over the desk. "By the way I see it, it appears you do your best work while so unwell that you could barely get out of bed."

Alexia thought her face was going to self ignite. Shuffling and squirming uncomfortably in the chair, she was aware that he had worked out the deception, and even worse, that Kevin had lied to cover for her.

"I... I'm sorry! It's... When I... It was me. I made him promise not to tell anybody. I needed... to get it done ..." Her words trailed off for fear of worsening the moment.

Bernard said nothing and mercifully, kept his eyes lowered and fixed on to the pages in the holder, magnanimously aiding in easing her discomfort.

"What does Melissa think of this? Shouldn't she have brought it to me?" he enquired after some more moments of reading.

"She doesn't really... um... I came straight to you."

"I see." Bernard said simply, then after a short pause, "I really would prefer all employees get along — and that includes with managers. I'll have a word with her."

The look of sheer panic that descended on Alexia's face prompted him to raise a palm.

"Calm down," he reassured her. "I'm on your side too. Nobody's in any sort of trouble. If anything, you might be very pleased with what I'll say to her. She might be too. It's how I like to run things. But you both must commit to trying harder to get along."

"It's not me! It's never... I don't really have any problems! It's always from her!" Alexia blurted out in defence far too quickly before immediately regretting it. It was never a good idea to say bad things about your boss to their superior. "I do really like her," she tried retracting her words. "Maybe it's because I'd prefer working in the labs but I'm not officially qualified. Maybe she thinks I don't really want to work with her."

From his expression, Bernard was well aware the words were an attempt at covering for the situation. Remaining diplomatic, he appeared to appreciate the effort.

In the end, all was forgiven. Clearly impressed, he picked up the phone, called an immediate halt to all non-essential operations and requested that everyone attend an urgent meeting. Swiftly closing and then sliding the holder back across to her, he stood up, buttoned his jacket, deftly walked around the desk and motioned for Alexia to follow.

"Time to sharpen up Alexia!" he snapped authoritatively. His face and the tenor had increased in urgency. "You're about to make a presentation to the scientists and to most of the attending engineers in the facility!" One look at the alarmed expression on her face prompted him to reach over and place a comforting hand on her shoulder. "Okay, I'll do the talking. How about you come over and stand right next to me, just so they see the mind that came up with this?" He paused and tilted his head ever so slightly. "And by the way I see it, you should try not to wander into any more daydreams that will make you blush."

Her head dropped and she buried her face into her hands.

She was no qualified scientist. An enthusiastic amateur, Alexia was biding time as an office assistant who had seen the core of the facility once on the day of her introductory induction and once more when tasked with personally delivering a machined thermal casing to the head of engineering. She searched for opportunities to help in other sections but the core was controlled as a sterile working area. Scientists and researchers were cleared for access and high level trained cleaners looked after the hygiene. Untrained staff and facility non-scientists like Alexia were rarely allowed unsupervised in the laboratories.

The raving project; a multi-hundred million, state of the art, plasma flow conversion engine, peaked at more than twice the thrust of large jet engines. Nearly twenty percent smaller, with lower mechanical maintenance and far lower fuel costs, excitement had peaked among talk of catapulting the aerospace industry into the future.

Many nations were plugged into the high-stakes venture, giving technical, financial and physical assistance and several were keen to inject resources for a piece of the valuable, futuristic pie. Dignitaries and heads of state were personally involved and notable names adorned the guest list for launch test day.

Alexia's knowledge of sections she had never seen consisted of information gleaned off reports she printed, forwarded, documented, stored, filed, made copies of or bound into folders. More came the way of brief, live training sessions and nuggets picked up doing tasks in the facility. She pored over, mesmerized by technical aspects, while printing specification sheets for engineers.

Irresistibly drawn to a well known problem with a vital aspect of the newly designed engine, Alexia mentally wrestled and pondered a solution. A daily talking point for the engineers and scientists, a formidable obstacle was holding up the work setting the entire programme back by a decade: the state of the art, plasma stream regulator module quickly faltered when tasked with directing consistent flow for the core of the brand new engine to operate. Dismayed with each test, tense engineers watched the system destroy itself shortly after start-up, as peaks and subtle troughs in the directed plasma stream led to low, and then too quickly, to excess flow, fatally overwhelming stability components.

Unable to calibrate for variation in output, the frustrated engineers tinkered with adjustments. The plasma stream flow would not run within tolerance without highly strung, specialized installations. Frantic meetings and brain-storming marathons ruled out all solutions; the added expense would force the final price and the size of the engine beyond anything economically or financially viable.

The solution detonated like a firework in Alexia's mind when daydreaming in the shower while shaving her legs. In the rising peaks of uncontrolled variation, the excess plasma could mechanically be shaved off and siphoned away from downstream components. It was similar — or so her mind had thought in the moment — to the simple way she solved sprouting bristles on her legs. She didn't try to find a way to stop the hair growing; allowing it to happen, she simply reached down with her trusty pink razor to sever off the growth and keep it under control.

Having heard of a little known marine experiment on the other side of the world, Alexia remembered a gizmo inside the equipment protecting all vital sensors in the core. After carefully reading up on technical details, she had tried to figure out how it spun out sorcery to save all the widgets and hidden machinery from extreme exposure and certain cremation. The concept was adaptable as fitting in an air filter — or so she decided — and the facility was filled with capable specialists.

As the scientists and engineers gathered for the meeting, Alexia stood facing them, with an optimistic attempt at looking calm and dignified. After confirming attendance, Bernard began by thanking her and passing on full credit for the proposed idea. Flawless and meticulous, his crystalline tenor then outlined her concept to the attentive audience.

Loud applause spontaneously erupted at the end. Astonished by the simplicity of the solution, the gathered teams surged forward to congratulate her. Everything blurred into wide smiles, handshakes, soft pats on the shoulder and loud, unheard questions that Bernard tried to answer for her.

Many enquired how she had come upon the idea and she stumbled endlessly at the limits of her knowledge. Everybody chimed in and helped to fill in the gaps. Going away from the meeting, Alexia found herself propelled into celebrity status within the facility.

For many weeks afterwards, top scientists personally came to her desk to request or deliver documents and schematics — a transparent strategy; they rarely, if ever, had done such a thing before. Bypassing long established facility couriers, the visits were open excuses for encounters.

"Jeez!" Kevin exclaimed in awe and envy after the head of laser research walked away from Alexia's desk. "They all proper just want to hang out with you! Miss big celebrity... Miss princess Alexia! Hey, I want ten percent of your bonus! Remember, don't you? I helped to cover for you." He paused. "Or just buy me a case of beers."

Alexia smiled sweetly and wallowed in the moment. She would gladly buy him even twenty cases of the finest beer! On a far lower salary than qualified scientists, the management had offered twelve months extra pay, tax free, in one lump sum, as reward for her major contribution to the project.

"Oh dear God!" Kevin suddenly whispered with urgency before turning to walk away. "Here comes another one!"

He whirled around and hurried off as the deputy head of laboratories strode into the office and walked straight towards Alexia.

She didn't mind in the least — it was helping her career; considering she intended to transfer to laboratories.

Every once in while, random scientists and engineers would meander to her desk to unfurl their blueprints and draft plans of projects they were working or engrossed in, or were tasked with manifesting into reality. Most sought her opinion — fresh eyes for inspiration — and the rest bore questions on lingering setbacks.

"You know the biting teeth part of a standard can opener that clamps and grips tightly on to the edge of the can?" she enquired of one engineer, who paused and nodded thoughtfully, with only a vague idea of exactly what she had in mind. "Couldn't you build a larger one that clamps across this way?" She ran her finger along the troublesome casing in the plans. "It could clamp on to this edge and then let go when it needs to. With that little space it's the only thing I can think of."

His eyes and face faltered and then lit up so dramatically, she chuckled and basked in his adoring gaze. He wasn't going to build a can opener mechanism; the suggestion had nudged his mind into a better idea.

"She's an utter gem!" she heard him openly declare to Bernard as they passed one another when he stepped on to the corridor.

Bernard turned to look at where she sat immersed in schematics, then nodded stiffly and waved a single palm in acknowledgement. Melissa, who had just walked into the room cast a cold glance, then carried on walking to her office.

Chapter three

On the day of the launch test, Alexia's name was well known as the amateur scientist who had saved the plasma engine. She had laboured, unsuccessfully, to obtain a pass for Kevin, who had all along been desperate to attend the event. Nine heads of state from other nations were in attendance and even though everyone remained polite and formal, the atmosphere was positive and charged with optimism.

Alexia stood stiffly by, mesmerized by the ceremony and infinitely grateful that Bernard was by her side. She smiled warmly and shook hands with officials, several heads of state and eventually, with the Prime Minister and his entire entourage. Out of her depth and prised out of her comfort zone, she struggled to string together words for conversation.

Bernard did the talking and the formal introductions. She had not needed to ask him; one glance and her distressed expression reached out — and he duly obliged. A natural with officials and with diplomatic etiquette, he never once forgot her and was skilful at including her in all parts of the process. Every once in a while she would glance upwards into his eyes, radiating intense gratitude from her own and each time, he responded with a subtle, reassuring nod, aiding to partly alleviate her unease.

"You're doing great!" he remarked at exactly the right moment when she needed to hear it. "You're a natural at this! By the way I see it, I might as well have taken the day off!"

Too nervous for laughter, her lips parted in half a grin. Bernard reached over and softly squeezed her shoulder.

"You really are doing great!" he said with sincerity.

She decided to believe him.

After the flurry of greetings, polite conversations, many congratulations and a myriad of ritualistic diplomatic formalities, everybody was seated in the designated area two hundred metres from the large demonstration plane. Twelve hundred officials from across the world had arrived and together with the scientists, the world's press and journalists from selected and related enthusiast media, the event was to be witnessed by nearly three thousand.

Alexia sat among them, three rows into the crowd and behind the Prime Minister, who was sat on the front row with other heads of state. Bernard was confidently settled by her side, and around them were management, along with a gathering of scientists and engineers who had drawn lots to settle which lucky ones would attend. Everywhere else was a collection of officials, civil servants, professionals and appointed representatives, many of whom had travelled thousands of miles to be there. Twenty university students sat near the rear, on the verge of self igniting with pent up excitement: having won in national essay writing competitions, they were a mishmash of diversity and the keenest of the keen.

The plasma engine was mounted into the body of the plane which ordinarily, carried four jet engines on the wings. The standard engines still hung solidly from their mountings and were newly re-conditioned and fully operational. The plane was scheduled to taxi slowly up and down the runway using the four standard engines for the first two runs, then engage the plasma drive to show and test the raw power along with six stages of throttle response.

The lone plasma engine, at ninety percent thrust, would be mightier than all four jet engines combined and could propel the plane with ease in the second part of the test while the other four engines remained fully powered down.

When the moment was finally called, the four jet engines flawlessly fired up drawing premature cheers and heightening the excitement. Tensions were high but the mood was airy and light as every eye and every camera was focussed on the craft. A new wave in aviation history was unfolding and everyone present appeared humbled by the honour.

After the first run up and down using the four engines, the large plane gracefully trundled a u-turn then lined up once more at the beginning of the runway. The engines were smoothly powered down to full idle and the giant plane stood hissing on minimum power. A few tense moments ticked painfully by before a sixty second countdown cautiously commenced and the process was initiated to start up the plasma drive.

Eight minutes ground by as perspiring technicians tenderly coaxed the complex system into life until finally, a wave of gasps erupted from the crowd as the pulsating whooping and low whistling shriek of the plasma engine carried across and rapidly grew louder. The pale greenish, yellow gush of high speed molecules became faintly visible, even in daylight, spewing from the grey-lined flow assembly outlets.

Frantic commotion broke out over the viewing area. Cameras beeped and whirred as every capable device was pointed to capture the incredible scene. Everyone began to shake hands with all around them and excited chatter rose above the howl of the engine.

Heads of state were smiling because the event would change history. Scientists had bigger smiles for the era of technology. Investors carried the widest smiles for profits they saw coming and for all concerned a new future was unfolding before their eyes.

After a final check on systems, the go-ahead was given to increase power and to begin taxiing using the plasma drive. Everybody watching suddenly forgot how to breathe. No eye and no camera was focussed anywhere else and every one of the spectators — including the Prime Minister — unintentionally leaned forward and craned their necks.

Alexia held her breath. Her hands, with all fingers spread like claws, grasped and clamped firmly on to her tensed up knees. Her sincere promise to Kevin that she would take plenty of pictures lay with her brand new, miniature, multi-media camera inside the handbag sitting silent and lonely on the ground and leaning, long forgotten, against the metal leg of the chair.

The deep whooping, whistling noise grew louder and more earnest and the greenish yellow flow from the engine expanded. Some moments went by before the large plane, as though suddenly prodded awake and startled by the altered pitch, lurched forward and its nose momentarily rose higher as it began to gently trundle, with restrained urgency, along the recently re-laid, tarmac on the runway. Another loud cheer broke out across the crowd but instantly died down with everyone's eagerness to focus on the event.

The whooping, whistling sound grew steadily higher in pitch as the plane picked up speed and gracefully trundled faster. The test appeared flawless and going as planned but Alexia shuffled and perked up, then leaned further forward and instinctively turned an ear towards the accelerating plane. A curiously gurgling and crackling noise, barely audible at first, had alarmingly begun to increase in intensity.

There was a sudden and fleeting moment of silence and then strange things seemed to begin to happen in slow motion. The centre and rear sections of the enormous plane appeared to expand in to a thousand pieces, like an inflating jigsaw puzzle, with every piece moving away from all the others around it. A greenish glow pulsed and radiated from within, followed by an intense flash so bright and overwhelming, it blinded every eye that was locked on to the spectacle.

Alexia recoiled and blinked, instinctively trying to regain her vision and her hands, which had began to rise to rub her blinded eyes, suddenly changed their trajectory and headed for her ears as a rumbling, deafening roar tore through the shuddering air, shaking the ground and reverberating painfully in her eardrums. A moment flashed by before she felt the whole front of her body savagely compress, as though a giant padded fist had slammed into her.

She was weightless for a second, flying backwards in the air as the shockwave caught up and barrelled through the crowd like a lightening gust of punches delivered all at once, sweeping objects and hurling humans like they were rag dolls. She landed heavily on her back, arms flailing and legs scrambling and her brain and eyeballs jarred as her head bumped and bounced into the polished, wooden decking.

Halfway to losing consciousness and gasping for breath, she blinked rapidly, desperate to regain her vision. The world descended into fogginess and dull noise and her brain and body felt disconnected from each other. Her mind swam in rolling waves and all of a sudden, she felt the pain as the back of her head began to swell. Blind, dazed and deafened, she fought her body's strong urge to descend into a darkened, temporary sleep.

Alexia stirred after a few moments and made a brave effort to stand but something firm and bulky was pinning her down. Incessant ringing in her ears, loud and only just bearable, blocked out the commotion rampaging in the viewing area.

Dust, smoke and the chemical, musty smell of jet fuel clogged her nostrils and scraped at her sinuses and an unknown substance, with a sharp taste and a mild sting that vaguely reminded her of printer ink and scalded plastic, gathered in her teeth and coated the surface of her tongue forcing her to do battle with a relentless desire to gag. She reached up with one hand to brush off coarse particles lingering on her eyelids.

Her vision slowly began to return as darkness gave way to an unrealistic, dusty, other-worldly grey. She tried once more to move or to roll to one side but the heavy, fleshy bulk holding her down would not shift. With one arm firmly pinned underneath her own back, she reached up with the other and felt that a bulky man, knocked unconscious, had been flung and tumbled backwards diagonally on top of her. He was breathing — which was a relief — but she shuddered at the thought of lying there, helplessly trapped underneath a dead body. She could feel his chest gently expanding and contracting and she wondered whether to try calling out to wake him up. Gritting her teeth, she moved her shoulder and strained with the physical effort of trying to pull hard to get her trapped arm free.

She turned her head to look at a grey movement on one side. The heavy gloom gently birthed a hazy, ambling figure which gingerly approached and then cautiously stretched out its spindly, tentacle hands as though reaching out for her. The dark space where a mouth should be was pulsing and yawning and as her hearing began to return, she heard Bernard's voice shouting out her name. He lifted away the scientist, placed him gently on one side, and then knelt beside Alexia, his face grave with concern.

Struggling to hear, she managed a quick nod to let him know she would be fine and with his help, Alexia shakily got up on to her feet and gradually began to regain her senses. Sirens wailed in the gloom and security personnel were already on overdrive, scampering about with the unsheathed urgency all trained professionals defaulted to. She felt faint and it took all of her energy to focus.

The ringing in her ears continued to slowly subside, but she winced and tensed up as pain swam through from the back of her head, bounced around to her forehead and then shot down to the neck, igniting and flaring each section in turn. Several moments went by before the agony diminished and she lifted her hand to feel the sore area where she had slammed into the decking. There was another peculiar noise and she looked up and saw Bernard asking if she was okay. When she was finally able to answer, he asked for her help checking up on other people, starting with the scientist who had fallen on top of her. Alexia had a sudden uncomfortable thought — was the Prime Minister hurt?

Chapter four

After the plasma drive exploded, authorities quickly confirmed there were no fatalities — even the two pilots and a technician were spared inside a blast proof, protective shell installed into the cockpit in case of an emergency. Many officials were injured by hurtling pieces violently flung away from the disintegrating plane and some suffered small burns from droplets of airborne, mechanically heated fuel which, after covering the two hundred metre span, had cooled to lower than the boiling point of water.

The Prime Minister was injured by a piece of alloy casing and had mild burns on his arm and shoulder from some of the droplets. Impact from the debris tore a cut on his temple which gushed a worrying flow of blood and caused a near concussion. His fortune at narrowly escaping serious injury did not help to quell the widespread speculation.

The world's media went in to an unleashed frenzy! News outlets screamed of the near fatal incident and pictures of bleeding and injured officials flooded into and circulated in the newsfeeds. Dramatic images surfaced of the Prime Minister and other visiting heads of state from eight different nations, each one covered in fine, powdery dust, with ashen, crimson, vertical stripes where fresh blood flowed from newly inflicted wounds. Vague, dusty figures could be seen stumbling to and fro, disoriented and half blind, amidst broken chairs and swathes of mystery debris.

In four of the images was a dishevelled Alexia, barely able to stand and being helped up by Bernard. One was a powerful image of the scientist on the ground and Alexia halfway to standing up, with smoke and dust in the air, and distant objects fading and dissolving into the gloom.

She was also in the background in the most famous and captivating picture of the day. A photographer had captured a well timed image of the injured Prime Minister, blood pouring from his wound and being helped by security, with two medical personnel running to his aid. Not far from them within the visual frame of the image, was a dazed Alexia, desperately clinging on to Bernard's arms, looking groggy and unsteady, covered in dust from head to toe — the moment when he had helped her up and was asking if she was okay.

The dust had barely settled and the injured taken to hospitals when questions began about the sequence of events. Investigations were hastily assembled and launched. Agencies and regional police swooped in and promises were announced about establishing the whole truth. Everybody's activities, what they were working on, their education, backgrounds and even their families were all to be scrutinized — and many of them questioned. Police, security services and a myriad of investigators swarmed the facility and records were opened up for detailed perusal.

And then Alexia's name came up.

Chapter five

Five days after the accident, Alexia was in her sitting room, wistfully staring at the angular, elongated, window shaped island of morning sunlight brightening a portion of the opposite wall. Her mind strayed and went away to explore the facility, wondering whether they would ever be allowed back to work.

She glanced up at the virtual clock. The pale-blue numbers glowed 10:28. Getting up to pick out yet another book from the shelf, it was easy working out she had been up for less than two hours. She walked back and stretched out lazily on the sofa. No need to go for a run today. She went for one yesterday; and it was twice as long — twice the distance and not even scheduled — well over an hour and blitzed through double the energy! No! She would stay in and have an easy day... but eat only half the calories just to be safe. There was some fruit, some mushrooms, and chopped kale in the fridge... and maybe have toast later, but strictly no butter! That would absolutely have to be all until tomorrow, if it was going to be a lazy day, she should stay within the limit.

With her elbow well supported by a pair of soft cushions, she decided to relax while doing some more research. Pausing to think, her eyes momentarily lifted to stare at the silent screen of the television, wondering whether to bother watching the main news again. News reports had descended into events to avoid; mainly to get away from wild speculation and pundits who carried hypotheses and theories and little information that was based on real data.

She had also minimised contact with any other people, only accepting phone calls from Oscar, Kevin, Bernard and two scientists employed at the central facility. She jumped slightly, startled by her suddenly awakened phone as it chirped with a brief, urgent message from Kevin, earnestly asking that she put on the news.

"Jenny! Visual!" she commanded, before remembering she had turned off the voice command feature the day before. Reaching for the remote, she held down the power button.

Alexia froze when the television flickered into life. Her face was on the screen with her full name underneath it in a "Breaking News" official update report. The picture alternated with a catalogue of images, including the one taken while she was helped up by Bernard and the image of her in the background not far from the dusty and injured Prime Minister.

She cranked up the volume. The voice of a female reporter chattered urgently on about how it was now believed that Alexia's recent modification to the engine was responsible for the failure and for the terrible blast.

The walls of the room began to flex and sway and she briefly closed her eyes to fight a wave of nausea. She turned up the volume another fraction higher as an unflattering, social media picture of her graduation splashed on to the screen. The report continued and explained how Alexia, despite having no known background in science, had vigorously pursued a position at the facility and strived to ingratiate herself with the scientists. The reporter described her as far too friendly and keen to learn the inner workings of all departments and to be allowed free and special access into them. Alexia leaned towards the screen. What the reporter was implying was clear to anyone listening.

In an educated accent, the classy female reporter's terse, polished and scripted monologue narrated how it was suspected that all of Alexia's actions could have been deliberate, and that she may have planned for the catastrophic failure. The husky, smooth, sedate and overly practised voice added that investigations were yet ongoing, and that there would be further updates on any developments.

The reporter then shuffled some important looking papers in a convincing, conclusive and professional manner and went on to introduce a suited, well read pundit and a career behavioural expert, who would both apparently analyze and help to break down all the complicated details of the story for the viewers.

Alexia sat paralyzed, with mouth half open. The television remote slowly trembled from her fingers and fell to the floor with a reverberating, hollow clunk. After a while of staring blankly at the professionals, she swung her legs from the sofa and made an effort to stand up. Her throat and stomach seized and it took all her willpower to wrestle down the overwhelming, incipient retching. Staggering to the toilet, she was violently sick until the spasms became drawn out, crushing waves of agony as her stomach convulsed and painfully squeezed trying to force out contents that were no longer there. She began to cry in heaving uncontrollable sobs.

The sound of the phone ringing obtruded from the hallway and after some hesitation, she gathered up her strength, staggered out to the sitting room, scooped up the device and answered it without looking.

"Did you see it?" Kevin's voice burst through with urgency.

Alexia was unable to speak.

After a short pause, Kevin vented his frustration. "Whatta proper pile of horse barf! Proper dumb binheads! Did you see that pundit!? Holy mother of newsfeeds! He gassed up the airwaves like King Kong's farts! I saw your papers. What they're saying doesn't make sense!"

An involuntary sob escaped from Alexia.

Kevin waited for a moment before speaking again. "This could be big — they'll proper throw us in it, big time! I dunno what they're up to! This sucks major ways!" He paused and let out a long, deep breath. "I'm trying to get hold of Bernard. In the meantime, close your curtains and proper lock your door. Do not answer it to anyone apart from the police... well, and me of course! I can come over right now. Would that be okay? Shall I come over now?" Kevin paused for a response he suspected would not come.

Alexia remained silent. He could hear the pained breathing so he knew she was listening.

"If you can, start going over all that stuff again, I mean proper PHD, telescopic detail! I'm on my way. Is there anything you need from the shop?"

Alexia's voice remained trapped inside her throat.

After a long pause, Kevin confidently reached out again. "Hey, come on now Alexia, you got to keep it together. I'm proper on your side and I will do anything I can. Bernard will too, we both know he absolutely will! You know how he is. I feel sorry for them lot when he gets started! I am on my way. I'm gonna stop at Veenoz to get some stuff. Is there anything you need? Anything you'd like me to get?"

Waiting patiently, he was rewarded with a resigned voice. "Yes. I... I don't know... I need marmalade and... a pack of green tea."

Kevin breathed a sigh of relief. "Okay, yeah. I got your back. I'll be there in a bit."

He was about to hang up when her voice came over the speaker again.

"Wait!"

"Yeah, whatsit?"

There was another long pause but he was careful to be patient.

"Could you bring some purple berries?"

Kevin did not hesitate. "Done!"

He waited again in vain as Alexia fell silent.

"See you soon?" he asked softly. He could just about hear her breathing.

"Okay," she finally managed a reply. "Thanks," she whispered.

Alexia disconnected the call and crumpled into a broken heap on the sitting room floor.

Kevin was at her door nearly an hour and a half later carrying a small brown bag of basic groceries in one hand and a bottle of medium, red wine in the other.

"Your favourite!" he announced, holding up the pricey bottle. "Thought you might need a boost!"

And he was right. She did.

She immediately went to the cupboard, took out two wine glasses and then reached for a corkscrew that clung with chic style to the middle of the fridge door.

"None for me please, you go ahead and have…" Kevin started to say, but another look at the tormented soul standing before him and he decided there was no harm in having a drink after all. "Oh go on then!" he nodded. "I'll have one too, why not."

Supportive and genuinely concerned for her wellbeing, he tried to cheer her up, but Alexia was too distraught and in no mood to speak. Kevin duly obliged and did most of the talking. Taking the bottle with them to the silent sitting room, they perched on either end of the three-seater sofa. Alexia raised and folded both her legs underneath her and clasped her glass in both hands, close to her chest.

"Hey whatever happened to that friend of yours?" Kevin asked. "Cassie was it? Didn't you have a friend called Cassie?"

Alexia glanced sideways at him and then cast her eyes sullenly back down to her hands. Kevin was about to speak when the reply was mumbled into the glass.

"She went to Australia… her and Jeff moved to Australia. It was like, more than a year ago."

"Australia, huh!" Kevin responded. Then a thought came to him. "Wasn't your ex also called Jeff? Proper coincidence, ey!" he chuckled. "Hey, Jeff's coming over… Which one? Yours or mine?" He slapped his knee several times and chuckled at his own humour.

Out of the corner of his eye, he saw Alexia stare at him coldly.

"Oh…" he exclaimed.

There was a lingering, awkward silence.

"I see…" Searching for a way out, Kevin wanted to kick himself. "Good riddance! If you ask me, Australia isn't far enough!" He glanced at Alexia. "So that's the reason you broke off the engagement? Or..." he tried to be careful "did it happen... um... before?"

She nodded slowly, keeping her eyes firmly fixed on the glass.

"I'm... sorry!" Kevin mumbled. "I didn't mean... you know!" he shook his head and desperately grappled for the right words. "We only ever talk about work stuff and... I didn't... know. I totally really didn't mean to pry!"

He stopped talking and sighed.

Alexia shrugged and waited a moment before venting her thoughts.

"I hate pretty girls!" she spat.

Kevin was shocked by statement.

"Like Jessica! Her silly face reminds me of Cassie!"

Kevin stared at Alexia. "You! Of all women! You could be jealous of anyone!? Have you ever looked in a mirror at any point in your adult life?"

He meant every word.

She stared coldly and then looked back down into her hands. "I'm not stupid! She's prettier than me!"

"No!" came the quick reply. "She's Barbie doll pretty and you're intelligent pretty!"

"Well, Jeff clearly decided he prefers Barbie doll pretty!" she retorted, before withdrawing more into herself.

"His loss!" Kevin responded. "The proper blind fool!"

Alexia smiled just enough that Kevin knew he had redeemed himself.

As the evening wore on, Alexia hugged the glass to her chest, occasionally lifting it to quietly sip the red wine. Losing all desire to speak, she sat and whiled away her turmoil. Kevin loyally stayed and carried a one sided conversation. He talked about work and then he talked about Canada, where he went hiking in the forests and saw grazing wild moose and a mother grizzly bear casually hunting in the woods with her two fuzzy cubs bouncing playfully in tow. He talked about the economy and then he talked about her brother working so hard in Spain and how his new catering business was sure to do well. He talked about the brand new, pricey night club in town and then he talked about the best club he had been to in Egypt, where he travelled two years before on a week long holiday.

With Alexia still silent and grateful for the distraction, he carried on and talked about not understanding fashion. Who actually wore the clothes proudly paraded on the catwalks? Nothing he ever saw on ordinary people in the streets came close to resembling what the models showed off. Then he talked about his new girlfriend whom he had started going out with only five days before. Wondrous and intelligent, she had once dreamed of carving out a career as a scientist, but she ended up in languages and landed a well paid job in a text translation company. She didn't know what to make of the big accident at the facility and was fascinated that he was caught up in such a major event.

Alexia wanted Kevin to stay, so he settled down for the evening and dozed off on the sofa at four in the morning when she finally went to bed. She tumbled into troubled sleep and had a strange dream where she plunged backwards, kicking and screaming, over a thundering waterfall, and another where a tall, sinister, long haired figure, carrying sharp sheets of paper, chased her into a building and continued to pursue her after she climbed out of the window to get to the street again, where she tried in vain to gain traction with her slippery, half-hovering feet so she could carry on running to a police station around the corner. She woke up just after 11am to an enticing aroma wafting over from the kitchen.

Kevin had just made fresh pancakes for breakfast and was stretched out on the sofa munching hungrily on one of them. The television was on and showing a national news channel but he sat up and hurriedly turned it off when she walked in to the room.

"Good morning, you!" he called out with an unconvincing smile.

"Goody, good morning." she muttered, mid way through a giant yawn. Drained and still tired, she felt tempted to go back to bed. She turned to casually glance at the silenced television screen. "It's that bad, huh?"

He nodded. "Even worse! More than you know!" He looked up and sympathetically shook his head. "The whole thing's becoming a proper cosmic gas-fest!"

Her shoulders slumped and the sitting room descended into forlorn silence.

"Hey, you want a coffee?" Kevin tried to sound enthusiastic. "I made some pancakes."

She attempted to smile but with every cell unwilling, opted for a grateful nod. Settling down on the sofa, she reached up to massage a dull ache in her neck.

The pancakes were incredible. He had added coconut milk, sugar, a pinch of salt and powdered cinnamon when mixing up the batter and had not used any eggs. A texture a world away from any she was used to, every bite was chewy with a lingering flavour. She always spread marmalade on pancakes as she ate them but on that occasion, the jar stood lonely and all but forgotten.

After the breakfast, more talking and a long hot shower, Kevin duly insisted they carry on with the research. "I don't know too much about it all," he shrugged. "But from what I saw, your idea straight up made full sense!"

She nodded in agreement, just as puzzled by the bizarre analysis in the media.

"Besides," Kevin added, "they all proper took a look at it and then totally agreed it was a great idea! Otherwise, why would they have gone ahead and built it in to the engine?"

They paused, mystified and in deep contemplation.

"If it wasn't a good idea to make that alteration, why would all the engineers have gone along with it? And then why would they actually have gone ahead and built the thing?" Kevin was absent-mindedly thinking out the words.

Alexia stared blankly, half hoping he had the answer.

"They're the ones supposed to know far better than you, aren't they!? They're the engineers!" He shook his head at the contradiction. "Why blame only you for the whole thing going wrong?"

Staring up at the wall, he squinted into the distance, wrestling with suggestions and negations that troubled him. Then perking up so suddenly that he made Alexia jump, he blurted out a new theory. "Hey! Maybe there was nothing wrong with the actual idea! Then they proper messed up by how they went about it? Or maybe they messed up and built it all wrong, you know! Now they're like... you know... just trying to save their own skins!" He swung an open palm in a gesture of disgust.

Alexia and Kevin stared thoughtfully at each other, both suddenly aware there was more to the story.

Kevin stayed the rest of the day and helped with the research. Alexia made fresh pasta salad for a late lunch and it was already getting dark by the time he stood up, wiggled an aching shoulder and then reached for his jacket while announcing it was time to go.

Chapter six

The following day – eleven twenty in the morning.

Two uniformed police officers, a man and a woman, turned up at the door.

"The neighbours will love this!" Alexia muttered to herself.

The marked police car was strategically parked in the way they tend to park when attending to business. She let them in, ushered them into the sitting room and then offered tea or coffee, to which they replied they would both love some tea.

After polite and standard, customary formalities, they carefully explained that she was not under arrest and that there were no charges levelled against her. The intention — they said — was to gather information for making a full and coherent report on how various actions led to the accident.

The welcome information helped to settle her nerves.

They began by asking how she came across the idea presented to the scientists back at the facility. Alexia guided the officers through the whole story — as far as she could remember it — which was no different to what she had told Bernard or anybody else. They requested to see the mentioned shaving razor, and the female officer asked to see and then to take a close up photograph of the mostly healed, inch long cut, vividly visible, half-way up on the inside of her thigh.

They flipped through the books she pulled from her bookshelf and requested she log on to the websites she spoke of. They asked to see the logs on her library account so they could list what she borrowed: they would go to the building later to validate the titles.

They asked for how long she had worked at the facility and why she specifically chose that career. And then they asked why she helped out in other departments despite having no official background in science. Finally, they enquired about Bernard's reaction when she made the presentation, and the reactions from scientists when they learned of her idea.

The last part of the questioning seemed odd to Alexia. Why would they need to know the scientist's reactions? As far as she could recall, everyone who worked there appeared impressed and very glad to make progress.

The officers implied that they were satisfied with the answers. "You're rock stone solid!" they confidently posited, apparently a phrase the local police liked to use. Her story entirely matched up with the evidence. "We will be back if anything considerable changes or if there is information that may concern you."

After pleasant and warm goodbyes, they politely made their way out, shut the door behind them and were gone before Alexia could register her relief. The visit had lasted a tense two hours and both officers genuinely seemed to be on her side. Her eyelids closed as she took a step forward and her head and one shoulder leaned heavily against the door. A long, drawn out breath escaped from her pursed lips. With eyes remaining lightly shut, she stood against the door calmly absorbing the silence. An unbearable weight had gone from her shoulders with the opportunity to tell her version of events. The police were satisfied and every detail checked out, but as Alexia was brutally going to discover, none of that would matter.

After a while, most media became unbearable. Her face was on news channels as the woman who came close to murdering the Prime Minister. It seemed not to matter that police were investigating. Someone wanted her guilty and the media played along.

Her phone rang endlessly with unknown numbers and there was banging from earnest figures at the front door. Impetuous reporters, gunning for exclusives, joined the lurking mystery figures in persistent knocking. Alexia was grateful her flat was on the first floor; they couldn't elbow each other to peek through her curtains. Everyone was keen for a picture or a word from the infamous woman who was rapidly becoming public enemy number one.

Alexia gasped and violently jumped early one afternoon and then cowered in terror, after a small brick crashed on to the centre of her front window sending large cracks radiating from the impact point. Had it not been formed from layered double glazing, the entire pane would have shattered into countless pieces.

Several raw eggs were also hurled in her direction, most of which smashed and splattered against the window sending viscous gloop dripping slowly down the pane.

Later in the same afternoon, Alexia was curled up in a corner of the bathroom, fighting back tears, when she heard a familiar voice shouting from outside. Bernard was demanding the reporters back away. After inexplicable noises, muffled scraping and vexed grunting, there was urgent but polite knocking, and then he was calling out her name. She ran to the door, unlocked it, took a moment to compose herself, and then swung it wide open.

He stood there, in the usual dark suit, with Kevin next to him, each carrying a small grocery bag in one hand and sympathy in their faces. She jumped out and hugged them and only then noticed Oscar, standing immediately behind, having secretly flown over from Spain to lend his support. The trip had been arranged with Kevin and kept as a surprise. She jumped up like the little sister and ran straight into his arms.

"Hey Lex!" he chuckled. "Is it good to see you or what!"

She buried her face in his shoulder and knowing her voice would not let her, did not bother to speak.

"I don't believe a word of it, Lex! Not one word!" He gently stroked the back of her head and leaned his cheek into her temple. "Together with my new friends Kevin and Bernard, we're gonna fix this!"

Alexia broke down and sobbed like a little child.

Chapter seven

Events spiralled as time went on. Alexia stared in horror at reports that she was officially the most talked about and the number one most hated individual in the country. There were accusations of missions to kill the Prime Minister and conspiracy theories of links with foreign governments. There were wild insinuations of espionage and sabotage and of planning a devious sequence of events that led to the catastrophic failure of the engine. Some groups began campaigns calling for charges of treason.

Kevin and Oscar's unwavering support eventually hurled them into near fatal encounters. While out rallying help for Alexia's cause, Kevin was savagely set upon by a baying, irate mob. Barely conscious when his rescuers got him to the hospital, concerned doctors chose to medically induce a coma.

Oscar, who narrowly escaped the angry mob, was later picked up by agents and detained for questioning. Wanting to know more about Alexia's interests, the interrogators asked why she had turned down the offer to relocate and work with him, and instead chosen to work, far too keenly, at the facility. They wanted to know why she put in so much effort when pursuing that particular job.

They produced records of her keenness to help out in departments she was clearly not qualified for and implied it was likely a deliberate ploy to gain access to sensitive areas of the facility.

"A carefully calculated plan!" the agents insisted. "Designed to get closer to spy and gather data and to carry out the pre-planned sabotage of the work!"

If Oscar had not known his own sister so well, he might have been convinced by their version of events.

Only six months earlier, a man had stayed at Oscar's hotel for four days and five nights. After leaving the accommodation, he turned up in two other countries over the next week and a half, before returning to England to go about mystery business. An acquaintance of a known spy arrested less than two months before the major occurrence at the facility, the man's conversations, plans and intentions were as yet unknown to police or the agency. They wanted to know what Oscar had spoken to him about.

With a befuddled look on his face, he stared for a moment before attempting — with visibly suppressed irritation — to answer as truthfully and plainly as he knew how. He had no idea what man they were talking about.

Pushing further with tactically combative interrogation, they implied that he might be involved in a conspiracy, and may have been working together with his sister to plan and carry out the entire operation.

Stammering from the absurdity of the allegation, he insisted that every word of their theory was wrong. The man, if he had stayed at all, was a random visitor and any encounter would have been routine as with any interaction with every paying guest. He could not remember a stranger who stayed six months before.

The agents went on to propose an idea that Oscar had somehow helped his sister to plan and carry out the sophisticated sabotage, and the man in question assisted in coordinating with other individuals and various accomplices. They suggested the man then went to meet Alexia to pass on some pre-approved engine alterations.

Oscar felt his face tighten and, too late, he noticed both his fists were clenched. Relaxing his hands, he made the effort to appear calm but he knew from the glances that they were trained to spot it. The sudden thought occurred that the rage he felt might be to his advantage: guilty men would not be so quick to lose their tempers.

When she heard about her brother being picked up for questioning, Alexia knew it was only a matter of time before they came for her. She wasn't too worried about answering their questions; her actions had all been honest and legal and bore no resemblance to the media reports. But the truth, which happened to be her version of events, was one perspective. The sour, sinking feeling in the pit of her stomach came from knowing that her fate lay on what version sensationalists preferred to go along with.

She stayed indoors and tried to keep her mind occupied. Three attempts to go and see Kevin at the hospital were thwarted by mixed mobs and enthusiastic reporters. Deciding it was safer to remain inside the flat, she relied on Bernard for all information.

Between watching the facility, numerous press conferences, high level meetings and visiting Alexia, Bernard seemed the busiest one of them all. At one point, three full days had gone by since she heard from him, and by noon of the fourth day, she began to wonder if he was picked up for questioning.

As she sat alone in the sitting room, sipping on a glass of water, pondering the future and poring over the data again, she looked up and saw him walk up, live on television, to a cluster of microphones in a "Breaking News" incident investigations update. She scooped up the remote and swiftly cancelled off the mute as the camera zoomed in on him and his full name and title popped up in a white banner underneath his image. He shuffled some papers, nodded to acknowledge reporters that stood beyond the visuals and then began to read a pre-written announcement.

After a summarized description of the incident, Bernard's next words made Alexia recoil. The statement spelled out how her suggestion for the engine caused the catastrophic failure, and the cascade of terrible consequences that followed. He was blaming her for the series of events and was taking responsibility for accepting the idea, and for helping her to pitch the flawed concept to engineers.

He announced that it was looking more and more like sabotage, so sophisticated, that the trusting scientists, in their quest for progress, could not reasonably have been expected to spot it. He conceded that she liked to move around different departments and the reasons she applied for the job were not clear. More investigations were going to be carried out with a new focus and a detailed look into her background.

Alexia reeled as a wave of nausea engulfed her, growing in intensity until it consumed her. She tried standing up but her legs shook and wobbled and the room swayed and danced shaking off all sanity. She let her eyelids close as her neck muscles seized from a sudden, hair bristling pain in her forehead. Trying to focus on breathing, she lost to the nausea and her upper body shook with violent retching. As the trembling wave shut her mind and her body, she crumpled like a woollen doll and fell to the floor.

Chapter eight

When she came to, Alexia could taste vomit in her mouth. She retched again, three painful times, straight on to the floor, then in a daze, struggled shakily on to her feet and stumbled to the bathroom to get cleaned up. After a quick shower, during which she cried the entire time, she went into the bedroom, pulled on a flowery dress, took one look in the mirror at her haunted expression then pulled it off and cast it roughly to one side. She reached for a black skirt and a plain pink top. She really was not in any mood for flowers.

After cleaning up the mess on the sitting room floor, she absent-mindedly loaded up the washing machine and tried the control panel several times before remembering to push in the fused switch on the wall. When it finally got going, she paused for a moment to listen to the muffled, mechanical whoosh as it sucked mains water into its bowels. Unsure of what to do with the rest of the day, she was still standing next to it when the wizardry determined enough water had sloshed in to begin tumbling the drum for the washing cycle. She leaned with one hand on the kitchen counter top and the other placed tenderly, with a flat palm, on to her chest, unconsciously massaging her traumatized soul.

Shaking and unable to focus, she turned her head and glanced up through the open door at the virtual time hovering on the sitting room wall. The sharp edged, blue numbers glowed 15:45. It was three and a half hours since Bernard was on television.

Feeling drained and weak, she stumbled to the bedroom and collapsed on to the bed. Her life was over! Her career was over! She shuddered at the thought of being in prison. Wincing and with eyes welling up with tears, she turned over to her side, pulled the covers over her head and curled up with knees folded up to her chest. Trying hard not to cry, she whispered out to whatever gods were listening. All this was far too much for her to handle.

"Pleeeeease! Please! This is not fair!" she suddenly wanted to scream out. She was not a secret spy! And she had never thought about assassinating anybody! Wishing he had been more persistent, she viciously regretted not taking up the offer to pack up and go to work with Oscar in Spain. "I should have gone! I should have gone! I should have packed up and gone!" she muttered miserably to herself over and over again.

Wracked with fear and a ferocious sense of dread, Alexia tumbled into a deep, disturbed sleep.

She woke up on the following day to find the night and the morning had stealthily crept by and it was already noon. Gritting her teeth with a crippling migraine, she crawled out of bed and staggered to the kitchen in search of pain relievers. After taking two tablets, she stood with eyes tightly closed, willing away the agony, wishing she was in a different body.

Gently massaging her temples and the front of her head, she glanced to the side, switched on the kettle to make some coffee, and then turned it off again after deciding not to bother. With one hand tenderly massaging her temple, she winced and grimaced, then stumbled as a piercing pain shot through the inner left side of her skull. With eyes closed and body feeling frail and nauseated, she steadied herself, leaning right up against the kitchen counter, waiting for the wave to pass. Suddenly feeling faint, she crumpled slowly to the floor and wished all of existence would come to an end.

In a daze, and petrified by what was coming, Alexia crawled into the sitting room and sat up on the floor, resting her aching back against the front edge of the sofa. She jumped and froze as a loud thud reverberated from the large front window, as another raw egg thumped into the pane. Reaching up to block her ears, she felt the crumpled box where her fingers still clasped the small pack of painkillers.

Unable to stop tears tumbling freely down her face, she lost all remaining desire to move an arm and wipe them away. A sinister calm descended into her swollen and glazed eyes as her willpower and all rationality evaporated. She placed the small pack on the table, steadied herself to stand up and with considerable difficulty, staggered back into the kitchen.

Wracked by another torturous spasm from the migraine, she fought to remain standing long enough to grab hold of the small blue box where she stored all the tablets. After steadying herself on the counter to regain some strength, she turned around, staggered painfully back into the sitting room and sat on the floor again with her back against the sofa. Standing on the coffee table was the half glass of water left over, unfinished, from the previous afternoon.

She picked up her phone and sent a text message to Oscar and another, slightly differently worded one, to Kevin. Given their situations, trying to dial any of their numbers would be futile. Then she paused for a moment, deep in thought, tapping the front edge of her phone against her forehead.

Blinking away the tears, she wiped her cheeks and then dialled Bernard's number. It went straight to voicemail. Barely able to speak, she managed a pain laden whisper.

"You lied to me! You said... You promised..."

She choked and her voice trailed off, trapped within the effort of stopping herself from crying. Losing the battle and all ability to carry on speaking, she stopped and sobbed quietly while holding the phone away. A few moments ticked by before she could carry on.

"I'm sorry... I... just can't... anymore!"

Shuddering in a sob, she disconnected the call.

Alexia emptied the entire contents of the blue box on to the floor, broke out all the pills and tablets from their secure packaging and then reached for the half glass of water on the table.

Less than forty minutes later, lying on the sitting room floor with legs tensed up in a spasm, mouth foaming and barely conscious, Alexia could faintly make out dulled, rhythmic, noises that sounded like somebody was breaking down the front door. She slowly opened her eyes and tried to lift her head to look but it was too much effort — her head fell to the floor again. With heart pounding against her ribs, literally for its life, she trembled and shuddered from a surging wave of agony.

Her body twitched and quivered in futile protest against the deadly substances rampaging within it. Her brain, immersed in a foggy haze and mellowed by gruesome shock, accepted what the rest of the body had not yet figured out.

Just before she let her eyes close once again, she saw Bernard — or a blurry figure that somewhat looked like him — come running into the room and desperately reach for her. She saw two lighter circles where his wild, panicked eyes revealed the whites of his eyeballs, and the dark oval in his face where his mouth was shouting.

Her eyelids, feeling like each one weighed a ton, drew slowly back together again and everything went dark.

Chapter nine

Alexia slowly opened her eyes and then quickly shut them again to block out the bright light. There was no feeling and no noise. It took all of eternity for her eyesight to adjust. Wondering if it was possible that she might ever see anything but excruciating brightness, she tried to move but there was no response from her body. Was she dead? Was this the after life? She strained and tried focussing to listen out for any sounds.

As her eyes slowly adjusted and the light began to soften, she turned her head to look to her left and saw she was in hospital. Her senses gradually, very slowly, began to return and peculiar, faint noises registered in her ears.

Moments ticked by as she allowed her eyes to close again and consciousness unhurriedly emerged from the gloom. The noises gradually resolved themselves into muted, earnest, mechanical sounds which she recognized as coming from a myriad of gadgets and a plethora of ultra modern, life giving machines.

Monitors, pumps and plugged in equipment whirred, clicked and beeped in the background and beyond that, hovering some-where on its own terms, was the barely audible hum of the sterile air conditioner. As her eyes slowly focussed, she turned to look the other way and saw Bernard sitting in a chair next to her bed.

Their eyes locked and a solitary tear rolled down from hers. The sight of him sat there made her blood start to fizzle. A bitter, unpleasant taste grew inside her mouth and she wanted to lean forward and spit it straight at his face.

With her body too ravaged to obey commands to move, hot tears of frustration trickled from her eyes, down along her temples and on to her ear lobes and finally, fell on to the allergenic pillows. She swallowed hard, engulfed by intense loathing and her ribcage shuddered as she fought powerful sobs. All she could feel was overwhelming hatred and staring into his eyes, she wished with all her being that he would drop down and die.

Averting his gaze, Bernard slowly got up, turned to step around the chair and then walked across the room to the end of the wall on the right where Alexia suddenly noticed the door was located. There were no other beds or any patients in sight; she had the generously sized intensive care unit all to herself. When he reached it, he gently opened the door a few inches and then cautiously leaned forward to peek outside. Then he stepped back, pulled until it was fully open and then nodded slightly as two uniformed figures stepped inside.

The figures shut the door behind them, smiled briefly, nodded their heads and then stood there, side by side, watching and saying nothing. After a quick glance at Alexia, Bernard casually walked back and then slowly and deliberately settled back into the chair. It took only a fleeting moment to recognise the pair as the two police officers who had visited to question her.

Alexia felt a wave of icy fear and deep dread as the truth painfully dawned on why Bernard had saved her. Death could not be permitted — not just yet. There needed to be show closure so the issue could be settled. There had to be the big ending to sell to the public without which, the story would still be lingering. The media and officials had whipped up a frenzy that had to culminate in an earth shattering climax. The villain was to be led off, clasped in chains, to serve the full deserved punishment, before any part of the story could be allowed to rest.

Pictures of her captured, restrained in handcuffs and being carted off to prison, were going to be broadcast live around the world and only then, would events be allowed to slowly settle. The facility, the laboratories and the company that owned them would have endless sympathy from media and the public. The innocent scientists — unknowing victims of a devious, attractive and cunning foreign agent — would be hailed as heroes furthering the cause of science. Funding would pour in to rebuild what was destroyed and extra time and more freedom given to complete the work.

The story and the drama had to be allowed to play out. There could be no ultimate villain if she died too early. The earth shattering climax, so carefully choreographed, would have ended up a forgettable, anaemic puff. The Alexia saga had to be controlled to a crescendo that would peak into a roaring, thunderous finale. Alexia had to live! The ending could not be robbed! There could be no roar or thunder if the star turned up dead!

Alexia closed her eyes and turned away in frustration at the vile hatred for the man sitting in her hospital room. She could no longer bear a single glance in his direction. He appeared to be mocking her and scoffing at the very nearly successful attempt at ending her own life. She choked as she tried opening her mouth to scream at him and the heart and blood pressure monitors spiked and beeped faster. Her breathing turned more laboured and she felt her temperature rising as her entire body trembled with uncontrolled rage. If she could move, she would have jumped off the bed and clawed at him.

Bernard began to speak.

Chapter ten

"They lied to me, Alexia!" Bernard spoke gently. "The chief scientist, the director and the head of laboratories conspired and systematically lied to us all." His crystalline tenor was intentionally mellow. "Too much had been invested. A lot of time, large amounts in third party funding and serious resources had gone into the project. Powerful reputations and many careers were at stake."

He cast his eyes downwards, searching for the right words as though they were carved into the sanitized floor.

"It went higher than any of us. This was global!"

He paused for a moment to see if she was listening. It was difficult to tell with her face turned away from him. He carried on regardless.

"They desperately needed a plausible scapegoat and a way to buy some more time to keep the project alive. They were scheming the entire time until you happened to come along!" He bit his lower lip in frustration at the treachery. "Your idea was workable! It brought the project forward by... in my estimation, maybe four years or so. But even with the new changes, they were still another two... maybe three years behind with the various complexities. I just didn't see it because I trusted my scientists. They misled me about the readiness for launch date. And they were convincing. Exceptionally deceptive! But good as they are they couldn't hide it forever."

He paused again and closed his eyes, regretting his gullibility and how much pain it had ended up causing her. Clearing his throat twice, he lifted a hand and meaninglessly ran one finger along his right eyebrow.

"You gave them a great way of buying some time, Alexia. By the way I saw it, your idea was workable. But with a small tweak, an incredibly tiny, subtle one, the altered engine was deliberately rigged to fail."

Alexia opened her eyes and slowly turned her head towards him. His sincere and earnest gaze remained locked on to hers.

"By the way I see it, it was a genuinely clever plan. Unbelievably genius! Very worthy of the scientists who colluded to pull it off, and difficult for those not in the loop to spot the problem. I only uncovered it because I went searching and even then, only because I felt there was a reason to look."

He paused and waited, as if to allow a moment for the information to sink in, then he suddenly looked away and shifted uncomfortably in the chair. Putrid hate was gushing from Alexia's tortured eyes and Bernard winced, clearly wounded by what he saw in them. Trying, unsuccessfully, not to let it bother him, he carried on speaking.

"By the way I saw it, it did not make sense why they failed when designing your idea into the engine. Something didn't add up! I had to find the reason. Such a level of professionals should easily have pulled it off."

He paused again with eyes closed and shook his head in frustration at letting something so enormous slip by him unnoticed.

"They hadn't planned on the failure being so catastrophic. They meant only to destroy the engine but the calculations were slightly off. It was a great unknown with the brand new plasma inducers, new re-modulators, new casing, new second phase boost initiators..." His words trailed off at the glaring irrelevance. "It would have been a miracle for anyone to work out right!"

He stared, apologetically — deep into her eyes.

"I wish I had known that before I read the press announcement!"

"Do you, really!" Alexia desperately wanted to scream. "Well, Mr 'by-the-way-I-see-it', it's far too late now!" But the only sound that came through the breathing mask was a whimper.

The bitter rage and hatred were far from mellowed.

Bernard was yet to discover that the chief scientist and the head of laboratories both knew the solution long before Alexia happened to stumble upon it. Aware of the older, sprawling, marine experiment, they had studied how the exposed components were saved. Having buried their research and wiped all the data, they scoffed at the office lady who thought she had dreamed up the idea before them.

Bernard would have known too — if he had been looking. But with a site filled with scientists and sixteen smaller, hi-tech projects in progress, there was no luxury of indulging in the minutiae. There were group-leads, project-leads, section-leads, shift-leads, day-leads, floor-leads, department-leads, stage-leads, and that's before getting to the head of laboratories — no shortage of people to trust with their duties. With every critical report, the head of laboratories and the articulate chief scientist were meticulous in explaining that the work was under control.

Having brought the Financial Director into the loop, it was decided by the three men to keep the information buried until they had solved another problem in the development.

"So if the plasma stream is entirely resolved," enquired the apprehensive director, "there would only remain the headache of magnetic confinement?"

"Just that," responded the articulate chief scientist. "Generating and confining such an intense field, *and* keeping it all cost effective for airlines is troublesome within the current size of a plane."

"But there's good progress on that?"

"Absolutely!" replied the chief scientist with certainty. "But we need time. Enough time. And we all know who's going to offer to step right in! They'll smear their stuck-up noses all over the whole thing!"

Having magnetic confinement as the only outstanding issue would trigger a large, multi-national aircraft manufacturer being muscled in to contribute as an equal partner — rather than consultant — for their technical knowhow on total weight and shielding. They would siphon a large portion of the available funding, take over much of the work, and when all the development was finally complete, claim and wallow in the glory, and then suck up much of the billions anticipated in earnings. No! The project had to remain within the facility and for the time being, the engine had to be considered the absolute main focus until they completed the work on confinement.

The two men could barely believe their luck when attending Bernard's meeting, called to announce Alexia's *new* idea with the BZ-241-GL7 equipment! The scheme to buy some more time finally had a clear way. With only a tiny adjustment to one or two components, the engine would destroy itself, and the lowly office lady was going to take all the blame! A small story planted here, a little planned encounter there, and when the time came, investigators would be steered to her. With help from the director and a few of his high level friends, events and strategic, planned leaks to the media would help to guide opinions. It was perfect! They almost giggled when their eyes met. The glee easily passed as joy for the good news.

Bernard stood up and casually walked towards the end of the room where the foot of the bed was facing. With her head propped up by the medical grade pillows, Alexia's eyes followed him, until, after seven or eight purposeful strides, he could go no further — stopped by what she then saw were wall to wall curtains, stretching down from the ceiling all the way to the floor. She squinted in attempt at working out what he was trying to do.

With a flurry of movement and a flick of his arms, he pulled both curtains all the way open, one after the other, revealing a large group of die hard reporters waiting outside behind large, reinforced glass, ceiling high windows that spanned nearly the entire length of the wall. With the curtains fully open, they could all see into the room with a clear view of Alexia lying helpless on the bed covered in medical wires and a plethora of paraphernalia that plugged her body into the life saving machines.

Commotion broke out as cameras began to flash and reporters burst into inaudible questions. As Alexia watched Bernard walk back to the chair, she wondered why he was doing whatever it was he was up to if he wasn't going to help her.

Lifting up his transparent, double screen, flip phone, he touched the lower screen, looked up into Alexia's eyes, then called out a number "Eight" which appeared to be linked to somebody programmed on speed dial. With the phone to his ear, he waited patiently while it connected to whoever "eight" was on his dialling list. The call was answered immediately.

"She's awake."

There was a brief pause.

"She will be fine. It's a go!"

After waiting for a pre-arranged confirmation from number eight, the phone came back down and the two screens came together to disconnect the call.

He glanced at the two officers and then turned back to look at Alexia. "You were in a coma for fourteen days." He delivered this news in the most sensitive way, but in a tone that suggested there was more to the information.

Alexia was disappointed that she had woken up at all.

"You died four times, entirely, and they had to resuscitate you."

She couldn't help thinking that they needn't have bothered.

"We've been very busy!" His expression was resolute. "At this moment, information proving what I have just told you has began to be delivered to all news organizations with an office in the country. Digital copies are going to law enforcement agencies, to authorities, officials and to countless people with any amount of influence! Many bloggers and vloggers, reporters, many active internet enthusiasts with substantial followers and considerable audience will be receiving a copy — in all known social media and all available platforms! *Doc-nami,* Kevin called it. First time I've heard the term. They'll unleash a doc-nami of this information... they're sending it to all platforms and all at the same time.

Alexia blinked and stared, trying hard to understand.

"Oscar, Kevin and many others are helping with this. We managed to bring together several hundred of your keen supporters, nearly one hundred and ten or so in this town alone. Every single one of your neighbours is in on it too."

Alexia's eyes were glued to his, her mind struggling to absorb the reality of the moment. Bernard kept his eyes squarely and passionately fixed on hers.

"Melissa eagerly joined us," he added as an afterthought. "She may have disliked your unqualified ambitions but she's not evil. She couldn't stand by and watch you go down in such a way. She has done exactly what a good manager should have — she backed you up."

Alexia felt a pang of guilt, and new respect for her manager.

"As you are aware, Melissa is a qualified scientist who wasn't quite at the level required at the facility. Well, we have decided to give her the opportunity. She jumped at the chance with no hint of hesitation. I have no doubts there are bright things in her future." He paused in a way that said more was forthcoming. "She pulled me to one side and asked for a favour." He paused again to see that Alexia was listening. "She asked when all of this was over, if we could transfer somebody else to work with her — somebody keen who was also seeking an opportunity." He gestured with an open palm. "She asked for you to move to the laboratories with her... if you would still accept her as your manager."

He saw behind the breathing mask, the tubes and the pale skin, the sort of expression he had anticipated. Nodding in acknowledgement, he waited just long enough before changing the subject.

"Oscar and Kevin were here by your side and they agreed to leave the hospital only when it was clear that you would be okay. Kevin has to wear a bolted, metal neck brace for a while and his left leg is still encased in one of those plaster casts; he has to walk using crutches for another two weeks at least. You should see him! Poor kid can't stand having to use the things! Day before yesterday he came close to flinging them straight out the window!"

Alexia could have sworn there was a faint hint of a smile — an occurrence that, on its own, would be worth surviving for. Nobody would believe her if she told them she had seen him smile.

"He's a tough nutter!" he declared about Kevin. "He desperately wanted to be out and about helping. By the way I see it, if I was to honestly state the fact, it was all of out and out impossible to stop him!"

Glancing at the two police officers near the door, Bernard lifted a palm to gesture towards them. "These two kind officers never stopped believing in you. They came to see me on the morning after the press announcement, concerned the official story did not seem to match up with any of their findings. They were also very concerned that the findings from their investigations were being ignored."

Alexia closed her eyes as hot tears obscured her vision.

"Of course I already had my suspicions by then, but at the time, I had absolutely nothing to go on." He glanced again towards the door. "The support of these officers helped strengthen my resolve." There was the briefest of pauses before he quickly added. "Of course all the results of their investigation were added to the documents being distributed."

He waved once again in the direction of the pair. "These two fine officers stood by you the whole time, and it almost cost them their jobs. It apparently had something to do with your story being 'rock stone solid'?"

The hatred within her had nearly all melted away.

Tilting her head slightly to look at the reporters, Alexia saw that one by one, they were beginning to fumble and reach for their buzzing phones.

Bernard spoke again.

"Alexia, we need you alive! You have been the most talked about person in the country. You have, without any doubt, been the most hated one in all of the media." He looked deep into her eyes. "That's going to change now. You are about to become a hero. The people responsible for why you are in this hospital are going to prison! We need you standing with us while we work to bring them down!"

As he spoke the last few words, a frantic commotion broke out among the reporters. Cameras began flashing to capture photos of Alexia covered in wires and confined to a hospital bed. Across the nation and worldwide, national and international live news networks suddenly began to flash "Breaking News" banners. More reporters were stampeding to the hospital and social media began to churn with new activity.

Bernard glanced at the uniformed figures by the door. "These two fine officers will stay for a few days just to be sure you are well and very safe. By the way I see it, no one could have picked a better pair. And they both vigorously requested the assignment."

Alexia let her head settle into the allergenic pillows and allowed the rising tidal wave of feelings to consume her. The hatred and last vestiges of anger had evaporated leaving behind a gaping chasm and a ravaged, wounded soul digesting miraculous news of its redemption.

She closed her eyes and tried, but failed, to fight back the torrent of tears. Her chest heaved and shuddered and her body shook with sobs as she lost what control was left over her emotions. She felt a damp cloth dabbing her temples and earlobes as Bernard leaned to wipe away the flow from her eyes. Over by the door, the officers had pulled out their handkerchiefs and he glanced over as a soft muffled sob carried across.

Thank you Bernard! Thank you everyone! Alexia thought over and over and after a while, her head and body began to feel much lighter, and every muscle less taught.

All of a sudden, she was feeling overwhelmingly tired. The heaving sobs softened and her breathing grew gentler as Bernard, with the damp cloth, dabbed tenderly at her forehead and the corners of her eyes.

As she drifted off to sleep, her mind left the humming hospital room and wandered away to the moon bathed, sparkling city centre. She was strolling amorously down the dusky, starry high street, side by side with him, looking sharp in his fancy suit, walking along with his steady stride, and wanting to be nowhere else but there with her, holding her hand...

By the way she saw it, it was the most beautiful of evenings!

The End

Moine Together

One – Before Visitors

"Not upon all occurrence of life point within time!" the faction head's raised voice thundered to thousands of members at the hurriedly called meeting filled with everyone who could attend. "Distant the point may it be catapulted beyond the faraway! We cannot stand for it! May it be upon all of those who thrive with this to strongly cease!"

Most of the crowd violently cheered.

Moine-E-Ghome casually watched and nodded in agreement.

Some days had gone by after the controversial meeting and crouched in position, he glanced briefly at a large snake gliding up a giant tree a short distance away. The creature was not hungry. The casual, graceful way it slithered suggested it was not a threat—not for the moment anyway. That did not mean it would be wise to linger near it. He was glad it was just far enough away to ignore; he could hold his position. It had turned into a matter of life and death that all fighters, at any cost, must stand at the ready.

Heavily built and towering a full head above most others, Moine-E-Ghome strode as the most daunting fighter of his generation. Rippling with the blessings of nature and training, his bulk twitched, sparsely wrapped in ceremonial battle gear, presenting a sound, hulking, formidable figure, impressive in appearance and dominating in character.

Despite his size, a disarmingly mild mannered charm and a moderated, soft way left everyone around him engrossed and at ease. The piercing, deep charcoal eyes and sweeping, mind settling gestures reassured all that, though superior in every physical way, he possessed infinite patience and the wide open mind to insist upon your freedom to be yourself in his presence.

The great "cycle of seasons" battles and tournaments were fast approaching and fighters of strong ambition were swallowed up in training. On most days, he was drawn by a potent compulsion to the corner of an open field, where for most of the daylight, he would lunge and thrust and swing his weapons, in a never-ending quest at mastering four of them. He had met two of his challengers—and Dorrne-E-Jonkuhe, who came startlingly close to being a formidable opponent in the last season's battles. And he was even stronger this season!

"Who marches head up and arm out and eyes upwards to face upon Moine-E-Ghome this closing end season?" an excited fan, hard at work, called out to the rest of the group of highly skilled bridge technicians he was out on a job with.

"Hehsseeh—e!!" a craftsman next to the foreman exclaimed. "They have well winning narrowed and left it called upon the final four, each one great at near most in their own tribes and factions!" He paused before lifting a hand and waving it from side to side. "But knowing I have mind upon none as great like Moine-E-Ghome!"

"I mind upon my thoughts he may, Dorrne-E-Jonkuhe, upon of the final four mostly may be!" the technician offered his opinion.

"Hehsseeh—e!" some in the group exclaimed in agreement. "Would be a mighty mind day to watch his style against the Grendje! Would be very, very most upon a very dearly day!"

Such was Moine-E-Ghome's, never questioned domination, excitement never revolved around who might defeat him, but who would venture to be the next to face him in battle.

Small tournaments—with a gradual increase in intensity—led up to the famous greater fights, and as fierce arena battles raged with injuries anticipated, and fighters in agony when weapons made contact, not a single life perished. The great annual battles were for power, speed and artistry; to hurt opponents so they bowed to superior talent. Grievous injuring was frowned upon and strictly forbidden having long been declared taboo in civilization—the sort of thing that only fresh amateurs would do.

"I mind make upon like this... and this... and this way!" explained a well trained fighter swinging one of the legendary weapons in a field, mid-way through an impromptu training session.

With squinted eyes and tensed shoulders, he stomped swiftly forward again, swinging the odd contraption in a rapid, oval arc. A deft snap of his upper arms, a flick of rippling muscle and the weapon changed trajectory and momentum at the final moment, faster than the eye could see, raising a puff of dust from a bag an onlooker was holding.

"Make upon to flow like this upon, strong here... and here!" he clarified, while tapping with one hand, the relevant portions of his well honed anatomy to have the most power for control of the weapon.

101

"Hehsseeh—e!" the small gathered crowd exclaimed in awe.

Experienced fighters all acquired power so precise, that a calculated lunge could dislodge a single leaf from the branch of a tree, or shatter and pulverize a large rock to pieces. Wielded by a seasoned and experienced combatant, a full force lunge from a legendary weapon could reportedly annihilate up to nine opponents—nobody knew for sure, and nobody dared venture a trial.

"Upon it may be done to march up with eyes up and arm out to face Moine-E-Ghome this biggest end season?" an excited group of bystanders called out to the fighter. "We call it may upon become the mighty biggest battle!"

There was a flash and a whoosh as the weapon arced in empty air, defying all reality and dancing in a magic realm.

"I march up, my head up, my arm out to face him!" the bulky fighter replied. "Upon of the last battles when in three well remaining, I face Moine-E-Ghome, full-way, with honour and glory!"

He swung his weapon once again purely for the theatre.

"Hehsseeh—e! Woh! Woh! Woh!" the onlookers cheered.

Two young males stared with mesmerized eyes.

Never deployed for bringing death, the great weapons stood as roaring symbols of restraint. Top fighters mastered unwavering self control, harnessing their own unique ways to win battles while avoiding the embarrassing label of *Amateur*.

Superior control, without inflicting grievous injury, was touted by those in the know to be like skilfully hurling a large rock down a hill at an opponent standing still all the way at the bottom, and having the rock slow and then come to a dead stop at just the right moment, and in just the right way to only graze his shin and cause no further damage. Means to master such feats eluded most beings making the seasonal tournaments a highlight for crowds travelling to witness the extraordinary fighters in action.

Moine-E-Ghome—unquestionably the most extraordinary—cast legendary focus and glowed with dedication. Close to mastering four of the six deadliest weapons and wielding them all with frightening skill and speed, his precision stung so faultless, live audiences frequently disbelieved their own eyes.

"Moine-E-Ghome upon the great most thrust and spike, speed, sway! Speed, sway! Most unstoppable! No stopping!" declared an excited fan looking forward to the tournament. "Speed, sway! Speed, sway! Upon whom of each four venture to even merely resist?! Even merely!? Upon whom?" he asked his large group of similarly excited friends.

"Hehsseeh—e!" exclaimed a keen battle enthusiast. "Not one! Not four! Not upon any may wander and venture forward from any near or distant land!" He raised his arms and wiggled his hands and head in barely contained excitement, then jumped up and down in unrestrained, comical glee, drawing laughter and exuberant support from the rest of the group.

Moine-E-Ghome treasured his favourite weapon, known by all as the Grendje, a long and innocent looking, toughened alloy, forged pole birthed from intense work by forgers and alchemists, with hexagonal, bulbous masses fused to both ends—each one nearly the size of an average height, adults head.

Well balanced, infinitely strong, the weapon swung like a charged up extension of his arm and wielding it with all his power, aware of its indestructibility, attacks flew with vigour borne of well tested certainty that every lunge would count.

He examined and carefully checked his Grendje before every event, looking along the entire length, eyes settling on one end, then scanning with deliberate focus, until they reached the other. There was never any need to; only a personal ritual. Every fighter had their ways and their own superstitions. When speaking of the issue, he declared a strong connection to the blood of the giant Metoa-ea-Nogoro tree that gave its essence when wrapping and curing in the delicate process of building the bulbous ends. Only the sap was ever used leaving the tree alive and strong and he launched every strike as though its living soul guided him.

Wielding the weapon, he erupted in a display of skill and ferocity of such intensity, spectators and gathered crowds gasped in awe. Few fighters had mastered its swaying, hypnotic style, smashing rocks, bringing down small, stone buildings in choreographed demonstrations, and demolishing structures erected purely for the show. With energized movements, they lunged at targets in mesmerizing, lightening fast, technical attacks, decimating them one by one, with flair and theatre, giving the best entertainment for the awestruck spectators.

But the great tournaments carried an intentional purpose.

Moine-E-Ghome's lively swagger, his pulsing, throaty, easy laugh and the universally infectious, positive outlook, laid bare his love for the sport and for current day life. But only a few generations before he was born were unhappy, turbulent and tumultuous times. Life in bygone eras was short and brutal and the days were unbearably fast and savage. With a handful of leaders seeking ultimate power and pursuing full victory with no regard for the costs, clans and factions endlessly battled each other and countless, beastly wars raged and savaged the land. Had he been a child in those ferocious and unstable times, it is unlikely Moine-E-Ghome would have lived to see adulthood.

Loathing had festered of the war torn existence as many desperately hankered for a settled way of life. Nascent factions for peace took root and began to collude and as they grew stronger, others eagerly joined them until looming change bore down like a rain storm hovering in the horizon after a long and difficult drought.

The great warlords, in the end, were resoundingly defeated and the remnants clinging to power were overrun and wiped out. Ghorron-E-Khomelo, the most powerful and well armed was the final tyrant to perish in the onslaught.

The peace factions grew, and eager covenants bound them to peaceful living alongside one other, settling on a system that was satisfactory for all, where no faction sought to dominate any other. Life flourished and the ways thrived. Everyone sought groups that led the path they yearned for and keen alchemists, scientists, inventors, scholars and uncountable myriads of innovative minds rose into the new ways, and the realms of all factions churned with creativity.

The battle tournaments were birthed into this new world out of sheer necessity and for entertainment. Lingering aggression that may have tainted new ways would instead be vented in training and fitness, conquering discipline and mastering the weapons. Spectators would pile into splendid venues to watch fighters do battle for 'Glory Of The Title', which came with the season end 'Box Of Known Valuables' holding twice the value of other combatants rewards.

"End season battles make upon good and great peace!" a wise faction elder explained to a group of children. "One here, one there beings inner quiver and yearning, upon energy and excitement, upon speed and power, upon loud and glory, upon thrill and danger! Troubled waywardness of beings upon set on good path! Seasonal tournaments upon peace and make good!"

The children listened keenly as he spoke of their culture, all glad to be living in the happy and peaceful times.

Moine-E-Ghome manoeuvred each day with gratitude, hurling frequent comments and rolling out niceties wishing all he encountered a long life and good health: it was pleasant being alive in the times he grew up in, where life had evolved beyond all recognition.

With limited technology, the civilization meandered into alchemy, architecture and large scale construction. The lands, the vast seas, heaving oceans and the clear lakes sparkled, rolled and chimed with stewarded purity, and the air was clean and blew so crispy clear, when deeply inhaled, it was believed to soothe ailments.

"Intake deeply one breathing good breath, more again and another until all of eight upon!" a wise faction elder guided a trio of youngsters, one of whom complained of some fogginess in her thoughts. "Clear mind, clear inside, clear thinking and clear health. Upon good air inside and clear mind and good body."

He laughed and nodded approvingly as all three youngsters immediately began a series of eight inhalations.

As seasons passed in time, giant buildings rose from the ground, sprouting and growing from their buried foundations while tiny clambering figures, dwarfed by the vast scale, added ever more rocks and materials enhanced with a myriad of powders and wonder and minerals, commanding the behemoth to bludgeon all common sense. Bridges spanned un-navigable, travel defying obstacles and sprawling new structures swelled, clawing for the skyline and worrying distance hills of being outshone in magnitude. Moine-E-

Ghome marvelled at alchemists and scientists who conjured hardness of such durability, dwellings and architecture spawned of the substances stood strong in defiance of the elements and of time. Some later, extreme creations extended to such great heights, they would take a full morning to climb without mechanical aids.

"I venture up! Upon step! Walk only! All up!" he overheard a youthful tribal member declare to a group of friends as they stared at the highest standing behemoth in their region.

Adorned with several viewing bays, balconies along its height and a flat area spanning the top, designed for sightseeing, it presented a challenge to any set on roof top viewing who chose to ignore the travel mechanical conveyors.

"Upon the new days of three, I venture step and walk way up!" the young male declared with the keenness of his low age.

"Hehsseeh—e!" exclaimed the group of young adults.

"Not half-way, even upon, fearsome, foremost exhaustion! You will downward under falling, breaking, doof, boof, kapang!" taunted a youngster amidst a wild eruption of guffaws. "Much asleep beyond surpassing, very a tired, like tired baby, upon two days, asleep, even more, upon it be!" he added as Moine-E-Ghome, standing a few paces away, joined the rest of the group in hearty, uncontrolled laughter.

"I show you!" countered the youth. "I show upon your own eyes! No under, boof, doof, and no upon I go kapang!"

He gestured mockingly, rousing howls of laughter from the boisterous group, and Moine-E-Ghome chuckled as he turned to carry on walking to his second favourite fruit market only a short distance away.

Peace, reigned in all the land and life trundled happily on. Moine-E-Ghome stared at new sunrises every day, earnestly wishing for a reply from his beloved, before gathering up the weapons to set off for training. He had to be certain to fend off all challengers in the tournament finals.

He had to once again defend his 'Glory Of The Title'.

And then the visitors came.

Two – The Dwelling

The strange flying structure emerged gradually from the skies with a non-stop noise like ongoing thunder. With simple lives in nature, Moine-E-Ghome and all others of his civilization had never encountered such an astonishing creation. Descending from behind the clouds, it floated by its own power, with the focussed intention of getting down to the land. Spellbound, with all activity frozen mid-motion, everyone witnessing it stood silenced with awe.

A few offered opinions of it being a flying dwelling, but as the apprehensive, growing crowds watched it hover downwards, bewildered by the size and frightened by the resonating noise, they stood perplexed, gesturing upwards and slowly shaking their heads, asking why anyone would want to create a home floating above the clouds, when there was so much space still available on land. No faction came forward as the owners of the structure. Probably some errant scientists from a faraway region had created it to show off their talents in construction.

Moine-E-Ghome was settled on a hand woven bench-chair in the rectangle of open space behind his large, stone cabin, having a broth and a weave bag of fresh purple berries when an out of breath messenger, impetuously fidgeting, arrived with startling news of the dwelling from the sky.

Head shaking in frustration, he frowned at the strange news and how it might adversely affect his situation. Having recently declared and confessed to a female, six days had gone by while anxiously awaiting ceremonial delivery with word of her answer. Solye-I-Bhove, the focus of his "heart thirst", ran a weaving enterprise with her sister, Konko-I-Bhove, right next to their sprawling, well decorated, parents home.

Back in the days of turmoil, females agreed to partner with any attractive males who declared and confessed to them. Tiring of joylessness and misery of uncertainty, and having to raise children—frequently without support—in a random, unfocussed, unforgiving existence, they met to discuss new proposals and solutions, and ways to make males more thoughtful and responsible. After collusions rippling across all the land, announcements reverberated like thunder of the intellect, shaking up society, that they would no longer be rewarding any males who were trouble makers, wayward and un-liked in any faction.

The resulting adjustment juddered and quaked and barrelled through communities, demolishing complacence. All males strived to be hard-working and honest so their quest would not be rejected when the time came. After declaring to a female, there followed a long wait while proving his honesty and worth in the community. The pause or "The Angst" announced a male's inner turmoil endured in the lengthy wait for word of her answer.

It was always easy to spot which were lingering in the angst; they scuttled about, the hardest working, most polite and most helpful, going far above and beyond what anyone would expect of them. Living in such a way had to be well proven for many days until sufficient numbers had taken word back to the object of their desire, and to all of her family, that he was an upstanding member of society.

When the lady was satisfied and happy with the efforts, she would send word, asking for strange and rare gifts—like a fruit that only ripened once every four seasons, or a flower that only bloomed in a long, perfect spring.

The male was to search—wallowing deep in the angst—until the item was obtained and the ceremony ordained, after which she agreed to give herself in the way he wished, and with great celebration and blessings from the community, they were partnered forever in the physical life.

Moine-E-Ghome stared at the sky pondering how it birthed the dwelling. What faction created it? What tinkering got it to fly? Sweeping his eyes across the partly cloudy expanse, he scanned to see if there were any more unusual objects. He saw a few birds, a moon, the usual entities and nothing resembling a descending giant.

Turning to look to the right, he stared with wistful eyes towards the cluster of rock pylons towering in the distance. Constructed to catch and channel wind to giant water pumps, they hissed softly and trembled as one walked in their presence. Solye-I-Bhove lived in the large settlement to the right, near their majestic shadows, so close, that when you stood in the rectangle of open space found outside of every home, the humming of the pillars carried over with each un-caught breeze. He had walked with her to the pylons and stood by the mightiest one, as the whistling of the channelled gusts reinforced his confession.

He promised that if she took him, he would be as reliable and by her side for as long as the winds had ever blown over all the land. He saw as her grey eyes gazed upwards into his the brimming urge to say yes—and she feigned nonchalance in pretence at considering. She would still make him wait: females needed to be sure. He had to prove his motives and intentions were noble.

Staring at the pylons, he ached with the savage, primal yearning for her essence and cast the ever-ether with wishes for the angst to end. Forcing it to the back of his mind, he was curious what her thoughts would be of news about the flying dwelling descended from the sky.

Settled in a thriving community a while away from the odd events, news arrived to Moine-E-Ghome, with updates from travellers, a trickle of reports from agitated messengers and keen-eared sources of reliable information. They told of a flying dwelling floating slowly to the ground with a great, thundering, bellowing noise, while belching dense fumes that lingered heavily in the air like a sour laden, oily soup, making sinuses sting and leaving a bitter taste in the mouth.

When the dust had settled and many moments passed by with no activity, the placid locals walked up to the humming, monstrous structure and began, with great curiosity and endless touching and prodding, to keenly study its walls and its cave-sized, belching ducts—still hot and pungent from gushing out the fumes. The exterior felt peculiar and strangely cold, as though metallic, but forged from a material they had never come across before. Two alchemists declared it was a blend of different metals, melted and blended and baked with minerals, and then processed for ultimate strength and durability.

Another alchemist produced a sample concocted seasons earlier inside his specialized workshop. Never utilized, it had nestled on a long, creaking, overfilled storage shelf that sagged under the weight of other substances and alloys that he hadn't got around to inventing a use for yet. A blend of three metals carefully melted together and strengthened with a tincture of four, rare chemicals, the sample came closest to matching the substance covering the exterior of the enormous structure. The alchemist had long abandoned research on the alloy and offering reasons, in his own learned opinion, insisted that the process of forging useful quantities was uncomfortably toxic, and the end result was not nearly as strong as a multitude of similar materials that he and other alchemists succeeded in concocting.

The strange dwelling hummed and stood, near silent and ominous, for nearly two days after which, without warning, a section that appeared to be a doorway opened up, like an eyelid over a giant, gaping eye socket, revealing a cavernous interior of mysteries. Real life beings—only a small group at first—emerged and tentatively made their way down a sloping, serrated ramp that had slowly extended out as part of the floor.

The beings all stood smaller than Moine-E-Ghome's people and their bodies were entirely wrapped and covered in what appeared to be sealed, protective materials—as though they feared the air. Their small, piercing eyes gazed from inside the darkened, frontal section of the bulbous covering that hid the rest of their heads. They walked on two unsteady legs and swung two spindly arms, striving to learn how to move in a strange land—which wasn't too much of a bother because they seemed to learn quickly. They appeared to tire easily, as though something squashed them down, with a few aimlessly striding about and then stopping for a rest, suggesting their bodies were a heavy load to carry. The locals watched them curiously, perplexed by their presence and amused by the movements of the odd, alien beings.

The first group to emerge clutched strangely shaped hand tools they pointed excitedly at anyone who approached them. Wary of the locals, they were unmistakeably keen to keep a safe distance away, which in the moment and at the time seemed reasonably excusable.

The strange beings then went about as though busy with errands that, to the locals, clearly appeared pre-planned, collecting fist sized samples of soil, water, rock and anything else they could cut or break a sizeable piece of. Various small portions of material they dug up were carried into the dwelling for what, at the time, were unknown purposes.

They brought out, as time went by, varieties of strange tools that hummed, pulsed and clicked under their own power supply, then used them to dig in selected patches of the ground into which they inserted long, cylindrical devices or injected a substance resembling a translucent gel.

After several days had gone by of this peculiar work, bigger and more powerful humming tools were gently trundled out and small structures begun to spring up all around the area, each bustling with odd, inexplicable activity. They collected greater amounts of buried clumps and samples and appeared to be conducting planned experiments on them. Keen alchemists and scientists of Moine-E-Ghome's world watched carefully, well aware of what the visitors were doing.

"They are looking upon about and under for a mineral, or some other material of to them, great preciousness and intense value!"

they declared, having done similar exploration work themselves. "Looking and appearances of it are that they have upon uncovered good and mighty size, plenty, fine portions of it!"

The locals were incensed! "Never upon this occurrence of life point within time!" they cried out, feeling disrespected and highly insulted. "Distant the point may it be catapulted beyond the faraway! May the beings show the meekest testing of courtesy and reach and make to ask us who walk the land first!" they vigorously protested. "May the ever-ether upon grant reason and thoughtfulness!"

After brave attempts to communicate with the visitors, decisions were made to let them carry on with digging. In the little interaction where anything was learned, they introduced themselves, explaining that they had travelled from their world far away, whose name was as strange as the name of their species—with a location so distant, they aged slightly on the journey. They spoke in a different way, with noises, pitch, gestures and a language so alien and indecipherable, that it may as well have been the rattling of a bag of pebbles.

With ever increasing difficulty in understanding each other and after a few exchanges amongst endless futile attempts to find out more about their odd activities, it became clear they had no further interest in talking. Before long, they rejected anyone going near them and when anybody got too close, they emitted panicked, warning shrieks and hoarse howling noises that to the locals, resonated like desperate alarm calls. Once in a while, they reached for the hand tools strapped to their sides and lifted them up to point at whoever was approaching. It was suspected that the strange tools were in fact, a type of weapon and the locals trod with caution so as not to cause alarm. The decision was made to suspend attempts at contact until the visitors felt more settled in the environment.

Frequent news filtered through to Moine-E-Ghome, mostly of stories about the visitors digging up samples of soil, or their strange, full coverings, or ever more descriptions of dwellings and other structures they were earnestly building. No ill appeared to be done and nobody was yet harmed and after some pondering, he supported, in full agreement with the elders' decision, to stay away and let the beings carry on undisturbed.

The visitors ambled and shuffled, studying materials and carrying out mystery experiments, digging and analyzing. More structures sprung up and when left alone to carry on with their peculiar work, all appeared to run fine: the locals could almost ignore them. But after many days of the site bustling with activity, just as all were getting accustomed to the alien presence, events altered and their bizarre presence turned ominous, and news carried on by later breathless messengers and more reports trickling from desperate travellers began to turn sinister and increasingly unpleasant.

Two enormous flying dwellings, similar in size and shape, arrived and firmly perched themselves in close proximity—on the same piece of land where the first one stood. Before they were settled and before a single being had obdurately trotted down the slanted, serrated ramps, a fourth colossal dwelling appeared, hovering high in the sky and with a non-stop bellow, descended and gradually set down, like a herculean beast, close to its smaller friends.

More of the strange visitors poured out from doorways and began to help with collecting samples of soil and rock. Odd looking materials and components were wheeled out, some of which they used for building large shelters on the land and others which they joined together and drove into the ground to create a metal boundary fence—as though marking out land duly declared as theirs.

Larger tools and structures tore up yawning holes in the ground and then descended into them, guzzling dusty, frothing material into their metal mouths. What they swallowed was swept along vibrating, mechanical intestines to vanish into grating bellies of larger, hungrier structures. Processes were applied to the rocks churning within the bowels to extract whatever part the visitors desired and the deadly waste excreted was pumped raw onto the land, where it soaked and then trickled, snaking into pristine waterways.

Local plants began to wither as their essence was savaged by the vile substances attacking and settling within them. Nearby animals showed anguish, and then perished, after drinking from the rivers or consuming the tainted wild growth. Children fell ill shortly after playing near the water and felt very unwell after swimming downstream; several succumbed after eating fruit, seeds and sweet plants, growing or rooted along the flowing, poisoned waterways.

"Within all in perception, far and near, high and low, not upon this occurrence of life point within time!" the burly chief of the local region cried out to a gathered audience. "Distant the point may it be catapulted beyond the faraway! And we may, unforbidden, converse with them all and make it upon the now and present that their waywardness must not be!"

The decision was made to once again talk with the visitors to work out a different way for running their processes. Their clumsy methods could not be allowed to go unchallenged and the chief wanted suggestions on how to proceed. A group of eight, wise individuals and two high level alchemists was assembled and tasked with the formidable errand and after gathering up assorted gifts, and a ceremonial head-wreath, they adorned themselves in grand, formal attire.

At the appointed moment, cautiously approaching the cordoned site, they made every attempt to appear as friendly as possible. They were yet some distance away, purposefully striding, when shrieks and muffled howls erupted from among the strange beings as all activity ceased and barely controlled panic ensued. Roughly half the visitors gathered up a myriad of paraphernalia and made their way to the ramps to climb back into the dwellings. The groups that didn't run teamed into clear defensive lines and lifted up the strange weapons to aim towards the casually approaching band of locals.

Bearing no ill intentions, the wise individuals and alchemists moved forward, with backs straight and arms down to avoid looking threatening. As they closed in on the entrance to the boundary fence, the wise leader raised his arm and called out the friendly, universal greeting, casting the ever-ether with wishes of joy.

Everything in Moine-E-Ghome's world changed from that moment.

The tools the visitors brandished sparked up and flared with bursts of sharp, crackling noises erupting out of them. Small, carbon based projectiles hurtled towards the individuals faster than any of them could move to get out of the way. One by one, as the small objects pierced their bodies, they stumbled and fell and their eyes glazed over. Gentle breathing turned into rasping gasps, sucking air into ravaged organs tortured by mortal wounds.

The carnage did not cease until the entire group lay dead.

Some distance away, terrified locals stood watching, horrified by the intentional ending of so many lives—a scene not witnessed by any who had walked the land in multiple generations of Moine-E-Ghome's people.

More visitors poured out of the ominous doorways, marching down serrated ramps, while wielding larger and more sinister looking weapons that began flaring out endless torrents of projectiles. Charging beyond the structures and the self declared boundary, they ventured further out, beyond where they had been working, seeking all locals who lived across the nearby land. All native beings encountered—fully grown or newborn—felt hurtling projectiles pierce their bodies and by close of the rampage, all who inhabited surrounding areas, and others who only happened to be travelling through, lay motionless on the ground or had fled for their lives.

The visitors, as the alchemists and scientists warned, desired a rare mineral ore of great value in their home land. Preparations were under way for more digging and transportation to where, back on their world, they would earn great rewards.

Harbouring little compassion for other life or beings and spurred on by what they had discovered in the ground, nothing was to be permitted to interrupt excavations—certainly not the locals, soon regarded as pests. It seemed the visitors had come to their own conclusions that the inhabiting people of Moine-E-Ghome's world might rise up and strive to become troublesome obstacles.

Among spiralling woes, groups of locals were sent out, carrying gifts and trinkets in desperate supplication, with hopes of finding new and fresh ways to communicate. Efforts were made on reaching out to restore calm and to try and understand why the visitors were vicious. Expeditions arrived, laden heavy with offerings, accompanied by wise aids, enlightened negotiators and at one point, by a celebrated dancing troupe adorned with ceremonial, woven, leaf-totems of friendship and painted in the colours of lasting tranquillity. A messenger was finally sent in with a peace recital, carrying messages of forgiveness and great new beginnings. The attempts remained futile and most proved deadly; the messenger's carbon projectile ridden corpse was retrieved much later, from where the heartless visitors had coldly discarded it.

Gathering each day after descending from their dwellings, the visitors ventured out further from the boundary, eliminating all beings not from their own world with no regard for status or thoughts of compassion. As Moine-E-Ghome glared at the distant hills, pondering the insanity, biding time in wait of announcements from the urgent, elder's meeting to make new plans, the truth about unfolding events seared on his soul: the locals, regardless of age or faction were under extermination, and at the end of ideas to appeal to the hunters.

Three – Urgent Times

The atmosphere simmered in grim, unrelenting dread, sunk in grave times, where ways buried deep in legend may have to be revived. Long forgotten, ancient tactics living only in old tales were up for consideration, if the people were to grapple with repelling the invasion.

Moine-E-Ghome leaned back in the woven chair outside his home, his charcoal coloured eyes locked, unseeing, on the horizon. Standing up to briefly gaze at the distant rock pylons, he thought of Solye-I-Bhove and longed for her presence. At other times, he would compulsively be out practising, refining new moves in preparation for the tournaments. But all recreation was forgone and forgotten; greater issues raged within, intensely occupying all minds.

He scanned the faraway hills at the edge of his faction's territory wondering when the visitors would come pouring over them. Unlikeable solutions may have to be unearthed, dark answers contemplated in any realistic quest for confrontation and he was certain, just as many in all the communities were that, even though he would support it, he was not going to like it. Unwilling to stand, uncalled, to make the difficult decision, he left it to the gathered, community group of elders. A meeting was already planned to announce the conclusions and every able bodied being was eager to attend.

During the meeting, the unthinkable began to be discussed. Endless options were offered up and heated words exchanged as passions rose and strong feelings vigorously erupted. Some tempers, made fragile by recent occurrences teetered on the edge, erratic and difficult to control. They had to fight back—some seething locals forcefully argued—but others remained fearful of awakening the consequences.

"Not upon this occurrence of life point in forever time!" a fiercely angry local hurled, while waving curled fingers in the universal gesture of rage. "Distant the point may it be catapulted the furthest away! We must! We must rise to give and to cease and to end, or they will finish us!"

But others feared resurrecting a slumbering demon.

It was finally settled, agreed to by all, to send a small group of fighters to warn—but not to kill—in the same way factions gestured to one another during difficult times when disagreements were rife. It was hoped such a message would be laden with clarity so they would alter their ways and begin to make amends.

On the planned day, selected fighters gathered up, out of sight, confirmed the final strategy, and then launched their mock attack, swiftly overrunning the new self-made boundary. The strange beings, cowering inside their coverings, were mesmerised, having been caught off their guard. Eclipsed by superior speed and power of the locals, they scampered, defenceless—in simulated danger from fighters with clean and meticulous skills, arcing lightening lunges that landed like feathers. It was only a warning after all, and an honourable action of speaking to beings in the language of warriors; a small tap—a gentle wave of a hand—to caution the wayward ways were unwelcome.

The visitors were not as honourable as the locals had hoped.

When it dawned on them that there was little danger of injury, they turned and struck back with their own lethal weapons, lifting and pointing with no apparent restraint, manoeuvring them to cause mortal damage. Mute in the language of honourable warriors, they meant no part of the reaction as a warning. Devoid of compassion and with no such morality, no thoughts abided for other living beings. Moine-E-Ghome's people would soon come to conclude that not a sliver of honour could be found within the hearts of all the new beings put together.

In the wake of the bloodbath, every fighter lay dead. Witnesses bore claims the slayers cackled with glee. The visitors then formed groups that ventured out and indiscriminately attacked more of Moine-E-Ghome's people. Hundreds were slain as extermination speeded up and the land spiralled into deep turmoil and sorrow.

Another meeting was called with all factions in attendance, where urgent discussions flared, lighting up emotions. Bold options were tossed about, pummelling the conscience and Moine-E-Ghome, with great reluctance weighing down his heart, put forth his opinion, fully agreeing with the majority. The decision was finally made and all consequences accepted. The civilization would fight back but this time, it would be different: it was going to be for real!

Every fighter was called up and all factions scrambled to put forward their very best to go into battle. Selecting their weapon, each hulking figure stepped forward, ready to depart—to abandon morality and strike with intention. Avoiding serious injury was no longer the rule; the taboo was to be lifted and temporarily set aside. The visitors were officially proclaimed as the enemy, a discordant force to be eliminated at all costs, and every faction tasked to do their part to go and stop them. Buried ways of legend were once again to be revived and Moine-E-Ghome's people prepared for the unthinkable.

An alchemist, working with scientists and inventors, constructed large devices designed and calibrated to catapult globules of fiery, explosive gel great distances over the air with frightening accuracy. Moine-E-Ghome, the elders and a gathering of fighters stood watching in silence during a live demonstration, occasionally murmuring of terrifying precision, and marvelling at the destruction after detonation. They taught a handful of fighters how to use the devices and concocted far more than the requirement of substance so no visitor's structures would be left undamaged.

Filled with wonder at the sight of shaped alloy shields that fit with acceptable comfort over the body and the limbs, Moine-E-Ghome thanked the alchemists and the scientists as he fastened on the last of the segments over his upper arms. Light weight and tough, assurances were given by the enthusiastic creators, that the shields would absorb most of the impact of the carbon projectiles the visitors sent from their weapons, and stop them from piercing the bodies of the fighters.

Moine-E-Ghome stepped up to lead the front combatants that would make the first contact and begin the lethal attacks. Five other groups would follow with a wave of reinforcement, rising shortly after the first strike had taken full effect. Approaching three from the rear and one each from either side, the targets would be swallowed in the legendary pincer. The elders were insistent that though an old formation, the element of surprise swung success in their favour and after long discussions, painstaking considerations and endless revisions of scenarios and tactics, the plan was finally ready to go into motion.

As Moine-E-Ghome and others toiled in a field in preparation, approaching sounds of children and wind chimes floated in the breeze. Everyone perked up and silence descended. Recognition brought smiles and a sparkle to the air and another male who had also declared, stepped forward to stand beside Moine-E-Ghome, waiting in breathless anticipation; it was customary to remain still and absolutely silent, especially if your name might be one of those called.

Before long, the three cheery ceremonial messengers stepped on to the field, with leaves in their headgear and contraptions holding large, metallic wind chimes dangling in mid-air behind their backs. A sizable crowd followed, many of whom were dancing and giggling children, swept up in the popular, irresistible spectacle.

Everyone knew what the trio represented.

With great drama, the messengers began to pretend to search, scanning across the entire crowd, gazing into the distance and hilariously, one of them searching underneath a twig. Finally, with exaggerated exasperation, even though they could see him standing a short distance away, they called out the name of the individual they were looking for.

"Where upon, would we know, this walking, breathing, fighting one called Moine-E-Ghome!?"

The shoulders of the other male slumped, and he slowly stepped away. It was not his time yet; his angst would fester a little while longer. Messengers for him would turn up only two days later.

Moine-E-Ghome stood silent and quivering with anticipation.

"He there upon! Only over there!" the entire crowd chanted.

With musical clinking and clanging from the wind chimes, the messengers skipped forward, going too far to the left, pretending not to see him and acting like he wasn't there.

"Eeeeeeeeeeh!? Where upon this walking, missing one called Moine-E-Ghome?" they called out in exaggerated dramatics and wonderment.

"Noooooooooooooo!" screamed the giggling crowd. "Too far upon one way! Turn and go upon the other! Moine-E-Ghome be very near!"

The messengers whirled around and enthusiastically skipped past him in the other direction.

"Eeeeeeeeeeh!? Where upon this walking, breathing, invisible Moine-E-Ghome?"

"Noooooooooooooo!!" the crowd yelled in rising laughter. "Too far upon other way! Turn and go back upon but only for a small way!"

With loud, skilfully calibrated tinkling from the wind chimes, the messengers skipped closer to him, and then turned to look the opposite way from where he stood behind them.

"Eeeeeeeeeeh!? Where upon this breathing, never finding, Moine-E-Ghome!?"

"Noooooooooooo!" the crowd responded even louder. "You are looking upon wrong way! Turn back! Turn baaaaaaack!!"

"Eeeeeeeeeeeh!? Go back home upon all you say!?" the messengers shouted in mock disappointment. "Okay, we upon begin to take back the sent message, and say upon the sender, Moine-E-Ghome is not upon for finding on this land!"

"NOOOOOOOOOOO!" the crowd screamed in hysterics.

The ritual carried on and by the time the messengers finally stood before Moine-E-Ghome, and with dramatic gestures, enquired where on the land he had been hiding, much of the crowd was rolling on the ground in laughter, with children laughing so hard, tears flowed from their eyes.

The messengers delivered word from Solye-I-Bhove and the request was simple—only two gifts in total. He was to deliver the same number of purple berries as the number of rock pylons where he declared and confessed.

The next request consisted of only a name—*Moine-E-Ghome*!

Every adult fell silent at the profoundness of the words. Children—with tender age denying them wisdom—broke into joyful, exuberant cheering.

Tears flowed among the crowd at the strength of the message; he was to come back alive! It was simple and succinct. After setting off to fight with great bravery and vigour, he was to stay alive and ensure he returned with the others. She was wishing him well, yearning for and accepting him. And when he came back, *he* would be the gift she wanted.

Moine-E-Ghome, never once known or heard of to cry, stood staring at the messengers, his eyes brimming with tears.

Four –Lurking Moine

On the day the true fight back was set to begin, events were worse than ever: the visitors, on a rampage, advanced so quickly, they were fast approaching Moine-E-Ghome's home and his community. All the young and the sick, the non-combatants and the elderly, were moved to hidden caves a safe distance away. The strong ones and all the fighters positioned themselves in pre-planned, ancient, tactical, battle formations.

A sense of sadness swam heavy in the air and many movements lumbered, slow and hesitant. Murmurs, sombre roving of eyes, multitudes of gestures in incensed resignation, and the instinctive absent-minded clenching of teeth whispered out to the ever-ether, reporting that the locals harboured no desire to kill: legends of turbulent times fuelled intense revulsion of lethal actions. But each hand was forced and every fighter coerced, every weapon newly wielded to its own full potential. With all nerves frayed and with questions festering, Moine-E-Ghome embarked on his new role of commanding the hastily assembled battalions to victory.

Using abundant thick trees in pre-planned strategy, they concealed themselves. Moine-E-Ghome endured an ever rising wave of nausea but he tried to hide it well so other fighters would not see. Also devoid of any real appetite for killing, he tamed every movement, successfully hiding the lingering, unwilling, shaky, tell-tale signs of a hesitant soul and a pounding, racing pulse. Killing went against every teaching of their world and rubbed raw the deep roots and saviour of their culture. As the spearhead—the one the fighters were all looking up to, it fell squarely upon him to exude bravery and when the moment came, there could be no hesitation.

Tasked with timing and launching the wave, all eyes would be alert, trained on to his every move, and he had to be certain not to let everybody down.

With the fighters all assembled, they lurked among the spaced out trees, silent, primed and ready, hidden behind the trunks and the undergrowth. Large, nesting, fearless Chuiku-ma-impye birds hissed, hooted and cheerily chirped their eerie, juddering, low pitched melodies, high up in the upper-most, leaf-laden branches. The resonating ballad pumped from their trembling throats, rolled and tumbled through the foliage and funnelled into every ear in waving, hypnotic pulses, playing subtle tricks on the mind and strumming hidden strings in the heart. The birds were alien to the visitors and their haunting harmonics made for a welcome distraction in Moine-E-Ghome's favour. He guessed they were disorienting to ears that didn't know of them.

A small, agile, four armed Komoi-nta-fyirie ape whooped, shrieked and bellowed a shattering, frantic call to its troupe and with rustling in the leaves, they made a hasty retreat from the growing tension permeating the mild, disturbed air drifting upwards towards them. With four strong, elongated arms and two powerful legs, the apes could leap among the branches at such incredible speeds, that locals were never tired of being fascinated by them. Feeding only on green foliage and bitter, pink berries, they flourished in the green heights for entire seasons of time, only descending to the ground to drink fresh river water or to occasionally explore new scenery for fun.

An enormous, transparent and luminous Junsa-ui-myapa snake slithered grumpily from the ground and glided up a thick stemmed tree, more through suppressed annoyance and intense irritation at the bi-legged land creatures stomping all over its territory, than a need to gain elevation. Moine-E-Ghome cast another glance in its direction just to be certain it was not going to be a threat. The Junsa-ui-myapa despised any intrusion into its carefully chosen home and was sometimes known to lunge to ward off trespassers. In full daylight, the snake was more difficult to see, but the moody reptile lit up, glowing in a pale green light as soon as darkness descended, making it conspicuous and far easier to avoid. Incredibly strong, partly venomous, thicker than Moine-E-Ghome's leg and longer than three times his height, the snake lit itself up to warn of its presence so creatures could stay away from where it was always trying to sleep. It turned off the luminosity and slithered at speed in full darkness only when hunting.

It was a well chosen spot to lay an ambush for the visitors; with endless cover among the gently swaying, giant trees and noises from creatures he guessed were alien to them, the strange beings would all be considerably disoriented, lending a true, tactical advantage to the fighters.

Moine-E-Ghome tightened his grip on the handle, planted his rear foot on to an outgrowing root and consciously paced and controlled his breathing. Behind the trunk and drooping leaves of a yellow weeping tree, he crouched low, invisible to all on the other side. The other fighters, in their hundreds, were all as cunningly concealed, each one brandishing their personal choice of weapon and spread out, stretching beyond the trees and into bush-land that sprawled away to meet a thriving fruit farm in the distance. Those within sight of him watched intently, staying well hidden and poised, keeping track of all movements and waiting for the first lunge.

Moine-E-Ghome angled his chosen weapon, the Grendje, and out of sheer habit, glanced down, first at the handle and then slowly along to each dense, powerful, bulbous end. There was never any need to check but he did so anyway—all fighters were creatures of personal ritual.

Foreboding sounds of the visitors sporadically echoed and scattered through the singing woods, tarnishing the prescribed music of life with riotous, impish, sinister clamour. They were fiendishly noisy, randomly letting off their brandished weapons with sharp, grating cracks, muffled lightly and then dispersed in rolling, stuttering claps by the abundant, low hanging, vibrant vegetation. "Krrakkat... kakkat... Krakkakkat... Phroooo... Krrrakkakkakkat!" the whole forest heard them approaching. They were far too careless and fatally overconfident.

Moine-E-Ghome looked upwards, his eyes swivelling thoughtfully, scanning one side to the other, searching for the source of a new, pulsing sound filtering faintly from beyond—a different noise, not coming from anything within the woods and not from the same direction as the advancing visitors; a droning sound so faint, that though he was aware of it, he could not be sure it was coming from outside his own ears.

Perking up, he closed his eyes and temporarily ceased breathing, straining to listen and to discern its origin. Gradually, the faint droning melted and swelled, forming a thundering bellow that grew incessantly louder, until there was no doubt about the otherworldly resonance. His heart sank. There wasn't one... or two... or even three. From the rolling, reverberating, pulsing grunts, it sounded like several more of the dwellings had arrived.

Struggling to peer through the cascading foliage, he caught glimpses of them descending, some through clouds and some in bright uninterrupted air, hovering down, resembling fume belching, behemoths and even from a great distance, way up high in the sky, their monstrous, scarcely believable size was perceivable. Six more flying dwellings, larger than the ones he knew, had emerged from the brightness and were lumbering purposefully to join their friends. He groaned inwardly, glanced around and slowly shook his head. Cautiously, with great care, he gently gestured upwards to warn any lurking fighters who didn't already know. Many more of the troublesome visitors were on their way!

The plan had not allowed for unforeseen increase in numbers but Moine-E-Ghome felt prepared and steadfastly carried the calm appearance of being ready. Camouflaged spotters scattered across the battalions would already stealthily be setting out to survey, and both wings of the pincer and the gel globule launchers were stirring to shuffle to adjusted positions.

A deeper, more concerning truth subtly bothered every mind: once the visitors were defeated, even more might arrive with endless waves of reinforcements and more tools and weapons. Their wrath and quest for vengeance would know no limits. Moine-E-Ghome cast a vow that he would spend his next days lending all possible efforts so if that were to unfold, the factions would all be ready.

Far more likely they might see his people as too much trouble—he found himself hoping—and not worth fighting with only for the mineral. Whatever their intention would be after the battle, now their presence was known and their ways observed, the factions would ardently focus on preparing and from what had so far been achieved in such a short time, he was certain that as the days passed by with more work, his civilization would be a formidable foe.

Pondering the spiralling descent into savagery, Moine-E-Ghome adjusted his grip on the Grendje. The visitors only wanted what they found in the ground. Alchemists had offered to devise better ways of extracting whatever substances the visitors desired and having personally witnessed their remarkable work, he was in no doubt that they could have done so with ease.

From any way he looked it appeared the visitors had come from a frightening world, where listening to reason was a deep flaw of character. He was certain they must have acted in similar ways before: these were not actions of unknowing amateurs or of first time explorers setting out to find another way. Wherever they had come from, he guessed their trodden path lay fouled with destruction, and churned lands bathed in the tears of survivors. Shutting his eyes, he bowed his head and cast the ever-ether with all wishes and good blessings to any beings, yet unknown, who may have endured the calamitous encounters.

When he was finished, he glanced up, his face resolute.

"Not upon this occurrence of life point within time!" his deep voice mumbled in the language of the region. "Distant the point may it be catapulted beyond the faraway! As sure as we make it be, as I, in unit and in force with my Grendje, and all factions upon rows and swells of our living and seeing and hearing and being, coming together, the waywardness of the visitor, the callous, un-thinking, un-charity of the reprobates is now, as I wield upon, to each of them, fatal!"

Taking care not to move from the cover of the tree trunk, he swayed the Grendje slowly so everyone could see. Cautiously, he glanced first to one side and then to the other, in the directions of the concealed fighters all around him. Unable to see most of them, he raised the Grendje, ever so slightly, as a sign of encouragement and confirmation of the plan. The immediate responses were mostly hidden from view, but it caused him no concern: everyone knew by heart that they were behind him all the way.

Scanning from behind the tree, he saw the first of the visitors still some distance away, shuffling in his direction, rude to the vicinity, and with no apparent knowledge of battalions in waiting. He glanced towards the tree the Junsa-ui-myapa had ascended. It had vanished into the foliage. It would stay there for a while yet. The fighters anywhere near would all know to be cautious—and they would warn others behind them.

In the distance, beyond his view, he guessed more of the visitors were pouring out of doorways and down serrated ramps, built bigger and longer, extending from the larger dwellings and reaching down like course tongues to vomit out inhabitants. Even in such a troubling time, he toyed with the idea of asking a scientist to devise a similar walkway for his home. He imagined it would look impressive stretching out from the entrance, and each step he trod on it would invoke memories of the victory he was certain would be had on this day. He wondered what Solye-I-Bhove would think of the serrated ramp. Now he knew she had accepted, it was wiser in such matters to be sure to consult her.

The moment was almost upon them. He estimated more than five might perish with his first strike. There was still no desire to kill. With the will now forced, all weapons stood wielded in a shadow of reluctance. His mind trailed away to what he heard about their species: more fragile and smaller than the people of his world, their outer clothing cocooned them—as though the air he breathed might injure them in some way. Their bodies appeared frail, lacking the bulky, hardened muscle of the people they found here, and inside the toughened shells they wore over delicate looking heads, their tender skin was visible, and their small eyes stared, strangely coloured and icy cold, like those of Muntie-Oa-Keyerie cave dwelling, lake hunters. Pale-white eyeballs, with dark circles inside them, darted back and forth as though searching, with a great thirst and a fiery pent up instinct, for the next band of objects to acquire or to kill. They lacked the soft compassion in the steady gaze of his people.

Pondering what they called themselves, he tried to pronounce the name. They said they were "Humans" and they had travelled a great distance from their home called "Earth".

He was curious how far away this Earth world was and whether there was violence there. There must surely be for a species so drawn to brutality! And why did they use names with only one word in them? How did any of them know what they were talking about? How did any of them know *who* they were talking about? How could they describe their home or their species or their factions when using only one word to name or speak of them?

Peeking from behind the trunk and through the yellow foliage with eyes so focussed, the trees could almost hear them strain, he locked on to the nearest figure—the one most likely to reach him first. With the target drifting closer and the gap gradually shrinking, he consciously lowered his head, tensed his foot and readied the weapon.

Time slowed as it ran out; the leading group was nearly upon them. Noisy and rowdy, they were close to the marked point, blissfully unaware that the locals were waiting.

Three... Two... just one... more... step...

Moine-E-Ghome lunged with the most spectacular attack the lurking fighters and every pair of eyes had ever seen. For the first time in many generations of his people, a full force lethal attack was unleashed on living beings. Eleven visitors perished with the Grendje's first blow and as the other fighter's weapons flashed on the way to make contact, an eruption of head sized, semi-solid, gel globules rose in a silent, foreboding swarm from an array of widely scattered, camouflaged locations, their trajectory leading them to the settled giant dwellings.

The humans did not stand a chance!

The End

Rachel's Dog

Chapter 1 – Stirrings

Rachel heard a soft metallic clatter as the small knife fell on to the concrete path an instant before the tall man disappeared. He was right there, his eyes a few inches away staring curiously, almost with a hint of compassion, back into her own as she pleaded with him, hoping he would speak up with an order to the other two. His expression froze at the same moment the strange, sharp protrusions appeared out of his face and then, without any warning, he vanished from her sight.

She heard a muffled, gurgling noise and her head instinctively snapped towards the other man. His hoodie looked much wider. With minimal visibility in the darkened alleyway, his head appeared to have separated into two halves joined together at the jaw, giving his face a wide, grotesquely stretched expression—like a comedic, fleshy grimace with the eyes parted twice the distance they should be from each other. His nose was leaning to one side and his lips thinned and drawn out, nearly to the limit. And then, he too was gone, before she knew what he was doing.

Rachel had declined the generous offer of a lift home, deciding instead, to travel on the late night bus. It was not unusual; she had done it several times. Having had four cocktails at the company party, she was well aware of being in no mental condition to drive. Preparing for that beforehand, she had called for a taxi. Her cute little hatchback remained parked outside the house. Had she opted for a taxi on the way back home, all the rest of her life might have turned out very different.

As she sat on the front left seat, in the pristine upper level of the mostly empty double-decker bus, Rachel let her mind wander, carried away by memories stirred up and roused by heart-rending conversations openly exchanged with her partying workmates. She could remember both drawn out incidents from childhood, when a large, scary dog saved her life two times. She didn't mention it at the party, even amidst a torrent of touching life stories pouring from tongues loosened by colourful liquids freely obtainable by a walk up to the company funded alcohol counter that remained open for the night.

One of the receptionists had shared a detailed narrative of a frightening experience she endured when a little girl. Classy, over-friendly and spectacularly well spoken with a hint of a Scottish accent, she possessed a helpful niceness so far decoupled from her jaw dropping appearance, that anyone who encountered her came away convinced she had no idea of her beauty. A growing crowd, mesmerized by every word she uttered, listened ardently, and drifting figures paused to boost their numbers. With her tongue and her usually well contained emotions liberated by yet another tasty mouthful of the third free cocktail, each sip of the green drink had appeared to wash away another segment of her reservations, until, finally overwhelmed by a therapeutic desire, she opened up and passionately told her story.

It was a mesmerising tale from over twenty years before about how she had accidentally fallen into a fast river. She was swept along, defenceless, for close to four minutes before several brave people who jumped to the rescue, caught up, saved her and carried her to safety.

The harrowing story stirred long buried memories of Rachel's own incidents and got her analyzing murky details all over again. At the time, her parents did not believe her version of events. Nobody did. Everyone was certain that it was a dream. In later years, when she went to school and told her story, the teachers, though kind and patient, did not believe her either. Only a child and caving in to popular opinion, she resolved to keep memories of the big dog a secret and never to speak about it to anyone again.

As the years went by, Rachel wondered if she really could have been mistaken. The incidents lingered and played in her memory, refusing to mould into bland, saner versions. Could she falsely remember in grinding detail, or imagine an experience with so much clarity? As she grew older, Rachel was no longer sure.

Approaching the age of twenty six, Rachel was thriving in the comfortable office for a company that manufactured specialized stationary. With a beaming smile for her colleagues every morning, she revelled in her work space, tackling complex tasks—the more complex the better. She lit up with excitement when the challenge was impossible: no allocated zinc to make the coating on stencils ordered for an engineer and expected in five days time? Excellent challenge! She would almost rub her hands with glee. It helped that time among her workmates was enjoyable and she woke up each day bubbling with positivity.

It was a happy time for Rachel. Only three weeks had gone by since her boyfriend surprised her with a romantic evening out when, halfway through the glorious meal, after watching an art show, a violin band spiritedly walked up to their table, stood professionally and smartly—two on one side of her and another three on the other—lifted their gleaming instruments to their shoulders and began to play in unison with stunning precision. A tall man in coattails and the shiniest, narrowest long hat she had ever seen, charmingly sauntered over and with the greatest charisma, presented a well crafted, polished, mahogany box in which, after theatrically opening the lid with a white gloved hand, nestled a beautifully hand-made, diamond engagement ring on navy blue, pristine, velvet padding.

Her eyes and mouth flew open and her utter surprise beamed out for all the other guests to see. The shock lasted through her boyfriend's eager, well rehearsed words, spoken earnestly on one knee, with an enthusiastic expression and a focus in his eyes that sincerely promised every word he uttered was true. Through an unrestrained grin she had no control over tumbled out the word "Yes!" which she meant with all her heart.

The applause from every guest in the mostly full restaurant was loud and rapturous, and a bottle of champagne appeared, courtesy of the house. It was the most wonderful night she could remember in a long time fulfilling her dreams of the magical moment. The wedding was in the planning for five months time and excitement grew with every day that went by.

Her husband to be, an up-and-coming, recently qualified architect was putting in monumental efforts to build his own company. After her choice to remain single for nearly a year, she had eventually said yes the sixth time he asked to take her out for a subtle dinner.

They finally moved in together and bought the three bedroom home which came with a garden, and a first floor master bedroom at the front of the property. She loved that the master bedroom had its own bathroom; their future kids could have the other one all to themselves. Money was tight, made worse by his having to fly around the world to meet potential clients and to show up at seminars—a necessary process in pursuit of his enterprise. Every trip was one step closer to his dream.

Her parents eagerly came over for a lengthy visit every month and she saved one of the bedrooms so they always stayed the weekend. An only child, she felt eternally bound to their presence and in between the visits, barely two days went by before she wanted to speak to them on any number of random issues. With their own spare key, they could let themselves in if she happened to be out or at work when they came by. Grateful for the fortunate and priceless situation, she endlessly remarked on how they would soon make the most wonderful grandparents, when the highly anticipated time finally came.

The bus trundled along, almost on soft, velvet wheels, past a jolly looking, tipsy man pushing a high-end bicycle. She guessed it was expensive and she guessed he was jolly: in the pale glowing street lights, she hadn't seen his expression. There was something about the way he walked—a carefree, springing happiness and lightness of the feet—that implied some sort of life burden recently offloaded. He appeared roughly the age her older brother would have been and she wondered whether he would also have ridden such a bicycle... or maybe a motorcycle, and he would be six feet tall... and a boxer... no... a kick boxer. And he would probably own and run his own amazing company, but he would still come to visit every month with her parents.

She occasionally went misty eyed at thoughts of her brother, Philip, who perished in an accident when she was only a baby. With no memory of knowing him, she remembered nothing about the time but there were plenty of photographs, and she had listened to endless stories of how much he had loved her, and how her parents loved them both. The aching, forlorn look lingering in their eyes every time they spoke his name always made her want to reach out, like a little child, to comfort them.

They had gifted to her a framed picture of all of them together. Professionally done in a studio using high quality print, her parents sat side by side in the image, with backs straight and hands clasped, tenderly leaning on each other, their love plain for anyone beholding it to see. Before them stood her brother—ten years old at the time— toothy smile, sparkling eyes, looking gleeful and content, holding a five week old sleeping baby in his arms.

Philip resembled her father and he had her mother's eyebrows, and she recognized her chin and her ears from his image. The photo hung high, proud and true in her sitting room, in a prominent location on the largest span of wall, playing its part, with great effect, to make the house more sentimental. She often wondered what he would think of the place if he saw it. It may not have been the most spectacular of properties but to Rachel, it was a wonderful space she could call their home.

Chapter 2 – Memories

On the night of the third incident, as Rachel sat in the silent bus, mind wandering among countless thoughts, weighing up stored memories, she thought about her workmates chatting at the party. Then she thought about the bus driver and how comfortable the ride was. He was being very considerate and when she focussed on it, she appreciated the smoother style and gentle braking manoeuvres; little things like that mattered. Then she thought of her fiancé away on yet another trip. It was going to be another six days and she felt a pang of longing as she missed his cheeky smile and the silly way he chased her, petrified and screaming, all around the house pretending he was holding a spider. She giggled softly to herself. It was funny when she thought about it, even though not remotely amusing in the moment.

Pulling out her phone from the small, long handled handbag, she looked at the time; it was three minutes to two o'clock. She glanced out the window. The flicker of street lights matched the speed of the bus in the opposite direction. They glowed, momentarily, off the chrome edged window sill, after glancing off the chrome hand-rail fastened to the cream ledge spreading away in front of her, and leading to the span of glass shielding from oncoming wind, faintly marked and speckled from a very recent bus wash. Faded houses floated by, nearly all with darkened windows, tightly drawn uncoloured curtains shielding mystery night murmurs. A tall, spiny hedge sprinted unceremoniously past, quickly giving way to a sprawling, empty, supermarket car park. *Fourth stop after this next one!* she thought silently to herself. The roads and streets were deserted—typical for a Tuesday night.

Looking down at her phone again, she typed out a message—
Missing you—and sent it. He was busy in a meeting but would smile
when he saw it later; it was only two and a half hours since she last
spoke to him. Sliding her phone back into the handbag, she crossed
her hands over it and then let her mind drift to wallow in luxurious
daydreams. The ride on the near empty, brand new, two-level bus
and the peace of the ghostly, half faded, moon coloured streets was
an ideal opportunity to reflect and meditate.

She tried to think back to when she was three years old and her
parents had taken her to Wales for a weekend. As they frolicked
by the lakeside, she had wandered off unseen and made it further
down, exploring alone, before she went in the water.

It was a picturesque setting, with rocks, thick ancient trees and
age-less wild bushes covering much of the lake shore—and most
of the land beyond. Several tourists, merry and mellow, jauntily
mingled with locals, who grasped opportunities to enjoy the dreamy
scenery, and to bring their young children to play outside in nature.
Everybody pitched in to look out for each other and they all helped
to look after the giggling, buzzing toddlers, happily playing away
from their half-vigilant parents.

Perhaps some rocks or bushes had obscured her from view, or
maybe the parents were distracted, preparing sandwiches, light
snacks and purple berries for all the kids to nibble on. Nobody could
explain how she managed to get away and end up near the far side
in a different part of the lake. A large, natural rock formation and
several broad, mature trees stood squarely in the way, hiding part
of the open lake shore where all the families gathered, and having
made her way past it, was shielded from where most of the other
young children were gleefully playing.

Another little girl watched and had seen her wander off and then tried, three times, to point to where Rachel was. When the girl's mother looked to where her daughter was pointing, the trees and the rocks sat neatly in her line of vision. Later, utterly distraught, she explained that at the time, she thought her daughter was pointing out the beautiful scenery.

Rachel had no memory of wandering off on that day but she could remember fighting to float and breathe in the water. She also remembered brief, watery glimpses of the shore—too far away to reach or for anyone to hear her—and the lanky branches of trees swaying over the lakeside like giant, sentient tendrils grieving her demise. The large rock formation seared itself into her memory as she tried to reach and clamber up on to it for safety. She drifted further away, floating beyond the shallow areas and before very long, there was nothing else around her but the cool lake water that was much too deep for a tender three year old who was out on her own.

She could vividly recall the coughing and intense pain as lake water filled up her nose and her airways. She tried crying out but pressure sealed up her lungs, clogged up both nostrils and stung in her sinuses. Stretching out her little hands, she grasped with clawed fingers, trying to feel for something rigid to hold on to, but there was only empty air.

Looking up from inside the water, her face an inch away from the surface, she tried to lift her head up higher and she tried climbing out. She tried reaching for the rocks or for anything that was solid. She tried reaching for the trees and to a large cloud in the sky. She even reached for two birds flying high above the lake but her pleading, outstretched hands flailed in the air, eventually sliding, with great protest, into the sun soaked lake.

Her muscles tensed and contracted in unrelenting waves sending her body into convulsions as it tried to expel the water. Desperate gasps of breath only sucked in more liquid, triggering ferocious waves of retching and coughing. Her arms and legs hurt more than she had ever known they could and her muscles clenched so hard, she felt her back was going to snap. The lake was unmerciful, savage, overwhelming, water filling her nose and lungs seared like acid.

She wished for mummy and daddy. Sliding deeper into the depths, mouth wide open inside the lake, with every fierce convulsion, her soul sought her parents. As the surface drifted further away, a crimson wave of anguish and deep loneliness engulfed her. If her face had not already descended into the water, her guardian angel would have seen the tears flowing from her eyes.

Just before she bumped the clay and powdery silt at the bottom, the convulsions began to slow, and the eyelids over the little hazel eyes began to soften. With a glazed look, a merciful peace slowly descended upon her mind.

But the gods and her guardian angel had not abandoned her. In the cold lake, the dog appeared, raised her back above the surface and paddling swiftly, swam gracefully back to the shore. It supported her barely conscious, still convulsing body until the coughing had subsided and she was breathing well again. Walking away from the water's edge, it laid her gently down upon a soft, level, patch of spongy, moss covered ground. The dog sat next to her, watching and waiting, until the glazed eyes brightened and colour began to return to her pale, damp skin.

It was not long before panicked voices carried through the trees and drawing closer, transformed into screams calling out her name. The big dog bounded off and melted into the bushes moments before one of the leading groups emerged from the greenery.

Rachel told everyone exactly what had happened. She said she was in the water and it was going in her nose and mouth and hurting her a lot, and then the big, scary dog came and carried her up and helped her and took her out of the water, and she was coughing very strongly and it was hurting very much and the water all came out until she could breathe. And then it put her on the green ground where she was very tired, and she was resting and falling asleep while the dog was watching, until they all came and found her, and then the dog ran away.

Nobody believed a word of it!

They were all in agreement that she must have fallen asleep and had a really bad dream. She almost believed them, she was only a child after all. But they were unable to explain the symptoms doctors found that clearly indicated a near drowning event.

Within a few weeks, when she was fully recovered, life was almost back to normal, with the exception that her parents endlessly showered her with affection and never let her wander anywhere out of their keen sight. She remained as safe and happy as a child could ever be.

Two years later when she was nearly six years old, sound asleep in her room late one chilly, breezy, autumn night, she awoke when a soft, unusual jostling shook her. Wallowing in a dreamy haze, her mind not of the living world, she saw—like a hallucination—that a big dog had wrapped some of the bedding all around her and was lifting her up to take her away from the bed.

In the darkness, softened by the mild, amber light from the street lighting leaking in through the drawn curtains, looking up at the strange dog, and then at everything else around her, it all appeared to be a dream and she wasn't sure it was happening. She tried stretching her arms and legs to stand or to sit up but in the half-reality, her body disobeyed. They both floated down the stairs, out the door and to the front garden where it laid her, a little roughly, down on to the dewy grass. It disappeared back into the house and a brief moment later, came bounding out with more bedding wafting in its wake.

Amidst the strange sensation invoked by being outside on the grass in the front garden late at night, she tried once again to move but her body, too weak and tired, continued to disobey. Her mind, hazy and groggy, only just about processed enough to understand that what was going on was not a dream. She watched, helpless and silent, as the dog clumsily placed the covers over her whole body and then turned around, intentionally ran towards the family car and bumped sideways into it, setting off the alarm.

It stood by, appearing to be waiting for something as the high pitched, pulsating wail screeched into the night. That was not good: in the silence and the dim, tranquil calmness, the car alarm screamed like an air-raid siren. Rachel knew the loud shrill was going to wake the neighbours and she winced and wished she had the little button to make it stop. Fairly certain by then that the dog would not harm her, she started to worry about what other people would think if they saw her sleeping under her covers, out on the front lawn.

"I am dreaming! I am dreaming! It's a scary dream!" she muttered, more for reassurance and comfort than a question to her senses. But it felt too vivid; the night air was too crisp, and the mild breeze ruffling her hair felt too airy. Even the wailing car alarm hurt her ears in a real way. She tried again to move but it was too much effort.

The neighbour's upstairs bedroom light suddenly flickered on and a moment later, a corner of the curtain lifted away. A figure appeared in the space and its head moved about, craning an urgent neck to see about the screaming car.

No lights came on in the windows of her parent's house.

As the car alarm persisted with the pulsating shriek, the dog bounded to a tree, snapped off a loose branch, then disappeared into the house, taking the branch along with it.

Puzzled and slightly alarmed, Rachel lifted up her head and with some difficulty, attempted calling out to her parents. Her soft voice, barely a whisper, was swept into oblivion by the sharp siren incessantly reverberating into the street. Through the thickening haze gradually engulfing her foggy mind, her vision began to blur. Momentarily closing her eyes, she allowed her head to settle on to the pink cotton covers.

The big dog reappeared only a few moments later, lurking near the walls as though to hide from any peering neighbours. Opening her eyes again to look for her parents, she watched as it nimbly bounded away across the lawn, out on to the street path and with one leap, crossed the road, deftly touching down straight on to the other side. It stopped for a brief moment and turned to look back and even from that distance, she could have sworn it appeared satisfied with the work. Suddenly turning around again and with one powerful leap, it merged into the gloom and was gone away forever, leaving her alone in the covers on the front lawn.

The curtain in the neighbour's window lifted once again and the shape, after having disappeared for a moment, reappeared with a second slightly smaller one for company. The larger one was pointing at the spectacle outside that to them, appeared to be a random bundle of bedding covers inexplicably laid out on to their neighbour's lawn.

The larger face disappeared back into the room and moments later, the downstairs light came on—quickly followed by the porch light. The front door opened and Mr. Xiang gingerly stepped out, craning his neck to take a look over the conifer hedge, before tentatively stepping around to walk towards Rachel.

Her parents half tumbled out the front door and shouted to her, calling out her name when they saw the pile of bedding. Stumbling forwards, they staggered towards her, each straining with the effort of helping the other to walk. Mr. Xiang, who by then had reached the well mown lawn, looked puzzled as he made the quick decision to hurry to them and help them walk towards the covered bundle on the grass.

Her mother screamed with relief seeing her daughter was alive and both parents crumpled on to their knees and held her. Mr. Xiang shouted to his wife to call for an ambulance. Rachel and both her parents looked very unwell.

Inspectors later confirmed that a fault in the gas boiler gradually flooded the house with deadly carbon monoxide. Entirely without odour and invisible to the naked eye, the gas, once inhaled, caused their bodies to start shutting down. Her parents were grateful to Rachel for saving them by apparently, using the branch to bang on their door and on their bedside cabinet until they were awake.

Rachel told her parents, the doctor, the nurses and anyone who would listen, that the large dog had saved them. Nobody believed her. She tried to explain that if she was going to wake her parents, she wouldn't go outside to get a branch from a tree, or intentionally jolt the car to set off the alarm.

It was argued that effects from carbon monoxide and the oxygen depravation had caused her to hallucinate. It was far more likely—they confidently deduced—that she had set off the alarm by bumping into the car after staggering out of the house in a weakened daze.

Rachel admitted it was a more logical explanation.

Bunches of flowers and an endless flow of gifts arrived and the local media soon got wind of the story. Presenting and reporting it for many days to a keen audience, they aired learned experts, all with theories of how it must have happened. It was a heart-warming tale about a five year old girl who not only saved her own life, but dramatically and heroically, also saved her parents.

Her mother and father, with gushing smiles on their faces and hearts welling with pride, told everyone who would listen about their wonderful little girl. They indulged in tours of very keen local media, telling mesmerizing tales of her rescuing them from death. Experts made guest appearances offering more theories explaining how her mind had to imagine she was a dog, so she would have strength to keep going when her body was so weak.

Before long, Rachel gave up on her version. People looked upon her strangely—usually with pity—when she implied in any way that it was not a hallucination. Others who survived very similar occurrences came forward to tell how they too, had seen or experienced strange entities. One of them, at the time of her harrowing incident, insisted she had genuinely been captured by aliens, who carried her in their small craft and took her to the mother-ship, where she spent days among bright lights and shadowy figures. It later transpired that the other-worldly visitors were simply the doctors that saved her life, and the small craft was the ambulance driving her to hospital.

Rachel began to believe them, questioning her own mind and all the blurry, troublesome memories of the night. She ceased entirely, speaking about the strange dog, ignoring many vivid thoughts that lingered and troubled her.

Chapter 3 – Alleyway

A familiar street view loomed and nudged away her daydream and Rachel saw, almost too late, that she was at her stop. Nobody else was getting off. It was fortunate the driver tried to keep to the schedule and run on his timetable; nearly two minutes too early, he needed to pass a little time.

Hurrying down the narrow stairs, she fluttered out the door after hurling a quick "thank you!" to the considerate driver. She immediately wished she had paused to complement his driving. It would have been nice to tell him he was appreciated. With a sudden resolve, she decided to email the bus company the following day.

Buried in her own thoughts as she leisurely walked home, she pondered the incidents that occurred in her childhood. Casting her mind back, she tried once again to replay the ghostly, distant, flittering details. With a sigh, she concluded that she should have told her workmates, if only just to get their honest thoughts and opinions. Nodding slightly to herself, she came to another decision: if the mood carried over, when she got to work in the morning, she would share both stories if opportunity arose.

She walked around a corner, turning away from the main road, and into the long alleyway to the estate where she lived. As she neared the halfway point, an uneasy feeling hinted that something was not quite right with the night. Her mind snapped back and only then did she become aware of two men loitering a short distance ahead. Both the mid-point, main light and the one at the end were broken, and the area was plunged into uncomfortable semi-darkness.

From the meagre glow cast by the only light at other end, she could make out that their heads were fully covered by hoodies. Too close to turn back, with a sinking feeling, she wished she had taken up the offer of a lift home. Fighting the urge to scream, she stopped walking and reached in to her bag to get her phone.

When they saw she had stopped, the men took a step towards her. Rachel panicked, turned around, started to run back and crashed head on into another man she hadn't even noticed had come up behind her. His head was also inside a hoodie and a mask covered half his face.

"Where you going?" he asked in a nonchalant, husky voice and in one quick movement, snatched the phone from her hand.

Wide eyed and in blind panic, all she managed was a feeble "Please!"

As the other two caught up, she glanced sideways towards them and in the gloom, their faces were only barely visible. They seemed young—late teens or low, early twenties—and one of them reeked of cheap, spray deodorant. The man she had crashed into positioned himself in front of her. Taller than the other two, he looked to be of larger build; a physic bred by gym equipment rather than hard labour.

"Lemme see that bag!" he demanded, snatching it from her arm.

Too frightened to react, she nearly caved in to the urge to scream and seeing her expression, he raised a small, sharp blade and pressed the edge against her neck.

"C'mon now! You wan' somma this!?"

Rachel quickly shook her head.

The man opened her bag and using a small light, looked inside and began rummaging through the contents of her purse. One of the other men, who by then, stood to the right, suddenly took a step closer.

"She's well nice!" he mumbled.

Rachel saw that his gaze was fixed well below eye level and she regretted choosing a low cleavage dress for the party. The man raised his hand but she leaned away, brushed it off, pulled her coat around her and clutched the lapels to hold it closed.

The tall man with the knife once again thrust it against her neck.

"You going somewhere?" he asked.

Biting her bottom lip, Rachel shook her head. Clearly the one in charge, he seemed in control of the other two.

"Please! Just take the money," she desperately offered. "And my bag is expensive! You can take it if you want!"

The men laughed.

"You wanna han'bag?" the tall one asked the man on her right.

"Yeh!" came the quick reply "Am gonna give it to yo mom and then ask her to—"

The taller one's eyes instantly narrowed.

"—um... nah! Don wanna bag!" came the reconsidered reply.

The same man suddenly reached up, pulled her arms away and spread her coat wide open. She started to step away but the one behind her blocked her path.

"She's in a hurry!" he chuckled gleefully to his accomplices. "You lot well boring her!"

Rachel burst into tears. "I have a little money in the bank," she volunteered in a sob. "I will get it for you. And I promise I won't tell anyone!"

The men burst out laughing again, careful to keep their voices low.

Reaching up, she pulled her coat tightly around her.

"How much you got?" the one standing to her right asked.

"I don't... it's... not that much," she stumbled, unsure of the balance. "Three hundred and sixty... no... eighty! Three eighty I think! You can—"

"No time for that!" the tall one aggressively interrupted, and even though he was looking at her, it was obvious his words were directed at the other two.

"How 'bout suttin else?" the one to her right muttered.

She felt fingers on the back of her neck fumbling below her collar as the man behind began to unclip her favourite gold necklace. Even though the ruby pendant was a gift from her fiancé, in that moment, it didn't seem wise to object. He lifted it over her head, carefully and gently, guessing from her attire that it had to be valuable. It was difficult to see the quality in the semi-darkness but he seemed to know by appearances that it was worth taking. A flash of anger flickered within her, quickly subdued by fear.

"How 'bout suttin else?" the man to her right said again, with leering eyes once more focussed below her face.

Suddenly lunging forward, he pulled her arms away and once again, grabbed at her coat and spread it wide open. Unable to step back, she quickly forced it closed and in a mini wrestling, tug-of-war, they both began to struggle. Instinctively, she started to scream but as the sound left her throat, she felt a savage thud and her head snapped back as his fist smashed into the side of her head.

A dark fog descended and her knees began to buckle. Reeling and struggling to remain on her feet, the dim alleyway swirled and swayed and slowly began to fade.

Oh God! No! she thought. *Please, please! Oh no!*

She didn't want to be unconscious surrounded by such men.

With tears streaming down her face and in a last desperate effort, she looked straight into the eyes of the tall man in front of her. In a choking voice so soft it was barely a whisper, she reached out, attempting to win him over to stop the other two. Under the hoodie, his dark, unflinching eyes stared back and a flicker of sympathy revealed he was not a ruthless man. She kept her eyes locked on to his and without another word, silently pleaded with him.

Then something very strange happened. His head jerked forward and his left eyeball bulged outwards—halfway out of the socket—as a slightly curved object protruded oddly, out of it. A similar sharp object had emerged at an angle from behind his left ear and another from the mask where his nose was concealed. Simultaneously, she blinked and instinctively flinched as a small amount of liquid splashed on to her face.

Time froze. For a moment, he stood perfectly still. His other eye was halfway closed and his face held an expression she did not understand, and then suddenly, he was gone and flying backwards through the air.

There was a blur of dark fur and the head of the man on the right seemed to split into two from the top going downwards—both halves contained within the stretched out hoodie. She felt another splash of warm liquid running down her face and, instinctively flinching, she blinked hard to stop it going into her eyes.

Unintentionally reaching up to stop a trickle of liquid sliding down her cheek, she moved her hand away and looked down at her fingers. In the dim light, the shade of the dark colour was indiscernible but the intense fear brewing deep within her gut let her mind know the vivid red her eyes would have seen had they looked at the substance in adequate light.

In an instant, the second man also disappeared as some force hurled him several feet into the air. Rachel stared as he landed with a sickening thud over ten feet away, where he tumbled twice and then lay twisted and motionless. She stood shivering, eyes locked on the contorted bundle. She expected to violently die at any moment.

There was a muffled, fearful noise and in a terrified daze, she whirled around to look at what was happening behind her. What she saw then, her brain had no way of processing, and she watched a macabre scene unfolding in the dimness. The man who had been standing behind her had already turned away and was running as fast as his legs could propel him.

In a flash, what looked like a hairy creature was upon him and tearing at his body with big claws and hairy arms. He fell hard, face first, skidding painfully along the ground, and made grunting noises as the animal tore into him. The savageness and fury, the ferocious ripping of flesh, the gurgling surrender from the disintegrating victim carried audibly, filling the gloom with sinister tones of slaughter. His legs and arms twitched violently as a large chunk was wrenched out, away from his back and flung with such force, it flew high over Rachel's head and landed several feet behind her with a sickening splat.

It was too much to process.

Rachel fainted.

Chapter 4 – Mum

When she came to, she was lying face-up on the ground, with her coat wrapped tightly around her body. Some moments passed by while awareness revealed she was still in the alleyway, but along one side where there was well maintained grass. Wondering if she was alive, she paused and tried listening out for any unusual sounds. Hearing nothing, she started to sit up, and then saw what looked like her handbag standing right way up, conveniently beside her. Without thinking, she slowly leaned over to scoop it up but froze in mid-motion as the dark, hairy figure loomed dimly into view, only a few feet away, sat still, silently watching.

Trembling, she kept her eyes fixed on the ground, too frightened to look up in case she provoked it. A tear rolled down her cheek. The memory of the three men came rushing back and a soft, subdued gasp escaped from her throat. She didn't want to die out there in the alleyway.

Slowly, she let her eyes drift up towards the creature until, gradually, they settled and then focussed on the dark shape. It hadn't moved. Squinting to see, she leaned forward another inch.

It seemed to be a large animal, like nothing she had ever seen, crouched in the semi-dark, near silent alleyway. A diabolical monkey, or a bear, or dare she think it... a giant dog with the shadowy appearance of a man—as though a crazed witch had flung a hairy Doberman, a wolf and a human into a cauldron, then churned and brewed it, casting fiendish spells, until a hellish beast was spawned from the infernal simmering. An anomaly in nature and a blasphemy of life, it was a heinous creature—sinister, abominable and terrifying to look at. The devil's own guard dog had broken its chains and found a way to wander into the world of the living.

Suddenly, Rachel was not as frightened as she ought to be. If the creature had wanted to harm her, it would have done so already. She knew then that the animal must have placed her on the grass and then wrapped her coat around her to try and keep her warm. Faint wisps and slivers of distant, scattered memories stirred hazily from foggy dreams of a sunny, tree-lined lake. Like fearsome puzzle pieces falling slowly into place, gradually, the incidents from her past began to make sense. Something about the hairy creature was oddly familiar.

Memories from childhood occurrences came flooding back. She swallowed hard several times and tried to calm her shaking limbs. Wanting to ask the question, it took several moments to compose her senses and regain the use of her throat. When she was finally able to speak, with all the courage she could muster, she stared into the fiery, unblinking, orange eyes.

"It was you!" her voice tumbled out in a shaky, hoarse whisper. "All those years ago? Back then? Was it you?"

The creature sat silent, with orange eyes glued to hers.

She leaned forward. "At the lake? At the house? The tree branch?" her voice steadily grew more urgent. "Nobody believed me! What are you? Please tell me! I need to..." she paused.

The orange eyes, calm and luminescent in the semi-darkness, had not so much as blinked or shown any recognition. She leaned closer towards them.

"Can you speak?" she whispered.

With no warning, the creature swiftly rose, stretched to full height, sniffed the air and then took an athletic step towards her. She gasped and jumped back, hands flying up to protect her head as she crouched down and cowered near the grass in fear. When no attack came, she opened her eyes and turned her head to look. The creature, with one of its thickset, hairy arms, gestured for her to stand up. Still shaking, she slowly and silently obeyed.

Its full stretched height reached well over six feet and the orange eyes appeared to have absorbed light into them. Mesmerized, she stared into the two glowing ovals wondering what sort of beast was watching from within. Slowly reaching up, she touched the dark, unflinching, hairy face. It felt tough and leathery and the hairs felt course. She could feel the gentle warmth radiating from the skin and hear the soft flow of air rasping through the leathery nostrils. There was a moment of connection, as though she already knew the creature, but it quickly passed as the hairy head shook her hand off, and a hairy arm pushed and gestured for her to walk.

Looking around, she saw why it was so keen to get her away. There was dark liquid everywhere which, if there was good light, would show up as rapidly hardening, crimson red. The bodies of the three men lay scattered around the alleyway and it was only a matter of time before somebody else came by.

The creature lifted an arm and gestured again for her to start walking. Bending down for the handbag, she suddenly remembered her phone and the pendant. Frantically scanning the concrete path, she found the phone lying where she had stood with the three men. After hurriedly scooping it up, she desperately continued to peer and search the ground for the necklace. It was important to find it. When the bodies were discovered, she didn't want possessions leading the police to her door.

She was about to check whether the light on her phone still worked when the creature pointed at the ground a few feet away. She stepped gingerly towards it, crouched low to have a look and saw the vague, near invisible glint where the man had dropped it. She snatched it up and grasping it tightly in both hands, held the gold necklace close to her chest.

For the third time, the creature gestured for her to start walking and, unsteady on her feet, she began to walk to get away as fast as she could. The creature went with her, keeping a few paces behind.

She tried not to look at the men, stepping as far off as possible, past the lifeless, mangled body of the man who died last. It was best not to leave any footprints in the dark liquid, but she would still have to throw away her shoes, just in case. The sweet, sickeningly musty smell of clotting blood hung in the air and trying not to retch, she kept walking, glancing once to check the creature was following.

It walked along behind her, moving stealthily, in perfect silence. There was no audible sound; she wasn't sure it was there unless she turned back and saw it, which she did, several times, just to check that it was following. Rachel felt safe with the beast walking with her; an invincible bodyguard ready to tackle all foes. Struggling to walk and with eyes beginning to squint from a looming headache, she tried to avoid contemplating the aftermath of the carnage. Thinking about it, the men didn't really deserve to die, but it was no time for pondering; there was going to be consequences. She would have to be careful to avoid being caught up in the raging storm she had no doubt was coming.

The creature followed her all the way, then stood by as she hastily fumbled for her keys and quickly unlocked the door.

"Come in," she offered, turning towards the glowing orange eyes. "Please!" she said, desperately hoping it would obey.

Under the unbroken street lights, it looked more terrifying, with longer snout, intense expression and impossibly large muscles tensing and twitching under the dark, coarse fur. The hair, though not as dense as had appeared in the alleyway, was still generous, tough looking and impressive from up close. Shaking its head, the creature reached out one of its arms, as if to give her something. She extended an open hand and a faded, black, leather necklace with a silver spider pendant, fell into her palm.

The creature turned, extended a claw and slowly carved the word *mum* straight on to the bricks on the inside of the garden wall. When it was finished, it turned, briefly stared with the orange eyes and then suddenly looking upwards, it crouched down low and with a powerful leap, jumped on to the wall, skipped up on to the roof and with a silent, athletic motion, was gone from the night.

"Wait! Please!" Rachel tried not to call out too loudly. "Come back!" She craned her neck, looking desperately upwards. "Please!" she whispered.

But she knew it would not return.

Looking down at her hand, she stared blankly at the necklace. The pendant was nearly an inch and a half wide and uncannily resembled a fully grown house spider—so realistic, if it were not silver, she would have dropped it in fear that it would come alive. She looked up at the word freshly carved on to the brick wall. Was the creature looking for its mother? Did it want her to be its mother? Gripping the necklace in her hand, she looked upwards again and stood waiting, hoping to see two orange ovals. After a while, she lowered her gaze and stared at the door handle. Fighting back tears, she reached for it, hesitated, then slowly opened the door to go into the house alone.

Chapter 5 – Baby

Rachel could not sleep a wink that night. Just after 4am, she dialled her mother's number. After several rings, it connected and nearly five seconds went by before the sleepy voice came over the speaker.

"Rachel?" her mother asked. "You okay honey? It's after 4 in the morning."

Some moments went by as Rachel silently fought back tears.

"Rachel!" her mother called out, sounding more alert. "Are you there? Is something wrong?"

There was some mumbling as her father, also awakened, enquired about the late night caller.

"I think it's Rachel!" her mother answered. "I think something is wrong!"

The low mumbling resumed, sounding distinctly more alarmed.

"I don't know! She hasn't said a word ye— No! Just... stop it... Let go!"

More urgent mumbling.

"No... Let go... I'll speak to her. Let go!"

"Rachel!" her mother was back on the phone again. "Are you there?"

"I'm here mum!" Rachel hoped she sounded calm.

"Good God!!" her mother exclaimed. "What a fright!" She exhaled slowly. "What's wrong honey? Are you okay? You sound like you're upset!"

"Mum," Rachel breathed, a little more calmly, into the phone. Clearing her throat, she made an effort to sound casual. "Can you and dad come over first thing in the morning?"

"Yes! Of course!" her mother replied without any hesitation.

There was more mumbling as her father demanded to know what was going on.

"She'd like us to go over."

The mumbling rose in urgency.

"I... No, I don't know yet, give me a moment to find out."

There was a pause.

"What are you doing?" her mother was suddenly asking. "Not right this moment! Get back in bed! She asked for us to go in the morning—Rachel, will you be okay until morning? You said morning, didn't you?"

"Yes mum!" Rachel almost broke into a smile.

"She said morning... You... Yes! It... Yes! Just... Yes, just get back in bed!"

There was another long pause and some back and forth mumbling.

"We'll see you in the morning Rachel," her mother was back on the phone. "I'll bring some low fat, cinnamon brownies. I baked two full oven trays and another half of them today. I was going to freeze them and bring them over to you for the weekend, but I'll bring them with us."

Her parents woke early, made the three hour drive and were at her house with her just after 9:30am. She had already called work to let them know she would not be going. After some pondering, she called again to ask for the rest of the week off.

When her parents arrived, Rachel was still dressed from the night before. The right side of her face was swollen and a dark purple shade was welling up under her eye.

"O-O-O-O-H M-M-M-M-Y GOODNEEEEESSS!!" her mother's panic-stricken shriek seemed to carry through the house and out into the neighbourhood. "Are you okay Rachel?! Oh dear God! Oh sweetie! Come here! What happened? Are those blood stains? Goodness me! What happened to you? Goodness, goooooooodness me!" Holding Rachel by the shoulders, she scrutinized the swelling. A sudden thought occurred to her. "Why is the alleyway closed off? Why are there police everywhere? Did something bad happen to you? Were you there in the alleyway?"

"Come on!" her father sternly demanded, grabbing Rachel by the arm. "We're going to the hospital!"

Rachel pulled her arm away then held it up to silence them.

"I'll be just fine," she said, eyes welling up with tears. "Actually, I'll be better than ever. I just... I... need only you for now. Only you! No doctors and nobody else."

She fell into her mother's arms and sobbed uncontrollably into her shoulder. Her father stood next to them, rubbing her back and mumbling soothing words of comfort. She didn't hear most of them, but she liked that he made the effort.

With her turmoil sufficiently vented, Rachel took a deep breath then looked at her parents. "Sit down please." She spoke calmly and felt more composed than earlier during the phone call. "I need to tell you something"

Suddenly very aware that she needed to get changed, she tried to excuse herself. The police would undoubtedly be visiting every home and would knock on every door in search of potential witnesses. Three gruesome murders was no small matter. With evidence pointing to some sort of animal or a savage individual, she could take solace in the fact that, being on her own, she would not be a suspect.

She had to get cleaned up and put her clothing in the wash. Her coat was dry clean only: she would have to figure out a way to remove all the bloodstains before going to the cleaners—or else she would have to very carefully dispose of it and buy a new replacement one the following day, just in case at some point during the investigation, someone came and asked if they could check her clothing. And she had to think of a story to explain not just her bruised face, but how she got home that night. The cameras on the new bus would have filmed her—with a time stamp. She would just have to say the path was clear when she walked through. With no cameras in the vicinity, they had no way to check.

There was so much to do!

"I really am doing just fine!" she said to her parents. "But I'm glad you're here. I'm going to have a quick wash then there's something I need to ask you."

Her mother looked unconvinced that Rachel was okay. "Is that your blood?" she wanted to know. "What on earth happened to you? Shall we go see a doctor? Or shall I call an ambulance? We could call an ambulance!"

Rachel looked her in the eye. "Do that, or call anyone—anybody else—and you will lose your daughter in more ways than one!"

Her mother's mouth flew open but Rachel remained calm.

"I love you mum and right now, I'm asking that you trust me."

Her mother backed down and nodded. "I love you too honey," she returned. "Don't be too long!"

When Rachel got back, all cleaned up and in fresh clothes, she was eager to speak with her parents. "Sit down please," there was a resolute and urgent look in her eyes. "There is something I need to ask you!"

They pulled over two chairs and sat across from her.

"We love you Rachel," her father said, meaning every word. "You know that we always have. Whatever it is that happened, we are here for you and we always will be."

Rachel nodded, leaned over and placed the faded leather necklace into her mother's hand. "Why is this familiar?" she asked. "And what could it mean to anyone?"

With a haunted expression, her mother held it tenderly, with both hands cupped. Her parents froze, each staring as though they were looking at a ghost.

"Where did you get this!?" her father finally managed to whisper.

Her mother, visibly trembling, was physically unable to speak.

After a long while, with her father's arm firmly around her mother's shoulder, they began to tell the story.

Rachel had always thought her older brother died in a car accident on a family trip to Eastern Europe. But the truth about his demise was far more bizarre. When she was a baby, the family went away on a foreign holiday, in a densely wooded area near a small rural village kept hidden from mass tourism, but open to outside visitors. During the second night of their stay, a vicious creature attacked the area and wreaked carnage in their cabin.

Brandishing a wooden chair, their father was injured and knocked unconscious trying to protect the family and in final desperation, eleven year old Philip shut his mother and baby sister in the small, metal wardrobe and then ran out of the cabin to draw the fearsome creature away. He was never seen again but his shoes and part of his shirt were later found in the forest, all covered in his dried blood.

Her mother bought the leather necklace, with the silver spider pendant for his tenth birthday, just before she gave birth to Rachel—her father explained with the occasional pause as he plunged into the memory. After Rachel was born, Philip showered her with affection, lighting up, mesmerized that he was an older brother. He loved to hold and carry her and every time he did so, her tiny fingers clasped on to the necklace and the spider. It became their favourite toy and they both played with it together for hours on any day, with Philip pretending that it could walk. When her brother disappeared that fateful night, he had the necklace on him and had been wearing it all day.

They sat quietly as Rachel digested the information. She stretched out an open palm and her mother carefully placed the necklace back in to her hand. Clasping it tenderly, she raised and held it close to her, next to her heart.

"But..." she hesitated, her voice choking with emotion. "Who is in the grave? If they never found Philip, who is buried in the grave?"

Her parents winced with heartache.

Her father found his voice first.

"It was some of his items—and some things he loved."

"We buried the shoes and the piece of shirt they found while searching for him," her mother managed to add in. "And his favourite jacket, a cinnamon scented candle he always wanted lit, a photo, and letters we both wrote saying how we..." her voice trailed off wrenched away by intense grief.

"So..." Rachel began to ask with dawning awareness. "Uncle John, Aunt Esther, Uncle Stuart, Emily..." she paused and shook her head. "They all know about the grave? They know Philip was never found?"

Her parents nodded slowly.

"You were only a baby at the time," her father responded. "We intended to tell you when you were older, but the years just, well... just went on by and we... um, the opportunity just never arose. We never knew how to bring it up."

A heavy silence descended, randomly broken as her parents looked up to speak more of little Philip. Rachel sat consumed by emotion, tears flowing down her cheeks and on to her cotton blouse, and occasionally, dripping on to the tightly clasped fingers wrapped protectively and delicately around the precious pendant. Slowly rocking back and forth, the final pieces of the puzzle began to fall into place.

She winced, almost in physical pain, at the heart rending sadness of young Philip's stolen life. She ached with the inadequacy, or the means to show gratitude. How do you thank a person who gave their life to save yours?

Her heart broke with thoughts of his forced desolation, living out there, alone, away from his family. She nearly screamed out his name. She wanted to see him again. She wanted him to know how they all desperately missed him. All of a sudden, she began to wonder if he was proud of her. After saving her three times, did he think she was living each day as well as he would have wanted her to?

Her father, with tears in his eyes, was making heroic efforts to console her mother who, like Rachel, was lost in a ferocious world of grief. A solemn silence eventually cast a cloud into the room.

Her father stood up and saying nothing, walked over to the wall where the framed family photo was hanging. Carefully unhooking it from the gold plated mounting, he studied it closely—as though in meditation—and then slowly turned around and with an expression she had never seen before, walked over to her.

"Look again at the picture."

167

He placed it into her outstretched hands.

With a blank expression, she glanced down at the photo. She had seen it hundreds of times. She looked back up at him with questioning eyes.

"The spider pendant," he said softly. "We never told you about it. There was never any reason to. But now there is."

Utterly puzzled by his words, she looked down at the picture and suddenly, she saw it! With a loud gasp, she drew the framed image closer to her eyes and staring in astonishment, leaned forward to study it. Every day she looked at the photo and yet, with the object subtly sitting in the image, she had never truly seen it. In the tiny hand of the sleeping baby, the hint of shiny metal was glinting among clenched fingers, with stray, silver, spider legs tiptoeing beyond the thumb. Around the wrist and draping down beyond the fluffy covers was the leather strap, just visible if the photo was studied closer. It was all she saw before the torrent from her eyes obscured her vision.

Philip

Linked to his sister from the day of her birth, Philip never knew a little bundle could be so loveable. He loved the new baby and he loved his family. He bragged to anyone who would listen about his baby sister. Welling up with pride, his eyes lit up with happiness as he spoke about all the things he would do as a big brother.

"I will always protect her!" he declared to his parents as they jostled in the studio on the day the photo was taken. "She will be the happiest little sister in the whole world ever!"

His bright, beaming smile and clear, over-eager eyes seared the special moment into their memories for a lifetime.

The noises woke him—deep in the wild forest—four days after the attack. Clearer and more pronounced than anything he had ever heard, he could identify each sound as though he knew what made it. A creaking tree trunk, a small singing bird, a toad crawling up a tree... incessant shuffling as a native mammal searched for its dinner; every sound was as though he had both ears next to it. Wincing, he turned his head and started to open his eyes. The light was far too bright, but his retinas adjusted unnaturally quickly.

It was that time of the day when the sky was getting darker. *Sundown time,* he usually liked to describe it. At school, they had all learned that it was called *dusk.* He looked around and there were trees and many plants everywhere. Dense, aromatic... very noisy trees. He could hear every sound—the stretching of the bark, the creaky swaying of branches, the rustling of the leaves in the evening breeze—and he could hear wandering insects and slithering worms as they went about their own ways of living in the woodland. He felt a sensation fluttering in his heart—a faint, persistent tingling, like a hook... or a magnet... pulling at his instinct from an unknown object.

He moved his hand and very cautiously, started to get up. There was a slight ache, and he felt strange, but there was no pain. He tried hard to remember what the monster had done. Casting his mind back, he replayed the events of the night: from shutting the wardrobe door, he ran out of the cabin and just about made the short distance to the forest. There was rustling behind him, the terrifying snarl and his legs were in the air when he could no longer run because something very strong and vicious had him in its teeth...

It was all he could remember.

He stood up. The hook, the magnet, the sensation, pulling endlessly at his heart purred and fluttered on randomly, growing stronger, and then weaker, then a little stronger again and just before taking a step, he happened to glance downwards and saw what he had become.

He could never go back home.

He hid and lived in the forests: a stealth existence. He knew of the creature's habits adapted into his cells; to move in a unique way, leaving no identifiable tracks, to steer clear of humans who, centuries before, had hunted his new species nearly to extinction, and he knew to groom himself relentlessly so there was never a smell—and never any tell-tale hairs left to become clues.

He fed on forest carcasses, and on endless bounties of flesh and organs discarded from a slaughter house, careful never to leave the slightest trace of his existence. And he knew that at one point, when he was much older, a time would come—a certain season—when hormones would flood into his blood and saliva, and he would get the overwhelming urge to travel very far and select one human, and then bite them as though he was beginning to feed on them, so the overflowing saliva would gush into their wound, and several days later, they would wake up where he left them in a safe and secluded place, with a fresh carcass close by because they would be hungry, and in that way, their species would carry on living, just as they had successfully survived all these centuries.

It wasn't long before he discovered what the inexplicable sensation in his heart was. When he strayed further from it, he immediately wanted to return so he could enhance and amplify its calming tickle. He knew when they eventually left the village to travel back home and it drew him towards them like a beckoning beacon. He travelled too, in stealth, hidden from civilization, skulking in foliage and lurking in dense woods. He slunk through the continent, swam across the channel and journeyed tirelessly towards it, just to be closer, and much later, when they travelled to Wales to spend some time by the lake, he skulked and lurked some more, making his way to be nearby—to keep the sensation tingling a little stronger. Nobody ever saw him. With over heightened senses, multiplied strength and near telescopic eyesight, it was easy to keep it that way.

He was dozing, in Wales, hidden in a clump of bushes, when intense panic crackled fiercely in his heart. The sensation was thundering, the hook was gouging and the magnet heaved with unrelenting ferocity. Every muscle and every animal sense rippled with energy. Crouched like a coiled spring, trembling with power, at first, he had no idea what was happening to him.

And then instinct kicked in.

He had to get to her. He had to get to his little sister. The sweet little bundle of joy's heart was calling. The magnet, the hook had fired up full throttle, thundering in cosmic waves of anguish. Their two hearts connected, he knew exactly where she was and he dove into the lake as though his own life depended on it. She was near the silty bottom when his hairy arm reached her and the hook, the sensation, was beginning to let go.

Filled with panic and dread that she would perish, he lifted her to the surface and swam to the shore. There were a few tense moments before the magnet resumed, and his fear subsided with its gentle pull. Then he put her on the soft moss and waited until the others came, bounding off to hide and watch them gather round to help her.

Rachel and her parents allowed a long while to pass as a solemn calm descended on the sweltering grief. Rachel eventually broke the silence.

"The police will be round soon, looking for witnesses."

"Yes they will," her mother responded. She looked at Rachel with a squint in her eye. "Yes, they absolutely will!"

Her mother knew her too well.

"I got this bruise when moving a full box of books to store them up in the loft," Rachel candidly declared. "It slipped off my hands and... well!" She pointed at her face.

"Box of books!" her father interjected. "Good enough story! That should do for them."

He wasn't falling for it either. But the box story would just about be adequate for the police.

She had genuinely moved the books to the loft two days before and while halfway up the ladder, pushing the box ahead of her, it slipped, started to fall and nearly landed on her head. She managed to catch it on her shoulder, saving it from tumbling down to the floor.

With a slight tweak, the story would be that she moved the box after the party, and it fell on to her head causing the injury they could see. She could show the police the evidence if they needed any, complete with the dented box which she had left as it was. *Shoulder* would be substituted with *head* in her version, making as convincing a story as any she could think of. The expressions on her parent's faces, besides a hint of irritation, showed they would support her. She wanted to get up and hug them.

Her parents sat in silence, watching Rachel expectantly with looks that promised they would eternally understand.

She took a deep breath and began to tell her story.

"Mum. Dad..." she wondered where to begin, "you want to know about the alleyway and why there are so many police?" she glanced down at her clasped hands. "And you want to know how I happened to come across this necklace?"

They remained silent and, holding on to each others hands, braced themselves and nodded. She paused and stared pensively at the crafted silver spider.

Suddenly looking up, with a loud gasp, it dawned on her that she knew how to get Philip to come so they could see him. All the three times he appeared, she was in danger—or in great distress. Something about any threat to her seemed to summon him; he had to be tuned in to her aura in some way. The only way to find him again was to call him to her in another situation where her life was in danger. Maybe her parents could help—but not with a physical attack: they would never agree to it, and even if they did, she couldn't take the chance that he would appear and attack them to save her. Maybe she could try drowning herself in the bath with the doors and windows open so he wouldn't have to... No! Wait! Not in the house. Too risky. Somebody might see him. She knew the perfect spot by a river in the woodland. *Oh dear!* She thought, immediately remembering the lake. *It's really going to hurt, but it's going to be worth it!* All she had to do was convince her parents to go along with a plan.

She looked again at the spider, then took a long, deep breath and raised her head.

"Do you remember when I was 3 years old and I told you that a big, scary dog saved me from drowning?"

The End

Kiibe's Tales

Chapter 1

Old man Kiibe reached the end of his story and finished with the usual words, "Yes, that is the way it was, and the way it has been."

His captivated audience broke into jovial smiles, nodded exuberantly and murmured endless remarks of approval.

Even while lying on his death bed in his homestead, on the edge of the sprawling, old-centuries, African village, old man Kiibe was encouragingly cheerful and still telling tales to entertain his visitors. In times when all nations still used horse carts and gathered coal and firewood as main sources of fuel, his tales came more alien and fantastic than others, each told with passion, heightening the drama. Surrounded by most of his close family and friends, all solemnly clustered around the narrow wooden bed, he found it impossible to resist telling another tale and as soon as he was finished, even more after that.

Old man Kiibe glanced up at his eldest son, Muume, standing bold and tall—in a courageous attempt at masking his distress—next to his brother, who sat distraught and silent at the foot of the bed, barely maintaining his own fragile composure. Muume had aged well and grown in to a strong man with three, good children and a good hearted, happy wife—a partner whom he genuinely took to be his other half and in whom he entrusted his soul and his being. Old man Kiibe was as proud of him as the rest of the family and he was sure they would all thrive and live very well.

Looking at his son's unmistakably distraught eyes, and his strong chin framing a determined yet friendly face, he knew with every instinct the right moment had come and he was ready as he would ever be, to handle the great truth.

But first, old man Kiibe wanted more time with the family, to tell them more tales and enjoy their warm company. He glanced again towards his son, and with eyes sparkling, betraying yet another looming series of stories, he slowly settled into the grass filled, reed-cloth pillow, cleared his throat and began to tell another strange tale.

He spoke of a land he visited where the ground was white as the peak of a frost covered mountain. A land where in some seasons, the sun refused to set, its never-ending beam glowing as far as the eye could see. During these seasons, it was bright at midnight as in the middle of a normal day, as the sun lingered shuddering in fear of the horizon.

In this land, the shining sun brought only light, losing entirely, the battle to carry through any warmth. The bitterness of the wind blew sharper than a new spear, and far worse than lashes of the coldest river water. The chill of the land beat the sun so resoundingly, that a bowl of boiled soup, left out in the glaring rays, would turn cold then turn to stone in less time than it took a herder, working at his usual pace, to finish milking three goats.

Old man Kiibe said if anyone was foolhardy enough to venture out on this land, they had to cover up with layers of the warmest fluff cloth and that no living person dared tread the earth with bare feet, or both would turn into darkened and departed stone, and then shrivel and fall away, separated from the rest of the leg.

Yes, that is the way it was, and the way it has been.

He immediately went on and began to speak of animals that were half dog and half fish, and larger than a grown man. They travelled faster in water than they did on dry land, at a pace many times that of the fastest human swimmer. Old man Kiibe asked if anyone remembered Magimbi 'the fish' and they all loudly proclaimed they could never willingly forget him.

Magimbi was a man who thrived in the neighbouring village, in the previous generation, back when current day elders were still only babies who had not long been born and were new in the living world.

Magimbi, who in those times was dashingly handsome, was the fastest swimmer all the villages had ever known. More impressive was the undefeatable feat of holding his breath and swimming deep in the water, submerged for so long, that some women had sworn they had cooked and served up bowls of millet porridge while he lingered in the water without taking a single breath.

Some of the eldest in the village had attended events when they were younger, where most of the community, and many visitors who came travelling from far beyond, gathered a short distance away from the waterside, near a large, clear pool fed by the waterway headed for the main river. Restless and joyous and fidgeting with excitement, they were keen to catch a glimpse of the legendary Magimbi.

Tall, lanky and lean with muscles rippling under dark skin, Magimbi 'the fish' emerged from the canoe repair hall he ran with eight of his close friends, where their highly skilled work was as famous as his swimming. Dressed in a waist cloth, a cowrie shell necklace and the infectious smile that made him so instantly likeable, he strode out light footedly and confidently made his way to meet the eager crowd, densely gathered and waiting in the afternoon sun.

He would stride, sanguine and happy, to the clear water's edge, pause to wave at the villagers and to his many female fans, and with a dextrous movement, remove his waist cloth and carefully place it on a moss-free, natural rock jutting out close to the healthy-reed covered waterside, leaving only the white groin cloth he wore underneath.

After stopping to calm and slow his heart, he gulped in great mouthfuls and deep breaths of air, huffing and puffing out inflated cheeks and breathing through pursed lips, and after one last look back, he would plunge feet first into the river, slipping smoothly and elegantly underneath its surface.

As the ripples died away, settling into a soft shimmer, all who didn't know would watch for what at first seemed an alarming, and then stretched to a distressingly long period of time.

The moment Magimbi's head disappeared with a subtle splash into the pool, the villagers jovially began to sing a lengthy folk song, telling a well known tale about a fish on a journey, swimming earnestly among the sunny rocks and the reeds searching long and persistently, from one location to another, trying to find the most worthy home for his family. He would search under one rock then look through some reeds, then move to scour another rock and then on to more reeds. The song described the tiny flaws he saw in

178

every place he looked and how determined the fish became to find true perfection. There was not the tiniest flaw in the love from his heart so there could not be any flaw in the home for his children.

The tone rose, matching the frustrations in the wandering fish until, near the very end, it burst into a triumphantly high, cheery, musical pitch as the ideal rock, enclosed by vigorously growing stems was stumbled upon and proudly proclaimed to be the new home.

With cheerful smiles, the villagers would wave their arms and bodies, mirroring the fish celebrating its success, and as the singing peaked to a high pitched, jubilant conclusion, and having stayed submerged without a single breath the entire time, Magimbi's head would break the surface at the centre of the pool, and as it rose, until the water parted for the shoulders, his bright white eyes, crowned with dark brown pupils, scanned the river bank from one end and slowly along to the other.

His big, toothy smile flashed at all who were present and after taking in a deep breath, as the folk song was winding down, both he and the villagers would raise their arms high, jump joyfully into the air and make loud whooping sounds to mark the exultant, celebratory dancing of the fish.

Old man Kiibe claimed that not even Magimbi could have been a match for the half dog, half fish creatures. Even on their worst day, they could swim faster than anybody had seen him swim, and any one of these animals, even the youngest of their children, could have swam inside the water without a single breath of air, and watched as Magimbi went up to breathe three times.

Yes! That is the way it was, and the way it has been!

The audience gasped and shook their heads at the thought of such creatures. They nodded in appreciation, murmured in approval and clapped their hands in awe at Kiibe's wild imagination.

He told another tale about mighty and ferocious bears whose hair was white as the land they endlessly roamed, which in turn was as white as clouds that carried no rain, or the palest of the purest white, mashed sweet potato. There was no tree and no shrubs as far as any eye could see—and even further away than that—in these deserted, empty plains. These mighty bears bred their young, lived and hunted, strolling and ruling majestically over all they beheld.

Old man Kiibe described the scene so vividly, that if the audience did not know better, they would readily have believed he had travelled to see the white land with his own eyes.

"Yes!" he declared after nodding to reinforce it. "That is the way it was, and the way it has been!"

Other tales he told were just as fantastic. He described a distant land with an incredibly tall tower which had many bright lanterns scattered all over it. Constructed using forged metal and without an outer covering, it rose to such a great height, that birds flew around, rather than bother to go over it.

"Even Kimenju tree," he declared, describing the tallest tree in the village, "could grow to twice its full height and not yet be halfway to the size of this tower!"

He told of a giant ship, built painstakingly from planks and logs and stretching out so vast and majestic on the ocean, the whole village could clamber and huddle in its chambers. The villagers could travel on the water for many days and never once endure tightness or the lack of any space.

He told of a land where people built a high and wide wall, so long, you could walk on it as though it was a wide path. The greatest wall standing in all the lands that people walked, and the longest thing built by a tool-wielding community, you could travel from the early dawn, all day, until dusk without coming close to being within sight of the other end, and all along the way, you would see that you were treading on the same form of building work as in the place where you began—each portion as masterful as any of the others. Such was the great and profound skill of the creators.

"Yes!" he declared once again after these tales. "That is the way it was, and the way it has been!"

His dazzling stories may often not have been believable, but in a world of mud huts and clay pots and earthen hearths, each tale was fantastically entertaining for the villagers.

After some time telling tales as he lay on his death bed, old man Kiibe requested that everyone else leave the room so he could have a private word with his son, Muume. Courteous sayings were exchanged along with wishes of good health and after calming and gentle touching of his arms and shoulders, the visitors departed with his promise that they could return.

When they were alone, Kiibe called his son to move closer and in a voice soft as a whisper, asked for a great favour. He wanted to go to a secret place that was dear to his heart and needed only his son for company to help him make the journey. He had to see this place again—he begged—for one last time but it was important that nobody else know the location.

Muume agreed without hesitation.

Early the following day, along with a large group of villagers, old man Kiibe and his son set off on what was believed to be their last journey together. Along the way, Kiibe told more far-fetched tales about faraway lands and the people who lived there.

Everyone huddled closer and eagerly clustered around, desperate not to miss out on his cooked-up narratives. They knew the fanciful stories grew only in his mortal mind, but each one was told as though he saw all the mysteries and traversed the odd places he was spiritedly describing.

He told tales about a land harbouring a stone bridge, built by enterprising people, crossing over a swirling river, joining one bank to another, standing so thick and solid, even the worst flood would flow by like a teardrop. He walked on this bridge—he said—built big and wide enough to carry a path for people—together with their animals—and yet have so much space available to spare, that all along the length, on both sides overlooking the water, were stone huts and buildings planted firmly into the floor, so solid and strong, the river glanced up and shook its watery head in disbelief. The stone structures all housed a myriad of ventures from which earnest sellers enticed wandering passers by.

He told a tale about a sunny, faraway island, thriving with dense forests and standing so remote, native wildlife had never seen or encountered a human. You could walk up to small animals and brightly coloured birds and stroke them or carry them like you were holding a pet, and they would never once run or try to bite you in defence and never once howl out or raise a claw in protest. The island sheltered a river and streams flowing so clear, you were only able to see the water because it was moving. The streams, if you had a drink, tasted so refreshing that from then on, you never wanted to drink anything else.

The group huddled closer, silent and breathless, as old man Kiibe told of a mystical land floating by in grey darkness, where another gargantuan world filled a portion of the sky; a mighty, supernatural ball adorned with radiant trails of vivid decorative clay and floating high up above the land, it was many times larger and far grander than a moon and just hung there, held aloft, the mightiest of entities, making miniscule all other objects hovering in the sky. In the long nights, this giant moon filled the ground with smoked light and bathed all un-shadowed land in ashen, crystal clarity.

The villagers listened, carrying distant expressions, their minds away with visions of a shadowed ashen world—an odd place, one too fantastical to imagine, every detail contradicting its existence along the others. They leaned in to listen as Kiibe cleared his throat and continued with the tale of the stark, crystal, ashen land.

Gazing at the great darkness beyond the gigantic moon, in the haunting, upper, empty sea of endless deep nothingness, every star shone so clear, so vibrant to your eyes, you felt sure they lit up in full honour of your visit. It was never dark in this world. The sun brightened the day and the giant moon lit up the night and though there was not a single tree or shrub as far as you could see, there was no lack of rock formations where one could sit to ponder and enjoy the dusky, glorious view.

Yes, that is the way it was, and the way it has been!

The stunned silence among the villagers lasted many moments. Old man Kiibe had described the bewitching and bewildering land in such great detail, it was as though he had been there and seen it for himself.

After travelling all morning, they stopped in a grass field where a clear stream bubbled on its way to join the big river. The cool water was ideal for washing and drinking and they talked about making camp for the rest of the evening. They lit a small fire and cooked a batch of fresh, millet porridge, served with purple berries picked from clumps of spindly bushes, and everyone settled to slowly slurp on the late lunch.

When every belly was filled and gurgling with contentment, old man Kiibe asked that everyone else stay behind so he could carry on with only his son to help him. After much deliberation and protests from the villagers who were reluctant to leave the two while Kiibe was weakening, they begrudgingly agreed to start shoring up the camp so they could remain in the area until father and son returned. Before they were allowed to leave, they spent some more time singing songs, drinking fruit beer and enjoying another one of Kiibe's imaginary tales.

As father and son eventually prepared to depart, the villagers gathered around knowing it was likely the last time they would see old man Kiibe alive. With little time remaining, he appeared to be weakening and a long journey without them would probably be his last. He explained it was a sacred journey, very special and dear to him or he would never have ventured to leave their side at such a time.

Father and son collected provisions the villagers wrapped for them and amidst a final wave of lengthy, emotional goodbyes, prepared to leave the safe camp site and walk into the forest.

Old man Kiibe and Muume set off on the last part of the journey with Kiibe self assuredly pointing out the way. Muume obediently supported his weakening father, curious to arrive at whatever mystery lay ahead. With ever increasing difficulty and as Kiibe grew weaker, they journeyed on all evening, deep into the forest and up the gentle slopes at the foot of the great mountain.

Stopping to make camp in the forest for the night, they ate some dried, sliced cassava, drank some more fruit beer and then slept soundly—with a crackling fire warding off wandering beasts. Early the following morning, after a bowl of cold millet porridge, they gathered up their supplies and set off trudging up the slope.

By mid-day, the path narrowed, faded away and then disappeared as they entered the thickly forested face of the mountain. After another long session of difficult trekking, the trees and wild undergrowth suddenly thinned out and then entirely gave way to open into a small clearing, approximately thirty generous striding steps across.

Some large, sturdy rocks, the size of boulders, lay in the middle, piled as though the earth around them had worn away. One especially large boulder straddled the top like it had settled there for as long as the mountain had stood. As they neared the rocks, old man Kiibe—by then weak and struggling—raised his arm and with difficulty, motioned for Muume to stop.

Chapter 2

After taking a break to catch his breath, old man Kiibe began to speak. "Muume, my son, I have brought you here to change your life. From this day, everything you know will be different. The thing I am about to show you changed me many seasons ago and it has all been a heavy, yet wondrous burden to bear."

Muume was watching his father with questioning eyes.

After a short pause, Kiibe took a breath and continued. "I do this now only because you are my eldest child and you have grown up to be a good and intelligent man. You have strength and wisdom enough to bear the hefty burden and a good mind to contrive good ways to proceed. No other soul can know the thing I am going to reveal until such a day comes when you know of a person in whom you will have as much faith as I have in you."

Muume was suddenly very alert. His father had never spoken in such a way before and he began to wonder what secret the old man harboured.

"Do you know why I say the words 'that is the way it was and the way it has been'?"

Muume shook his head. Like other villagers, he assumed it was a style of speaking.

"It is because every word of the tales I told was true!" Kiibe casually declared. "Every word of each story I ever told was the truth and the places I spoke about are all very real..." his voice trailed off for the briefest of moments. "There may have been only a little embellishment for drama—but only a small part. The stories were always true."

Muume stared in silence. The worry for his dying father had just intensified.

After a short pause, old man Kiibe carried on speaking. "The places all exist, Muume. I went to every one of them and saw all of those things, just like in the stories. I saw the places, the people, the beings, and all the creatures, living and breathing as clearly as I see you now. I felt the heat, I felt the cold, I saw the heights, I saw the depths, I saw the beauty with my eyes, in this living reality, with a very clear mind, while breathing and walking. It was not in any dream and it was not imagination."

Unable to think of anything suitable to say, Muume remained silent and stood staring at his father. Kiibe appeared to have the same taut expression and the stern look he carried when discussing serious matters.

Muume was suddenly confused. He did not want to doubt his father but nobody could travel to imaginary places. Maybe it was all a shrewd test or a riddle, or a cleverly concocted puzzle he was expected to solve. Wracking his brains, he stood baffled and disconcerted, unable to think of any puzzles hidden in his father's words.

"I do not understand. How can... What do you..." Muume's words trailed off and he waited for an explanation.

"Listen carefully Muume," Kiibe spoke a little slower. "I say again that every word of those stories was true. I visited those places and saw everything I spoke of. It was no illusion or any imagination. The places and those events are not only in my mind. They exist just as our own village does." Shaking his head to stress the absence of any imaginary thinking, he leaned forward and looked his son straight in the eyes. "I went there as sure as you are standing right here with me. Everything was the way it was, and the way it has been, even up to this moment."

Muume was lost. He shrugged, tried to speak and then raised the palms of his hands and shook his head slowly. For the first time, he began to consider the real possibility that his father, in his final days, was losing his mind.

Kiibe was immediately vexed. "Remove that look from your face! I say one thing your mind is unable to grasp and you begin to doubt my sanity?"

Muume instantly felt ashamed. Such odd words must have been uttered with good reason. He cleared his mind, relaxed his posture and waited for an explanation. There had to be a purpose for making such a long journey.

Kiibe continued, "Muume my son, what I am about to share with you will astound not just you, but anyone else you ever make the decision to reveal it to. I know you will do the right thing and will not exploit it. I have brought you up myself so of this I have no doubts!"

Muume nodded in agreement, and swore never to betray his good upbringing or his father's unbounded trust.

"Do not take this lightly!" Kiibe urgently cautioned. "If what I am going to show you is learned by others, the consequences may be beyond what I can express. Terrible anguish may befall you and the whole tribe and destroy much in this living land that you have ever known! You must never reveal this to anybody that you are not certain you can trust even with your own soul, and you must guard that no one can ever stumble upon it!"

Muume once again began to feel increasingly worried.

"Muume, my son," Kiibe said after a long pause, "I have told you that every word of my stories is true. I travelled to those places and saw them with my own eyes. It should not be possible. But I ask you my son, that if no way you know of can surely be possible, how then, in any way, can it also be true?"

Lowering his gaze to ponder the puzzle for a moment, Muume reached up to scratch his head, searching his mind until, all of a sudden, his face and eyes lit up as the only obvious and simple answer revealed itself. "Then it must surely be a way that I do not know of!"

Kiibe nodded, his face warming with a bright smile. "Yes, that is correct Muume!" he enthusiastically confirmed. "That is the one very simple and very correct answer! I used a means to get there that nobody is aware of!"

Muume stared in wonder. What path could one travel to imaginary places?

"Muume," his father said in a slow and deliberate voice, "what I am now going to show you, no other person knows. And you must keep it that way until the day you trust your own son or daughter, or other person of your choosing, enough to be certain that they are fully worthy."

Muume nodded and agreed.

"Let us walk closer to those," Kiibe said, while pointing to the pile of large rocks in the centre of the clearing.

As they approached the boulders, he slowed and then raised his hand to point to the largest one. "Look at the big rock on the top, the widest one with the strange shape."

Muume studied it carefully but all he saw was plain rock. The biggest one perched on the top was an impressive object, far taller than he was and much wider than its height. The same colour as the others, it was nothing out of the ordinary. He shook his head. Nothing was unusual in any way.

"That is no rock," Kiibe profoundly declared. "It may look now like a rock, but I can tell you it is no rock. I will show you in one moment."

When they reached the pile, Muume took a few moments to look at them. The big one lying on the top was even larger up close. It was rare, but not unique; he had seen bigger ones. Turning to look at his father, he frowned and slowly shook his head.

"Climb up and look at the big one," Kiibe casually encouraged.

There was a healthy stride's worth of space around the large rock. Looking closer, he saw the rock was smoother, well formed and was perched as though a giant hand intentionally adjusted it. Though a little strange, it was not too extraordinary. He had seen column shaped rocks—some standing on their edge—randomly propped up by the forces of nature. Though uncommon, it was not worth puzzling over.

"This one is a little strange," he called out to his father. "But it is nothing very special. I have seen others more majestic and even more outstanding, like the big one near the waterfall." He gave the example of a giant, embedded, square shaped boulder, lodged beside a waterfall located nearly a morning's walk along the main river.

"Help me up!" Kiibe called out after a moment.

Muume leaned down to pull his father up by the hand. Walking gingerly on the narrow space, Kiibe paused to glance at Muume before nodding reassuringly. Then he stepped forward, reached out with the flattened palm of his hand and almost touched the large boulder. What happened next shocked and startled Muume so profoundly that he spun around, jumped down and sprinted away in terror.

Kiibe calmly steadied himself and sat down on the lower rock with his back against the smooth boulder. Folding up his aching legs, he placed his elbows on his knees, made himself comfortable and patiently settled down to wait for his son to return.

Chapter 3

Muume eventually reappeared and slowly inched his way back— one cautious step at a time. When he was close enough, his father reached out to reassure him.

"Come near! Do not be frightened! It will cause you no harm. This is how I went to those places. It is as safe as a warm, big hut in the homestead!"

Muume stared at a thing that could not possibly exist. Even in the wildest stories of fantasy and witchcraft, his imagination never conjured up such an entity. Barely restraining himself, he stayed only because his father was unafraid of the object. Its presence appeared to have a homely, calming effect on him and he seemed to have instructive control over it. Muume stayed and walked forward only because he trusted his father.

After allowing his son a little time to calm his senses, Kiibe stood and turned to face the large rock again. Reaching out once more, he held up his palm and as his hand got closer, the boulder reacted in the same way it had done before.

The surface appeared to shimmer and tremble in waves and a barely audible hum pulsated within its belly. The entire rock began to change colour to a dark green and its shape altered slightly to look flatter on one end. There was a slight hissing noise and a small part of one side opened up, revealing a dim, hollow interior. Though darker than the afternoon daylight outside, the soft illumination within revealed strange items and fittings that could not have been part of any rock.

Muume's eyes were wide with fear, but he remained calm only because his father looked to be in control of the entity. Kiibe glanced at his son before calmly stepping forward to climb into the rock through the door shaped opening. Muume stood outside baffled by what was happening and some moments passed by before his father's head peeked out.

"Are you coming in or are you going to stand there like a pumpkin?"

Head forward as though trying to listen out for a heart beat, Muume plucked up the courage to begin walking closer. When he reached the oval opening, he leaned forward and cautiously peeked inside. It was so far beyond anything he had ever even imagined, that he suddenly felt faint and he reached out to steady himself.

When his hand touched the surface, it felt nothing like any rock he had ever seen or known of, or he had ever touched. He ran his fingers along the substance, trying to understand. Smooth, rubbery and green, it reminded him of the surface on the leaf of a banana tree. He caressed it for a moment trying to make sense of the texture and how it had got there. The entire outer part looked to be of the same material.

This, he thought to himself, *is not made of any rock. And this green substance is not banana leaf!*

Bracing himself, he took a slow and overly cautious step, climbed up and tentatively went through the opening.

Muume was greeted by the unexpected, stunning sight of a softly illuminated, hollow interior, with an array of organized panels, some tubes along the ceiling and the strangest, inexplicable objects jutting out in odd places. A peculiar, narrow, waist high pedestal stood lonely—but strangely purposeful—against one wall, and four large illuminated panels hung, near vertically, at one end of the tidy and well-planned space.

His eyes swept disbelievingly from the top and down to the floor and then from one side to the other. Suddenly whirling around, he stepped back outside, jumped off to the ground, ran a few paces away, and then stopped to turn back and stare at the pile of rocks. Shaking his head, he walked all the way around them in a wide arc, with his eyes glued to the largest one, and when he had gone all the way around in a circle, he turned and started again in the opposite direction.

After walking around twice more, he paused and stared blankly before hurrying back towards them. Jumping on to the rocks again, he stepped back inside to find the same scene confronting him. He was unable to understand. The interior seemed bigger than the rock looked on the outside. There was far too much space—much more than there should be; as though he stepped into a house, but once inside, saw a space as big as a meeting hall. It appeared more than twice the size he saw from the outside. His mind grappled with trying to figure out the illusion.

A few paces away to the right, he noticed there was a large chair that was different to any piece of furniture he had ever seen. It appeared to have no legs but was suspended, in mid-air, by what looked like a thick rope attached to the ceiling. A second thinner rope ran from the floating base of the chair and down into the floor, seeming to secure it from movement. When he looked closer, he saw his father was settled upon it, calmly using his fingers to manipulate different lights on the four large panels hovering before him. Behind it were two similar chairs which, though smaller, were just as impressive and sturdy as the bigger one. In one quick movement, Kiibe swivelled the contraption and turned to face his son.

"Try one of them," he suggested. "Have a seat for a while, gaze around and give your troubled mind a little time to settle."

Muume slowly and tentatively walked towards his father. Stopping by the smaller chairs, he reached out to touch the one closer to him. It was made of a material he had never encountered before that felt like softened cow hide mixed with reed cloth—a peculiar combination as the two could not be woven together.

He took another look around and glanced again at the chair before slowly settling into it. With the strange sensation of a floating, strong hammock, it was more comfortable than any furniture he knew of.

"Good chair, is it not!" his father confidently exclaimed. "It keeps your body supported and works together with the light to take away discomfort and to sharpen your senses." Kiibe watched as Muume gazed around in awe. "The chairs were not set before for the people of our world, but a simple thing to change them when you learn of the maker's tools."

While nodding in approval, Muume suddenly froze.

What had his father just said!

"Our world?" he asked, convinced he had misheard.

Kiibe smiled. "I was waiting for just such a question. Look around you Muume. What you see could never have been built by any people of this world. There is not such materials or even any of the knowledge for us to have created such a thing as this." His smile stretched wider. "No matter how you heat metal, weave cloth or cure wood, you could not create the things as they are in here. One day we may be able to, but now it is as difficult and undecipherable as the most powerful magic. I know this because I have seen with my own eyes, much of this world we all live in at the moment." He shook his head. "No, Muume. This is a powered... I still don't know how to describe it! A wagon... No... well, some sort of entity. And it came from a world beyond this one we are living in."

Kiibe paused to let the startling information sink in.

Muume was staring at his father, silent and very still.

"And there is more," Kiibe continued after some silence. "I know the direction in which lies the world that this very thing came from. It is far away! Very far! Up into the sky! Much further than I can describe in any words I know. I have not travelled to see it. That may not at all be wise." He sternly shook his finger back and forth to emphasize the point. "If I did, the people there might not let me return. And if they could build such a thing as this so long ago, by now, they must have much bigger and stronger ones that would make this one look like a child's toy wheel."

Muume stared at his father and as though afraid of the answer, half spoke and half whispered, "Which powered... wagon?"

"Wagon is not a good name. It does not describe it well. Muume, my son, I would like you to meet *Walvenye*. A thing which when you get to know, you will become good friends with."

"Wali... Whe... What?"

"Walvenye. *Walvenye*."

Mumme stared at his father.

"It is what it first said to me when I first encountered it. Listen—"

Turning towards the panels, Kiibe pointed out a curved line of light nearly as long as his finger. It glowed and dimmed by itself in constant rhythmic pattern. "This light is always doing that. It was the first light I touched—out of sheer curiosity—and listen to what happens."

He touched the light with a finger. It responded by coiling itself into a circle and then glowing in bright yellow. A sound filled the interior with what to the human ear, was likely a spoken name.

"WAELNVENIHE!"

The circle opened up again and changed back to a curved line.

Staring around at the walls, Muume tried to see where the sound had come from. "What did he say? Who was speaking?" he asked trying to see where the hidden being was lurking.

"There is nobody. Just this entity." Kiibe casually replied. "Listen again," he instructed.

He touched the line once more and the same strange word reverberated from the walls.

"It does the same every time." Kiibe said with a shrug. "*Walvenye*! Every time I touch this curved light."

"It sounds like it is saying *walinevinye*." Muume remarked. "Yes, I think it was walinevinye."

Kiibe played the sound again, three times in succession.

"Now I am not sure." Muume declared with a furrowed brow. "I have never heard such a sound. It is like a bull trying to talk—but without any air in its lungs, and then it says a word in a language from a faraway land. I cannot understand it."

"To me it sounds like Walvenye. That is what I decided to call it. I have no idea what it means. Maybe it is the entity's name, or maybe it is a greeting. Or maybe even all it is actually saying is 'Welcome'. But I do not know the dialect and I have never learned the purpose. So until we find what it may mean, I will assume it is saying its name. That is what I have always called it since the day it spoke that word."

Muume nodded in acceptance.

"How is it able to speak?" he asked.

"I do not understand the workings but I know the objects that make the noise. They are hidden in the walls, I will show you all that later." Kiibe was looking at his son square in the eye. "Walvenye can do many things. It is powered by a mystery force and needs no person or oxen or even a single donkey to pull it along." He nodded as though to confirm the accuracy of his statement. "It travels upon its own power, which it absorbs from the sky... or the stars... or the sun, I am still not sure. And it goes about, moving from one place to another using only this power and nothing else that I know about."

Taking a deep breath, he stared thoughtfully at the floor, allowing a few moments to pass by before he carried on speaking.

"I suspect that it drinks in some of the mighty warmth bathing down from our sun. Maybe one day, when you have learned more of its workings, you will strive to find out. It would be a good thing to know."

Muume was gazing as though staring at an apparition.

Kiibe casually continued. "I have more news to astound you. Walvenye, using the power that it drinks from the sun... or maybe from the stars, travels up in the air, higher than any bird could dream of flying. And that is not even a small part of what it can do." Lowering his head, he waved a hand in a gesture that more was forthcoming. "It will also happily go on to the surface of any lake, or sail well on any sea, like a very strong canoe, and once there, will float all day long without a worry, teasing waters tickling its belly trying to find a way in."

Kiibe paused to allow his son to process the information.

"And yet even that is nothing, because it can plunge into the depths of those waters and travel far down and all around in the deepest parts for as long as you desire, without even one tiny drop getting inside. And it can do all this while we sit here within it, comfortable and dry as if we were still on land. Walvenye would easily make Magimbi 'the fish' look like a new born baby a countless times over."

Staring at his father in awe and boyish wonder, Muume wished that every word he had spoken was true. How could anything made by beings fly in the sky? He had not seen feathers or any wings on the outside. How could it fly without them? Maybe they were hidden and tucked into its side in the same way all birds fold away theirs. It could be like a large bat or a very large insect; bats are all featherless yet have no trouble flying. Half fearing the answers, he hesitated to voice out the lingering questions and obstructive doubts. What if his father had only imagined he was flying? What if some part of what he said was only in his mind?

Noting his son's expression, Kiibe cleared his throat and spoke again, "Cease your worrying Muume. I am as sane as the lively breath of wind fluttering in the trees, and as the bright, shining warmth of the morning sun. Every word I have spoken is heavy only with truth. You will find out soon, Muume. Settle your rising doubts." He nodded to reassure his son. "You are fortunate Muume, because you have me to show you all that I have learned and that I know about this thing. When I discovered it out in the forest many seasons ago, I was all on my own and fortunately for all of us, I told no other soul. I had only myself for the journey of discovery and the same terror consumed me as causes you to worry."

Kiibe took a long look around the whole interior, his eyes eventually settling to gaze at the entrance. The daylight outside fluoresced the oval shaped opening in a door sized, doubly bright, flicker free lantern. A round edged patch of sunlight, shining through the doorway, had serenely settled, sprawled like a luminescent doormat. The substance covering the floor appeared to absorb half the light, leaving a feeble reflection—with the effect of glowing clay—in the exact shape of the round edged, textured patch of sun. He had seen it before a countless times but he saw it all anew again, as Muume, a new pair of eyes was going to see it.

"Only my deep curiosity pestered me and brought me back." he looked up and continued. "And I am very glad because this became one of the greatest blessings, not only upon me, but for all our community and all of our tribe."

Feeling overwhelmed, Muume stared and chose to remain silent. Kiibe looked and sounded sane but every word was too incredible. If half of what he said was true, then even more remarkable was the keeping of such a thing a secret for so long. Making the decision to carry on trusting his father, Muume committed to abandoning the lingering doubts.

"Muume my son," Kiibe spoke after a long pause, "tell me any place far from here that you would like to visit, a place you might have heard of or you may have wanted to see."

Muume pondered, his mind weighing up possibilities.

"What type of place do you mean?" he enquired after scouring for options. "Anywhere I can think of? Even a place I may have only heard about from other people?"

Kiibe nodded. "But it has to be of the physical world, not one existing only in enchanting tales."

Some moments went by before Muume suddenly perked up. "Father, you have said that all the stories you told were true, and that is the way it was and the way it has been. You told of a distant village with a tall metal tower that has many bright lanterns all over inside it. I have tried imagining such an incredible thing but my mind does not let me. I would like to see this village and the magnificent tower."

Kiibe nodded. "Very well. We will go so you can see it."

Turning around to face the panels, he used the tips of his fingers in sweeping motions across several symbols and translucent images. Then without looking back, he lifted one hand and tapped on the upper edge of the back of his chair.

"Do you see those two, white things on your chair?"

Muume turned to look and easily located the two objects.

"Good," Kiibe said encouragingly. "Pull them out and two ropes attached to them will follow them. No need to pull strongly. Pull down and attach each end to those two, grey bulging objects on the sides of the chair."

Kiibe swivelled back around, gestured how the straps should go and then pointed to a section located near Muume's hips. The strange straps were comfortable and held him firmly in place. Kiibe pointed to two levers underneath the armrests and showed him how to gently manoeuvre them to free the straps. Muume did so and they detached with a soft noise then moved away and upwards back to their original position.

"My own design," Kiibe said. "I did not like what was there before. It had not been made for us and the size and shape of our bodies. Within Walvenye are some tools you can use to change a few small things. But I will show you all of that later."

Muume wondered what bodies the chairs had been designed for but before he could ask, Kiibe gestured once more.

"Now put them on again so I can show you something with these lights."

Whirling back around to face the four vertical panels, he pointed to one of them. Among other symbols and strange dancing patterns, a flickering line glowed, branching off towards one corner.

"You see this scraggy line loitering over here?"

Muume leaned his head to have a look then confirmed that he could.

"Look—" Kiibe said before using three fingers to gently swirl the line and disrupt its solitude.

It shuddered then curved upon itself to form a circle, which flickered, turned yellow and then shrunk into a small symbol. The straps released themselves without use of the levers and moved away back to their original position.

Muume was immensely impressed.

Kiibe spun around, a childish grin glowing on his face. "Magical!" he giggled out. "Amazes me every time!"

Muume nodded in agreement.

"Now pull them down and put them on again so we can see this tower!"

Swivelling back around to face the four large panels, he pulled down and attached the straps on his own chair and then raised his fingers to touch the patterns in three places. There was a light jolt followed by a low, droning hum and after carefully watching the lights, he nodded enthusiastically.

"We are on our way," he announced in a soft, mumbling voice. "It will take a short while for Walvenye to reach there, so get comfortable for now. Ready yourself for a surprise!"

Muume once again began to worry that it might not be true.

"The lights show we are moving even though you can barely feel it." Kiibe suddenly called out. "There is much I need to teach you and very much you will have to learn. But first we go to see this place and look upon the tower. You will learn much quicker once all doubt has left your mind."

They sat in humming silence while Kiibe studied the four panels. Muume gazed around the interior, marvelling at the lighting. Looking up at three tubes trailing along the upper wall, his eyes followed them until they merged and swelled into a protrusion expanded to nearly the width of his head. He made a mental note to ask his father what the object was.

Before long, and very much sooner than he expected, there was a slight vibration and a barely perceptible jolt. Kiibe detached his straps, deftly touched two of the panels, swept his gaze across all four then swivelled around to face his son.

"We have arrived!" he announced with a curiously cheeky smile.

Muume yet again wondered if any of it was real. He willed it to be true, if only as proof that his father was sane.

201

Glancing down at his hands, he pulled on the levers and quickly stood, eager to see if they had left the forest. He immediately stumbled backwards and fell back into the chair. Eyelids shut tight, a strained groan escaped from his lips. Ferocious spinning in his head forced his face into a wince. Sitting very still, he braced and waited for the wave to pass, struggling, with great difficulty, to remain seated upright.

When he could focus again, sounds of hearty laughter registered and he looked up to see his father's face staring back at him. Still sat in his own chair, Kiibe was leaning forward, hands on knees and heaving with unrestrained chuckles.

"You will soon be fine Muume!" Kiibe reassured his son. "You are feeling the effect of going very far and very fast. Within a short time, you are no longer where you were and it takes your body a while to adjust to the new place." He paused as lingering laughter shook his lean shoulders. "I was going to tell you about it before we began the journey." His shoulders shook again. "But I decided it would be more entertaining this way."

Muume, fortunately, appreciated the humour.

"There is no harm," Kiibe said after regaining composure. "The same will happen every time you travel very fast to a place that is far away. But you will get used to it, just as I did." And as though to prove the point, he stood up, raised his arms and comically stretched them upwards. "You see!" he said with confidence. "Steady as a rock." After standing to attention and then waving from side to side, he lowered his arms again. "Rest for now and feel better and then we will prepare so you can go to see this tower." He looked down at the woven cloth that was standard village attire. "We must change our appearance so we look like those who live here."

Something was strangely new and different about his father but in that moment, Muume was unsure of what he saw. Unwilling to dwell on it, he leaned back into the chair to rest until his head had finally ceased spinning and his body and limbs once again felt like his own.

Kiibe walked over to a large, rectangular compartment and pulled out some strange clothes, hats and walking canes. Though the cloth they were sewn from was vaguely familiar, Muume had never seen such odd attire.

Handing one set over as soon as his son could stand, Kiibe held on to the other, and then carefully demonstrated the best way to put them on. As his son was getting dressed, Kiibe walked over to another compartment, pulled out two objects and walked back with both carefully draped over his arm.

When they were dressed up, he stressed that there were rules for behaviour and strictly forbade Muume from speaking to anyone.

"You must only observe and carefully follow my directions. Do nothing that is different and do not get distracted!"

In Muume's mind lingered suspicions of a deception. His father was well known for elaborate pranks but there had never been anything remotely as peculiar.

"One more thing," Kiibe said as he reached across to place on Muume a translucent strap that wrapped loosely around the neck, down the chest and to the belly and around the back and to the front along the circumference of his waist. "Do not take this off!"

He placed and carefully fixed a similar looking strap over himself.

Satisfied they were suitably clothed, he looked at his son. "We are ready," he announced. "Come, let us see this tower."

Making his way to the door, he touched a curved protrusion on the wall and a section moved away revealing the oval shaped opening. Daylight flooded into the craft. The partly cloudy day lit up harsher and brighter than the soft illumination they were accustomed to on the inside.

Kiibe took one last knowing look at Muume and after a short pause, turned and briskly stepped outside with a sideways glance indicating for his son to follow. Shifting and fidgeting uncomfortably in the strange clothes, Muume briefly tested his weight on the cane and then stepped forward to follow his father into the brightness.

Chapter 4

It took only a moment for his eyes to adjust and Muume stopped and stared, breathless and stunned. Kiibe glanced at his son and recognized a face bathed in a wave of the emotions that had also engulfed him, when he too saw it for the very first time. Turning to look, he beheld it again—through his son's eyes—awed by its complexity and obscene extravagance.

Rising up from the ground some distance away and piercing the sky higher than anything he had imagined was a magnificent tower, made entirely out of metal, bigger than any man-made building Muume had ever laid eyes on. Proud and majestic, it stood out in the landscape, a spectacular example of mechanical architecture. Kiibe stood and waited, savouring the occasion, allowing his son time to process the reality.

There were more strange buildings and structures in the distance, some huddled close and others appearing randomly spaced out. Many stood in clusters intentionally planned in rows and others gave the impression they were added as an afterthought. Muume was about to step forward to have a closer look when he felt a firm hand on his chest holding him back.

"We will go together!" Kiibe instructed in a low tone. "You must stay beside me for every single moment. Say nothing, do nothing and above all, do not stare. If you catch the eye of any people, smile and keep walking. We cannot stay for too long. We have to make our way back to Walvenye very quickly."

Some time later when they got back to the craft, Muume sat in stunned silence, in attempt at processing everything he had just seen. Together with his father, they had walked among the bustling community of people who wore strange clothes—and closed shoes made of hide, and had a very different culture to any other he knew. They had walked among the stone buildings and then right up to the tower, and he felt the cold metal as his fingers pressed against it. Everything was as real as the trees or his arm; none of it was imaginary. And no part was a lengthy and elaborate joke his father had cunningly rolled out for him.

Muume asked many questions that were churning in his mind; how the people were so different and how the straps worked. "If these straps made us look so similar to them, how come I could see you the same way you are now?"

"They have a stored power." Kiibe ventured an explanation. "A stored strength which releases to hide the wearer. They were made... or they belonged to the builders of Walvenye and must have been used when exploring our world, likely so as to avoid panic among those encountered."

Muume began to ponder every stranger he had ever walked past.

"The straps can be changed to have a stronger or weaker power." Kiibe pointed to the narrow space in which they were hanging. "And they must also be carefully stored in that way. They gather power from Walvenye, and they can only do that when you hang them back in the right way after using them. When they have no power, they will turn a dark grey—like the clay near Nyandaro in the grassland by the waterfall." He lifted the palm of his hand in reassurance. "But they can last two days before the power fails and they begin to turn slowly as you lose their protection. As long as you return to Walvenye in that time, which is easy to remember, then you will always be hidden and remain well protected."

He walked over and unclipped, then removed and brought the one Muume had been wearing. The next few moments were spent carefully demonstrating the best way to adjust them.

"You were able to see me the same way as always," Kiibe explained while his son tried the adjustments, "because we know each other well and we are in Walvenye together. The straps can not overcome this even with their strongest power. But they hide us from the others and make us appear as one of them as long as the difference is not very great, and also if we do not remain outside for too long."

Muume was suitably impressed. "Have they always worked for you? How big, do you think, is a difference they can not hide?"

After pausing to ponder, Kiibe slowly shook his head. "I am not certain what is the greatest difference they can hide and where the line is that they begin to find that they can not. But it is always best to avoid much time with strangers. The straps cannot hide language. I try to avoid people and I pretend to be deaf whenever I must encounter them. It is much safer that way."

Muume understood entirely.

Almost as an afterthought, Kiibe offered an example. "If you put the straps on a cow or something else like a sheep, it would be a big difference that is too great to hide. The people will not behold the sheep as though it was a person."

Chuckling involuntarily, Muume tried to imagine a cow wearing the straps. "Did you try them with any animals?"

"Yes I did," Kiibe nodded, his face lighting up with a smile. "I took a small goat along on a test trip to another land, but nobody was fooled. Even imbued with the strongest power, the straps could not hide it. They must have thought a deaf man decided to keep a goat instead of a good dog as a helpful companion."

The sound of hearty laughter rang out, brightening the interior before instantly melting into the sound absorbing walls.

Other thoughts worried Muume. Knowing for sure that every word his father spoke was true, he began to wonder about the beings capable of building the craft. Why had they gone away and left it? Where were they at that moment? Why would they abandon such a functional thing? What would happen if they turned up to reclaim their property and found him and his father freely playing and travelling with it as though they owned it?

Kiibe appeared to read his mind. "Are you wondering about the creators of such a thing?" he enquired before shaking his head to reassure his son. "There is not the furthest worry worth disturbing your mind for. I have lived all my long life from back in late childhood when I stumbled upon it, until this day we sit here peacefully inside it. If they were meaning to come back, they would, as sure as rain is made of sky-ward water, have done so by now. And if they had meant us any harm, you will know, when you find out what Walvenye can do, that there is not a thing in this world that could have saved us from their wrath." He paused and shook his head. "No Muume! There is not a slither of worry to be had. If they were ill willed, then you and I would not be here now living well in this moment!"

Muume felt more at ease. If the builders of such a thing had come to cause harm, they would have known of it back when his father was only a child. "Have you seen them?" he enquired. "Do you know anything of them?"

Kiibe paused, and then shook his head. "I never saw, or to my knowledge, encountered any one of them. This thing appeared abandoned as far as I have ever known. The little that I know of them is from what I have seen here. Maybe they left it to test us. I can not comprehend how beings capable of creating things like this would simply go and forget it. Probably it was intentional. And probably they have been watching while hidden all the time. Sometimes I look at strange rocks, or strange bushes, or strange trees and think it might be another one of them watching in silence. We would never know. They could hide just like Walvenye. I will tell you the story soon, of how I stumbled upon it while running away from forest dogs all on my own. But that is for another time." He waved his arm in an arc from one side to the other. "There are many signs inside here of how the makers lived their lives. I am certain that they live even now, very far away, in their own homes constructed and gathered in another land."

Swivelling in the seating contraption, he turned to face the other way. "There is great wealth of information harboured within these." He gestured towards the panels at what Muume, by then, assumed to be the front of the craft. "It is very possible they left Walvenye as a test, and also possible that I was selected to find it." A distant look lingered, towed along by a memory. "But I have only broken the skin and have not even began to feast on the main flesh of the fruit of vast knowledge lying within it." He gestured once again towards the illuminated panels. "I will teach you as much as I have learned of these things and it will be upon you to diligently carry on learning!"

In the following three days, they went visiting and saw another half a dozen places, three of which Muume asked to see from past stories, and three destinations Kiibe eagerly suggested. In all of them were glorious, unimaginable features, sprawling architecture and land-scapes magnificent as the giant metal tower; every one of them strange as a live-action dream.

They saw varying seasons Muume never knew existed and weather so extreme, he could not bear walking in it. Some places were so cold that however warmly he was dressed, his toes and fingers went numb in a way he had never felt before, while some were so hot, potatoes could bake in the sunlight—or at least he believed they could—the heat was that unbearable.

And they saw many people Muume would never have known of; every style, colour, size, fashion, language and appearance, some of them so strange, they might be from another realm, some lifestyles so bizarre, he gazed in fascination at their simplest rituals.

He was humbled by many animals roaming many lands and endless forms of untamed creatures hunting in the forests. He stared, mesmerized by the white bears on white land and later, at the dog-fish entities Kiibe had described—more remarkable in real life, the dog-fish were formidable and even more unusual than his father's words had made them seem.

"Magimbi the fish surely would have been shamed against these swimmers!" he exclaimed as the entities disappeared into the depths.

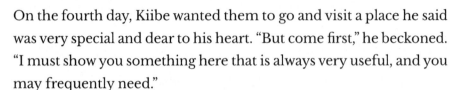

On the fourth day, Kiibe wanted them to go and visit a place he said was very special and dear to his heart. "But come first," he beckoned. "I must show you something here that is always very useful, and you may frequently need."

After stepping outside, they turned back to look at the craft and touching the side to close the door, Kiibe pointed to a slightly rougher part of the surface.

"You see over here, Muume?" he asked, while hovering an instructive finger over the strangely speckled section. "This is where you put your hand to make the surface show its colour. You hold it near here to open the door and change the appearance. It will do nothing if anybody else puts their hand, but now Walvenye knows you, it will respond to your presence."

Moving slightly to the left, he pointed to a smoother section, barely perceptible in texture from the first. "Do you see this part?" he asked, while swirling a finger over the different surface.

"I see it." Muume replied. "It is smoother than over here."

"Good. This is where you always put your hand near to so Walvenye keeps itself hidden. In places you do not know, it is wise to remain hidden. It will hide in plain sight by pretending to be a rock... or a giant bush... or a mound of sand... or... I do not... many, many, other things. I do not know how it sees and then thinks so it can decide, but it looks at the surrounding area and hides itself the best way."

Muume nodded and reached up to try both surfaces, marvelling at the magical and smooth transformation.

"It probably uses the same ways to be unseen when flying." Kiibe added with roving eyes wandering up and down the craft. "I have wondered many times how come nobody has ever seen it for all these seasons, visiting so many places! If it could not hide, somebody would have seen or heard it. It wanders like a spirit among the world of the living, travelling here and there as though in full spite of seeing eyes!"

After climbing back inside and settling into the chairs, Kiibe tapped and slid his fingers over the four hovering panels, exciting the flickering, dancing lights and with the usual jolt and a low, droning hum, they were on their way.

When they arrived at the destination, Muume was consumed with wonder at the purity and beauty of the forest covered island. It was just as his father had described in the tale. Remote and teeming with life, no humans had lived in the pristine jungle that sprawled all around him, serene and untampered with. Honed over eons, it was nature's art in detail—a cacophonous world where all lived in blissful balance. Tailored abundance was in infinite variety. The trees and bushes appeared to have lived for so long, they made homes for things Muume had never seen or heard of.

Captivating, bird songs bounced off thick foliage and massaged his eardrums while swimming through the lively air. Desperately searching for the sources of the ear nectar, glimpses of plumages under clusters of dewy leaves, vivid and impossibly bright, stroked his eyeballs and bewitched his senses.

Small animals scampered by, adorned with furry, glossy coats and so lacking in fear, one brushed past his ankle and, utterly unconcerned, wandered off along its undeviating chosen path to whatever errand the island maternally decreed. Another brown, hairy quad-ruped, a short distance away, allowed its furry head to lower and its eyelids to droop shut as it took an undisturbed rest—or a casual nap—fully out in the open, unconcerned about the visitors or any hostile beasts.

Another creature, similar to a small grey pig covered in the glossiest coat of all, grazed and chewed lazily on succulent, low leaves and occasionally churned up earth using tough, stubby tusks protruding from its lower jaw, to coax up delicacies the island had stashed within.

Most astounding was the calm, untroubled friendliness of life. Muume was able to walk right up to a myriad of creatures, stroke their smooth coats and gently rub behind their ears. Some sauntered over to him of their own free will and gently sniffed and nudged his leg in innocent curiosity.

He scooped up and held aloft a grey, furry animal and studied it closely. Except for shorter, glistening fur, stouter ears and a leaner body, it would have passed for a brave rabbit. Utterly calm and fear-less and happy to be handled, he had never seen anything resem-bling such a life form. There was not a hint of protest as he stared in to its blue eyes, and then placed it on to his shoulder, where it nervously nuzzled slightly alarmed about the height.

He gently placed the furry animal back on to the ground and walked up to the branch of an unfamiliar broad leaved tree, where an oddly colourful bird was perched, beak pointed into the air, shrieking and chirping out a surreal, exotic song. It made no attempt to fly away, but paused momentarily, as he reached out and stroked its soft pink and blue feathers.

They walked further into the forest and stopped by a bubbling stream. He stood and stared for a long while, hypnotised by its clarity and the fist size, rounded rocks covering its meandering bed. It was just as his father described; he could barely see the water. Only the dancing sparkles of light flickering from the surface revealed that there was any liquid winding its way beneath.

At his father's eager request, he knelt down, leaned over the edge, cupped his hands and scooped a helping of the mineral rich water. Raising it to his lips, he closed his eyes as every sense was wrestled and enchanted, immersed in a crystal world of purity and essence. He took a long drink with eyes remaining blissfully closed and after a few moments pause to believe and to savour, he leaned down, scooped up more and drank the same again... and then again after that.

The purest, freshest liquid he had ever drank or tasted, nothing else could beat the pleasant, quenching sensation. With an awestruck expression, he turned to look at his father and as though both in the know, sharing a cosmic secret, they stared and knowingly mirrored conspiratorial smiles. It was just as Kiibe had told; once you drank this water, you never wanted or desired to drink anything else.

Muume would gladly have carried on exploring the island but Kiibe was insistent they not stay for too long.

"There is very much still that I need to teach you," he explained. "I have been here many times and you can come back to visit as often as you wish. It is important that no one else know of its location. When you tell of it, let them believe it lives only in your mind. I fear for the safety of these wonderful creatures should their presence and mannerisms become well known."

Muume nodded in agreement. He too, feared for the creatures and the island.

"You would also not be able to explain how you travelled here." Kiibe cleverly pointed out.

Muume understood completely.

After several more visits, informative conversations and time spent with his father learning more about the craft, Muume sat in silence with elbows on his knees and with forehead resting heavily on tightly clasped fingers. His outlook on reality lay bludgeoned and battered, his view of the living world reordered and altered. Long held memories were quickly unwinding and all he had ever known was slowly re-forming. A soft whistle—almost a sigh—escaped from his lips as he wrestled with a different world, grossly departed from the simple one he thought he knew.

Regarding his father with a newfound respect, he began to understand his actions over the many seasons; the strange disappearances, the differing opinions, the selfless, enthusiastic embrace of all life—all while gently sowing seeds to prepare for the future. The tales were entertaining, the moments turned more precious by wisdom and patience from secret endeavours.

Chapter 5

On the fifth evening, with a solemn expression weighing down his face, Kiibe swivelled around in the chair to look at his son. There was an unusually long, unnerving pause before he spoke.

"My life has been very good," he began with a soft voice. "I am truly honoured and blessed. If the spirits were to ask me, I would do it the same once more; I would marry your mother again without changing anything of her, and I would pray for the same five children, and the same grandchildren, and not one of you would come out changed in any way."

Deeply humbled, Muume bowed his head but quickly looked up again. The depth of his father's words implied more was forthcoming.

"Everything has to come to an end," Kiibe solemnly continued. "It must do so, not even the spirits can decree it may not. The cycle needs to carry on as life finds a new place and the world rearranges as many find a higher form."

Familiar wisps of worry began stirring within Muume.

"My time in this world is no different," Kiibe concluded.

Muume was taken aback. "Why do you speak in such a way? You look more alive than I have seen you for many seasons!"

"Yes I am," Kiibe agreed. "And I feel very good. I am more alive but it is all Walvenye's doing."

Muume sat up an inch higher. What did those words mean? How could it be responsible for keeping his father healthy?

Kiibe fumbled for a way to describe what was really happening. "When I am inside... When you step into... There is a living power within Walvenye when you are inside it that I am as yet to learn its strange way of working. But it is all around us." He paused to search for clearer words. "Once you come inside and make the internal connection, it has a way of hiding you and boosting your life force. But it will only do that while you are within it."

He waited to see if Muume grasped the implications.

The next words were spoken slower, for clarity and certainty.

"In all the passing moments you are sheltered inside, time hunts on relentlessly. It does not cease the search. If you venture outside and stay away for too long, the protection from Walvenye will erode and wear away. If you do not return quickly, time surely catches up, all in less than a day, and restores every one of the ravages bundled up, stored and declared as destined for you."

Staring with a furrowed brow, Muume tensed with an almost physical pain in his stomach. It was all too clear what his father was suggesting.

Kiibe lowered his eyes and after taking a few moments to select his next words, looked again at Muume. "In the outside world, I would probably have passed on two days ago. I am here now because Walvenye is sheltering me."

Muume shut his eyes and his face tightened up in an involuntary wince. Kiibe placed the palm of his hand on his son's shoulder.

Muume suddenly knew why on the first day in the craft, something appeared oddly different and unusual with his father. The change—glaring and obvious—was so sudden and profound, he was embarrassed it had taken him so long to see it. His father looked healthier—filled with more energy: anyone could have sworn he was several seasons younger.

On their trek up the mountain, his father was very weak, floundering at the limits even of ordinary walking. At some point, soon after they climbed into Walvenye, the transformation took place and he was visibly more alive. Easier to see, should have been when they arrived after the journey to the land with the magnificent metal tower; when he arose from the chair, Kiibe needed no support to stand. Muume should have seen it then, and had his senses not seized up, cudgelled by the incredible events on the day, he might have been more aware of his father's drastic change. Muume tried to think back to when the transformation began but memories of the first day were blends of awe and wonderment.

"Muume, my son," Kiibe softly continued, "my existence in the outside world has already been called up and time is now anxious and prowling in full hunt. I cannot be outside for too long without it pouncing."

"But father," Muume harrowingly blurted out his words, "then you must remain inside here. You must never... you... never leave!"

Kiibe slowly shook his head. "What sort of existence would that immerse me into? How could I stretch on my time, on and on without limit?"

"There are many places yet to see!" Muume desperately pleaded. "We could travel together to many more, see endless wondrous sights and find another island with more friendly creatures, and with sweet spring water!" Glancing around wildly, as though another idea might be lurking in the walls, he unintentionally spoke louder. "We could go into the ocean and into the great lake and you could tell all the villagers many more..."

His voice trailed off as unbounded truth dawned.

If time took less than a day to catch up with its prey, then his father could never go back home: he would never make it! He had to remain nearby and never venture too far to return to the shelter before it was too late. Relocating Walvenye to a spot nearer the village was too risky an option and besides, he could never be outside of it for too long. It had to remain where it was, safe and well hidden, and he had to be within it each day to be protected. Such a life would be difficult and unbearably lonely. Muume would be on endless, long journeys to see him all planned without revealing the destination to anyone and in between visits, his father would be alone living fully isolated from the rest of his people.

Kiibe reached out once again to pat his son's shoulder. "I have lived a long and happy life. I had a wonderful family and friends in a thriving, wondrous land. And I truly have the best children any man could wish for." Lowering his head, he stared downwards towards the floor. Sorrow flashed across his face as memories flooded his mind. "Your dear mother—may she be blessed—before she passed to the spirit world, was the most warm hearted wife any man could pray for. I was filled with joy long ago when she accepted me. I would not change a thing if the spirits made it be and granted that I could live my life all over again."

They sat in silence, listening to the faint humming eternally purring from deep within the craft.

Kiibe eventually spoke again. "My allocated seasons for this world are all spent, and they were spent very well. We have a lot to talk about and you have much more to learn so I am going to stay for now until you are Walvenye's very good friend."

Muume struggled to hold back tears and Kiibe leaned forward again to squeeze his shoulder.

"When morning comes, go quickly down to the camp and tell the villagers we are both fine—or they will come looking for us. Then come straight back so we continue with your learning."

Muume sniffed and nodded.

Late the following evening when Muume returned bearing gifts and a large, full gourd of sorghum bear, his father looked especially cheerful.

"I have saved a special trip for our last, long journey!" Kiibe excitedly announced glowing with anticipation. "We must have a good rest. We will set off tomorrow first thing in the morning when we are both well refreshed." His smile grew wider and his head tilted to one side. "Now is that sorghum beer I see looking so good?"

Chapter 6

After a mostly sleepless night of tossing and turning, they arose to begin the trip in the early hours of the morning.

"Now settle in the chair," Kiibe spoke with suppressed eagerness. "I promise this is going to be very, very special."

It was a longer journey than any other Muume had been on and they travelled much faster than at any other time. Kiibe took the opportunity to teach his son more about the craft's light based, navigation system.

After travelling for a long while, eventually, there was the usual mild vibration shortly followed by a slight jolt. Kiibe pointed out to his son the light patterns on the panels that showed the description for their current location.

"They look very different to other ways I have seen before!" Muume exclaimed while trying to figure out the configuration.

"That is because this place we have come is more special and it is a much greater distance away from the others! It is also very different from others you experienced and will look nothing like anything you have ever seen." Kiibe was careful not to give anything away. "When your body has adjusted, we will begin to get ready to go outside. It will be easier to understand when you see it for yourself."

Kiibe also had to wait in his chair for a while. They had travelled very far and incredibly fast.

"Clothing ourselves to go out in this place is a most serious matter of life and death!" he cautioned in a surprisingly urgent tone. "We must do it very carefully and cover up completely!"

Muume remained seated much longer than his father. His body was still new to such extreme travel.

"When you are sufficiently rested, bring out two of those outer garments I showed you from inside that door over there." Kiibe pointed to an area that looked to have nothing but a series of long, shallow, vertical lines.

When he was able to stand, Muume walked over, lightly touched the panel on the wall and watched it slide away to reveal a tall, spacious compartment, inside of which hung seven full-body garments, far stranger than any other clothing he knew of and made of a substance that he did not recognize. Held between his fingers, it felt like softened, well processed ox-hide, but smoother, much tougher and could stretch beyond the limit of any high grade, well refined hide he had ever seen. Deep-green in colour, the material carried splashes of random patches that in the soft illumination turned a contrasting blue.

"The blue parts have functions," Kiibe promptly explained, "one of which is to gather power, probably like Walvenye."

The colouring in the patches seemed to pull any staring eyes into a vortex. Muume got the impression that if he looked closely, and stayed looking for too long, his eyes and mind would tumble into the blueness forever.

"They are strange ones, those patches!" Kiibe was watching his son's reaction. "They seem to suck your mind and soul... like wet clay pulling on your feet."

Muume blinked twice, paused and vigorously shook his head. He had stared for too long and his eyes felt tingly. Selecting the first two garments from the right, he pulled them out of the compartment and with a conscious effort to avert his gaze, walked towards his father, bearing them like he was holding infinitely priceless, golden cloaks.

Kiibe and Muume were yet unaware that the makers of the garments called them "Species Protector Suits". Part of full body, self powered environmental suits, they protected the wearer from the most extreme weather, from a wide range of temperatures and other hostile elements lurking in places and many distant planets that the maker's own species could not resist visiting. The suits also helped protect vulnerable species from any organisms the wearer might be harbouring.

"I used two of those tools to change the shape of the garments to make them fit better." Kiibe calmly informed his son.

After finding eleven all together, he had altered only seven. The first three went wrong, but he carried on trying and the next four turned out looking near perfect. Later, he would show Muume the unaltered suits to give him an idea of how different the creators were.

"The shape of the makers is a not far from ours but is nothing that you can mistake for one of the villagers."

Muume stared in awe at the other-worldly garments while trying to keep his gaze away from the blue patches.

"Let me show you how they go on," Kiibe instructed, while hoisting up the comfortable cloth he was wrapped in that was standard and regular attire for the villagers.

Tightening it around his legs, he stepped into the one piece suit, pushing each foot gingerly into either leg section and pulling the whole garment higher, right up to his hips, before reaching down with both arms to coax it over his upper body.

After pushing both hands into it, he tugged gently at the edges until the whole unit settled into a perfect fit. Muume wasn't sure, but the garment appeared to change when on his father, as though adjusting itself to form a protective hide. Trying not to be surprised, he silently instructed his mind to no longer question unexplainable occurrences.

Kiibe reached across the front, pulled the edges to close them and then tugged at a strange material that ran all the way and sealed tight the entire seam. With a big smile, he comically wiggled his shoulders, hands and all his fingers and then stood with arms straight, like a soldier standing to attention.

"Have you ever seen me looking so smart and handsome?"

Muume doubled over with laughter. In a close fitting garment covering every part of his body all the way up to the neck, his father's trim frame fully enclosed within the material reminded him of a long-fish wrapped in river reeds. Still laughing, he lifted up his own protector suit and began the same motions his father had demonstrated.

With a little help from Kiibe, Muume tugged, pulled and shrugged until his own suit fit like a protective hide. Easier than he had expected, it rolled, moved and slid with ease as though the makers had carefully deigned it to. Running his fingers along his arm and down one leathery leg, he marvelled at the sensation and indescribable comfort. He could move his arms and legs without any restriction and felt secure—protected from all that could cause harm. Soft as tender hide and tingling with its own life, his entire body, from shoulders to the tips of his toes, felt as safe as a baby tucked inside the mother's womb.

They stood in silence, staring amusingly at one another and then both, simultaneously burst into laughter. Long isolated in his knowledge of the suits, Kiibe was seeing, for the first time, another being encased in one.

When they were finally calm again, in between hearty chuckles, Kiibe pointed to a compartment next to the one the suits had come

from. "Now go and bring out two of those head bowls I showed you."
Still overcome with laughter, he barely managed to speak the words.

Muume walked over to a long, horizontal panel, gingerly touched
the lower corner and stepped back as it revealed eleven small, inner
compartments, each holding what appeared to be dark-purple pots
displayed upside down and all facing the same way.

Picking out two, he closed the panel, walked across the floor back
to his father and handed one over. He lifted the other to eye level
and carefully studied it. The material felt metallic, but tougher and
much lighter than any metal he had ever known and eerily smooth,
with a hint of what reminded him of tough, polished stone.

One half of every bowl was clear and transparent as though made
of a layer of clean, curved, solid water nearly one of his little finger's
width in thickness. The weight of the whole bowl was not just in
balance but unrealistically low; it may as well have all been made
from light wood and nothing else. Holding it aloft, the rounded
object he stared at in no way matched the low weight he felt in his
hands. Bewildered by the material when his father had shown them
to him, he had given up attempts to figure out how the makers could
possibly have constructed it.

"Even these bowls defy belief!" he whispered to himself.
"Walvenye's builders must surely be the greatest living alchemists
or the most powerful magicians any village has ever seen!"

"I did not use the tools with these." Kiibe pointed out. "I attempted
to but nothing happened." He shrugged as though it didn't matter.
"They would be better a little smaller, but they work well as they are
so it is not going to be very much of a bother." Holding up his head
protector, he pointed along the open edge. "You see this folded part
along the inner lip of the bowl?"

Muume looked closer at the soft, dark coloured material that curved inwards and fully covered the swelled, inner edge. Using two fingers, Kiibe softly pulled to unfurl it. It unwound and slowly stretched out to nearly four times the size.

"You pull it out like this," he instructed, "and then it will attach to this tough, dark material around my neck... here... on this outer line."

Muume took a step forward and leaned closer to have a look.

Turning the protector so it was upside down again—to what Muume would soon know was the right way up—with the palm of one hand, Kiibe tapped the transparent section.

"This clear part goes at the front, over the whole of your face so you are able to look and then be able to see out of it. You have to pull the bowl down over yourself like a hat so that your head goes inside it, all the way up to the neck."

Muume looked at his father and they struggled to suppress laughter.

"Okay, serious now!" Kiibe was trying hard to remain composed. "This is how it goes, look... like this. Let me show you."

Carefully raising the head protector, he lowered and gently shifted it until his head was all the way inside—right up to the neck. Reaching up with both hands, he manipulated the strange material that lined the open, inner edge, until it fully attached and clung to the toughened layer around his neck.

When he was satisfied it was secure, he let go, wiggled his head to confirm a good fit, and then trying hard not to laugh, suddenly performed a short, comical dance and then stood to attention, with arms hanging by his sides and with wide eyes staring through the clear, front portion.

Muume collapsed into howling fits of laughter.

Struggling to catch his breath, and with random bursts of chuckling disrupting every movement, Muume raised and turned his own clear fronted bowl and regarded it with glee. With great difficulty, distracted by spasms of laughter, he duplicated the motions of fitting his head into it.

Frowning at the sensation of having his head fully covered, sounds from the outside were muted or muffled and only reached his ears by an enhanced, working design of the bowl. Noises were gathered and replayed to him by unknown contraptions inside the head protector. Sounds reaching his ears rang vivid, with unnervingly startling clarity, and were highly exaggerated, crackling from everywhere around his head. The built in, specialised, self powered acoustics of an advanced space helmet was not a concept any humans were as yet aware of, or even close to imagining. In a world where nations used horses for transport, there was a while to go before such objects were required.

He imitated his father and stood to attention—with arms straight by his sides, and wide eyes glaring out through the clear front. It was Kiibe's turn to fold over in hysterics: another face staring from inside a head bowl was a phenomenon he had never experienced.

When he was calm enough to turn and look again at Muume, their eyes met, causing both men to double over, clutching their bellies once again in roaring laughter.

The head protectors, once connected physically to the suits linked their communications and as both men clutched their sides, bellies seized tight and struggling to remain standing, the sound of the other laughing beamed all around their heads, multiplying the hilarity, until finally, light-headed and muscles aching from the spasms, the moment was equally tarnished by agony. In between gasps for breath and pursed lips forming feeble obstacles for laughter, each man focussed on begging the other to stop.

When the humour subsided and both men could speak again, Kiibe motioned to his son. "Now we check if the garments cover us completely—" He paused to suppress another eruption of chuckling. "Come over here to this small patch of brown roots and let Walvenye have a look." His hand waved to a palm-sized, light brown coloured, rectangular cluster of what appeared to be a collection of rounded, fibrous roots, all of similar width but each unique in vertical length—roughly that of an average human index finger. The roots appeared to sprout from the top of a narrow pedestal rising to near waist height and installed very close to the wall.

With fingers spread, he gently placed his left palm on the cluster and then stood still—anticipating some sort of reaction. The thick roots came alive, glowing in dull yellow and then stretched out and wrapped delicately around all of his hand. A moment later, his entire suit, from the neck all the way to the toes, and then the outer layer of his sealed head protector, shimmered softly in a subdued wave of the same colour.

Kiibe remained still, his hand resting on the pedestal, patiently waiting for something else to happen. A few moments went by before the roots flashed, went dark and then reverted to their light brown colour. As he lifted his hand away, they loosened off, shrunk back and softly settled down to their original position.

Muume stared in wonder.

"It is well fitting and very good." Kiibe declared with a nod. "Now you must do the same so we can know that your garment and head bowl are well fitting and that you will be protected."

Muume stepped forward and placed a hand on the cluster, positioning it the same way he had seen his father placing his. It lit up once again as the roots came alive, extended upwards and then wrapped themselves around his hand and all his fingers. A strange sensation cascaded up his covered arm as tendrils of light pressure ran through the material. The same barely visible wave of dull yellow light swept up along and over all the surface of his suit.

Remaining calm and standing still just like his father, he suddenly felt some tightness as the roots stiffened around his fingers, and the panel changed alarmingly to a bright, purple light. A tingling began around the base of his neck and an alternating buzzing noise droned in his ears. Trying not to panic, he turned to look at his father.

Kiibe lifted the palm of one hand to reassure his son. "It is nothing serious. It is only a simple problem." He pointed to a section just above Muume's shoulders where the unfurled material overlapped with the suit. "The small area around your neck is shining in that same colour you see on the patch of roots. Walvenye is telling you your head bowl is not well joined with your garment, which would be very bad because of this place we are going to go."

Muume reached up and with careful adjustments, aligned the material until suddenly, a new soft and subtle sucking noise popped into and swirled around inside his head protector, as the suit pressured up its own internal circulating air. He looked over at his father.

"There was a strange sound inside my bowl!"

"Did you hear the air?" Kiibe asked.

Muume nodded quickly, aware of what signs to listen out for the next time. Reaching out to place his hand back on to the cluster, he waited as his covering, from toes all the way to the head, shimmered in dull yellow. The roots, finally happy that the suit was fully sealed, flashed rapidly and went dark, then settled back down into the original light brown.

"Very good!" Kiibe exclaimed. "They are happy with your garment!"

Muume smiled and performed a short comical dance, drawing more laughter that took a long while to fizzle out.

"Now another important thing," Kiibe said when calm returned. "Walvenye and the garment make and keep air for you to breathe."

With the palm of one hand, he reached around behind Muume and tapped the upside down, triangular, bulbous protrusion swelling out between the shoulders and tapering downwards all the way along more than half of his back.

"It is kept in this pouch here. Can you feel this part all over here going all the way down to just... over here?" Using two fingers, Kiibe pressed below his son's neck and then lower down his back near the base of his spine.

Muume nodded, "Yes, I can feel it now!" he responded. Wriggling his shoulders, he marvelled at the new, very peculiar sensation. "It feels like a pouch which is quickly filling with air."

"Good," Kiibe continued. "Once the head bowl and garments are fitted and closed together, they begin to make air and send it there to fill the pouch. It will become full and nearly hard as a rock, and that will be very good for you." He nodded and once again tapped the pouch with his hand. "When it is finished, yellow light will show for a short time on your forearms, and you will feel some slight shaking here on your back, just here on the higher part in between your shoulders. That will be the garment saying the pouch is ready."

Muume was overcome with wonder.

"That air in the pouch will be enough for only a certain time," Kiibe sternly warned. "If you want to wear the garment to protect you for a long time, you must attach on to your back an additional, bigger pouch so it can carry more air. I will show you all of that later because for now, we will be out for less time than a morning. When we come back, I will show you how to fix on the extra pouch."

Muume, still in wonder, stared blankly and then nodded.

"What will happen if the air I have in this pouch is finished?" he suddenly thought out aloud.

"When we are inside, the garments will keep making air so the pouch will always be full," Kiibe reassured his son. "So not a worry when in here. But when we go outside, it does not seem to be able to, but it will always tell and show you if the air is not sufficient." He gestured towards the forearms. "It will shine here softly, and show the second colour that you saw on the roots when your head bowl was not properly fastened to protect you." He reached over once again and tapped Muume on his back. "It will also tremble slightly on your back and on your arms."

Muume made a mental note and hoped to remember to stay calm when he felt sections of his clothing vibrating.

"When that happens," Kiibe continued, "we will make our way back. The garments will let us know with time to return safely."

Turning swiftly around as though he had suddenly remembered something, Kiibe walked towards the wall next to where the suits were stored. He paused, pointed, and then reached up to open two hand sized panels, revealing two more sets of root-like structures, one grey in colour and the other, immediately below it, a pale light brown.

"This is important to know," he said, gesturing towards them. "The top one turns off the illuminations in your garment so it can only talk to you by various ways of trembling. It is useful for where you may not want to be seen, or when you may be where it is best to remain hidden."

Reaching up, he placed a palm on the upper, grey set of roots. They stretched out, gently wrapped around his hand and all his fingers and began to glow dull yellow. His entire suit flashed twice in a wave of the same colour and then suddenly went dark. The roots shrunk back and returned to a soft grey.

"The illumination is turned off." Kiibe spun around and announced. "The garment will only speak by various ways of trembling." Gesturing to the lower cluster, he placed his hand over it. "This one makes the illuminations all come back on again."

The roots enveloped his fingers, glowed alive in the usual yellow, and his suit responded twice, flashing the same dull colour.

"Now the illuminations are on again," Kiibe joyfully declared. "I much more like and prefer it like this. I think it looks much better."

Muume very much agreed.

"Do you have any more questions?" Kiibe asked after a short pause.

Muume slowly shook his head.

"Okay, now another strange thing that I must show you."

He walked to the other wall, touched the protrusion to open the door, and then paused momentarily to wait for the opening. Covering the entrance after the door moved away was a strange substance that looked like a thick, vertical sheet of water. Kiibe reached out and pushed his hand, and then his arm, through it.

"This is a sealing material that stops air going out or any water coming in. For example, when we go into a lake or a sea, this miraculous material keeps the inside dry. So far, I do not know what it is or even how it appears—maybe you will learn that in time as you know more of the workings. For now, Walvenye always knows when it is needed and each time, after the door opens, this strange sheet appears. It will not let you pass through unless you have touched the roots to check your garments and head bowl are well secured. Better to leave it that way I think. It is much safer. I doubt anyway that Walvenye would let you remove it."

As he pulled his hand and fingers back, the strange substance over them clung and stretched slightly before breaking contact and springing over the doorway again.

"You see!" he glanced sideways at Muume. "It grasps on to the garments so nothing else can go past as you walk out or walk back in. And it lets you go easily whenever you move away."

Staring at his fingers, he was suddenly as impressed with the morsel of information as he knew Muume must be. It was indeed a magical substance. He had gotten too used to it—almost to indifference.

"Are you ready?"

Muume nodded.

After a last glance at his son, Kiibe cautiously stepped outside.

Chapter 7

Muume stepped forward to the oval shaped exit and stopped dead at the sight of the insanity that lay beyond. Behind the clear viewing shield, his eyes and mouth flew open. His body and both legs forgot how to move.

Eyes darting back and forth with visual senses pummelled raw, he struggled to accept the grotesque magnificence blanketing an endless, physical existence that in no possible way should be seen outside a dream. A sight wilder than his mind could conjure in a fantasy, what lay beyond the door was a world that should not exist.

Taking another step forward, Muume moved to the edge of the entrance, pushed his fingers and then his hand into the substance and then quickly pulled it back. He could feel the touch as his arm went through—like a subtly tightened bracelet moving along the protective suit forming a seal to stop air escaping from the craft. Staring blankly at his fingers wondering how the sheet worked, he was briefly distracted before his mind snapped back to the unrealistic landscape waiting beyond. Stepping closer to the material, with barely contained enthusiasm, he leaned the front of his head through to look outside.

The violent land and beastly features stretched in all directions, churning and writhing away to crash into the horizon. With little flatness to the terrain, everywhere was marked with deep valleys, craters, hills and infernal rock formations. The scene reminded him of the big lake in a grey, twilight storm, when the water was seething and crashing down upon itself. If time stopped and the sharp edged, jagged plumes of dark water froze solid in mid motion, it was surely what the resulting silent view would look like. The craft had searched for and perched upon a flat topped hill and from his perspective, he could see most of the landscape, giving the sense of witnessing—from a privileged vantage point—the motion stalled darkened waters of a stormy lake.

What appeared to be solitary wisps of feathery, floating dust wafted ominously by, like heinous apparitions on a detailed, slow-walk patrol of their life-bare haunting grounds. He watched two narrow clusters glide, ever so slowly, and then hover, contemplating and regarding their kingdom. One of them then gradually descended into the ground, appearing to merge with its essence, while the other distorted as it surged and set off gliding towards the horizon, its invisible cloak brushing gently along the churning surface.

The air was spectacularly and impossibly clear—and not in a comforting way. Untainted and unnatural beyond being realistic, Muume could see into the distance and then on to the horizon with unnervingly realistic and crystal clear clarity. Nothing he saw or focussed on appeared to be real. Blinking several times at the disorienting illusion, he stared at the jagged rocks, craters and dark valleys. It was as though, for all his life, he had viewed the world through fine dust and on the land he now beheld, it had inexplicably gone.

Carried away by the vision, he jumped visibly from a sudden light pressure on his arm. Looking down, he saw the fingers, hand and arm of the other garment.

"Come now," Kiibe called. "Inside there, you are still feeling your usual weight. Once you step outside, you will feel like you weigh only as much as a little child. You must walk and move slowly in a deliberate and different way, like you are walking in water, but without the weight of the water. It is quick to learn but be very slow and be very careful."

Muume was puzzled, but he nodded that he understood. He did not. He had no way to. His mind could not conceive of a world where the body, of its own accord, suddenly felt much lighter.

Kiibe suspected his son's difficulty with the concept. "Move slowly at first until your legs and your body all learn to be used to it!"

Unsure of what to expect, Muume nervously kept his hand clamped on to his father's arm. Taking a deep breath, he hesitated before tentatively taking a step forward to leave the sheltered safety of the craft.

Stepping out on to the landscape, he immediately began to stumble and lose all balance. His body and limbs, responding the only way they knew how, powered the rear foot, lunging onward with the other, making the logical worldly attempt to regain stability. Instead, he jumped into the air, awkwardly tumbled further forward and began to fall in slow motion, as though suddenly made of feathers. When his feet touched the ground again, his knees kicked back out as the legs—entirely of their own mind—set out to compensate. He bounced up higher and tumbled forward even faster.

While still up in the air, with both arms desperately flailing, his body began to roll in a slow, aerial somersault with legs going up, feet kicking helplessly behind him and his neck frantically craning to raise his head higher. He felt a hand on his arm as his father saved him from falling.

"Slowly now Muume," Kiibe softly reassured him. "Slowly!"

But Muume was no longer paying attention. His senses were seized and his gaze held fast by a gruesomely stunning and hypnotizing world.

Around him were riotous and violent eruptions of rolling, foreboding and jagged terrain bathed in dramatically eerie, yet mutedly soft light, broken by spatters of near black patches. Shaded areas lay immersed in close to pitch darkness, difficult to see as chasms carved out of pure coal. Day and night appeared to exist in the same moment, with visibility ascertained by which direction shadows lay.

Exposed portions shone with a disorienting grey—well stoked and ashy, appearing to be reflecting several moons. A mildly distinct sense loomed in his mind that the grey would be too harsh for all mortal eyes, were it not subdued by the witch doctor cast material making up the clear, front half of his head bowl.

He tried mentally digesting the unruly landscape; its brutal, jarring jaggedness, it's spattered, calming fury and its wiling, magical, witching tricks, wantonly conjuring and wielding light and darkness, playing games with reality—wrenching rogue impossibilities out into the physical realm. He stared in awed silence, intensely discombobulated. Denying it would be accusing his eyes of lying.

He looked down at the alien ground, made of a dark material, as near to black, ashen coal as anything he had ever seen. Resembling what, to the eye, was solid rock in most places, it mutated into fine, ashy clay in all the others.

In every direction, as far out as he could see, deep craters of every size savagely punctured and scooped out all efforts at creating flat surfaces. There appeared to be a corresponding cavity or valley for each of the motion-stalled, outlandish rock features.

In the distance to the right was an especially large crater, much wider and deeper than any other he could see. Half the hollow glowed bright in the same grey light while the other lay darkened by extreme nightfall. Muume marvelled at the bewildering clarity and the overwhelmingly extreme distinction between the two. The stark line separating them was abrupt and sudden as though drawn up and marked using a sharp, precise implement. Each entity, light and darkness, filled its side of the border—right up to the very edge— with no regard for fading to blend in transition.

By far, the most breathtakingly, glaring entity within the relent- less assault on his senses was a gigantic, colossal ball hovering in the sky. It was impossibly enormous! The most immense, fantastically awe inspiring, gargantuan thing he had ever laid eyes on—many times more mighty than the only moon he knew—it was so big, he unconsciously grasped for his father's arm, fearing he was going to fall upwards into it.

The powdery moon he always knew emitted a pale milky essence, but the hulking, mammoth ball bore no resemblance to it. With swirling, earthy streaks careening across its broad face, it hung there, silently hovering, majestic and mighty, with the definitive intention and the quench-less desire to dwarf all else, star or moon, in the edges of the sky it disdainfully left unhidden.

Muume searched the twinkling darkness but could not see the usual moon. In a patch of exposed sky on one side, hovered a tiny moon, meagre in size, meek, and of a different colour, yet far too bright next to the dominating giant. Its pale orange surface appeared to mimic the texture and the mushy, stringy pulp of an overripe mango.

From where he stood looking, even the stars were different—the entire sky was different. He had travelled up and down to various regions and territories and been far away visiting distant tribes but he had never seen the sky look as strange as it did then no matter how far away he ended up from home. Staring up at the vibrant stars and the gigantic entity, he recalled his father's tale of giant moons and smoked light. How far had Walvenye come? What forsaken land was this with a mighty sky giant and the small, mango moon and where the stars shone brighter from different locations? Where were the trees, or any river, or any stray grass? What dark ash and rocks were these covering the ground?

"Are we in the outer ends of the world?" he spoke into the head protector. "Have we travelled so far that we reached the end of the land where no life will thrive and where the spirits forbid our presence?"

Kiibe smiled warmly inside his own head covering. "It is not like so, Muume," he replied with understanding, remembering his own thoughts when he first saw the land. "We are on a different world, indescribably far from the one that we live on and know as our own home."

He paused to let linger the conflicted expression he guessed must immediately have adorned his son's face.

After all he had seen so far, Muume no longer had the desire to doubt anything, but another world was beyond his mesmerized mind to sustain. He thought to ask a burning question, but the right words eluded him.

Kiibe offered more information, "This world we are on is further away from our own than I can try to explain in any distance that we would both be able to understand. Even I, after this long, am unable to fully grasp it, but I know, with great certainty, that we are very far away."

Staring at his father, Muume blinked, attempted to speak and with the words still evading him, elected to remain silent. Too much already lay beyond his means to understand. Grappling with a mind reeling in a duel with doubt, he fought mentally and persevered, trying hard to comprehend, his brain wallowing and grasping having long shattered limits of all the knowledge it possessed.

He stood silent, pondering how big the world really was and what sort of shape it held. Did it look like a mountain? How would you know you were looking at it if you moved far away? Where would you stand to look back at what you left behind? Would you simply fall away? And if so, what substance would you fall away into? What were the garments and the head bowls protecting them from?

His questions, when they finally came, were endless and exhaustive. His words, when he found them, were teeming with curiosity. Kiibe tried to answer as best as he could with the knowledge he had gathered and the things he had seen.

"So that is not our world where we have come travelling from?" Muume asked while pointing at the colossal, hovering entity.

Kiibe patiently shook his head. After another barrage of questions half of which he had no answers for, he turned and pointed to an area so low in the sky, it was nearly at the horizon.

"Do you see that bright, yellow star over there? The one above the other two that are very close together... just below the brighter one?"

Turning to scan the speckled darkness, Muume easily located the star.

"Take a good look at it," Kiibe instructed. "That star is our one and only, great, shining sun!" He nodded with confidence, confirming the profound statement. "That is the same sun you see rising in the morning. The same one that comes up to shine upon our land and to warm up our village and to make our crops grow. That is the very same sun that shone joyfully upon us only a few days ago when we sat in the grass field drinking sorghum beer."

Muume stared at the star. His mind, having exceeded all processing capacity, was fighting to decipher what his father had just said.

"How can that be?" he muttered. "It is a star! I see a star! I do not see the sun! How can it be a star?"

His befuddlement came as no surprise to his father.

Kiibe attempted to explain. "It is the distance Muume. We are very far away. It is so far, that to us, our sun now looks like a star." He paused in mental search of a suitable example. "Imagine a vibrant cooking fire alight in the night time, but in the middle of the yard instead of the usual place."

Muume, listening keenly, turned towards his father.

"When you are close," Kiibe continued, "you can see the dancing flames and the embers glowing brightly among the hot ashes below. But if you move away, out of the village and far along the path, and then turn to look again at the same thing from a distance, it would appear to your eyes as only a spot of light, would it not?"

Muume nodded, and inside the head protector, his face slowly lit up with a comprehending grin.

"It is the same thing even now Muume. We have travelled very far and so from here, our sun appears to be a spot of light, or as we behold it, only a star in the night sky."

Muume turned towards the twinkling light in the horizon which had suddenly acquired a spellbinding significance. No longer just a star among many in the beyond, it stood out in the sky, its presence pleasantly wistful, its flickering, mellow essence, nostalgic and enchanting.

Eyes fixed pensively on the shimmering entity, his mind strayed to what had become an impossible measurement. "How far away is that?" he enquired into the head covering. "I am unable to even attempt to grasp such a great distance! Father, are you also saying that all the stars we see are suns just like the one that shines down upon us on our land?"

"Yes Muume." Kiibe confirmed. "Every star you see is a sun burning bright in the big sky. Some are bigger—as big as the main centre hall in the village when compared to a potato—than the one that shines down on us upon our homeland, but some are also smaller."

Muume reached up and tried scratching the top of his head. "Heh! Ah!" he exclaimed in unrestrained wonder, his mind interned in thoughts beyond what it could process.

"And that is not close to being all," Kiibe continued. "Nearly all those suns have other worlds of their own clinging endlessly, like little children latched on to their mothers, in the same way our world clings by the spirits will to our own sun, compelled by the force tying a calf to the cow. Without the sun, it would starve and then shrivel and wither!"

Muume squinted, lost in the scale of what lay beyond.

Kiibe nodded, very slowly, also awed by the revelation that he too became aware of not too many seasons before. "They shine down upon their worlds the way our sun shines on ours, pouring on bright light and great warmth of many strengths..." his words slowed and trailed off as he marvelled at the wonders. "Many, many... many... worlds!" he continued after a long pause. "One of which the builders of Walvenye live and thrive on, just as we and our village and the people live on ours."

He stared into the distance and they both stood in silence gazing soulfully at the twinkling entities scattered in the darkness.

Kiibe watched, overwhelmed, seeing it all anew again, the way he knew his son must be seeing it in that moment. Trying to think of a way to describe the immeasurable distance, he settled on an example.

"What is the fastest horse you can think of?"

Muume pondered for only a moment. "Gambari Sainti." came the answer. "The Arab trader's horse that used to win all the races!"

Kiibe broke into a smile. "That is an ideal example!" He paused to gather up the words to voice his description. "On the wonderful and very joyful day that you were born, imagine if that horse had immediately started running from our world, through the skies, making its own deliberate way to come here, and it ran every day and every night and never stopped; not to rest, not to eat, not to drink or to do anything."

Muume glanced at his father while visualizing the racehorse.

"At this moment," Kiibe continued "even though it ran without stopping for all the entire time, and was running even up to now at full racing gallop, it would still not have travelled half the distance to the way here." Kiibe saw the anticipated reaction in his son's face. "Not even half the way!" He emphasized the words *half the way*.

"Eh!" Muume exclaimed. "Even running? Without stopping?"

Kiibe nodded very slowly. "And there is more," he continued. "Even as we look upon it from this distance where we stand now, our world that the sun shines upon is too small in the great darkness for our eyes to be able to see from here."

They both paused to stare at the divine, twinkling entity. Muume struggled to understand why he could not see the world.

After a long while, Kiibe ventured an explanation. "Think again of the healthy cooking fire in the yard, looked upon from far off away, up along the path."

Muume turned to him and nodded.

"Suppose I tied a small fruit to the wall of the grain shed several paces away in the corner of the compound, could you see that fruit from the same distance along the path as it hang there in the dim light, even though in open air?"

Muume firmly shook his head. "No, I could not. Nobody could." He hoped it was not a trick question. "No person would have the eyes capable of seeing it in the dark from such a long way away from the homestead."

His tone carried the burden of lingering questions and Kiibe waited patiently, knowing they would soon be voiced.

"Is our world not very much bigger than the sun?" Muume innocently enquired. "It seems it surely must be because we may, when we do, travel far away from home, walking great distances all upon the living land and no matter where we go, the sun remains a hot, burning entity, floating high up in the sky; a ball not even bigger than the land hill it hides behind when going down to sleep at the end of each day." He looked genuinely puzzled. "We surely must be able to see our world from here, if we can see the shining sun?"

Kiibe understood the perspective. "I used to think the same Muume, we all did." he softly replied. "It appears that way when looking up from where we stand, that the land is truly greater and extends further in size. But there is much for you to learn the same way as I did over many days and many seasons about many of these things. Much about our world and far beyond will be revealed but for now, I can tell you that the sun is very surely many... very many times bigger than all of the world." He paused to glance sideways at the puzzlement in his son's face. "It is so big that our world could disappear into its body and the sun would carry on barely even disturbed. It would be like if you swallowed only one cooked bean seed. Would you feel the weight of that seed as it sat inside your belly?"

Muume shook his head. One seed would be of no consequence.

"It is the same with our sun. Our world is like a bean seed being compared to you. The sun only looks smaller because it is far away from the land where it shines to light up our village."

After some moments of pondering, Muume perked up and nodded. "I understand!" he proudly declared. "When I see the great mountain from a long distance away, it may be smaller than a rock which I hold in my hand. But if I travel to the mountain and stand upon the vast slopes, that same rock is small and insignificant next to it!"

Kiibe was smiling, impressed by the example. "It is exactly so, Muume." He was beaming with pride. "I could not, if I ventured, have said it any better way!"

Muume stood in thoughtful silence, trying to make sense of the new information. His eyes remained drawn to the faraway star, such a great distance, yet infinitely more enchanting.

"Another world!" he whispered, trying to memorize every detail.

"Ah!" he jumped visibly, startled by a sudden thought. "Are there any other people who live here on this world?"

Kiibe firmly shook his head. "I have come here many times and I have never seen another soul or any living being. It appears that life has not yet found a good way to come and settle down and start to thrive on this world." His eyes scanned analytically around the brutal landscape. "That is not saying that there are no small living forms that we can not see, or that we do not see as beings."

Muume stared at the landscape, eyes glowing with awe. "Would such living forms also survive on our world? Have you tried to bring any from our world to this one?"

Kiibe paused and pondered, surprised he had never once considered such an action. "I have not knowingly carried any creatures to this world." The words, as he spoke them, appeared to be directed not to Muume, but to himself, as though in reproach at never having contemplated such an experiment. "It would truly be a surprise if no small forms had succeeded in making their way, hidden on the garments or inside Walvenye. But it would be very difficult. That material that covers the door appears not to let anything it does not agree with to pass through without bother. Did you see how it clings to our garments as we came outside?" His face broke into a grin as a thought crossed his mind. "I should have tried to bring the goat!" he chuckled.

Each one suddenly found themselves stretching to maintain their balance as loud laughter rang out, reverberating with clarity inside their head protectors. Humour, as they were both finding out for the first time, felt different when experienced in very low gravity.

Chapter 8

Muume quickly learned to walk in the strange, grey and black land on which his weight was a fraction of what it was back home. It was an extraordinary sensation. He could jump high up into the air in any direction, but he had to be careful and consciously light footed when he got back to the ground again, or the whole manoeuvre would go wrong—a skill that he began to master with growing hilarity.

He fell twice on to his head protector, once on to his left shoulder and at one point, hilariously, straight on to his bottom. It was like learning how to walk all over again as a child, except his absurd exuberance brought great amusement. Before long, their bellies were hurting so much that Kiibe, barely able to breathe, was begging him to stop.

After another long and painful bout of all out laughter, Muume waddled onto his feet and, with some comical shuddering, prepared for another brave attempt at running. His father, still on his knees with one hand clutching his belly, raised the other high in a plea gesture begging for mercy.

Muume, far too excited, eyed up the ground and lined up an ashy, level stretch, determined to master moving fast in the bewitching land. He paused to glance around again at the undulating landscape. What a fascinating place! What a magical, brutal place! Walking in it was truly as his father had described; it was like walking in water without the weight of the water!

"You are fortunate that I am here with you to guide you Muume." Kiibe chimed in after yet another hilarious tumble. "It was a different experience for me—" he chuckled at the memory. "I came here, all on my own, without any knowledge that there are places where your body weighs less than that of a child. The first time was a difficult and brutal experience." Through the clear front, his smile had sunk into a sombre expression. "It is fortunate Walvenye would not let me come outside into this harsh world without protection of the garments. It was only on the third visit that I finally knew the reason." After a moments pause, he cleared his throat and nodded appreciatively. "Walvenye is a good protector!" He glanced in its direction.

"How did you know it was because you were not wearing the garment?"

"A matter of deduction," Kiibe truthfully answered. "When I went with Walvenye on to a choppy lake one windy day, I decided to try and open the door. It was the first time I saw the clear sealing material. While floating on the lake, the substance covered the doorway and worked like an oil-cloth to stop the water coming in. I touched it with my finger tips, but at the time I was so frightened, I was not in any way going to attempt to go through it." He turned towards the craft with the sort of expression one carried when looking at a long lost friend. "I tested it by travelling to different places until I knew it always appeared for protection. Then I opened the door when we were deep inside water. It opened like it always did, and the sealing material was covering the doorway. When I attempted, it would not let my fingers pass through and that, for me, at that moment in time, made good sense."

He turned back to Muume and gestured down towards the suit. "But one day, I tried on the garment and the head bowl and in mindless curiosity, I placed my hand on the roots. It would have been one of the most frightening happenings but I knew by then that Walvenye would not injure me." He looked again at the craft with warm, open eyes of friendship. "I guessed that it was looking for any leak in the garment and when the roots had finished and released and then moved away, I walked across to open the door, with my heart beating like the village festival drum." He chuckled lightly—almost half heartedly—at the memory. "When I reached out, trembling like a frightened calf—" he stretched out his arm, theatrically shaking his hand and all his fingers, "the clear sheet allowed my terrified fingers to pass through."

He paused and stared distantly into the rocky greyness, entirely consumed by the intensity of the memory.

Some moments passed by before Kiibe re-emerged. "I pushed through my whole hand and it went straight into the water. I could see the part of my arm that was immersed into the lake, but the rest of me that was behind the sealing material was dry as though I was still standing back on land."

He held up and absent-mindedly scrutinized his hand but from his blank expression, Muume, did not believe he saw it at all.

"I pulled my hand back in and stared at the lake water and the few Tilapia swimming by eyeing the new entity. I needed time to gather up enough courage to walk through so I paced up and down wondering if it was wise to do so."

Staring up at the giant ball with a bright, jubilant expression, his head shook from side to side, his mind all but swallowed away.

Muume watched his father and sympathetically re-lived the profound moment with him, wondering how he would have handled such things all on his own. Carried away by thoughts of what his father had gone through, he was overwhelmed by feelings of pride and admiration.

After a long while, Kiibe stirred, and then turned to look at his son. In a sweeping gesture, he slowly shook his head and shrugged:

"Walking into the lake was wondrous beyond all words that I could utter!"

Muume understood completely.

"We must go for our next trip, to the centre of the big lake." Kiibe suddenly decided. "We will go into the depths and put on these garments again. We will take two each of the small magical lanterns and we will walk into the water among the fish and the creatures—creatures never seen anywhere close to the surface and never witnessed or caught by any living fishermen—and you will see all of it with your own two eyes. Any words I speak to describe what you are going to see would shame all of existence with their great inadequacy!"

Kiibe smiled as Muume's eyes lit up with anticipation.

"It is very dark in the deepest depths!" he felt he should warn Muume. "Two each of the smaller lanterns should be enough. But also—" pausing to reach a hand up to his neck, his fingers stopped at the lower right section of his head protector. "You see this part here?" He leaned forward to show Muume and after getting a nod, turned away before applying pressure. "You press it in like this—"

Muume gasped as a row of lights came alive along the top of his father's head bowl, sending a beam volleying out into the greyness. Leaning to direct it towards a shadowed area, Kiibe illuminated the patch with near-white light. Muume's hand flew up to his own head protector and his beam briefly disappeared out into the greyness before he turned to guide it towards a dark patch. His list of new, magic toys had just grown by one.

With more practice, Muume mastered the light, gentle, rhythmic steps and arched swinging of both arms to walk safely and upright in the baffling terrain. Time flew by as they examined and explored the landscape and Muume gazed, mesmerized by every little detail. The giant ball was creeping across the glittering sky and was hovering in a noticeably different position. He struggled to absorb its overwhelming presence; no matter how long he stared, it refused to look real.

He was eagerly bounding away to see another crater when a sudden vibration rippled along his back and upper arms. Kiibe was a short distance from him studying a block shaped rock when the change in his son's voice to a distinctly panicked pitch, burst through, loud and clear into his own head protector. Muume glanced down at both the outer forearms of his suit as they simultaneously began to shimmer in dull purple light. When he looked up again, Kiibe was already by his side.

"It is all well Muume," his father spoke in a calm voice. "The garment is telling you the air you have inside the pouch is going to be finished soon so it needs to go and make some more." Kiibe gestured towards the craft. "We should start to make our way back. Probably, it would have been better if I had shown you how to attach the big pouches." Noting his son's fearful eyes, Kiibe reassured him. "There is more than the needed time to go back very safely. Believe me, if you ever have no time left, the garment will let you know. And if that moment ever comes, it will tremble and act in such a frantic manner, you will want to do nothing but return to Walvenye."

After the trip to the lake depths—during which they had a long, amusing tussle with a blind, tentacled creature—Kiibe spent the following two days teaching his son about the craft and how more of the unseen parts worked.

"You are fortunate Muume that I can teach you these things. I had to learn it all myself when I discovered this wonderful thing so many seasons ago." Smiling at the warm memories, he gestured broadly across the interior. "It is a good thing for all I had the sense to keep it hidden."

Muume was impressed his father kept it a secret.

Kiibe's face cooled to a more sombre expression. "If I had not done so and let it all be openly known, then others in many nations I had no knowledge existed until I saw them in my travels might have waged wars upon us so they could acquire it." His eyebrows lowered in contemplation of the consequences. "And then others would have waged war on those who took it, so they could take it away from them!" As the thoughts churned in his mind, his head shook, attempting to banish the terrible events playing out within it. "Great destruction and suffering would have befallen our world. The endless number of deaths would be impossible to count!"

Turning to look at Muume, he raised an arm and waved a stern, accusatory finger at hordes of howling invaders lurking in the distance. "I have seen what those who live across the great seas do to one another and to any communities they stumble upon. It is only fortunate and by the grace of good blessing, that our village and many others have so far been spared."

Kiibe leaned forward and spoke softly, almost in a whisper. "Heed my warning Muume, and heed it intensely. If they were ever to find out about Walvenye, it would be the end of us and the end of many others for sure." His wise eyes carried the dire admonition of his words.

Muume's eyes and expression showed he clearly understood.

"There is no need to worry for some time yet!" Kiibe reassured him. "They have not reached our land or come near our neighbours and I know you will protect this knowledge I pass to you. You must protect our people, our land and our world from itself and from those who may set out in rampage. You must prevent others from knowing of this thing until the world is ready and well to accept it."

Muume promised to follow his father's guidance.

They stayed several more days, during which Kiibe was careful not to leave the craft for too long. They were better friends than any other father and son and Muume strived to remember all his father was teaching him.

He made two more day trips to let the villagers know that all was still well, and to extend the warmest greetings. They were astonished, but pleased that old man Kiibe was alive and they desperately pleaded to travel up and see him. Muume apologetically denied them that permission with the promise that his father would see them in his own time—just as soon as he was finished with a very important matter.

Chapter 9

After another day spent practising with the tools that could alter the shapes and sizes of most objects, with a cheerful face and beaming with pride, Kiibe turned towards Muume. "I am very proud of you my son! You are learning very well. There is still more you need to know of many distant places, but you will learn now that you can use Walvenye."

He shuffled forward, right to the edge of his swivelling chair, wearing an eager expression that betrayed something profound lingering on his mind that, with the moment ready and ripe, was on the verge of being shared. Mirroring his father, Muume also shuffled closer.

Taking a deep breath, Kiibe spoke in a hushed tone. "Walvenye has a powerful weapon!" he announced with the flair and overly suppressed drama of a high official delivering an operations report.

Squinting and tilting his head as though he had misheard, Muume waited, expecting to hear other words that would cast a different meaning.

"A weapon?" he asked after a moment of silence.

"When I was a boy," Kiibe patiently began to explain, "I went wandering into the forest and got hopelessly lost. That was when those roaming wild dogs found and chased me. Remember the wild dogs I mentioned to you the other day?"

Muume, still perplexed, hurriedly confirmed that he did.

"There was not any possible way a grown man, let alone a boy, could come close to outrunning them, and I ran only because there was nothing else left to do. I ran and ran, they chased and chased and I did not even know in which direction I was going!" He closed his eyes and winced slightly at the frightening memory. "And just before they caught me, I could feel their hot, hungry breath blowing on my bare heels as I ran and burst into the unexpected, small clearing, where there was only plain, ordinary, green, unsuspecting grass." He paused, visibly shaken by recalling the encounter. "The last thing I remember—I profess truth before the spirits—was feeling a vicious, hungry jaw rubbing against my bare foot, a mere blink of an eye away from the first bite of its meal!"

Muume was leaning so far forward, he appeared to hover in mid air.

"The next thing to happen was I woke up at mid-day of the following day, lying face-up on the grass, sun shining high in the sky baking me so hot, I felt like a roasted cassava! My head hurt, my body hurt, my legs hurt, my toes hurt... the only part of me that did not hurt was my hair!"

Muume very nearly chuckled, but he was far too eager to hear the rest of the story.

"When I discovered I was not dead, and then looked to see what part of me was not yet feasted on, I saw with my own eyes—may the spirits never forgive me if I am not speaking only truth—two dead dogs on one side, already drying out, and two others behind me, also dead as logs fallen two whole seasons ago!"

Muume slapped his hands together and leaning a little further forward, lifted one palm to cover his wide open mouth.

"When I gathered strength to stand and begin looking for a way back, I heard your grandfather's voice, and voices of other villagers, faintly carrying through the leaves and the spinning, dancing, hazy branches, shouting into the forest searching earnestly for me. And it was not only the branches and the trees that were dancing: everything I looked at was spinning and tilting and looking very blurry, and my legs and arms felt like they were made from sweet potato peels."

Waddling and waving his arms, he acted out the motions like a floppy and drunken bird.

"I made my way slowly through the trees, towards the voices, wallowing and staggering, and when he finally saw me, I have never seen a father run to his child so fast! Gambari-Sainti would have scratched his long head in amazement." His eyes lightened at the memory of his departed parents. "My father ran back to the village carrying me in his arms. An astounding feat—only three others kept up with him: the other twenty six emerged from the forest much later." An indescribable expression formed and lingered in his face that left no doubt of the love carried for his deceased father.

"Only then," he continued after the briefest of pauses "after we reached the medicine woman, did I find out my face was much bathed in my dried blood, and my lips and nose were split open like trampled papayas. I understood only then why my head and my face felt as though Kimenju tree had collapsed and fallen on them."

"What hurt your face?" Muume desperately blurted out. "Was it the dogs when they caught you?"

"No!" Kiibe answered simply. "It was as though I had run blindly into a wall, or a tree, or a cliff... or... something hard and unyielding."

Muume was perplexed. "A wall? A tr... wh... you would have seen it!"

"Exactly!" Kiibe replied. "But as you know, there was no wall or tree there within the small clearing. The last thing I saw was only grass and nothing else!"

He took another deep breath.

Muume was at his wits end with anticipation.

Leaning forward again, Kiibe spoke in a dramatic whisper. "Walvenye can make an invisible wall to hide itself!"

His son's eyebrows shot up so high on his forehead, Kiibe feared they might disappear into the hairline.

"Yes it can!" he stressed while nodding to confirm the news. "When it is formed, nothing—and I mean nothing—can get through, but also, Walvenye itself, when you are outside the wall, is invisible and all you see is the plain, breezy air. When I was running from the dogs, it was that wall I ran into. It was hard as though made of wood, or formed from baked clay."

Muume leaned back, his amazed eyes so wide, Kiibe wondered if his eyeballs would fall from their sockets.

"And there is more," Kiibe announced. "It was not that wall that killed all those dogs. Many days later, when my own curiosity brought me back, armed with a bow and arrows, spears, a knife and a small shield—in case there were more dogs—I found their decomposed, dried out husks lying there." Lowering his voice again, Kiibe spoke in a whisper. "Walvenye had killed them with an invisible weapon!" He saw the expected reaction adorning his son's face. "I do not know what it was and I do not know how it works. I have not been able to figure out anything about it. Walvenye killed the dogs using that weapon to save me! And when I came back, it allowed me into the wall. I felt it as I walked past its invisible boundary!" Looking down, he brushed his fingers along his forearm. "It was like walking through a wall of dried leaves joined together. There was sensation on my skin... and sound deep inside my ears. The first time I felt it was strange beyond anything."

His eyes glazed over as he vanished into the memory.

Muume waited patiently.

Eventually, with his consciousness finding its way back, Kiibe glanced around the interior, eyes fleetingly pausing at every visible surface, as though within it lurked substance of infinite significance.

"You know the small clearing a morning's walk into the forest? In the direction towards of where Murwando cave was discovered?"

"Yes, I do," Muume replied. "I have not travelled to see the cave but I heard many things about the rocks and the darkness."

Kiibe reflectively pointed down towards the floor. "That was where it happened! It was where I stumbled upon this thing. In that clearing was where I ran face first into the wall." A distant look flashed, but his mind clung to the present. "I later found this space and brought Walvenye here so it would be further away. And it is fortunate I did because the village has grown bigger and people have become more curious and adventurous."

Muume voiced his support for the inspired action.

"Seasons later, when learning the workings of Walvenye," Kiibe continued, "somehow, I asked it to turn off the wall... or maybe I turned it off myself in some way that, up to now, I still do not know how." His arm briefly gestured towards the four panels. "I have not yet found how to turn it on again. It is fortunate this thing hides itself by imitating the appearance of unsuspicious objects. So you see Muume, there is a lot for you yet to learn in your own time, among other discoveries. Find how the wall works. It will be useful one day. And if you ever find how the weapon works, be careful!"

Both men sat pondering in the faintly humming silence as Muume digested this new revelation.

"Do you see now why it is even more gravely important that nobody else yet should find out about Walvenye?" Kiibe authoritatively enquired. "What carnage could be wreaked with malevolent hands!?"

Muume nodded, a grim expression darkening his face, chilled by thoughts of events in an alternate world where the craft had fallen into ill meaning hands. Both men leaned back, each contemplating their knowledge and the profound importance of meticulously protecting it.

"Ah!" Kiibe exclaimed, suddenly remembering something important. "I am so used to it that I have not told you all this time!"

Standing up, he swiftly walked to a section of wall, behind, and to one side of the hovering panels. With flattened palms, he waved his hands in sweeping motions. "All this wall here... all the way to here... and then all that way to across over there—" scurrying across the floor, he waved his hands over the other part of the wall "here... to here. You see all of that?" He hurried past Muume, towards the rear of the craft and waving his hands, marked out more sections of another wall. "You can actually see the line on this side... here... you see this line here?"

Muume hurried across, leaned to look, and then quickly nodded.

"So all this part... to here... You see? Over here! And all there where I showed you—" Kiibe waved his arms towards the front, "all those parts used to change, by themselves, to be as clear as pure water, so I could see outside as though looking through the clear sheet that appears over the doorway. It was like big windows covered with un-moving water!"

He paused just long enough to glance at the amazement glowing in his son's eyes, before taking a step to walk back to the swivelling chair.

"Astounding, is it not!" He let out a long, slow breath and with head shaking in frustration, stared down towards the floor. "That was many seasons ago. I was even younger than you. Also these here—" he gestured casually up towards the panels "could show me, like magic windows, what was going on outside! It was like there are some good eyes on the outside and their sight is carried to these so I could see on here what they... saw... it was..." he shook his head again. "Just like the wall, one time I must have asked Walvenye to set that aside!" His voice emerged carrying the annoyance at his blunder. "Many of these lines and lights are an unfathomable mystery. So you see again, like the wall and many unknown things, there is much to learn yet that you will be discovering yourself."

"How did you even gather enough courage to keep walking towards this thing and then step inside it? Were you not afraid? How did you first know to move the lights?"

Taking a long breath, Kiibe cast his mind to early days. "It was a most profound and nearly hypnotizing encounter!" he said, shaking his head almost in disbelief of all that had happened. "When Walvenye first let me into the invisible wall, all I saw at first was a big bush in the centre. As I pondered what magical thing I had just walked through, a doorway opened on the bush—the door as you know it. It was terrifying! Very, very so! But I did not run because it was obvious by then that Walven... well, the strange bush, meant me no harm: if it did, it would not have bothered to save me from the dogs—or that was my foremost thinking in that moment. I needed to know who the people were who chose to save me. Of course at the time, I had no idea this is what I was stepping into."

His eyes wandered again, wistfully scanning the interior.

"I walked forward and stepped inside with every part of me shaking, and with my heart beginning to threaten that it would jump out and run. And I saw all this as you see, but with parts of the walls appearing to be solid water—the parts I showed you—so I could see the forest outside very clearly through the walls. Everything looked as strange to me as it first did to you. There were no people anywhere! I knew nothing of the makers! And after a while, I began to touch and explore everything." He paused, lifting a cautious palm. "But I was careful, especially because I did not know if whoever lived in this thing would come back and be angry. Maybe they were out gathering food in the forest, or maybe they were fetching water. But

257

I stayed a while so they could meet the young boy they saved. But as you well now know, nobody ever came back."

His hands went up in a shrug.

"These here were showing the lights—" his palm swung towards the panels "and it was only a matter of time, on the same day, that I touched them. How could I not! Have you ever seen anything like them?"

Muume shook his head immediately.

"And when I did," Kiibe continued, "different things happened, which of course at the time I did not understand. I was alarmed the first time the purple colour happened. Here, come and try again. Here... swirl these ones and then put your fingers over here."

Muume did as his father asked and immediately, a purple light flashed around the interior, and a tone that reminded him of a horn blown in unrealistic, interrupted pulses, rang out a few times from hidden sound makers.

"You see! That is another way. It will not let you do some things. My suspicion is that those might be things that harm Walvenye, or maybe harm you by probably... maybe by changing the air or... maybe something else that might be very bad for you. In the first few seasons, I heard that sound many times. Some days it seemed everything I dared to touch was wrong. It was a long time before I began to know some basic things. So you see, as you continue to learn more and more, do not forget not to fear. It will not let you do things that might put you in danger. I am certain of that because in all these seasons, it has never once done anything to cause me harm."

"I think I would have been too afraid if it was me!" Muume said while waving both palms in hesitation.

"Not so!" his father countered. "I know you well Muume. You would have been even braver than me."

Muume looked unsure.

Kiibe suddenly chuckled aloud. "The first time Walvenye flew, I lay on the floor shaking in terror!"

"Eh! The first time? How? How did it begin to happen?"

"Well," Kiibe chuckled again. "I was playing with the lights and the straps came out the way they come out of the chair. It took me nearly two days to figure out they were meant to go over me and into these holders here. They looked a little different back then; remember I altered them all much later?"

Muume nodded.

"I was settled in and shuffling about feeling pleased with myself when I felt what you now know is Walvenye starting to move, and I saw through the water walls that we were going in the air!" With one hand on his knee, the other went up to cover his mouth. "Ah! Ah!" he exclaimed. "I panicked like a wildcat caught in a rope! I managed to remove one of the straps and then slid from the other. Then I tried to run—I don't know to where because the doorway was sealed. And then I lay down on the floor quivering like a frightened deer."

"Eh! You came out of the chair?" Muume slapped his palms in laughter.

"I am telling you! I jumped off! Faster than a cheetah! And when Walvenye saw what was going on with me, it turned and returned to the forest and settled down once more."

Turning to glance at the panels, he gestured towards various symbols. "It took a long time to figure out what I know now—like these signs here show where you decide is home and the others… like these ones here, show what is lakes and land and … you understand all that now, don't you?"

Muume nodded confidently.

259

"And there is still so much more that I do not know!" Kiibe humbly added. "What I know is even fortunate: if the walls did not used to look like solid water so I was able to see outside, it would have been impossible to learn anything with these lights. When I could see outside, it was very easy to learn; the lights looked one way and outside I could see trees, and then they looked another way and outside was a lake. It was clear they were showing what Walvenye could see. Before long, it was as easy to tell them apart as it is to know all the different plants in the forest: once you learn, it is simple."

Kiibe's face slowly settled into a sober expression.

"Now Muume—"

"Yes father."

"I have spent many seasons learning this thing and the world."

Muume nodded in agreement.

"It is very good that I did, and now, I think it is time to do more. There are still many things you need to learn that I do not know— like bringing back the wall, and finding how to work the weapon. And after you learn much more, then you can begin to use it to benefit the villagers and as many people as possible. But you have to do it slowly and without their knowledge. Maybe one way is to use these tools in here to begin to make other tools the villagers can use. But they have to be subtle so there is no suspicion. I think I have a good plan you can begin to consider."

Keen to hear the idea, Muume leaned forward.

"How about you find a blacksmith, a carpenter, a builder, and maybe another two people that you might be able to trust. Spend a lot of time with them and get to know them very well. Be sure they can all be unquestionably trusted. And then, if you become certain that it can be so, bring them here to Walvenye, just like the way I brought you. Be sure not to share with them everything at first, not until you are entirely and resoundingly certain. Then maybe they can slowly begin to use their skills to adjust and make tools and many other things. If, for example, tools come from the blacksmith, people might not be suspicious. And then maybe onwards to bigger things from there."

"And if I can learn and find out how to use the weapon, if ever there was turmoil or great troubles for the land, and if Walvenye can stay unseen—like the air in a breeze—I could use it to protect the people?" Muume offered, with eyes glowing in a wealth of new ideas tumbling into his mind.

"Absolutely so." Kiibe replied. "But be very careful. If the invaders know there is a secret weapon, they will amass numbers and come to try and capture it. Can you imagine the invaders from distant lands and the weapons they have? You saw them for yourself! Think of how much carnage they would come and cause. You have to use it only as a matter of last resort—if it only comes to that the whole land is going to fall. Then there would be no choice. But the black-smith and the others can make better weapons using Walvenye's tools. Then you will all be better armed. If the hordes ever come, you can defend yourselves. It is far better to keep back this secret weapon as something you can turn to using if all else fails.

Muume immediately agreed.

"I had to spend my life learning all that I did and much about Walvenye." Kiibe instructively continued. "Now I pass this on to you and you will judge what to do. Use it for taking our people to another level—with guidance from the spirits! Maybe one day the whole village could know about it. If they are aware that survival depends on keeping it a secret, it may be that it might be possible to show them. Decide for yourself many seasons from now. I have faith in your wisdom as you keep learning more."

Both men sat a whole day discussing different ways, both full of new ideas and new workable suggestions. By the end of the session, as they sat in the humming silence, Muume's eyes were alight with a new intensity and life for him had turned to become infinitely purposeful. He suddenly felt no number of seasons would be adequate; it would take three lifetimes to achieve what he had in mind.

After many moments had passed, Kiibe sat up and cleared his throat. "You have learned well Muume. Our ancestors and the spirits are beaming with pride! I have taught you nearly all I can, or all that I am able to. You learn so fast, even the builders of Walvenye would soon also have nothing left they could teach you!" Suppressing welling emotions, he paused and swallowed several times. "You must promise you will continue to love your children and all the grand-children, and bring them all up even better than I have succeeded in doing with all of you."

Muume vigorously shook his head. "Father!" he protested. "You are giving me an impossible task! No man living could make a better parent than you!"

Kiibe playfully reached out to punch his son on the shoulder. "You flatter me!" he responded. "Yet we brought you up well so I know you will do an even better job than I have done. I am proud of all of you. As the eldest one of my children, you must make it so that everything keeps on going well. And this secret, you must ensure remains just so!"

Muume hesitated with a reply as his eyes pooled with tears. "You have my word father!" he finally managed to say. "You have my full promise. But I am not ready for you to go. You must stay much longer!"

Kiibe squeezed his son's shoulder. "We are never ready to lose those who love and care about us no matter how long it may be that we spend with them. They always leave too soon." He leaned back and sighed heavily. "I was not ready when your grandfather and later, when your mother passed on and till today, I miss their presence and their inspiration. They helped to make me who I am, and they did a good job because we raised children more wonderful than I could have dreamed of." His eyes were carrying the sincerity of his words. "In the same way, through us, their inspiration passes to your children. We carry on living in this world through all the others, even as our life force leaves to go and join the spirits."

With great difficulty, both men struggled to fight back tears.

Kiibe rubbed his son's shoulder. "Walvenye has given us extra time together, and that is very precious to me. I have treasured each moment beyond what I could speak to say it."

Muume lost his battle and the tears flowed freely.

Two days later, they hesitantly stepped out and left the craft together. Kiibe would have less than half a day of good health before his heavily borrowed life force began to dissipate. There would barely be enough time to get back to the camp where the villagers remained with hopes of seeing him once more.

They walked fast. The way back was mostly downhill and Kiibe had the energy infused into him by the craft. Every once in a while, Muume would lose his composure and a subtle, stray tear trickled down his cheek. Each time, his father reached over and gently squeezed his shoulder while whispering warm, fatherly words of encouragement.

It was tough trekking. The journey was relentless and fast-paced and before the end of the morning, they had gone most of the way. Just before they reached the camp, Kiibe slowed as his life force, denied the replenishment, began to fade away. Muume broke down and could no longer hold back his tears.

"I will miss you greatly father!" he sobbed inconsolably. "I could not have asked or dared to pray for any better parents! As you watch from the spirit world, you will see, as each day passes, that I will sincerely keep my promise!"

Kiibe beamed with pride as he glanced over at his son. "I know you will Muume, I have not the slightest doubt." His voice carried forth the unshakable confidence. "And I will be watching!" he added with conviction.

A short while later, face bathed in sorrow, Muume emerged at the camp, carrying his father's lifeless body. All activity ceased as the villagers stood still, solemnly watching, amidst several dull thuds as a myriad of crude tools and daily-living items slipped away and fell from the grips of grief stricken hands. Overcome with emotion, some villagers fell to their knees and harrowing wails howled and echoed out into the trees. A brief moment passed by before the rest broke into mournful singing and surged forward to help with tenderly carrying the body, and with wrapping and placing it on to the ceremonial mat, on which, old man Kiibe, would make his last journey to the village.

Chapter 10

At the funeral, nearly at the end of the ceremony, Muume got up, tentatively ambled to the front and stood before the large and sorrowful gathering. Silent and staring at the ground around his feet, he appeared to be lost in a loop of reflection. The villagers exchanged discreet, mournful glances but patiently kept their heads bowed in sorrow. When he had gathered his thoughts, among memories of his father, Muume raised his head, breathed, and passionately began to speak.

He told the story of a great man on travels with his son, where he went to show him a magnificent, majestic tower constructed from metal bars with no outer covering, and so tall that birds flew around rather than over it. When the sun had gone down and darkness was upon the land, lanterns along the length—all the way to the top— twinkled brightly, like warm, glowing stars in the night sky, making the tower appear as though it stood in full daylight.

He told a story about a strange canoe impervious to any weather—a canoe solidly covered, then wrapped and sealed so tight, that water, try as it might, could never find a path in, and even the air enclosed within could not find a way out. You could walk in through a door which then tightly fastened over, keeping you safe, warm and dry and protected from the elements. Inside of this canoe, you would find a large room, vastly commodious and nearly the full size of a house.

This canoe needed no oars or rowing to propel it and moved using wizardry of stars and the shining sun. When you wanted it to sail, all you had to do was ask, which you did using power of directed daylight captured in a box and released in small flashes.

And he told of a room with lurking mystical power so great, it faced and brazenly defied death itself. A room which if you never left, infused vitality, so you remained alive, healthy and full of youthful vigour, walking tall among the living, even though your time allotted for this realm had long elapsed. Death's claim on you was brushed aside, just like a withered leaf, your heart still pounding fresh life to your limbs, your spirit ever living on, breathing soul into your body, oblivious to death's grim, portentous bellow.

You could only leave this room for half a day at the most at the end of which, if you did not urgently return, time itself, after tirelessly skulking and stalking, would swoop down, draw out diabolical claws and cling strongly to your soul, so that death, as restless as a starving reptile, could slither by and once again stake its cold claim.

When Muume was finished, the villagers were gasping in awe and a deafening wave of applause spontaneously erupted. There was not a single dry eye in the gathering of hundreds and the crowd began to surge forward to touch his shoulder.

"You are truly your father's son!" they broke out with admiration. "Those are the most wonderful tales we have heard since any past day before old man Kiibe left us! And even though all the stories may not be true, your father lives on within you! His spirit is among us! He lives on and thrives! We are honoured and greatly pleased!"

The applause was endless and the cheers were deafening.

Muume looked around at the crowd, from one side to the other. Pain from losing his father stung strong and relentless and some relief came from honouring his name.

When the noise eventually died down and the crowd settled in silence, he glanced around once more at the awestruck villagers. His sorrow was mingled with a mysterious sparkle as his eyes settled on faces harbouring no knowledge that soon, after not too many seasons had passed, their lives would change in ways none of them could fathom.

"Yes," he proclaimed, knowing it more then than he ever had. "That is the way it was, and the way it has been!"

The End

Mr. Magatti

Chapter 1

Standing at his favourite spot on the southern wing of the mansion grounds with both hands clasped tightly but casually behind his back, Mr. Magatti glanced down at his gleaming, charcoal coloured, hand-made shoes. He did not particularly like them, but that did not matter because everybody else did. The Italian designer had charged 12,000 Euros for them and the legendary attention to detail was worth it. People noticed. It was critical to Mr. Magatti that they did. Image was important to him and he grappled with unease when it was short of meticulous.

Mostly incapable of liking any clothes, he covertly relied on others for all cues. Fortunately, quality often went beyond the splendour appreciably soaked up by the casual gaze. The reassuring comfort of high priced designer wear was a pleasure enjoyed in a way known only to the wearer.

He adjusted the lapels of his flawless jacket and casually glanced down at the dark coloured suit. It seamlessly complemented the dark grey shoes. He did not particularly like the hand-sewn suit either, but everybody else did and that was all that mattered. The

Italian tailor charged 145,000 and fortunately, the quality was well worth the price.

Mr. Magatti felt suitably smart and supremely comfortable, a situation he considered second most important. First was that other people liked what he wore; image took full priority over personal taste. Time and effort went into carefully sifting out the best and mercifully, money was not remotely an issue.

Looking up again, he stared thoughtfully into the trees, sinking into the majestic, calming view. His heart warmed as it reached out to wallow in their aura. He took a deep breath, inhaling the late afternoon air and after slowly breathing out, inhaled deeply once more. The smells of the small forest and the carefree swaying of branches soothed and mesmerized him, bathing him with their essence. Every tree stood tall and whispered out enchantingly. Absorbed in the moment, he believed that if every other sound was turned down, he would have heard poems the trees were murmuring to him.

Focussing on the stems, he admired the way they withstood whatever compounding forces nature hurled their way; they didn't fight back! They toiled relentlessly along with it, grasping with their roots, waving by all natural challenges. Like advanced jujitsu fighters, parrying and deflecting, they fended off all the ancient forces besieging them. He smiled slightly and nodded. Trees were sturdy and strong. They were innocent and natural. Standing as nature's way of monitoring its own health and so tough, you had to use a chainsaw to bring one down. Watching in part meditation, he whispered another life lesson just gleaned from the towering giants.

"I harness willing forces of the ether to stay strong!" he softly declared. "Strong, just like the trees!"

Shifting his gaze to the foliage and the branches, he felt the mental tug as they soaked up his turmoil. He loved that the trees gave him oxygen he needed to breath — they gave without limit, without judgement or question. They couldn't loathe or resent or violate and abuse him. They would never beat him or hit him or hate him or reject him. He could stand there and enjoy their presence, absorb their essence, relax in the peace. And he could walk away and come back and they would still be there for him. They were beacons of love and unquestioning acceptance and deep in his heart and in a recess of his strange mind, he suspected that they actually, truly did like him.

Standing in the southern section of his private estate a short distance away from the seventy three room mansion, he slowly admired the view of the man-made forest. The modern mansion stood in the middle of the forty acre expanse of land that made up the serene gardens of his preferred residence. With a longer than usual drive from the main gate to the front courtyard, the opulent dwelling nestled in enhanced security.

Several guards, sensors, cameras, a variety of gadgets and other advanced technologies remained constantly vigilant and such was their effectiveness, the security team were quick to declare that no intruders could ever successfully skulk in. Within the large, square shaped, designer, open courtyard that everyone called the fountain area, Mr. Magatti felt relaxed, safe and very secure.

With stone flooring shaped from solid, dark, natural rock, the fountain area courtyard spanned twelve hundred square feet and was entirely surrounded, along its full boundary, by a three foot high balustrade, assembled from individually carved, miniature pillars of stone.

Standing majestically in the centre of the square, Mr. Magatti had commissioned an eight foot, granite fountain in the shape of three beautiful women wearing long, flowing dresses and standing back to back, facing three different directions, all pouring pure water from forged, brass urns which they daintily held aloft upon their feminine shoulders. The full size statues stood exquisitely hand-carved and planted on a rocky pedestal, surrounded by a clean and clear, circular pool of water held in place by cleverly engineered slabs of grey marble.

Mr. Magatti did not particularly like the granite statues, but everyone who saw them commented on their beauty — and that was important to him. And he was always soothed by the soft and mellow flow from the half tipped urns, calibrated for a hypnotic, bubbling melody.

Beyond the fountain area, the southern wing of the land was dedicated to tamed and domesticated forest. Standing close to the balustrade with the fountain behind him, Mr. Magatti was well into the racing second hour of meditatively staring at the abundant trees slowly swaying in the mild, late afternoon breeze. In his special, quiet spot meant for solitude and reflection, there was no need of worry or vexations of time. Individuals of consequence, including staff at the mansion, were under strict orders not to disturb him.

His staff and all employees appeared to speak well of him — at least everyone claimed they did — and they all said they liked him. Making sure to pay them well, he strived to be reasonable, even compassionate, and though exceptionally high standards were demanded, he made gestures conveying appreciation for loyalty. The gestures paid off; nearly all, including the highly experienced security team, had glued themselves on to his payroll for many years. Complaints were rare, and they worked with the type of unreserved dedication he did not see in most places. He didn't particularly care what any of them thought of him, but it was important that they settle into their roles.

Another large cash bonus was planned for the end of the year — the largest one yet — which as had become routine, would be announced as a surprise. It was a habit now, one that had endured for several years and from what he could gather, was a resounding success: his mansion staff and other employees in his businesses responded with resolute dedication and vigour.

He closed his eyes, took another long and deep breath and then opened them again to watch the captivating foliage. Beyond the courtyard, out in the forest, birds, insects, small animals and myriads of creatures chirped, squawked, squeaked and sang a rich, vibrant cacophony of nature's lively theme songs, breathing dynamic life in to the wooded area. The earthy diversion offered up a mental off-ramp from gruelling schedules, and vented dark and harrowing issues threatening to overwhelm him. Being a billionaire was hard work: too often, he needed a way to release and recharge.

It was beyond this mellow and thriving keynote of nature that he heard the faint, unnatural sound that didn't belong.

Deep in dreamy meditation, something starkly unusual nudged him back to reality. Out of place in the fountain area, the sound was hard to make out and most would have missed it, but to him and to anyone who was capable of knowing, it was chilling, very real and unmistakeable.

Though nowhere near as loud as he knew it should have been, no meaningful attempt had been made to conceal it — a deliberately slow and careful action by a professional, tactfully and stealthily announcing his presence; the careful sliding of the hi-tech mechanism to pre-load the chamber of a high powered pistol that Mr. Magatti knew must be pointed towards him. He froze and was very careful not to make any movements.

It was difficult to tell what model had made the sound, but that did not matter: such knowledge would not save his life. He guessed it would have a high quality silencer screwed on to the muzzle. When the moment came, he would most likely never hear the shot, nor feel the impact of the bullet — an ironic mercy.

High level professional killers possessed no desire to waste time watching a victim suffer. The job was simply to end a life and the quicker that was done the sooner it could be ticked off the list with minimum fuss, minimum risk and without getting captured. Most targets were dead long before they knew of lurking danger — merciful in a way, except for the perished, hapless victim.

Mr. Magatti, still standing and alive after a few moments, knew his killer harboured customary respect for status. It was not at all surprising and not entirely unexpected when the target was as wealthy and as high profile as he was, and the only reason whoever was assigned to be behind the gun had stepped onto the courtyard and intentionally allowed the sound to make his stealthy presence known. Professional courtesy was allowing his target a little time for introspection, and for spiritual closure.

Mr. Magatti sighed but remained perfectly still, resisting the urge to turn and face his assassin; any attempt to do so would immediately be fatal. Acutely aware that there were only a few moments to summon up his life's acquired negotiating skills to buy some more time for a plan, he dug deep into his mind, searching for the right words. Another moment went by before he took a deep breath.

"So" he tried to sound polite, "they settled on sending you?"

He paused, remained still, and waited for an answer.

His assassin did not speak.

"I do appreciate the respect you have shown me."

There was still no sound, but he remained alive, so he continued.

"It hasn't passed by me either the fact that they chose the best. In different circumstances, it might have been an honour!"

There was more silence. Still alive, he chose to speak again.

"Would you care to—"

A smooth, emotionless voice interrupted him, so softly, it barely rose above the bubbling fountain.

"And who, in your opinion, is the best?" it enquired.

Mr. Magatti was aware his assassin was checking to see if he genuinely knew his identity, or whether it was a weak bluff. Killers of such calibre were not just lacking in emotions and empathy, they were highly intelligent; a necessity for survival in high profile assignments where targets were shielded behind the best security.

Intelligence was tricky, but Mr. Magatti could work with it. Grinding his teeth together, he feigned calm while mentally assembling a strategy. They like to be flattered: not superficial flattery on vain simplicities as hairstyles or appearance, or the forward type of flattery about somebody's good work. Such gestures came across to them as frivolous and insincere.

The best route, he concluded, was undoubtedly their ego. One of the safer options was acknowledging their genius; a blatant implication that they alone stood out and that nobody could do better — or even come close. It helped to throw in sly comments wondering why those in the know did not recognise that fact, and how they must be mistaken.

In a quest to choose his next words, Mr. Magatti weighed up the most fruitful approach. Men such as these had a primal attraction to a need for their actions to be better than any other. Though extremely intelligent, they felt no joy from it, and they felt no regret, no remorse and no fear. Assassins at this level were all, without exception, highly dysfunctional human beings. Settling on a tactical nudge at primal craving, Mr. Magatti prepared to cast a shrewd verbal hook.

"There are only three professionals—" he was careful not to say 'killers' "—capable of such a task. One of them could never get past my security and I doubt the other has resources, or anywhere near the influence, to get away with carrying out such an assignment."

The statement was untrue. All that would matter was the assassin had to think that Mr. Magatti believed it.

He paused — purely for effect.

"That leaves only you."

He paused again, a little longer, before speaking out the name. He always thought it was an outdated, old fashioned name that though lacking in style, never failed to strike fear into anybody who knew of it, and was disturbingly fatal to anyone that encountered the individual attached to it. Still, it was impressive and fulfilled the criteria: high level assassins chose to have strange code names that when spoken out, sounded like names of race horses. Every one of them was inadvertently chosen and all had profoundly unsettling meanings. Mr. Magatti was respectful when he said it.

"Turquoise Arrow!" he spoke as though addressing a commander.

There was an immediate sense that his assassin had began to a smile. Real respect from men like Mr. Magatti was one of the highest forms of praise and flattery. Turquoise Arrow, or Mr. Maurice Burt Smith, was suddenly very pleased with how the day was going.

Chapter 2

Entirely hating his real name and spurred on by desire to abandon his past life, Maurice Burt Smith formed an alternate identity. Growing up immersed in memories of overwhelming fear, a dark glint in his eye hinted at searing burdens of savagely suppressed anger. A violent, repressed revulsion festered for his mother who unceremoniously abandoned him, his father who beat him when he was only a baby, and for all forms of authority — and all humans for that matter — who failed to intervene in any meaningful way to save him from suffering endured in his early years.

His mother, who lived on her own, at the limits of what an over-whelmed human could endure, tried to murder him when he was only a few weeks old — at first, by leaving him unattended and unfed for nearly three full days, during which he cried shrilly and pitifully the entire time, only stopping when his tiny body was so exhausted that it fell unconscious into a tormented sleep. She finally, perhaps troubled by the diminishing wailing, tried to smother him under the folded layers of bed covers, hoping that when she called for help, it would pass as an accident.

When the ambulance crew arrived, the tiny heart still sparked in the emaciated, scrawny creature desperately clinging to life. When it became apparent that he had not been fed, his mother hastily escaped the room, ran away to avoid arrest and was not seen again until four years later when her body was discovered in the North-East of the country, perished from an overdose of low grade heroine.

After a short while in care, he was handed over to live with the unreliable man who had made his mother pregnant. His father, a brash, extremely violent individual who also lived on his own in a small rented property in Northern-England, was rarely ever home. He neglected and beat him severely from the start. Little Maurice was left alone to cry for hours, usually for a day or two, and he was fourteen months old when authorities intervened, took him away, and sent his father to prison for eleven years.

With bruises all over his body, and two cracked ribs from his father's fist when he wouldn't stop crying, at the tender age of fourteen months, little baby Maurice already stared from lifeless eyes borne of lack of nurturing and of human connection.

He was taken to his father's sister, who was not much better. Having always hated his mother and alienated from her brother, she agreed to take him in and raise him — mostly to get the money. Behind closed doors he never knew what it felt like to have a caretaker show love or compassion. Neglect and the beatings continued from his aunt and her long string of boyfriends, each as sour as the next. Living with the sixth 'uncle' by the time he was ten and though nowhere near as crude and violent as the previous one, Maurice lingered in fear of his rage fuelled outbursts.

Maurice hated that his aunt cheered on the violence, staying silent and hidden whenever they were home. When he was six years old, he was traumatized from a thrashing doled out by the gruff, next in line, live-in boyfriend — a brutal man named Ronno — during which Maurice nearly passed out from crying. He fell to the floor, seized and desperately trying to breathe and as he lay there, hovering ever closer to death, Ronno coldly sat back, placed a foot on Maurice's head, and then proceeded to open a beer, while watching a championship game on television — using the young boy's head as a living, human footrest.

Maurice despised school, mostly terrified by bullying for always being dirty and endlessly hungry, and with no support at home, there was ever growing frustration and he hid within himself, cowering inside his own mind, feeling that there was nothing physical he could ever do. With a love for the sciences, mathematics and history, and an ever growing passion for all general reading, there was never a safe space to spend time with his books and he grappled with resentment and sank into despair. Unable to settle down and study at school or at home, his face locked and tensed up with stress and depression.

Having never learned how to be a real human being, he withered into himself and his mind began to falter, seeking ways to bury wounds of trauma and rejection. Maurice felt and knew nothing of love and compassion and he felt and knew nothing of connection with others. Gradually devoured by suppressed spasms of rage, an intense revulsion grew for his parents, his aunt, her boyfriends, for Ronno and eventually, for anybody else he encountered.

Some of Maurice's teachers reached out to the young soul, grasping for the sinking mind fading into turmoil. When he was eight years old, his class year teacher, kind Mrs. Milly Mayward, was touched by his torment. With two young children in her thriving, happy family, his craving for parental compassion was glaring and among kind gestures and smiles of encouragement, she offered up a soft heart, a shoulder and an escape. His aunt outmanoeuvred her every step of the way and with endless complaints and repeated accusations, Mrs Mayward was nearly suspended from her job.

When he was fourteen, Maurice gave up on attempts at fitting in with society, unwillingly sliding into beckoning darkness. After festering and simmering through his childhood years, it peaked in ferocity, overwhelming his psyche. Drained of all strength and any will to repel it, he dropped the last defences, stopped trying to care, and offered himself up, allowing it to devour his soul.

Genuinely puzzled by all human relationships, Maurice descended into a cloudy reality. Daily encounters became grainy waves of flickering acquaintances and half-life occurrences. His aunt's voice shrilled and cawed when in the vicinity — without any meaning — and fellow students crowed and cackled mystifyingly. Losing all feeling for everything and everyone, the cold, emotionless eyes glazed over for good.

When he was sixteen, Maurice packed a bag and moved out, surviving on odd-jobs and occasional shoplifting. A year later, finding himself near Manchester, he wandered into fitness and martial arts training. Waking up each morning was almost a pleasure, with a mind full of exercise, power moves and high kicks. Consumed by techniques and an ever swelling loathing of having to work with what he perceived as mundane people, he searched for new ways to intensify his training.

Towards the end of teenage years, as he approached nineteen, Maurice wanted to be the best in the world at something. He never truly understood the reason why he needed to be, but as the days ground on, the desire only grew stronger. He worked and trained harder, getting ever more extreme, pushing to the utmost limits of his physical ability. The world — as he saw it — was a festering wild-land and he had to be sure he was better than them all.

It was only a matter of time before his new life's path snaked into shady, grey worlds of rumours and contracts, and flutters of mentions of a world class assassin, and foggy fear across ways trod by high circles with covert hires by rich, nefarious entities — the great assassin rarely ever failed an assignment.

Helplessly mesmerized, Maurice greedily gobbled every morsel and flitter of the unspoken stories, vanishing into hazy worlds of dreams and fantasies and dread and focussed skill, and words most people never know were uttered. Bedevilled by a vision, he tumbled, head over heels, into a new mission and a new life calling.

Six days after a lonely, twentieth birthday, Maurice knew, with no doubts, what his code name would be. He stumbled upon the object in a renovator's waste dump while rummaging for metal fixings to hold up a punching bag. Lifting up an old door on a pile of discarded material, he saw, burrowed within the clutter, a bow and arrow symbol, mounted into the centre structure of a metal, garden gate. Traditional looking with a true and narrow, hand-struck, tapered point, the arrow was two feet long, forged from reinforced steel and was painted a bright, slightly weather worn turquoise. Staring in awe, as though it called softly out to him, he immediately decided it was the weapon he was going to use to kill his aunt.

When all the planning finally converged into a chosen night, he sat watching her building, waiting for the current live-in boyfriend to step out: his favourite football team would shortly be playing in continental championships, and his favoured bar, fifteen minutes walking distance away, was licensed to show a live broadcast of the match. That was well over an hour, likely two or three, that he would be not of this world, which was far more time than Maurice planned he would need. Waiting a little longer after the man emerged from the building to set off at a hasty pace towards a hope-filled evening, Maurice eventually stepped forward and made his way to the main entrance.

In the busy and noisy neighbourhood, with many people out and about, it was easy to blend in with a minimum of effort. A fake moustache, a cheap hat and a jacket that half the men on the street all seemed to be wearing in a variety of colours, presented such an average figure, that nobody would remember seeing a stranger in the late evening, dusty, darkening light. Making sure to check that there was nobody in the stairway, he climbed up to the second floor of the four storey building and cautiously approached her door.

Picking the lock was easy, but the door creaked alarmingly when he let himself in. From muffled, rhythmic patter of falling, sprayed water, it was clear that his aunt was in the bathroom having a shower. He didn't mind the noisy door. She must have heard it. She would assume that her boyfriend most likely forgot something. He shut the door, took a moment to carefully lock it, then turned around and surveyed the medium sized and surprisingly well furnished sitting room.

The furniture was cheap, but it was tidy and organised; impressive what could be achieved on a meagre budget. Slowly and deliberately, he scanned around the room trying to summon up faint stirrings of distant memories. Apart from the large cabinet against the main wall, the solid wood coffee table and a large corner unit, everything else was new and unfamiliar to him.

Maurice calmly took off the jacket, revealing a smart shirt and tailored waistcoat that complemented subtle, tailored, dark brown trousers. He glanced down at the hand-made, dark coloured but subtle shoes with a monumental effort in attempt at ignoring the hint of street dust that had gathered from his lingering. Giving up on the battle, he pulled out his handkerchief and polished at them vigorously, until the near perfect glint was fully restored. In the brighter light indoors, they were easily discernible by any curious, roving eyes as high priced designer wear. He didn't particularly like either the shoes or the trousers, but they were carefully chosen to blend away in evening light and fade into obscurity in the orange glow of street lights.

He pulled the arrow from its hiding place in a flat sheath along his back and carefully placed it lying diagonally on the table. Looking around at the main walls, he saw several photographs of his aunt taken together with her current live-in boyfriend. She had not aged well. Her tired eyes and lined lips bore pain of poor choices, and regular brand, dyed hair was not fooling anyone. Her appearance was not as much of an interest to him as the convenience of the pictures. They were going to be very useful. It was more than perfect! The plan was unfolding far better than expected.

On the main wall, in a prominent position to the left of an enormous, black framed, obscure brand television, mounted dead centre above a tacky glass fronted cabinet, was a large painted portrait of the two of them together, his aunt and her boyfriend, the sort done by a street artist rather than a studio. Fantastic! It was going to be far easier than planned. He knew just what to do and exactly how to do it.

Pulling on a thin pair of white, woven cotton gloves, he walked up to the portrait and roughly pulled it off the wall. Using a small knife from a concealed hip carrier, he slashed the canvas several times, taking care to focus on the area around his aunt's face. Pausing to be sure that the cuts would look just right, in one quick motion, acting as though he was angry, he smashed the frame hard on to the corner of the coffee table, and then flung the mangled mess, with great force, on to the floor.

Walking to the other side of the wall-mounted television, he pulled down a framed photo and threw it hard across the room, taking care to aim towards the opposite wall. It smashed against the plastered brick with a loud, echoing clang and disintegrated, spreading shards of glass in all directions.

The patter of water went quiet and his concerned aunt called out, wondering about the noise. Maurice walked calmly to a large shard of glass fallen on the beige carpet, reached into his pocket for a miniature vial and along one sharp edge, applied a very small spot of Ronno's blood carefully stored and carried as a key part of the plan. He dropped the piece carefully, from a low height, on to the floor, watching to be sure that everything still looked right. A couple more, very tiny, strategic drops, straight on to the carpet, completed a convincing, near flawless fabrication.

His aunt shuffled into the room wearing only a bathrobe.

"You!" Clearly startled, she was expecting to see her boyfriend.

Scanning around the room, her eyes and mouth flew open. "What silliness are you doing? You childish, stupid boy!" The same hatred dulled her eyes as he saw in younger years. "You idiot! You are well going to pay for all of those! And don't say you don't have money when wearing clothes like that!"

"It won't matter any more!" Maurice stepped forward calmly. "Not to you anyhow." He spoke in a soft and mellow voice.

A cold essence leaching from unfeeling eyes spooked her, and all of a sudden, she no longer cared about the damage. Disturbed by his expression, she only wanted him to leave.

"It's fine," she tried to sound dismissive. "Just get your silliness out! You've done your damage. Now get out! Go!"

"Not yet!" he said calmly. "I haven't yet done the thing that I came here to do!"

His eyes were fixed on to hers.

A cold shiver ran down her spine.

"Look, just get out! It will be fine. Just go! I'll tell him it was me. I'll say I broke them by accident. You can go now! Before he comes back. I will clean it up."

His expression did not change. He turned to glance at the arrow, still diagonal on the table and, following his eyes, she noticed it for the first time. She took a small step backwards.

"What's that for? Whose is that?" Her trembling voice had dropped almost to a whisper.

He bent down, picked it up and studied it closely.

"A thing of great beauty!" His stare was as though beholding a divine object. "Look at this tapered point—" he oriented the arrow so she could see the sharp end. "It's handcrafted you know. You can tell... here... see here... these wavy patterns! Irregular, unique, just... handcrafted and nice..."

His voice trailed off, mesmerized by the craftsmanship. A few moments passed by as he gazed at the arrow.

"A machine could never do this! Machines have no soul!" he declared after finally emerging from the trance. He ran his fingers slowly along the full length and the tapered point. "Takes a good blacksmith nearly twenty minutes of skilled labour! And that's only after they're done shaping up the metal. Takes years to learn it this way. Takes years just to learn to hand blend good metals! You can feel the soul of the blacksmith, buried well inside of this!" He nodded as if agreeing with his own information and then carried on silently studying the arrow.

Like a passionate lecturer instructing keen students, he held it horizontally in proud demonstration. "And the paint, this paint, this is a special weather proof blend. I looked it up. It's perfect! Whoever ordered this absolutely wanted quality." He lifted it towards her, wanting her to have a look. "Look at it! You see! Look how beautiful and balanced it is. Feels almost magical! Feels like it's alive!" he was slowly rocking the arrow, as though weighing a rare artefact.

She stepped further backwards, her eyes widening with fear. This was not a sane man! Something was very wrong with him! And there was something about his gaze, his dark eyes and his posture that was ominous and threatening, overwhelmingly frightening.

She was suddenly very fearful of being in his presence. Her hands began to tremble and then fell away to her sides. The untied dressing gown partially fell open, revealing her flabby front and quivering belly. Maurice was repulsed. A mild sneer flashed across his face.

"Wh... what are you going to do with th... tha..." her stuttering voice vanished back into her throat.

He took a gentle step towards her and she flinched and stepped backwards.

"I've planned for this moment for a long time now." His voice had lowered both in tone and in projected volume.

He walked up, stood barely two feet away from her and looked straight into her eyes. "Did you think I would never grow up?"

She stared back, unsure of whether he was waiting for an answer.

"I'm... I'm sorry! I'm sorry! F... for... everything! Everything! Forgive me! Please!" she stammered. "I'm really, truly sorry!"

He held a finger up to her lips.

"Didn't I beg? When it was me? How many times did I beg?" his voice was unnervingly calm.

Tears rolled down her cheeks, down her chin and meandered in between her breasts, trickling all the way down to her belly.

It repulsed him even more.

"You didn't listen when it was me!" His face briefly flickered with scorn.

"P... please! I'm sor—"

He held a finger to his own lips.

"You made me who I am!" he said softly after a short silence. "It could all have been different. I could have come another time carrying a birthday card, or flowers, or a cake, or a new hat and a case of fancy beers for your boyfriend! But now, I have this!" He raised and held up the arrow. "I'm only doing what I need to. I want you to understand that."

She tried again to reach out but the gentle wave of a hand commandeered silence.

"I've arranged it all and made it so that Ronno is going to get the blame."

She stared, slightly puzzled, then, unable to speak, shook her head, trying to understand what an ex would be blamed for.

Maurice leaned forward and looked straight in to her eyes. "Ronno is going to spend the rest of his life in prison — for your murder!"

She flinched violently, stepped back and instinctively began to scream, but no sound came out as the arrow pierced the base of her neck, penetrating two inches through her trachea.

She grasped at her throat with both hands, desperately trying to breathe, and her legs and spine buckled as her brain acknowledged the trauma. As she fell to the floor, Maurice jumped back, keeping a grip on the arrow, and it popped out from the wound with a dull, squelching, sucking sound.

With hands clasped around her neck, she spluttered and coughed, every breath rasping and gurgling in harrowing torment. Blood seeping through her fingers bathed the neck and shoulders, and flowed down to soak into the well cleaned carpet. Her toes curled unnaturally, and sandals flapped as bare heels thudded desperately against the carpeted floor. And watering, wild eyes glared, first at the ceiling, then swivelling to him, before returning to the ceiling among noises of drowning.

Maurice, very cautiously, stepped forward again and then, careful to avoid the blood, leaned down to look at her. Her tortured face stared back up at him and through the tears, her eyes carried raw intensity of a soul in pleading.

He stared down into them and for only a fleeting moment, connected with the human being, and the anguish he was certain she must be enduring. A brief flash of sympathy was swept away in a deluge of overwhelming memories of wretched tears of his own.

They looked at one another, and her eyes grew wider as he slowly and purposefully shook his head. There would be no forgiveness. There would be no mercy. She had drawn up her own fate and in her own ignorance, she made the appointment — the malevolent request. Both he and the arrow were only delivering.

With a quick thrust, he plunged the arrow downwards — straight through her ribs — and up towards the middle of her heaving chest, until he felt the crackly tear as it pierced through her heart, and he saw the cosmic shiver of a soul in surrender. She clamped her elbows tight to the sides of her body, shuddered, then stopped moving, and her blood soaked hands fell away from her neck.

Maurice looked down at the bloody, half naked, lifeless body, then closed his eyes and turned away, more repulsed than ever. Beyond the revulsion peeked slivers of gladness — very faint but present — and with her life extinguished, he felt his own was untethered to finally begin.

After cleaning the arrow with a leather cloth, he carefully replaced it into the improvised, hidden carrier nestling along his back. Not entirely happy with the setup of the scene, he smashed two more pictures, made extra adjustments, and then looked around to be sure everything was just right. After going through a detailed, memorized checklist, he pulled on and carefully buttoned up the cheap jacket.

Walking over to the door, he unlocked it, turned to sweep his eyes across the morbid room for one last time, and then stepped out into the hallway. He paused to listen out for any footsteps in the stairs and once sure there was no one about, he shut the creaky door in the most casual way possible — as though a usual resident was popping out to buy some milk. Some neighbours would hear it and it had to be forgettable. It had to sound the same as they had heard another thousand times.

It was nearly dark outside and he blended in seamlessly with the average, dusty streets of the still bustling neighbourhood. A vague, average, strolling figure, even the stray cat grooming itself on a wall at the end of the building wasn't troubled to look up, and barely acknowledged him.

Maurice kept a close tab and an ear out for developments, watching with satisfaction as, awash with clues, the police swiftly arrested Ronno for his aunt's murder. With chin in one hand and the other fingers drumming on his knee, a news report spoke to him, telling what he already knew; the evidence — every part of it — was simply overwhelming.

A brutal, short tempered man who had used fists, feet and any manner of crude tools to inflict pain on Maurice, Ronno stood at average height, husky voiced and rough as a grater. On the day he used the boy's head as a living, human footrest, they had stayed that way, far longer than Maurice cared to remember, until his aunt walked in, paused to survey the scene and then promptly kicked Maurice hard, squarely in the ribs, and shouted at him to go to bed and stop his silly whining.

The incident endured, pitiless, mauling his sanity, permeating depths from where it malignantly smouldered. The devastating humiliation, the grinding juvenile helplessness assaulted his subconscious thoughts and firmly wedged into them a mind engulfing desire to make the bad uncle pay.

Maurice had been training maniacally for over two years by the age of nineteen when he began to formulate the solid plan to kill his aunt and to entangle Ronno in a lasting web of misery. After learning about an organic blood anti-clotting agent that broke down ten minutes after exposure to breathable air, he acquired a small vial, hand delivered in two days from a secretive dealer. The extortionate price was well worth it for his next step. Before murdering his aunt, among the carefully selected events that had to run flawlessly, was a visit the engulfing desire chalked up as requisite — and one that he was very much looking forward to making.

He watched the residence carefully and memorised their schedules. He got to know their habits, their timings, all their comings and goings, memorable peculiarities and even their two most favourite foods. And he found out a possible date in the not too distant future, when mother and son were scheduled to be away for four days — another convenient piece freely offered up to develop the plan; the portion for his aunt would fit nicely into one of them, assuming a certain football tournament wasn't cancelled.

The small residence in East London was a small detached house with a symbolic small gate, and a front garden only just wide enough to park a car and grow a mini-lawn beside it. The half-homey neighbourhood, evidently cohesive, nestled in a safe and liveable part of the borough; where children played outside and where pet cats and puppy dogs were not at all uncommon with a flurry of doting owners — an ideal place to visit in unholy hours of the night when everyone was resting away daytime adventures.

Ronno had settled down with a shrill, scrawny woman nearly as vile as Maurice's aunt, who sold bootleg dvds, illegal downloads and piggy-back streaming services for money on the side. Their withdrawn three year old son, mistreated and neglected, carried a tell-tale furrowed brow in mental distress. When Maurice broke into the house in the early hours of the morning, the child was fast asleep in a separate room.

The lock in the backyard entrance was moderately easy to pick and he walked into the kitchen and quietly closed the door behind him. Using a small key fob light to check his surroundings, he walked into the hallway, paused outside the child's room and then gently opened the door to be sure he was fast asleep. The little boy's head peeked from under the covers and gentle breathing floated softly in the semi-darkness.

"Don't worry little guy," he thought out under his own breath. "I will make it so you have the best mummy you could want!"

Pausing to stare a while longer, memories flashed by of years when he was only a little boy himself. Blinking away welling tears, he breathed out to the sleeping child. "I'm sorry but your daddy won't be around for much longer." He glanced at the dark floor and then looked up again at the bed. "I have a strong feeling you will not be missing him. One day, when you're older, I will find you and tell you some things about your daddy. When I do, then you will understand."

After gently closing the door, he walked further down the hall and let himself into Ronno and his partner Shelly's, bedroom. With the miniature key fob light, he searched for and found the switch in the standard, universal location next to the door frame. Reaching up, he flicked it to turn on the main light.

Shelly was the first to stir. It took only a moment to focus and she gasped when she saw a strange man standing near the door. She shook Ronno to wake him. He stirred, lifted up his head, mumbled in lethargic annoyance, closed his eyes, let his head droop and drifted back to sleep. Shelly shook with more urgency and called out his name while pointing out with a hesitant finger, the stranger standing in their room. His head lifted and he looked again. A brief moment wound by before his eyebrows lowered and his eyes glared in anger.

"What the hell you think you're doing over in 'ere boy?" he recognised Maurice straight away. "Night creepin' whiny boy! Gettout of it! Go home!" He glanced at Shelly. "He's not even a burglar! Just look at him! Smarty, softy, creepin' prissy boy! Look there how he's all dressed up! You going to a smarty, fancy, mincy wedding, whiny boy? Come to show off your new gear? Eh? In the middle of the night?"

Maurice remained silent, staring with unblinking eyes. Shelly saw the warning signs and recognized the danger. Cowering in fear, she reached for her partner's arm. Ronno missed the look entirely.

"Gettout whiny boy! Stupid. creepin' prissy fool!" Stupid was pronounced *schoopid*.

Maurice stood his ground and kept his eyes firmly fixed on the pair.

Ronno started to get out of bed. "Am g'nna bash your whiny head in, night creepy git!"

Shelly fought to hold him back but he snatched his hand away, violently threw back the covers and jumped out on to the floor. With both fists clenched, he stomped furiously across the room.

When nearly upon Maurice, he swung his fist, aiming at the jaw. Maurice ducked and a dull thud reverberated from the bricks as the hand pounded into the wall, mangling three knuckle bones.

Ronno cradled his injured arm and doubled over in pain. Shelly snatched a pillow and covered her mouth to stop herself from screaming. Ronno flew into an all out, uncontrolled rage.

"Am g'nna bash you! Schoopid git! G'nna bash yo... your head in!"

Maurice calmly stepped away towards the middle of the room, but Ronno followed and tried swinging a punch using the other hand. Maurice dodged it, took one step back and brought down his right fist, straight on to Ronno's unprotected left eye socket.

Ronno fell to the floor half conscious and writhing in pain. Maurice watched for a moment and then slowly walked over to the bed. Stopping at its side, he stood quietly looking down at Shelly, staring at her face with a thoughtful expression. She stared back up at him with wide, fearful eyes.

After some moments of silence, he casually lifted an arm and pointed an accusing finger in the direction of Ronno.

"I want to tell you about what that man did to me."

She nodded quickly, her eyes never leaving his.

In a shaky voice, he told her all about the neglect, the beatings, the pain, the overwhelming dread and the incident where Ronno used a boy's head as a footrest. The astonished expression showed him she was adequately repulsed.

"Now, tell me, why did he think... why did he... that I would never grow up to be as big and as strong as he was?"

She shook her head, unable to think of anything safe to say.

293

"I grew up!" he continued. "And take a good look at me now. I am a man in whom such a memory and many others have torn and festered in my insides for all these years. Why did he never once see that such a thing could happen? Why did he do so many bad things to a small boy?" he asked and then paused, genuinely seeking an answer.

She stared up at him, far too frightened to speak. Shaking her head again, she pursed her lips and meekly shrugged her shoulders.

His face descended once more into an ominous expression.

"I also happen to know that you're not nice to that little boy, your own son, who right now, is fast asleep in the other room!"

Shelly's eyes began to water and she trembled into the pillow.

"P... p... please don't hurt me! Please!" she whispered.

"You touch her and I swear — I swear..." Ronno grunted.

Maurice's eyes didn't leave Shelly's. And his stare didn't soften.

"I will give you one chance—" he paused and slowly leaned forward. "Only one! No more!" He was staring straight into her eyes. "I'm going to be watching you, every now and then, just like I have been, anytime day or night!"

She nodded quickly, her lips and fingers quivering with fear.

"You are going to be the best mother a little boy could want! And if you slip up even one time, I will be back to visit you!"

Tears flowed freely, trickling down to the pillow. She was too frightened to wipe them away.

"Yes! Thank you! I promise!" she responded in relief. "I swear on my life, I will be! I will! Forever!"

Sincerity etched into her face confirmed she meant every word.

He turned away and looked at Ronno who was trying to stand up, still clutching his injured hand. His eyes had mellowed with a new recognition that the boy he tormented had grown up into a man who, apart from appearing to be slightly insane, was far more athletic and a much better fighter.

"It was your right foot!" Maurice said, speaking so calmly, it seemed to be an inconsequential, throwaway comment.

Ronno paused in bewilderment.

"On that day, as I lay on the floor?" Maurice reminded him.

He paused and waited as the puzzled look on Ronno's face transformed with the memory, and then tightened with panic.

"I need to make sure that foot always remembers never to do such a horrible thing again!"

Maurice took a few purposeful steps forward and Ronno, concerned about the posture reverberating savage intentions, started to back away. With the separation between them closed to striking distance, Ronno attempted to speak but before any words could emerge, Maurice's folded fingers stabbed sharply, straight into the middle of his throat, in a lightening speed jab.

Ronno fell to the floor, rasping and gasping for breath. Maurice calmly knelt down, plunged a syringe in to Ronno's leg, drew some blood from the muscle and then returning the syringe gently into its holder, placed it carefully back inside his inner jacket pocket. Then he reached down to lift the leg up by the foot, held it firmly in both hands and with a quick, twisting motion, dislocated the ankle and turned the foot all the way so it was facing backwards.

Ronno opened his mouth in a bellow but only a hoarse, grating noised filled the early morning air. Shelly let out a long muffled scream into her pillow and sat trembling violently, with tears flowing from her eyes. Maurice stood up, straightened his jacket and then turned towards her.

"Don't forget," he reinforced the warning. "If you slip up, even once, I will come back to visit you."

She nodded and sobbed uncontrollably in to the pillow.

Maurice walked towards the door, turned for one last glance at Ronno writhing on the floor, and then quietly left the room.

Shelly kept her word and from then on, frequent remarks told of what a wonderful mother she had suddenly become, and how happy and lively her little boy looked every day. Never mentioning the incident, a story had been concocted to explain Ronno's injury as a household accident.

Shelly took the planned trip with her son some weeks later leaving a fully healed Ronno — with persistent, dull pain as a permanent reminder — at home all on his own with no believable alibi. Maurice had Ronno's phone switched with a clone, carefully carrying the real one with him to his aunt's place.

Late that night when he crept in to return it, Ronno was snoring and alone in the room. Maurice kept the light off, pulled on a pair of surgical gloves, uncapped a tranquilizer syringe and with a careful movement, plunged it into Ronno's neck. There was a grunt and his eyes opened, and his head began to lift but the eyes slowly closed again and the head fell back to the pillow. A few moments went by before the snoring resumed.

After turning on the light, Maurice pulled out a small cloth and unwound it to reveal an inch long shard of glass from the builder's waste yard. Pulling out a small leather pouch in which was some cotton gauze, sterilizer, a plaster and anti-inflammatory gel, he laid them on the bed cover and then reached for Ronno's arm. After cleaning the glass and the hand, he sliced the skin of a finger with a swift movement, making sure to go the right way, just enough to be sure it bled. He waited to catch all the blood in the gauze until there was no more, then he gently cleaned the wound and after checking to see it looked right, unwrapped the plaster and applied it over the finger.

Satisfied with the result, he reached up to clean the small drop of blood on Ronno's neck, and then leaned to check the puncture wound was invisible. He applied the gel, waited a moment, and then wiped it off. There would be no tell-tale swelling or soreness by morning. Ronno would have a headache and feel very queasy when he woke up six hours later — with no memory of being sedated.

Maurice carefully returned the items into the pouch and then surveyed the scene to check he hadn't forgotten anything. He checked, yet again, before turning off the light and quietly leaving the room to disappear into the night.

Evading cameras was easy when travelling the streets — with meticulous preparation, and a new vital friend at a monitoring station.

When investigators analyzed the phone location data, Ronno was unable to explain why his phone was live and logged in the vicinity of the heinous murder on the evening, at the same time the crime was committed.

The cut on his finger was weakly explained as a slip while repairing a drawer in the bedroom.

During the intense proceedings, Ronno wisely refused to name Maurice as a suspect, certain that no proof would ever be uncovered — and revelations about Ronno's own activities from a well dressed, well groomed man he had mistreated as a child would do far more harm to the defence of his case. The argument presented — that an unknown man took some blood from his leg in an unreported incident, and then stored it for use in incriminating him sounded so far-fetched, it drew laughter in the courtroom.

The jury was unanimous and quick with a decision. Of all the people watching in court and on the news, only Maurice and Shelly knew the stunned and hollow look on Ronno's face was real.

After another two murders of people who had brutalised him in childhood years, Maurice let himself into the sprawling home of a troubled business man burdened with worry from a villainous competitor. One look at the stealthy, calm, well groomed assassin and out of fear, rather than any desire to do business, the offer of a permanent solution was accepted. The charge for the service was twenty thousand Euros.

Maurice had done his homework. It took all of five days to carry out the hit and when collecting the payment, a gaze of astonishment confirmed trust had been earned and a reliable contact inadvertently cultivated. The seeds of a deadly reputation were sown. Less than three months later, terms for the second tough assignment were laid out.

Turquoise Arrow was unleashed upon the world.

Maurice never forgot his kind teacher, Mrs. Milly Mayward, regularly checking and occasionally, following her to see if she was doing well and if anyone was troubling her. She never knew of his presence and if she had, would not have recognized him. He sent four separate, anonymous thank you cards and twice, without her knowledge, killed people who upset her; a drunken neighbour with whom she often had bitter feuds and a car salesman who sold her a faulty, unworthy vehicle.

After initially, resolutely denying that he had done so, the salesman had gone on to refuse to take any responsibility for the faulty car, or for having it rectified. The Maywards teetered on the verge of bankruptcy after attempting legal action, and then after having to pay a large bill for a repair shop to put the car right.

The car dealer was found dead very soon afterwards after, apparently, having a sudden and inexplicable change of heart during which he decided to process a full refund — and all costs incurred — directly back to the Maywards. Supposedly tortured by guilt, he then took his own life with no explanation given for why he thought he should die.

The drunken neighbour was found cold and dead on his blood soaked kitchen floor only a few days later. A large knife had torn through his shirt and his belly, sliced its way through his liver and gone halfway into a kidney. After passing out, deep in shock, he quietly bled his life away and his body was found the following day, when his grumpy wife returned from a weekend visiting their son.

Investigators leaned towards a night burglary gone wrong. Trace evidence found at the scene implicated a drug dealer, who then mysteriously and very suddenly went missing from his rented home and was never heard from again — Maurice took care of that too; the dealer was a personal project from a separate matter.

When police obtained a warrant and visited the suspect's home, the murder weapon, cleaned but carrying traces of the victim's blood, was found under the kitchen sink. A bag containing several items stolen from the dead man's home was found on the coffee table, and his watch sat in a cabinet in the dealer's bedroom.

Mrs Mayward spoke — with utter surprise — to anyone who would listen, about how two people who vexed her both happened to die within a few days of each other. Astounded by the incidents, she was taken aback by the slightly notorious reputation it bestowed. Strange rumours were whispered about spells and witchcraft and speculation suggested links to organized crime. Friends and acquaintances suddenly harboured superstition, and she paused in suspicion when they hesitated, hinting at fears of upsetting her. The headmistress regularly went over to say hello and her neighbours went out of their way to be friendly.

Chapter 3

Maurice stood a short distance behind Mr. Magatti, pointing the automatic pistol at his back.

"I don't suppose you could tell me how you beat my security?" Mr. Magatti enquired.

Maurice remained silent. The question was laden with transparent desperation — draped in a clinging wish and hopes of prolonging a life. He was unimpressed. Mr. Magatti was painfully aware that time was quickly running out.

"They sent you!" he offered. "My security is unbeatable. You are the only one who could have found a way if there was any. So here we are, unlikely as it ever should have been. I'll be a blue-breasted Robin if I could figure any way you did it."

Still alive, he knew he had recaptured his assassin's interest.

"Humour me!" he reached out again. "Just something to ponder in my final seconds." He tried to sound casual. "I'm doing you a favour!" he was scraping the bottom of the barrel. "Great skill... unmatched talent! Best in the world in my opinion! And yet, who else will you tell? Lonely existence keeping it all to yourself, isn't it?"

He appeared to have done enough to buy another minute or two. His assassin stirred and the calm, husky voice carried over again.

"Wasn't easy." Maurice replied with the casualness of answering questions about the weather. He paused for some moments before adding an explanation and outlining how the hard drive was hacked with write-over codes. At a pre-defined time, they launched a visual data loop.

"It's going to self-expire! It will permanently delete. They're never going to know. When they look, it will be like it was never even there." He paused to savour the satisfaction and to allow Mr. Magatti to digest the information. "They'll see nothing but static when they play it back later." he added with certainty.

Mr. Magatti remained silent, waiting for more information.

"The sensors were tougher." Turquoise Arrow verged on bragging.

The calm voice floated how an induced power surge had over-tasked the systems, and then talked about copper and aluminium powder sprays that cause read errors when sensors reboot.

"Takes three hundred and fifty seconds to re-calibrate themselves and another twenty minutes to soundly reconfigure the grid. That's after a few attempts. They'll be back on eventually. Won't matter on my way out!"

Within peripheral vision, just out of direct view to the left, Mr. Magatti suddenly thought he saw a movement in the trees; a fleeting shadow, brief and inconsequential. If he didn't know the woods well, he might have missed it. With both hands still clasped behind his back, he casually ran his thumb along the index finger — an ordinary gesture for anyone in deep thought, but a crucial, split second diversion to a trained killer; a quick glance down to distract his assassin's eyes.

"When you're done, make your way over to the right," he offered, hoping the attempt to sound calm would be worth the effort. "Stay at the edge of the trees and keep going all the way. Don't stop until you're practically under the large oak. There's a clear censor blind spot most of the way, until a few paces after it. If they're back on, that is going to buy you a little time."

For the first time, Maurice nearly broke into a half smile. It was utmost respect from a high profile target. Mr. Magatti was being truthful; the tone of voice assured that. He paused, impressed by the obvious, token reward; a barter trade for knowing how the system was beaten. Other men he assassinated who had the honour of knowing their fate all acted differently. Most made desperate attempts at deception. Others tried to get away and a few tried to fight back. A last-ditch plan was to resort to plain bribery. None had ever reached out with the level of respect that had just been shown. Maurice began to feel the same instinct towards Mr. Magatti as he did for the Maywards.

His finger hovered over the trigger. For the first time in his clean and untainted career, Turquoise Arrow hesitated with an acquired target. A thought flashed that he would not mind if Mr. Magatti lived. If there were ways to abandon the contract, he would have considered them. Faint sentiments of regret fluttered, and then faltered and shrivelled away before there was opportunity to blossom.

"Much appreciated," he mumbled, only loud enough to carry over the bubbling of the fountain.

Mr. Magatti nodded slowly. The gratitude from Turquoise Arrow was for the acknowledgement and not for the information — his strategy was paying off. His killer's hesitation broadcast cracks in the resolve and slight turbulence in his psyche, seedlings that could take root and be a game changer. With all means of stalling for time nearly exhausted, he asked the only other question to which he wanted an answer. Deliberately clearing his throat to warn that he was about to speak, he waited for a moment before summoning up confidence to hide badly frayed nerves.

"What kind of name is Turquoise Arrow? Did you steal it from an eighties movie?" He paused and closed his eyes, almost regretting the approach.

Behind him, ever so slightly, Turquoise Arrow's face lightened with a hint of a suppressed smile. In any other circumstances, he would have pulled the trigger. But a faint tug in unknown depths plucked at powerful memories of the kind teacher in school — kind... kind... Mrs Mayward. And spongy tentacles swirled and uncoiled from another realm, stretching out in realm-less length with padded infundibula. He saw them, waving in slow motion, some in embrace of restraint, a giant tentacle on his shoulder, and one around each leg, urging questions, urging thoughts, and feeling, and protection, and purging out just a few more consuming memories, and reaching out to stroke his hair, and finally, to place a giant, calming, fleshy pedipalp over his darkened, cold heart, with everlasting prom-ises the foamy jaws would never devour — for him, they would remain foam, even though not to others. But unforeseen mentions tumbled fleetingly in the haze, with feathery clues that they could remain foam for Mr. Magatti too. The conflict in Turquoise Arrow simmered, barely contained. He relaxed his stance and allowed his finger to move nearly half an inch away from the trigger.

"It's not my name." the reply floated — eventually — past gently writhing tentacles that only the assassin could see.

Mr. Magatti understood. It had to be linked to some sort of precious symbol, or an object bestowed with deep, personal meaning. They stood in bonded silence while he waited for an explanation.

"I found it in a builder's waste yard."

There was another long pause. Mr. Magatti was patient.

"It's twenty five inches long, half an inch in diameter, made of high grade, tempered steel and painted bright turquoise. Workmanship imbued with the real soul of the blacksmith! You can feel its essence! I used it to kill my aunt. It's in a crystal glass case now, professionally mounted."

Mr. Magatti understood. The name must be linked to his assassin's first ever kill. Pangs of sympathy flickered and he very nearly turned around. Turquoise Arrow was a consequence of trauma in childhood.

As Maurice described the killing, vague recollections stirred in Mr. Magatti's mind. He scoured for more details. Newspapers had said the cruelly murdered woman's boyfriend was convicted for the crime.

"Nice touch taking the boyfriend down," he tossed out casually.

Maurice was extremely impressed. Mr. Magatti knew of the incident.

"*Ex* boyfriend!" he corrected. "The one she was with did nothing to me."

"Hm! The ex!" Mr. Magatti nodded in approval. "The Reno guy? Did he do something?"

"Ronno! He did a lot of things!"

"Maybe one day you could tell me all about it." Mr. Magatti joked.

Both men genuinely smiled.

Another short silence endured as Maurice faltered among the tentacles, his finger wanting to go to the trigger, raging in argument about the assignment.

"Thank you!" Mr. Magatti said with as much sincerity as could be commanded in a voice.

Both men, in their own way, found they enjoyed the moment. On both minds endeared thoughts that in different circumstances, the likelihood was they would have ended up great friends.

Maurice stood with finger stalled a quarter of an inch from the trigger. It was going to be the most regretful kill for Turquoise Arrow.

Chapter 4

In a ramshackle, dusty, rough neighbourhood in South America, the desperately poor lady shuffled in the dead of night, with a blank look and eyes swimming in hollow submission. The little bundle she wielded was only two days old and she gasped into the ether when her fingers finally opened and allowed helpless Frederick to fall into the pit latrine.

Half an hour went by while he precariously floated — in a stroke of what some later described as good fortune, having landed face up — among wriggling maggots and squirming worms, on the four foot deep sludge pool of human excrement. Well into the second half hour, a wandering neighbour in need of the facility, perked an ear in disbelief at the muffled, pitiful cries.

Running from assumptions of an otherworldly spirit, neighbours were roused by panicked cries and screams of alarm. Gasps of horror reverberated when the truth became apparent. The entire neighbourhood tumbled out, brandishing heavy tools to dig beyond the latrine floor and retrieve the weakening baby.

He was adopted by a friendly American couple called the Malcolms and given the first name "Robert". The future looked bright until three years later when a change in circumstances forced them to a decision to pack up and go back home. The adoption papers for little Robert were slightly inaccurate and the courts would not allow issue of any travel documents. The Malcolms found it difficult to prove the origins of the boy and unable to locate the mother, or in any way explain the true identity of the father, it would prove far too complicated for the process to go ahead.

They travelled back home and left Robert with a nanny — along with all the money they could spare for expenses — but only a week later, on a trip to the countryside to visit her parents, his nanny was killed in a horrific, local bus crash and all contact with little Robert was lost.

Two years later, in a lavish cocktail party hosted by Mr. Magatti, a glum expression on one of the full time maids reached out through the sea of politeness and niceties. Among nods and friendly gestures, he eventually wound his way to intercept the gloomy helper and casually enquired about her wellbeing. She tried, but failed, to give a coherent answer, immediately breaking down, far too upset to speak. He did something unusual and asked her back to his study until she could calm down and compose herself.

In between shaking sobs, Katalina the maid spoke about a violently abused and neglected little boy she had been working to help, who lived back in her home country. He had suddenly gone missing. Mr. Magatti, driven by instinctive, primal sympathy, handed over a wad of money and sent her home on condition that she came back to see him the following day.

At they appointed time, they met alone in his study and, far more composed, she told him about the turbulent life of little Robert: After the tragic death of his nanny, the family had sent him a short distance away to a close and long-term neighbour, who then sent him to a cousin with four children of her own. The cousin's shaky relationship broke down a few months later and her abusive husband, a loud and brutal man named Alfonso, threatened extreme violence if she tried to take the children.

Poor Robert was left with Alfonso and his mistress, an opinion-ated, vicious and heartless woman with the unlikely name 'Joselin'. He was neglected, frequently starved and regularly attacked — even the four children took pleasure in inflicting injuries. A friendly neighbour finally gathered a large mob to rescue him and the family reluctantly allowed him out and let him go. Katalina, her family and a cousin whom they lived with were tasked with raising and taking care of the boy.

Katalina travelled to the United Kingdom a short while later to find a better paying job, and regularly sent money to help with little Robert's care. Traumatized and clearly psychologically disturbed, Robert Frederick seemed to be recovering well and had finally began to attend and settle at the local school. With word of his disap-pearance, there was good reason to believe that he may have been abducted and the family, assisted by most of the neighbourhood, were out in all hours searching everywhere for him. Katalina, over-wrought with worry, could do nothing but anxiously wait for any news.

Mr. Magatti immediately reached out with offers of help, suggesting phone calls he could make and funds to ease rising burdens. Six days later, little Robert was located, badly beaten, very unwell and locked up in Alfonso's home. Joselin had colluded, participating in assaulting him. Savouring the punishment, she was even more ruthless than her heartless boyfriend.

Mr. Magatti insisted on paying for Robert to be flown in to the country so Katalina could live with him and raise him as her own son. A little over a month later, when all the paperwork was complete, he glanced over at her grateful, sparkling face as she sat in the back seat of the Rolls Royce with him, while the chauffer skilfully guided them in an air-conditioned, gliding, soft classical music infused cloud to the airport.

When Mr. Magatti met him, he was disturbed by the haunted, detached look in the pained, six year old eyes. When opportunity arose, he whispered to Katalina that he would do all within his own power and ability to provide the sort of life the little boy must dream of.

With his wife and three children on holiday in Canada, he made the tactical decision, turned to Katalina, and asked if he could adopt him. Her stunned expression said more than the stuttered words tumbled out in disbelief among sobs of gratitude. But the deal had to be a secret. He offered to stump up for a three bedroom, furnished house, in which she could live free of charge while caring for Robert. To assist with household costs and for control of the schedules, he would promote her to oversee all mansion operations — a spontaneously made up role — to help quell rumours about how she could afford the home.

Katalina, without hesitation, accepted the new arrangement. In a three bedroom, detached home with a large garden and her own car, she could provide a life for Robert only ever dreamed of.

Over the years, Mr. Magatti frequently visited. Fond afternoons and evenings were spent playing football, computer games, going fishing, mock wrestling, mock fighting and working on hobby based projects until late in the evening when the tired boy went to bed. Then he would enjoy long conversations with Katalina where her joyful face and new-found laughter brightened up the charged night. She bore two more children, both boys who lived a joyful life, blessed with a doting mother who gazed at them with fascination.

Robert Frederick Malcolm finally had the parents he had always dreamed of, and though strictly forbidden from discussing the family secret with any outsiders, his eyes sparkled every moment spent in their presence. The secret was a great adventure, and he felt for his attentive, adoptive mother and father, the closest thing to what he imagined could be love for one's parents.

Robert, just like Maurice, could feel nothing else and a cold, blank stare filled the rest of his existence: hidden desires became evident one day when Katalina caught him just in time, about to kill the family dog.

Later on the same evening, both of his adoptive parents — two of the only four people he felt a connection to — began to teach and guide him to control the lurking impulses.

Robert stumbled upon his code name almost as inadvertently as Maurice happened to stumble upon his. When he was nineteen, he began intensive self defence and, driving himself to outer limits of human endurance, obtained a second level black belt within four years. He was disappointed. The goal all along was fifth level, but wisdom and inner peace and mental preparation took longer than a keen young adult dared hope for — especially when immersed deep in two other combat arts along with weapons training and high level survival skills.

When he was twenty three, using a false identity, he sneaked off after finding a way to travel by sea to South America. The well groomed, smartly dressed, extremely athletic man was a world away from the little boy who began a fragile life in unpredictable circumstances.

His destination, when he arrived, looked nearly as he remembered. There were a few different buildings, a new road, some new shops and a bridge halfway under construction less than half a mile away. The streets and the buildings looked far smaller and more cramped but he understood it was merely a matter of personal perspective: he had more than doubled in height since he last saw the neighbourhood.

The house was easy to find and he settled down across the street in a battered rented car adorned with customary tinted windows — a fashion trend he was pleased to find was raging in the nation; every other car boasted bright, luminous paintwork, garish racing stickers, stylish after-market wheels and nearly all had fully rolled up, darkened windows. Robert was eternally grateful for the unique trend as he sat, unseen, a short distance from the property. He cranked the whirring air-conditioning all the way to maximum and a dank, mouldy smell from the vents intensified. They puffed out just enough to keep the interior comfortable.

The house looked very much the same as he could recall, though smaller, far dirtier and with a new, foliage coloured door that looked hand-made to order by a qualified carpenter. He wasn't surprised they painted the door bright, leafy green. It appeared to be a trend favoured across the whole region and judging by the doors on some ramshackle properties, seemed to have been a taste spanning several generations. It clashed with the dull, matt yellow on exterior walls and with the brown, glossy paint protecting frames of hinged windows.

Nine days later, after meticulous planning, he let himself into the house in the dead of night.

Joselin and Alfonso, his former custodians were asleep in their bedroom and two of the four children, also young adults by then, snored softly in other rooms. After peeking in, he quietly shut their doors and let them be. They were young when they hurt him. They couldn't have understood.

He let himself into Joselin and Alfonso's room, switched on the ceiling light, and watched the rhythmic rising and falling of the two sleeping forms tucked under the covers. Airy, uneven snoring rasped from one of them and they occupied the same dark blue, metal framed bed from way back when he was a child; in these parts, beds remained as long as they were viable. He paused to see if either one of the sleeping forms stirred and when no movement occurred, he stepped forward slowly, treading softly on the handmade, designer, rubber soled shoes, until he saw the two heads sunk into matching pillows.

Gliding to the foot of the bed, he stopped and squatted down low, then reached to run the tips of his fingers down one of the metal legs. His eyes closed at the touch of the cold, visibly rough surface where flakes of paint had chipped away, ground off by a rope driven by juvenile anguish. He opened his eyes to check his wrists. Lines where the rope had burned were only just visible. He saw Joselin's face in his mind — gleefully callous — and he smelled the minty lotion she had always slathered herself in. He hadn't smelled it for years but the memories lingered. With no suggestion or even a hint of it in the real air, the distinct memory clawed painfully in his mind — and a minty elbow struck rudely against the side of his head, while minty hands, amidst grunts, tied his wrists to the metal, and all the little boy could do was sit murmuring in terror.

He winced at each incident — eleven of them in total, each one clear in his mind as though living it all over again. He saw the sneer on her face and recoiled at the whistle of the telephone cable swinging faster than his eyes could see, aimed at the unprotected body of the little child.

A shiver ran down his spine as deep in his troubled mind, he felt the pain once more, and relentless terror boiled like bubbling tar, tainted with tears and searing pain, churning into deep-burgundy, hovering lumps, each the size of a large pillow, scented generously with mint, crowding him, surrounding him, and more of them growing, sprouting out of nowhere, all of them with writhing skin that looked like raw flesh, and he didn't know whether they were friends or foes but their presence brewed a realm where sanity was banished in unwilling desperation. They were birthed here, first emerged here, and he saw them yet again — he saw them every single day. Even after he grew up, they never went away. At first, he had marvelled at how everybody else walked fearlessly through them, and how they ignored them. Only later did he know they appeared only for his eyes, and much later, he knew they lived only in his mind.

The fourth time he was tied up and the phone cable began to swing, he bit nearly half the way through the side of his tongue. She paused at the sight of red colour dripping down his chin, only to start again when in a stuttering sob, a little splash made its way on to her cream coloured blouse.

On one occasion, she left him tied up, half conscious, with no food or water for nearly two days, lashing at him several times during the agonizing ordeal and kicking or hitting him every time she walked past — until she sprained her own ankle when, in an absent minded kick aimed at his ribs, her foot made awkward contact in a way nature despised.

A more savage attack was unleashed, knocking out three of his teeth when, unable to go to the toilet, he let go and wet himself before the end of the first day. Joselin then pulled off his urine soaked shorts and pushed them over his head, covering his face all the way to the neck, and leaving him tied up and barely able to breathe, until late evening on the following day when they desired privacy.

Robert winced, closed his eyes and tried shaking off the memory. Slowly, he stood up, pulled a wicker chair standing unassumingly near the wall and sat next to the bed only two feet from Alfonso. Reaching to his leg, he pulled out a metal bar nestling in a purposed holder securely strapped to the outside of his shin. He gripped the end and lowered it until the bar was out of sight. A solitary tear rolled from one of his eyes as memories thundered, re-awakened by proximity to the couple.

He looked over at Joselin. Half her face was in the pillow, breathing rhythmically, with eyeballs dancing behind gracefully aged eyelids. Peaceful sleep appeared to hide the scorn he knew lurked beneath. He saw her real face again, not the peaceful sleeping one, all those years ago, when he desperately reached out to protect himself from a plastic coated, copper cable swung in demonic frenzy. She grabbed at his defensive hand and twisted the little finger away from all the others, until a noise announced it had disconnected from the socket. He cried so hard with pain, his voice was hoarse for days.

Watching the vicious, sleeping pair, Robert's mind vanished under the foreboding, burgundy lumps that only he could ever see, to replay the days when they stole him that last time and locked him in the back room. They carried on hurting him, even when he cried out for his unknown mummy, and they laughed out heartily when in desperation, he screamed for the president.

Only a child, Robert had heard stories of a man who was more powerful than everybody else in the whole town. He had a big army with metal tanks and big trucks and scary guns and many people had to listen to what he said. With no one else to call upon, he cried for this hero man. The man called the "President" was big and strong and powerful and if he came and told them to stop, they would have to obey.

Joselin and Alfonso laughed long and heartily and lied to him, saying the president was just in the shower — and then that he was doing his homework and would come when he was finished. Alfonso used a metal rod to hit his toes and ankles and Joselin whipped him with a frayed phone cable. Then she got a hammer, saying she would crack his head like a coconut. Choked with fear, drowned in pain, he sunk further into insanity.

Days passed in turmoil until good people nearby assembled by the front door and shouted at Alfonso. They stormed in, still shouting, loudly opened the door to the room and rescued him, while angry with Joselin and Alfonso. After a while, they sent him on a big plane to Katalina... sweet, kind Katalina, kind, loving, earthly angel — his saviour and his new mother — to whom his soul and mind became bound to forever, and daddy Magatti, his new, kind and wonderful father, who came once in a while to visit, and played football and wrestling and bought new computer games which they

314

both played together. And even though his daddy could play most games better, he always held back just so Robert could win.

Magatti and Katalina were earthly gods in his eyes and a twitch of homesickness flickered, a flash of two divine faces, their kind smiles and loving eyes, and he longed to see them both again, to be near them, to feel safe, away from burgundy invaders and time travel trips to minty torment and telephone wires.

The trip into his dark memories dissolved into their kind ways.

Joselin was the first to stir. Seeing the light was on, she began to raise her head to investigate but stopped dead at the bizarre sight of a man watching them. She gasped, jumped back in fear and then shook Alfonso to wake him. Robert looked them straight in the eyes and slowly raised one finger to his silent lips. Something about his expression betrayed the imminent danger. It was clear their coming ordeal would be easier endured if they precisely and calmly followed every instruction.

"Do you remember me?" he asked softly.

Joselin tentatively sat up. Alfonso raised himself on his elbows and they both nervously shook their heads. Much taller, extremely athletic, well groomed and dressed in a dark, tailored, designer suit, he was unsurprised by the lack of recognition. He stared for a few moments but both were too frightened to speak. Alfonso began to get up but Joselin firmly held his arm and pulled him back on to the bed.

Robert lifted one hand with the palm oriented towards them and with fingers tightly held together. It took a brief moment for the pair to notice the little finger was bent and slightly misaligned.

"You broke my little finger," he said, looking straight at Joselin.

The horror of why he was there dawned like a thunder clap.

He spoke slowly and very softly.

"I need both of you to remain still and very quiet and I will explain what all the pain you inflicted upon me does to a little child."

He paused to wait until they nodded, never taking his eyes off theirs.

"After you have understood, you will have five minutes to convince me of any reason why I should spare you."

The staring eyes and toxic vapours from the ice-cold demeanour cast to them that there was nothing within their combined power to uncover ways to turn him around and earn his forgiveness.

Almost in slow motion, all happening in a split second, Robert saw the narrowing eyes, the slight tilt of the head and subtle lean of her shoulders, and the tell-tale requisite intake of breath that told him, faster than the blink of an eye, that Joselin was in the process of beginning to scream. Before the sound could leave her throat, the metal bar slammed into her lower jaw with a squelching crack, splitting it into several pieces and dislodging it from its mounting.

Alfonso turned and reached for his wife who had fallen back onto her pillow. She spluttered and gasped for breath in his arms. He turned to glare at Robert.

"You animal—!" he began to shout but the second word barely left his throat when the metal bar flashed and smashed into his mouth. He fell backwards on to the bed, dazed and choking on fragments of teeth.

Already standing, Robert leaned and looked each one in the eye.

"I distinctly requested that both of you remain quiet!"

He recoiled as a watery cough sprayed substance into the air. There was a lot of blood, more than he had ever seen from up close:

he had never considered that humans carried so much inside the veins.

He watched for a while, hoping for a sense of accomplishment, or some relief from the turmoil and memories. There was nothing; no relief, no lifting of shadows — only pity watching Joselin cough and gurgle on the bed. Blood was creeping into her lungs and she was gradually beginning to drown. Coughing through a smashed jaw looked and sounded inhumanly excruciating.

Deciding to end her misery, he swung the metal bar, at near full strength, dead centre onto her forehead. It pounded with a sickening squelch and the front of her skull shattered and grotesquely caved in like a squashed, fleshy tin can. Her entire body shuddered and shook and he watched as it went limp and with a last judder in protest, finally stopped moving. Her eyes, still open, carried on rolling upwards until the irises vanished underneath the upper eyelids, leaving only the bloodied white eyeballs still visible.

He leaned down and looked into Alfonso's wide, frightened eyes, trying to understand the odd expression on his face. There was terror, distinct hatred and something difficult to decipher. Was he pleading? Was he still attempting to beg for his life? Surely, he couldn't expect any mercy! They were both beyond redemption.

"I did not cause this!" Robert snapped authoritatively. "I am not responsible for it!"

If Alfonso had listened to the cries all those years ago, he could have saved them both, maybe even saved Joselin! There would be no redemption. Alfonso made the choice for them. Robert was there merely to fulfil their destinies.

"It may console you to know this," Robert said to Alfonso's eyes, "I will spare your two children who are fast asleep in their beds!"

Alfonso tried to speak, but the metal bar came down again. For a moment, there was violent shuddering, limbs abnormally extended and toes and fingers curled beyond realistic physical limits. Robert stepped back and calmly watched the bloodied grimace gradually mellow into red, distorted emptiness. The body eventually relaxed, and the battered head slowly settled into the pillow.

Robert sat back down, mesmerised by all the blood. The metal sprung bed sagged noticeably in the middle, guiding all liquid to soak through the mattress and emerge in one elastic trickle from underneath the bed. There was still no relief, only mild satisfaction. It felt slightly better knowing the people who caused so much pain were no longer among the living.

As he began to stand up to leave, there was a jingling noise in the window. Their grey and white coloured cat jumped in onto the window sill and then down to the tiled floor. It froze and stood still, evidently wary of the stranger. He put down the metal bar, smiled, leaned forward with one hand extended and softly clicked his fingers. Deciding he was not a threat, it majestically padded over, rubbed across his shin and began purring contentedly.

Robert stroked the cat, scratched it playfully behind the ears, ran his hand along its back and gently tickled under its chin. After purring in ecstasy, it paused in curiosity at the dark trickle flowing from under the silent bed. Padding a few steps towards the ever expanding, crimson puddle, it leaned down to sniff and then recoiled in disgust.

The cat turned around, half-heartedly rubbed onto his leg and with some more jingling, jumped up on to the foot of the bed where it stood warily staring at its motionless masters. Looking around, clearly in distress, it meowed pitifully several times, as though calling to celestial minders to announce a great misfortune. After a short while of communication with the unseen, it moved back and sat in a corner, licked one of its front legs, and then reached up with a rear one to vigorously scratch its neck.

Robert sat captivated and mesmerized by the scene. Small metallic bells clinging to the collar around the hairy neck jingled with each motion, sending a mellow sound ringing into the room. As the cat acrobatically scratched behind its ear, the collar rang and tinkled with a soft, metallic note chiming a mystical soothing and a gentle climax to the harrowing and gruesome events of the night. He watched and listened, transfixed and hypnotized in an odd enchantment of the surreal moment. When the cat was done scratching, it paused to lazily glance around before punctuating the silence with occasional tinkling, cleaning and grooming itself to feline perfection.

Robert stood, stepped forward and reached over to feel around the freshly groomed neck. The cat leaned into his palm and rubbed affectionately against his fingers. Reaching around with both hands, he slowly unfastened the collar and gently lifted it away. The cat shook its head, scratched again, stared despondently at the two still forms on the bed, and then embarked on more grooming. Robert held the collar in between his thumb and index finger and raised it up to eye level. It was burgundy, made of waterproofed, heavy, interwoven cloth with five bulb-shaped, aluminium bells hand-sewn on to it.

A sudden decision — in a deluge of invoked inspiration!

A new career...

A new path...

A new secret life...

Very softly, he whispered what was going to become his code name.

"Jingle!"

Chapter 5

From the corner of his eye, Mr. Magatti saw the flash of light in the trees to the left, close to where he first thought he had seen a slight movement. He knew his assassin must have seen it too but that did not matter; some things happened in a way that was fast enough that knowing of them would be of no help.

A fraction of a second... and he heard a dull, metallic clang reverberate behind him, followed by the sound made by a human caught off guard.

"Ah!"

A series of metallic clattering clapped three or four times as a gun attempted to bounce on the stone floor of the courtyard and in that short moment, Mr. Magatti knew he was going to live.

He stood still and waited until a figure emerged from the shadows and for the first time, Mr. Magatti turned to see his assassin.

His first thought was that he was very impressed with the designer suit. He didn't particularly like it, but it clearly fit very well, and the dark material radiated quality of tailoring. Even while unnecessary, Turquoise Arrow clearly preferred dressing impressively. On his knees clutching his left hand, his eyes were closed in super-human effort at remaining calm. Dark red streaks dripping from in between the fingers of the uninjured hand trickled down to a small, expanding puddle on the stonework.

Maurice slowly raised his right hand to reach into his jacket and Mr. Magatti winced as he saw the mess left by the bullet. He was surprised to see that Turquoise Arrow was actually left handed, a small but very useful fact he had not been aware of. He remained calm as Maurice reached into an inner pocket; the man he was looking at was far too intelligent to be drawing a concealed weapon.

The dark figure that fired the shot emerged from the trees holding a high powered, stubby rifle — still raised and ready. Maurice, through a carefully controlled haze of agony, guessed the figure was not a policeman, or any individual with connections to security. If he had been, the weapon would immediately have fired again at the sight of the uninjured hand reaching into a pocket.

Few people had such intense sense of awareness and not many of those could be calm in such a moment. Only a similar mind would know the actions of Turquoise Arrow and Maurice suddenly guessed who the dark figure had to be. Few people were that stealthy. Few would have succeeded. He glanced up again to confirm his suspicions.

Very slowly — to avoid pain rather than for caution — he pulled out a handkerchief, shook it till it unfolded, and then used his teeth to help him fold it halfway into a triangle before wrapping it tenderly around his injured left hand.

Mr. Magatti watched in silence. Turquoise Arrow held himself well. Despite the obvious agony, he was eerily calm and made no unnecessary movements.

There were faint and careful footsteps as the dark figure caught up to them.

"You're late!" Mr Magatti called out without turning to look back.

The man walked up and stood two feet away from Mr Magatti's right shoulder. The high powered, stubby rifle remained aimed at Maurice.

"Every sign showed things were lined up for tomorrow," the man casually replied, with a hint of irritation at getting so easily fooled. "He's slippery. I must admit he's one of the best. My tracker couldn't find him and I figured there was only one place left to look." He nodded in acknowledgement. "He came a day early! Decoy plan! Very clever!"

Maurice cradled his left hand, kept his eyes on the stonework and focussed on breathing. Something was very odd about the new situation. Glancing at the two men, he tried to figure out what it was that bothered him. The way they stood... the body language... none of it was right. They stood too close together... spoke too casually...

He glanced at the gun on the floor, barely three feet away. It was too risky to reach for it — and besides, it had taken a hit and might misfire. There was still the small, six shot pistol hidden in his belt. He would have to use his right hand, which was a fraction slower — plus double the time for intense pain obscuring his senses. Even in the best case scenario, it would be at least half a second to retrieve and fire it — a grinding lifetime in the world of high level killers. Had the man holding the rifle been ordinary security, both he and Mr. Magatti would already be dead. Maurice settled on playing along to wait for an opportunity.

Mr. Magatti walked slowly towards the man who had nearly killed him. Careful to keep his distance, he stretched out a leg and kicked away the gun that lay within grasp of the assassin. After backing up a few feet, he looked at the kneeling figure.

"Turquoise Arrow!" he made certain his tone still conveyed respect. "Or shall I call you Maurice Smith!"

Maurice glanced up and very slightly bowed his head. Then he turned to look at the dark figure. The man was dressed in tight fitting, near black, cotton trousers, a grey turtle neck and a buttoned up, dark, tailored jacket. His face and head were covered by a dark-grey balaclava leaving only the sharp eyes, unblinking and resolutely focussed on the target. The athletic posture, impressive taste in clothing and the superb marksmanship were unmistakeable.

"I know who you are!" Maurice said, staring at the gunman. "Jingle!" He spat the name as though a clod of vile sludge. "Couldn't resist the money?" His tone was bundled heavy with scorn. The assassin's code strictly forbade attacking one of their own — and if it came to it, for four times the usual asking price.

"I'm not paying him a single scrap of anything for this!" Mr. Magatti interjected.

Maurice was puzzled. How could a man like Jingle take an assignment for no pay? He guessed it was not blackmail; some unfortunate souls had discovered — at a high cost — that blackmailing an assassin was a terrible idea. What sinister hold could Mr. Magatti have over such a man? Maurice had a sudden thought but then dismissed it from his mind: he would have known if they were related. Perhaps a distant in-law? Was he married into the family? Not a chance! Such a thing would be impossible to hide.

Mr. Magatti smiled as Maurice glanced again at the dark figure. Raising his hand with an open palm, he gestured towards the gunman.

"Mr Turquoise Arrow—" Mr. Magatti spoke with theatrical formality, "may I present the one and only, a stealth master, Jingle, or Robert Frederick Malcolm, who is, I am very proud to say, my son!"

He paused long enough to savour the stunned look on Maurice.

"High level killers do come up with the strangest names!" Mr. Magatti broke out again after a suitable silence. "Stroke of genius if you ask me. I could shout them out to a stadium well filled to capacity and everyone would assume I was talking about race horses!"

Maurice was no longer listening. Consumed by a raging, new reality of the situation, his mind was re-calculating, searching for an option, and replaying every word spoken with his contact. Did anyone else know about this? Was it all a set up? His eyes closed as another wave of agony tore through his hand.

Mr. Magatti nodded at the turmoil engulfing Maurice. Only two others knew the full story of little Robert; Katalina and the long time and very dependable chauffer. Turquoise Arrow had just joined a very exclusive club.

"Two out of three of some of the most deadly assassins in the western hemisphere!" Mr. Magatti remarked. "If only Hedgerow Pixie was here! We'd have the trio! I'll be a Shire horse if I couldn't figure what a party that would be! Wouldn't you agree?"

The two assassins glanced at him, surprised by his enthusiasm.

"I do honestly enjoy the way you happen upon your names!" he distractedly continued. "They have deep meaning. They define you and your journeys. Identities bestowed by the circumstances that raised the floodgates to your darkness, and released it upon an unsuspecting but complicit world!"

He paused and smiled, mesmerised and caught up in the moment.

"Yours are epic identities, unlike Laser Sam or Exterminator or the other fellow called Papa Pounder. Those names fester and repugnantly smother the tongue like a half melted, five year old mouldy tub of rancid lard!"

Lesser assassins repulsed him. Their approach was vexing. Their work tainted by shortcomings on professionalism. Laser Sam, Exterminator and Papa Pounder were lower assassins who never truly had what it took to be the very best. What they lacked in finesse and intellectual intelligence was made up for in brutality and with unbounded greed — a sure way to guarantee short lives for their careers.

Laser Sam, who earned the code name through his love of the laser sighter mounted on his favourite pistol, was captured by police in Chicago when, in an amateurish mistake, he lost the key to a door that was a crucial escape route. Sentenced and locked up for life after the trial, there were no realistic options for ever legally getting out.

Exterminator committed the forbidden, loathsome sin of accepting a hefty payment to kill the lifelong, best friend of another working assassin. It took all of half a day to track him down after the murder and fortunately for him, the hunter, whose friend he had just terminated, dispatched him near instantly with four gunshots to the chest. They could have done all manner of vile things in revenge, but by following the code, the assassin enhanced his reputation.

Papa Pounder, a thick-set, six foot plus, vicious hunk of a brutal killer, wasn't so lucky. His own fists served as the favourite weapon and on his last paid assignment, his victim's brother cancelled a trip and happened to walk back in just as he was beginning his work. The brother turned out to be quite a pounder himself and by the time they were finished, Papa Pounder could only be identified by the gold plated belt buckle forged in the letters "PP".

The two brothers succeeded in extracting from Papa Pounder, the name of the unfortunate millionaire who had paid for the hit. More vigorous pounding was dished out that evening. Bound and gagged, the businessman's wife watched in horror as her husband's life was unrelentingly pummelled away. They were kind enough to say goodbye and untie her before leaving and the whole troubling issue was finally left at that. In their world, it was wiser to leave all things be if an assassin or professionals involved in a successful hit openly faced vengeance from grieving family members. If friends or relatives of a victim happened to pay a visit, opinions by all was that the matter was settled.

Robert relaxed and gradually lowered the rifle a few inches, keeping a steady grip on the handle and a finger on the trigger. Body language from Turquoise Arrow suggested no immediate threat and Robert rode on instincts and subtle, leaking visual cues.

The great Turquoise Arrow appeared truly defeated.

Chapter 6

The Brankly's, a couple with one child of their own, adopted another, solely for the money paid to foster parents. With a spare room in their three bedroom, semi-detached property, they registered for the monthly pay to help an unwanted child. Outsiders described the home as serene — even joyful — but the violence and neglect indoors was wretched and ruthless. Bruises and injuries were explained away as accidents and few questioned why they tended to only happen to one child. Marko Bernard Brankly, the young adopted boy was marinating in turmoil and simmering in turbulence that would, some years later, serve up Hedgerow Pixie.

The couple loved a tidy garden. Mrs Brankly was often seen milling about with new buds and a handy weeding trowel. Edward Brankly loved wheeling out contraptions and tools with which he would gradually tread sections of the garden, like a militaristic surgeon, among twigs and shredded leaves, until every visible bush — and eventually, the living lawn — looked as preened as though sculpted by an artist.

Mrs Brankly swooned over figurines and garden statues, often hovering on the verge of declaring them sentient. The declaration hovered ever closer to reality when in the vicinity of a beautifully forged, two foot high, bronze pixie, standing on a painted plinth, strategically located in one corner of the garden next to a meticulously nurtured hedgerow.

Simon, the Brankly's son, took the greatest pleasure in brutalizing Marko and was a constant source of the bruising and scarring. Marko bore the beatings so stoically on two occasions that he suffered a concussion, a cracked skull and a broken nose before Simon's fists and shoes stopped raining down on him.

When he was eight, Marko lost four upper teeth when Simon, who was three years older, hit him with a brick. The Branklys refused to pay for dental implants and reluctantly settled a bill for cheap, plastic, gap-fillers after concern from his teachers grew into voiced protests.

The incidents were explained away as unfortunate accidents that happened while the two boys raced on their bicycles out in the family garden. If anyone had looked into it, they would quickly have discovered that both bicycles in the home belonged only to Simon, and that Marko was strictly forbidden from riding any of them.

Marko walked away from the home after turning seventeen, a disturbed, unstable, yet focussed young man.

Shortly after his twenty first birthday, Marko paid the Branklys a visit. Eleven weeks of careful planning had narrowed it to two evenings when Simon would be staying over to help with a new garden wall. With over three years intensive training, the family stood no chance against the intruder and three days later when their battered bodies were discovered, Marko was furthest from any suspicion. The contents of the safe and all the jewellery was gone and police deduced from strategic and haphazard evidence, that it had to be a heist gone terribly wrong.

Marko beautifully played the role of grieving son and brother; so convincing was the sorrow and forlorn expression that the home and all belongings were legally turned over to him. With no desire for a dwelling festering in sour memories, he touched hearts in the neighbourhood by donating it to charity.

Seven days later, he throttled down the power on a rented speed boat and casually watched the ripples as it coasted to a stop. Dancing gently on the ocean, he reached for the binoculars and scanned the grey waters. The silhouette of a large ship, made a bath toy by the distance, was silently crawling in the Western horizon. Nothing else but the sea and occasional scattered clouds were visible, even on maximum zoom.

Reaching into his leather bag, he pulled out a canvas pouch, laden with a lead slab on the inside for more weight, and bound up in home-made leather straps in loose knots — just enough to ensure the whole package reached the sea bed. The fine sand would swallow it, unquestioning and welcoming and in no time at all, the Brankly's jewellery — every painful portion of it — would be lost from human civilization forever.

Only one treasured object held value for Marko; if investigators of the killings had been more thorough, they would have picked up clues of an item missing from the scene. In the far corner of the garden, on the pristine lawn near an immaculate hedgerow, was a circular patch of earth less than six inches wide. If the statue mounted on the plinth whose base had obstructed the growth was located and examined, the weight and size, the surface and the dents and distortions would have matched expert's estimations of the murder weapon. Shortly after the spree, he had stared at it with intensity of priceless fascination, and then deep cleaned and polished it, re-coated the base plinth and kept it all locked away in a toughened crystal cabinet.

Holding the statue aloft on the evening after the gruesome night, Marko had stared at the dented bronze surface. In a flash of inspiration and a moment of clarity, he surrendered to the irresistible pull of a calling and with hypnotized eyes locked on to the object, he held it higher and whispered his thoughts out into the room;

"Hello, hedgerow pixie!"

Mr. Magatti had hesitated before making the call. It was impossible to be sure, but he was left with little choice. Going with the less likely option, he picked up the secure line, dialled the special number and asked for a meeting. Fourteen hours ground by before confirmation, and the hurried discussion was held three hours later.

With a fifty percent chance, his gamble had paid off and Hedgerow Pixie, not the one on the assignment, accepted a peculiar one for ninety thousand British pounds — paid in one lump sum of randomized cash.

Hedgerow Pixie flatly refused to stop another assassin, but he could look into who initiated the contract and deliver the information to Mr. Magatti.

329

Three days had already raced by since an edgy man asked Mr. Magatti for six, small gold bars in exchange for information.

"It will be your loss! Believe me!" the edgy man had warned when serious doubts were expressed about the deal.

He was glad he finally paid up when "Victor" — as the man anxiously asked to be called — revealed there was a contract and an assassin would be visiting. He would try and find out more, including who provided funds, and if he did;

"I will need... um, I will require payment... I want ten more gold bars if I find out and if you want to know!" he threw the words at the walls, glancing around as though being hunted.

With Hedgerow Pixie newly recruited on to the task, there was the option of quickly neutralizing the initiator, rendering the contract non-executable. Marko elected to covertly follow Jingle. His trusty field assistant would watch Turquoise Arrow.

Both assassins, professionals, were slippery as greased eels and when they suddenly vanished off the face of the earth, at the same almost coordinated moment in time, his well honed instincts drew him to the mansion with nothing more than stark, circumstantial coincidence. On the verge of sneaking in, his contact aborted the hack on the security system.

"The entire grid has shut down! It's like it's recalibrating! This makes no sense!" the voice announced in his earpiece. "The visual monitoring array is also sort of... iffy! Hard to tell! It's not right! Somebody's tampered with it!"

There was a brief silence.

"It's genius!" his contact breathed the words in fascination. "Dude! If I didn't actually know of the gutch code, I would never have sussed it was playing on a loop!"

He paused and whistled softly under his breath.

"And it's deleting the drive... dude... in... like... in real time!" His voice rose higher with each new discovery. "Woah! I've never seen the gutch code live! This is big time! Big shot! Something is going on! Someone was desperate for big time stealth!"

His voice was more urgent and he paused, suddenly wary of the symbols he was watching.

"It's designed not to bother to pretend it was never there!" his voice came back when half a minute had ticked by. "It's pretending just for now, but only until... well... until... checkmate!"

There was another pause.

"Wait!" he unexpectedly half shouted. "Wow! It's a decoy! What the... there's something else running in—"

Sudden silence, broken mid-way by a soft slurp as he took a sip from a straw immersed in a thick, mystery beverage.

"Someone's dove into this! I can't even figure it out! Gutch code as a decoy?! They're up to something big — something that... something... phew!" he paused to re-calculate his suspicion. "Something that is not going to stay hidden for too long! That's what this feels like! Watch yourself out there!"

"Seems we have a visitor." Marko whispered into his radio, careful not to reveal his own suspicions. His hunch had paid off; one of them had to be here.

"Careful though!" his contact warned. "The sensors will complete self calibration in a few minutes. Dunno how long the loop in the camera system will last but all the ones I've seen self delete in a couple of hours. All depends when it started. No easy way of finding out. I suggest—" he paused to decipher more information. "Do whatever you're up to as quickly as you can!"

"How quick? Take a guess?" Marko whispered into his receiver.

"For the sensors... I'd say likely ten to fifteen minutes. Aim for eight and no more. Don't be near them after that. For the visuals, indications are, I'd say, aim for thirty. It's probably more, but play it safe. After that just assume that you can be seen so, dunno, pretend to be the new butler or something. I'll keep you updated if you still have your comm. on."

When Marko made it into the trees he was wary and very alert. Eyes scanning the vicinity and ears catching every sound, he floated — at a faster than usual pace — from one tree to another, stealthily making his way to quickly get to the residence. The plan was to beat the hi-tech security system, get in to the mansion and locate Mr. Magatti. Time had suddenly become an urgent priority with the near certain presence of another lurking assassin. He hoped he was not too late.

From the trees some distance away, Marko stopped to listen for unusual sounds; a rustling of ground leaves, the snapping of a twig or compressing of vegetation beneath a human foot. Every sound in the air belonged serenely in the forest and every flickering movement bore no intentions. Lifting up a pair of powerful, miniature binoculars, he surveyed the area ahead, until the lenses hovered over a courtyard beyond the shadows, and found a magnificent fountain with three life-size statues. Mr. Magatti loomed into view, just recognizable with the distinct hairstyle and the firm, straight-backed posture. In very close proximity, injured and on his knees was Turquoise Arrow. A third dark figure, head inside a balaclava, stood holding a hi-tech rifle on the ready.

The scene was unexpected! Entirely beyond reason! Something about it was profoundly unusual! Adjusting the focus and squinting into the lenses, Marko tried working out why it was hard to accept. The dark figure was clearly not part of security; if he had been, he would already be on the ground, dead. His casualness in the presence of Mr. Magatti suggested they were more than occasional acquaintances. The whole picture — the unfolding scene — made no sense.

Marko adjusted the binoculars to full zoom and focussed on the image. Something in the posture of the man holding the rifle reminded him of a fighter... an obsessive athlete ... a well practised marksman. A startling suggestion lurched and stirred among his instincts and a name tumbled out of the odd gathering of skill sets.

Few mortal beings could outwit Turquoise Arrow!

"Jingle!" he whispered with lenses locked on the figure.

The day had just become a lot more complicated!

Staring at the spectacle, he watched, trying to figure out why Jingle was holding the gun. Why were they both there? He was breaking very strict rules if he was intervening. Both assassins would know it.

Focussing on Jingle, Marko slowed his breathing. It would take calm senses to cover the distance unseen and successfully take him down. Looking at the rifle and then scanning around the court-yard, his mind sparked with options, weighing a tactical approach. It was not going to be easy; Jingle, a stealth master, was teeming with sixth sense. But he had to be stopped. If he was paid to kill Turquoise Arrow, it was only a matter of time before he took money for someone else!

Marko watched Mr. Magatti walk away from Turquoise Arrow and stand next to Jingle. They stood too close to one another each comfortable in the other's presence. He tried to decipher what their postures were telling him. The familiarity spelled out an unlikely story, but it was undeniable; the two knew each other well. The longer he looked, the more apparent it became that they had known each other long before events of that afternoon. Something about the stand-off didn't fit with the picture. The whole scene was tarnished by missing scripts and missed lines.

It was impossible! He would definitely have known if one of his main rivals was good friends with one of the richest men in the country. Maybe they were more than friends. Maybe they were... No! Mr. Magatti was married! And the closeness bore no hints of clandestine romance.

After he was done with Jingle, he would have to kill Mr. Magatti —easier still, he would allow the other assassin to finish the job. It helped that there was already a contract laid out. Marko suddenly hated the day! It had become too complicated! As he watched the situation unfolding on the courtyard, he tried to answer how the two had stumbled upon each other. Peering through the binoculars, he contemplated his next move.

After watching a while longer, Marko made the bold decision to trust a gut feeling. Reaching into a small, hidden holster behind his back, he pulled out a miniature titanium pistol machined with a capacity of only four bullets. It was more than he would need. In the palm of one hand, he held it in place using only a thumb keeping the other fingers extended to hide it from view. With arms down by his side and an illusion of calmness, he stepped out from behind the tree and began to walk forward, in the direction of the three men.

Chapter 7

"I don't suppose you could tell me who hired you for the assignment?" Mr. Magatti ventured with Maurice.

After a short silence, there was the slightest, barely perceptible shrug.

All three men knew no information would be forthcoming.

Robert suddenly tensed up and glanced quickly towards the trees.

"Someone's out there! Approaching! Roughly at your eight o'clock!"

Mr. Magatti turned to check. Robert's eyes covered Maurice, waiting for a movement. The gun was fully raised again.

"There's a pistol in my belt." Robert murmured to his father, never taking his eyes off Maurice.

Mr. Magatti pulled out the gun, immediately released the safety and cocked a bullet into the chamber. He saw the figure straight away, he knew the woods well; a calm man with no intention to hide, approaching at a steady pace, with apparent purpose that telegraphed no ill will.

Tense moments ground by until the figure was closer. Mr. Magatti re-engaged the safety and slid the pistol back into his son's belt holster.

"You expecting someone?" Robert asked his father.

"As it happens," was the reply.

"Why is he in the trees?"

Mr. Magatti held up a hand.

There was crunching of footsteps as the figure approached. A well dressed man, approximately six feet tall, athletic, light footed and extremely well groomed eventually walked up and confidently stepped over the balustrade. Mr. Magatti watched, impressed by the tailored suit, the dark grey shirt, buttoned up but devoid of a tie, and the deep black hair that was stylishly slicked back. He didn't particularly like the suit but the cut suggested a British tailor, and judging by the fit and style, the creator was world class. The laced shoes were slightly higher at the ankles for comfort, and for a tighter, more secure fit for running and fighting. He appeared to be a man acquainted with the unexpected and from his intense eyes and open but fixed expression, was undoubtedly prepared for it.

"Excellent timing!" Mr. Magatti called out as the man walked right up and stood a little distance to the left.

Maurice and Robert glanced first at Hedgerow Pixie and then at Mr. Magatti, uncertain of whether he had planned the encounter. It could not be a coincidence that one of the few individuals both of them feared had suddenly just turned up. Men like these never just happen to be in the neighbourhood. Turquoise Arrow stared, bemused. Assassins did not believe in major coincidences.

Mr. Magatti cleared his throat.

"Isn't this an excellent moment!" he theatrically broke out. "I see you both know the identity of my new guest and I assure you, he is my guest, even though the great timing is purely coincidental."

Lifting his arm, he waved an open palm in introduction.

"Gentlemen, allow me to present Hedgerow Pixie — or Marko B. Brankly for any want of a real name!"

There was a short pause, not lightened even by the bubbling of the fountain.

"The 'B' is for Bernard, just in case you're wondering."

The subtle change in expressions forced him to quickly add, "But of course you already knew that!"

Robert reached up and pulled off his balaclava.

Maurice, still on his knees and growing weaker with blood loss, was staring at the new arrival — the one man, since he knew of him, he had never wished to battle with.

"Aren't you going to say hello?" Mr. Magatti commanded with humour.

There was a forced nod from Robert.

Maurice barely responded.

Marko curtly nodded back.

"Do you people even know how to smile?" Mr. Magatti taunted.

Marko and Maurice both locked their eyes on him. Robert cast a quick glance. The bubbling fountain had darkened into a sinister tune. Each assassin burned with questions of how the day had turned out.

"Well, good gentlemen," Mr. Magatti began to explain, "A few days ago, when I caught wind of something foul simmering in the circles, I, with Robert's help, looked into it."

He paused and as an afterthought, suddenly turned towards Marko.

"Rude of me!" he held up a palm. "My sincere apologies!"

Waving a hand towards Robert, he quickly introduced the two.

"May I most humbly present my son, Robert Frederick Malcolm, or Jingle, as both of you undoubtedly know him! I do sincerely apologize that I could not tell you before."

Marko was stunned! How had they kept it a secret! The bizarre situation finally began to make sense. It was a valid intervention! He took a breath and nodded. His entire day had just become a lot less complicated.

Turning to look at the man on his knees, he understood the predicament — but he was wary of the danger. The great Turquoise Arrow was a threat, even while injured, and he must have a backup weapon. Asking him to remove it was plain suicidal: a shot could be unleashed far faster than the eye could see. And approaching him to remove the gun would be outright fatal. With two assassins who could react fast enough if it was drawn, the wisest strategy was to leave it just where it was. Marko was about to ask why Jingle hadn't pulled the trigger, when Mr. Magatti cleared his throat.

"I will call you all by your first names from now on, if I may." With deliberate politeness, Mr. Magatti turned towards Marko "If you don't at all mind?"

Marko nodded his approval.

"You are men of few words!" Mr. Magatti observed. "Even my dear son here!" he gestured casually towards Robert.

Maurice leaned and moved to shift his weight on his knees. Weakening by the moment, it was taking too much effort to remain alert and upright. Going for the weapon was no longer an option. With slowed down senses, pulling out the small gun and squeezing a well aimed shot would take nearly a full second. Jingle would have all the time in the world to react. There had to be another way. There was always another way. And he had to figure it out before he lost too much blood to make the all important getaway. Ignoring the obvious mystery of why he wasn't dead yet, he clung to every extra minute, mind whirring to summon a plan.

"Maurice over here is in quite a situation." Mr. Magatti suddenly announced. "His life is in our hands, but I'll be monkey if I don't like the boy. You see, we had a snip of a moment before my son showed up. Good thing we did or it would all have ended very badly — and that's for the both of us! Robert here would have hunted him to the ends of the earth!"

All three assassins were mystified by his words. Sparing Maurice would be so far outside the code, that none of them could contemplate any move to justify it. Robert was about to speak when Mr. Magatti held up a hand.

"All four of us are much more alike than you all know!"

As he spoke the words, his face transformed. Robert saw a man he had never seen in his father before.

It took months of practice but was well worth the effort. Many years before, Mr. Magatti had persevered, day after day, standing in front of the bathroom mirror, until he mastered a happy expression, adorned upon a mask of an endless smile. His true nature, confined into an internal dungeon, was chained up and tethered down. It protested and fought back. Daily battles with it, reinforced by trees and happy employees, raged on — usually in Mr. Magatti's favour.

"Carbon Chisel!" Mr. Magatti announced into the air.

The rest of the world disappeared for all three assassins.

"The Colway family back in August 1989!"

He guessed they must have heard of it. The question lingered in all three pairs of eyes.

"I have scars all over my body, and two bones that were broken and never healed right. Lost half the vision in my left eye, which if anything, was lucky, because the older Colway boy nearly knocked it clean off!"

He stopped for a long sigh, absent-mindedly shaking his head.

"Then there was the uncle, a cousin and two family friends — in their thirties at the time!" A dark look engulfed his face. "Those four men took what was left of my soul and repeatedly violated me, in ways a four year old boy should never have to encounter in his wildest nightmares. The pain, in the many... many moments I was held down was worse than the beatings, and to this day, I can still taste what they made me swallow!"

Revulsion began to bubble within all three assassins and Maurice, for a few moments, forgot his own anguish.

"The Colways knew everything." Mr. Magatti continued. "They facilitated it. They charged the men twenty pounds for a night spent in my room and it seemed there was a never ending supply for the privilege; at one point, I believed they had practically moved in and I wondered whether to leave them a space in the clothes cupboard!"

There was not a hint of humour in the altered atmosphere.

"Mrs Colway provided clean towels for when they were finished — for which I found out they willingly paid a small, extra fee. She beat me so badly one day when I tried to refuse, she broke this bone." He pointed to the outer bone on the left forearm. "They never took me to the hospital so it didn't heal quite ri..."

His voice choked and trailed off. Some moments ticked painfully by before he could speak again.

"The pain was more than I have learned the vocabulary to describe. It took two months to heal. The men never stopped making their visits the entire time!"

Mr. Magatti stared into the distance, his eyes pooling with tears, and his shoulders shook several times before he could regain control. The three assassins remained silent until, with considerable effort, he blinked back into clarity and composed himself.

"Mr Colway had a fancy, wooden toolbox he seemed to love more than any other entity on this living earth. He bought a brand new, state-of-the-art chisel for his woodworking. From the moment I laid eyes on it, I knew our destinies were bound. It drew me in like timeless forces draw in the high tides and called to me in whispers that thundered in a gale force." He was staring into the distance at an invisible horizon, nodding subtly to himself and to whatever deity that commanded the supreme beckoning. "I'll be a gallivanting moose if I could do anything but listen!" he added, with words breathed as though he was humming them at the clouds.

After a moment of nothing but the fountain and birds, Mr. Magatti blinked and spoke again. "The blade is seven inches long and sharper than you would ever believe. Tough carbon steel! Tough as anything you could ever get. Unbreakable! Indestructible! You could tie it to a bulldozer and use it to tear down a house and it would barely feel a thing!"

He absent-mindedly swung his fist to tear down an imaginary house.

"The solid ebony, oak tipped handle bares the word 'carbon' smartly engraved upon it." He stretched the word 'carbon' while gesturing across the air, willing it to light up in neon before them. "It's the toughest sort of ebony handle fitted to any tools, and a narrow shaft of the toughened steel runs right through the centre, binding blade, handle and tip into a wholesome thing of glorious strength and infinite wonder. She is a thing of greatest beauty! A wonderfully glorious tool! Of that, I entirely promise you, she absolutely is!"

The three assassins saw that he must still be in possession of it. And they saw that it latched on to the wrath of buried fiends hurled into his depths by beasts paying fees for supplies of towels — pummelling a young soul to grotesque infinity.

Each one of the assassins understood him perfectly.

"I stole it just before I left the house at the age of fourteen and fanatically kept it close to me, as I roughed and hustled my way across many towns, wandering northward — adrift on a land-tide. I trekked across fields and meadows and farms and sprawling heath-land, and tree-dotted grasslands of aristocratic properties."

He smiled and cast his eyes downwards, and spent far too long a moment immersed in the past journey.

"I burgled two castles," he tossed out with amusement. "It wasn't easy! I didn't intend to. But hunger and the cold bit with potency and vengeance. It was deep into autumn, and the evening breeze came armed with saws and razor blades! And you know, the absolute most bizarre thing of it was that all I encountered was a total of five servants and two overworked butlers." He shrugged one shoulder. "It was easy to evade them as walking around a row of bushes. They were so busy cleaning, they didn't know their noses from their sweat laden eyebrows."

He shook his head in sympathy.

"I found kitchens and storage rooms and chillers and fancy alcohol cabinets, and a room with a fancy leather bag that I filled with all the food I needed." He flashed a quick, cheeky smile. "A full bottle of scotch happened to find its way in. I didn't want to take more and cause the servants any trouble." And as a quick afterthought, "A blanket and a sleeping bag *decided* they would come along." He stretched the word 'decided' with comically raised eyebrows.

He stopped to look at the other three with a gleeful glint in his eyes.

"Here's a happy and interesting fact." He appeared pleased with himself. "All the five servants and two butlers from both of the castles are now working for me, lured into my sphere with pay raises and bribery. They're all undoubtedly happier! And of course none the wiser about our close encounter — although one of them mentioned a past worry over a sleeping bag."

Even Maurice found the thought suitably amusing.

"But I digress!" Mr. Magatti declared with unhidden satisfaction after glancing around to confirm the desired reactions.

Robert's mind wandered to the servants at the mansion and the many drinks and fine foods they had laid out before him on uncountable occasions, and their silent, purposeful gliding — infused with soporific passion — with stealth dusters, sneak cloths and unheard scourers, and the whole mansion shimmered with kempt care bordering on clinical obsession. They loved their jobs and when he addressed them, he used their names — a touch of human respect daddy Magatti instilled into him. He accepted them as fellow people, helpful people, kind people, even though the entire team were unaware of the bizarre connection between him and their charismatic employer. Even Mr. Magatti's wife, happily married to him for over two, blissful decades, had no knowledge there was a son right underneath her nose, with a loving adoptive father, and a secret life making grown men tremble with fear — and occasionally, disappear.

In his father's home swirled a myriad of secrets.

"So I trekked and trundled and strolled and waddled." Mr. Magatti continued. "And yes! For more than three days, I was waddling!" He shuffled forward awkwardly on his feet to demonstrate. "I had jumped over a wall and got tripped up on the other side. Bam! Straight on to a rock feature in a flower bed. My backside felt as though a canon was fired at it!"

Robert smiled, Marko stared and Maurice appeared unimpressed.

"Then one day, I looked up and found myself in Scotland. I hustled hard and played and survived only on breezy luck and fried consternation, and fragments cast to me by what I can only assume were attentive guardian angels, which made me ponder where on earth they were when I needed them in my early years! Still, maybe one is born with limited portions of luck, and I was only beginning to unwrap my own providence. How I never got arrested I will never understand, and how I slept and obtained food is most of the way a mystery."

A thoughtful expression promptly replaced a dim smile. "Glasgow is a... let's just call it an interesting place and Edinburgh might as well be in another world. I loved them all! All those places have a unique way — even a little town to the north whose name I can never remember. I must go there again one day soon."

The last few words were addressed entirely to himself with a voice half lowered in volume, and with brow furrowed in access of a mental itinerary.

"Many months later," Mr. Magatti continued after slotting a subtle trip to the north into a 'to do' list, "before I left Scotland and came back south, I met the man who changed my direction in life. He sent me to another man, who sent me to the man who then flew me to the place where I began my training."

He settled his stance and stood with both hands behind his back.

Maurice glanced at Robert to see if he was distracted. One second was all he needed! He would have to take out Robert first and then Mr. Magatti. Marko was not in the fight and would not intervene. They could walk away together. He might even help with the escape: it was priceless to be owed a favour by Turquoise Arrow.

Mr. Magatti shifted his posture, instinctively uneasy at invisible vibes from Maurice. He glanced to confirm that Robert was sensing them too. He had every faith in Jingle, never having known him to lose a fight. But then again, in that moment, they faced Turquoise Arrow, and maybe Hedgerow Pixie, and a sense of foreboding came from not knowing which way it would go. For a fleeting moment, he wished that he hadn't put the gun back in his son's belt. Reaching for it again would trigger a cascade of action. He had to carry on and hope that Robert would stay alert and not get distracted. Another glance at his son reassured him he was in control.

"It took a mighty hell pile of planning," he continued amidst the rising unease. "But finally, back on that day in August 1989, when I was twenty three years old, I got all eight people to be together in the Colway house. There was the parents, the two sons and all four men who hurt me — all in the same place at the perfectly planned time. It was supposed to be a casual dinner party for fourteen but six guests, for various reasons, never showed up." He winked conspiratorially. "Four had several things go wrong and the others suddenly had to attend to urgent emergencies." He winked again and then cast another glance at Maurice. The sinister vibes appeared to have substantially subsided as all three assassins became visibly more attentive.

Mr. Magatti cleared his throat. "Sometime after the food was served and everybody was settled, I casually walked into the room, locked the door, and barricaded it. It was quite a moment! Very surreal! More than I expected! And not one of them had the slightest clue what was about to happen." He smiled, his mind massaged by a very fond memory. "It's a good thing they were not wealthy enough to employ servants; there was not another soul in the entire rest of the property. I made sure to detach the external wires to the phone line—" he raised a finger to make a point, " and I remembered to re-attach them when all was finished, just to add to the mystery when the carnage was stumbled upon."

The three assassins were unable to hide their anticipation.

Maurice temporarily forgot his escape plan.

"The two sons and the parents recognized me immediately. It took the other four just a little while longer. When I pulled out the chisel, I think they all believed that I was only there to give it back. Mr. Colway even had the nerve to ask for an apology! He did so dislike anyone meddling with his things — let alone stealing them."

He smiled at the irony.

"Mrs Colway was always more vicious than the boys. I would have preferred to do her last, but I didn't want her running around screaming the house down so she had to be the first."

He closed his eyes and sunk further into the memory.

"I walked up to her, looked casually around the table at each one of them, and then leaned down and placed the tip of the chisel on her chest, and do you know what she said? Would you like to know what she said?"

For the sake of continuity, humouring eccentricity, the three men each gave very subtle nods.

"Hm! She said she didn't want it! 'I don't want that!' she said. And she said that I should very well know who it belongs to."

He scoffed and shook his head, disdain darkening his expression.

"Everything was still calm. Not one of them suspected they might be in any trouble. I looked down at her eyes. There was no hint of remorse in them. I looked again around the table, and though shame effused from the faces of all the men, I saw no remorse showing on any one of them. Not one of them cared or felt sorry for what they did. None of them at all!"

He made a fist and thrust his hand gently but forcefully forward. "I looked down and slowly sank the chisel into her heart — through the ribs and straight in. And I felt the rip of muscle as it sliced into her coldness, and frantic effort to pump against icy, carbon steel. I felt it! Right through the handle! The heart fought bravely! But her face broadcast a dumb look of disbelief as her soul and the essence in her eyes dimmed away. Not one of them around the table ever expected it!"

His mind drifted away, irretrievable, ensnared. Half a minute went by before he blinked and re-emerged.

"All hell thundered and broke loose after that moment! It was almighty mayhem! The two sons jumped me — a futile endeavour!" He stretched out his hands in a martial arts pose. "I had been training nearly five years since after I was eighteen. It was easy as handling a couple of baby sheep." He swung four quick swipes, two punches and a chop. "After knocking them down, I stabbed the first one in the neck and then carefully made sure to stab the other one in the eye." He pointed to his left eye. "Payback for this!" and all three men nodded, each appreciating the drama.

"Then one of the other men came at me to fight back, which was not at all a problem. I took him down so easy, nobody else bothered to try again with that idea." Mr. Magatti nodded firmly at that segment of memory. "The rest of them spent the time trying to get away or shamelessly begging for their lives and offering all of their money." He shrugged nonchalantly. "They knew what they had done to me. Maybe they figured I would be a terrified boy forever!"

A look of scorn flashed again.

"I killed Mr Colway last. By then, he was resigned and sitting quietly in a dream world. And when his moment came... not a smidgen of resistance."

Mr. Magatti held his head up. "When I walked out of the house, I was a brand new man. I felt no joy and not even remotely liberated. But a sense of accomplishment nudged at my soul, warming the wasteland within. Persistent turmoil has always plagued my mind — like it does in all of you. For me I see... well... monsters and... it

347

doesn't matter!" His palm swiftly waved away the issue. "Then I felt I could do something! Become something! Achieve something! And I set out on a new life. Trotted into a new path."

After a very long pause, Marko was the first to speak. "I remember reading about that! The Colway massacre!"

Maurice and Robert also knew of the Colway killings — a media sensation at the time they occurred. Assassins were instinctively drawn to unexplained murders.

"That was you!?" Marko called out at exactly the same moment as Robert.

"You did the Colway massacre?" Robert asked his father.

One of the most infamous massacres of the eighties was known to most assassins as a major unsolved event. The lone surviving relative, a young man called Raymond, only lived because he was apparently too ill to attend the dinner. The killings were partly blamed on a well known London gang, riled by humiliating attacks on three senior members.

Marko had a sudden thought. "Wait... you're Raymond Colway!"

"Woah!" exclaimed Robert.

Even Maurice was intrigued.

"Yes," continued Marko with an expression suggesting his mind was reorganizing everything filed under the name 'Mr. Magatti'. "There was a Raymond who survived because he couldn't go to the dinner! That was you? You actually did it!"

Mr. Magatti smiled and stared aimlessly up at a cloud. "A story for the investigators! I convinced them I was sick." He appeared to be speaking to the sky. "Of course I was never invited, but everything was arranged just so — right down to the medicine partly discarded into the toilet so the level left in the bottle was entirely believable."

The Mr. Magatti they knew had evaporated away and before them stood a spectre so profound in intensity, they reeled in disappointment at never once spotting or sensing his aura. Having never known much about his father's childhood, Robert saw he knew even less about later years.

Mr. Magatti's eyes swivelled lazily back to the courtyard. "Yes, I *was* Raymond Colway. Two years after I disposed of all the other Colways, I made to change my identity. The sound of the name grated and hacked at my very soul! I could no longer bear it!" He made a sudden gesture desiring to clarify something. "Just so you know, the gang members who were suspected of attacking the Colways? It might have seemed that they may have possibly had a reason to." He winked and nodded, as a cunning smile once again erupted over his face. "I ambushed three of their high level members, covered up and all disguised! I made sure to leave them alive. I told them somebody sent me but I never told them who, so you see, pathetic efforts for revenge were fruitless. Babies were thrown with bath water... they threw toys out of the pram... use whatever metaphor to describe raging tantrums! You'd have thought it was the end of the world. Police were aware of murky goings-on afoot with the gang and eyes and ears were peeled out for ever pending troubles."

Mr. Magatti turned away to stare thoughtfully in to the trees. "I moved further southwest and changed my identity. I altered my appearance, my dress code... even the way I walk. It took months to save for the surgery on my nose—" he tapped the tip of his nose "and they did one hell of a job! Then I worked on changing my voice to sound much deeper, and I practised smiling in front of a mirror, hours and hours, for weeks on end, until I grew this charming look you all love so much." He paused briefly — non-committedly allowing for laughter. "Four years later I tested my new look and travelled to see some people who had known Raymond Colway. Not one of them recognized me, even as I stood barely three feet away and in full conversation."

Staring into the trees, he drew a long breath.

"Some time after that, I drifted in to a line of business. I loathed having to depend on people paying me to kill. I had to try something else. I had to find something different. One thing led to another and..." His words trailed off and he gestured towards the mansion. "Somehow, next thing I knew, I ended up with all this!"

"How do you stop the urge? Doesn't it ever overwhelm you?" Robert hoped for an answer that could solve his own struggles.

"It does!" Mr. Magatti replied. "Every now and then I feel as though I might succumb. That's why I come here. Right here! To this very spot! There is something about the trees. I promise you, believe me, the trees are alive! And I'm not trying to fool you! They help to calm and soothe me — one of the reasons I turned all this land into forest. It settles my mind when I spend some good time here. They're un-judging, living rods that soak away the sludge."

Mr. Magatti turned to look at Maurice, who was still on his knees and so pale from blood loss, he appeared close to passing out.

"Here's how we might be able to solve this situation."

Robert and Marko were curious.

Maurice harboured no hopes.

"We all went through a mighty hell pile of rough times back when little kiddos. It's why I felt so drawn to young Robert over here. He has his own story and it's just as bad as any other. It's also why I wanted to adopt him all those years ago."

Marko glanced over at Robert. Another piece of family puzzle had just fallen into place.

Mr. Magatti looked first at Maurice and then at Marko. "A while ago, I took the liberty of looking in to both your pasts. I may not have all the details, but from what my investigator found, some bad, nasty goings on went about in your childhoods. You had nothing even resembling any sort of a real father, or any sort of a father that remotely seemed to care. But I do care — even though you're far from family. It would be difficult not to with our shared situations." He spoke with real passion and undeniable conviction. There was a poignant pause before he spoke his next words. "And I would like to reach out and extend that to both of you."

All three assassins stared.

"You're still young and I know you're both intentional lone wolves with nobody else you can trust and nobody you can truly count on. Robert here can tell you how very different things could be having a father around that you can entirely depend on."

Robert nodded several times in resounding confirmation.

"And besides, look at the four of us! Who else would get us and what we're all about? My own children — my children — know nothing about my past and know next to nothing about Robert, let alone that he's their brother. What if the four of us ventured to look out for one another? Would that be the worst thing? Would it really be? Can you imagine the peace of mind? The endless possibilities?"

Marko's eyes began to glisten but he blinked away the tears.

The bubbling of the fountain had mellowed, the foreboding mostly dissolved.

"I know all three of you don't care about the money." Mr. Magatti resumed in persuasion. "But here's something enticing: I have an island with only one, lonely mooring berth. Robert here has been to stay over on many occasions. I will have three more, generously spaced berths constructed and you can all have your own boats, with their own spaces. And as for the cabin, I will have three, self contained extensions added on so you can have your own dens equipped however you want them. It's an ideal getaway. I'll be an eight foot grizzly bear if you could find better! I like to go there myself every other month or so."

Money attracted attention and brought responsibilities, two aspects of life skilled assassins shied away from. Marko and Maurice had both saved and invested for a quiet retirement — even though neither expected they would ever live that long. A dependable father and an isolated island were far more tempting for highly strung assassins.

Relieved of the burden of pre-planned events and the looming spectre of death, Maurice's vision, with no warning, began to fade and the tension left his stiff body. Allowing his eyes to close, he passed out from blood loss. Marko athletically bounded the few steps and caught him just before his head smashed into the stone paving.

Chapter 8

Six days later in a mansion in southern Germany, Mr. Bronentgen was shuffling out of the en-suite bathroom in the lavish master bedroom after his late evening shower. His wife and two daughters were away for four days skiing and visiting with his wealthy sister-in-law in Northern Europe. Keen to lie down and retire for an early night, he scrolled a mental checklist for the morning business flight to Hong Kong. Two designer bedside lamps bathed one side of the room in a luxuriously creamy and half-dimmed glow and once the bathroom light was off, the large bedroom remained softly lit only in the vicinity of the silk lined bed. The far corners of the room faded away in semi darkness.

He stopped dead and whirled around when out of the corner of his eye, a dark figure materialized in the chair by the far wall. The thick, white medical bandage around the man's left hand stood out in stark contrast to his dark coloured suit. It took a few moments in the low light to recognize the figure.

"Wh... wh... what are you doing here?" he demanded in a trembling voice. "You should not be here! You... you... should never come here!"

Turquoise Arrow calmly looked up but remained silent.

"Wh... what's the matter with your... your hand?" Mr. Bronentgen stuttered.

Maurice did not speak. Deliberately waiting for a moment to pass, he waved casually towards his right and in the dim light, Mr Bronenten saw the other two smartly dressed figures standing near the wardrobes. He jumped and stepped backwards.

"Wh... who is that? Who are you? Who are they? What are you doing in my house?" he demanded, pointing at the two men.

"May I present my two brothers," Maurice announced calmly. "Jingle—" he paused as Robert raised his arm "and Hedgerow Pixie." Marko gave a calm mock salute.

Mr. Bronentgen stumbled backwards and fell on to the bed. He knew well of the names. And he also knew that nobody survived a visit from any of them. To see all three in his bedroom was more frightening than he could bear.

"W... W... Why? ... wh... why are you..."

He was unable to speak.

"There was a problem Mr. Bronentgen." Maurice eventually announced. "Turns out Jingle here is actually Mr. Magatti's son! He's the one who shot me. Almost shot my hand clean off! It hurt very bad too!" Lifting up his left hand, he studied the sterile bandage. "Don't get me wrong, I'm grateful he only shot at my hand. Doctors say it will heal... though it might not ever look anywhere near as good as it did before."

Mr. Bronentgen appeared close to passing out with fear. When he hired Turquoise Arrow to kill Mr. Magatti, there was no information of relation with an assassin. Was it a child from an affair, or maybe a past relationship? Struggling to figure out the mystery connection and why there had been the need to keep it so well concealed, his face rose with panic as he grasped the situation. It was going to be a very bad evening for him.

"They... you... your... brothers... How—" Mr. Bronentgen started to ask and Maurice nodded very slowly.

Mr. Bronentgen, in a desperate effort, hoped to bargain with the fact that nobody was dead yet. There might still be a way out for him.

"I didn't know! You must believe me! I DID NOT KNOW! If I had even the smallest clue, then I would never, NEVER—"

Maurice held up a palm and the room went quiet.

Allowing a few moments of silence to tick by, he picked up a device resting innocuously on one lap. With a calm expression, he stood up and slowly walked towards the luxury bed.

Mr. Bronentgen cowered in fear and held his hands over his head. Maurice opened the flip screen device, placed it on the designer covers and swivelled it around so Mr. Bronentgen had a clear view. After barking out a four word command, he paused to watch the vertical screen flicker into life. A customary swirling logo and crisp software graphics splashed impressively in vivid colours, before Mr. Magatti's face and upper body appeared, filmed in high definition.

"Good evening Mr. Bronentgen. I hope you are safe and very well... for now at the least. If you are watching this, then no doubt you have met my two, wonderful, newly adopted sons — and Jingle with them."

Trembling in fear, Mr. Bronentgen lowered his hands and leaned closer to the screen. Sat in a hand-made bamboo armchair, Mr. Magatti's smiling form was staring straight back at him.

"For obvious reasons, a live call to you would be unwise, so I am making this recording right here in my study. Three days from now, my boys are scheduled to meet you and well... I am certain the pleasure will be all theirs." The tone was polite, bordering on being friendly. "I am sure you fully understand the new situation so I will save us both some time and get to the real business." Mr. Magatti made a deliberate effort to be diplomatic. "There is no way to save you so I will make no false promises. If it is of any consolation, they're all sticklers for the code. It will be very quick and clean and meticulously professional. There isn't a need to remind you that they are masters of their craft."

Mr. Bronentgen's clasped hands rose to cover his mouth.

"There is however, something I would like that we can bargain with. I need some information from you; information that will help me. I happen to also be a great stickler for the code so we won't bother trying to forcefully get it out of you and believe me, if these boys were to choose that option, they could get everything they need in minimal time. But that is all unnecessary. It's not our way."

Mr. Bronentgen sunk lower on to the bed.

355

Mr. Magatti's recording raised its hands in a question, "So what could I offer, from all the way over here, to make it worth your while if you were soon going to be..." He paused, entirely for effect. "I know you love your wife and your two beautiful daughters."

Mr. Bronentgen felt like he was going to throw up.

"No, no, no!" Mr. Magatti reassured, anticipating the reaction. "We would not dream of harming them! Not if you co-operate. Remember! We're all great sticklers for the code!"

Mr. Bronentgen breathed out heavily in relief.

"But I can do something good for them in return for information."

Mr. Bronentgen suddenly felt very keen to make a deal.

"I will ensure that your estate and control of your company goes to your dear wife, and that it stays that way. I will ward off and keep away those venture capitalists and the hedge fund you've been trying to fight off for a year."

Mr. Bronentgen was leaning forward, very focussed on the screen.

"And here's the sweet, creamy icing on this wonderful cake," Mr. Magatti teased with a smile, "Mrs Bronentgen, as sole head of the enterprise, will retain exclusive rights to the shipping supply chain for Western Europe. I will hand my controlling half over to her, no charge, and I will spend my days watching that she not only wards off any hostile take-overs, but that nobody tries to muscle those rights off of her."

Mr. Bronentgen's expression changed with doubt and sudden suspicion. What sort of information could Mr. Magatti need that was worth so much in return? What could he want to know that was so important?

"Now what could I need after offering so much?" Mr. Magatti had easily anticipated the question. "I have some new business opening in Asia and Canada. I need you to surrender the Atlantic shipping line — fully — to me, with no questions asked. I also need the contacts and production schedules of your facilities and subsidiary in Eastern Asia."

Mr. Bronentgen remained focussed, waiting for more demands but Mr. Magatti had finished. He raised his head slightly. That was it!? Was that really it!? It was either a bad joke or the bargain of the century: a barely profitable shipping line, some production schedules and contacts in Asia? It was too good to be true! There had to be something to it.

Mr. Magatti explained why he needed the information and with each word, Mr. Bronentgen's eyes narrowed with envy! The plan was so obvious, he wished he had thought of it first. Mr. Magatti stood to make at least another billion Euros within the following two years.

"So tell the boys how it's going to work out Mr. Bronentgen. Do lets, at the very least, make just one last trade! My boys there with you have the paperwork for the shipping route — all ready for signing. Hand over to them everything else and they will bring it over to me. Make sure it's all accurate. Turquoise Arrow has a recorder for any verbal information. It shouldn't all take you more than a couple of hours, should it?"

Mr. Magatti paused, glanced down, and then looked again at the camera with a solemn expression. "We could have done great business together for many years. We could have had a good run, just... so many opportunities!" He sighed and shrugged his shoulders. "You have my word. Mrs Bronentgen and your girls will remain well protected. My three sons will happily visit anybody who troubles them."

His expression promised that he meant every word.

"I hate to ask, but there's one more thing you could do for us. My boys can do it, no trouble at all, but nowadays with forensics, digital investigations, DNA matching and whatnots and all such..." His voice theatrically trailed off as he stared into the camera. "It would be so much easier if you helped with the process and made it look like suicide, you know, with the note and all that and... other things?" His right hand waved to conjure up necessary actions. "And it would go a long way to providing the incentive to look after those wonderful ladies you leave behind."

Mr. Bronentgen cast his eyes to the bed in resignation.

After another suitable pause, Mr. Magatti leaned forward and spoke for one last time.

"Goodbye Mr. Bronentgen!"

The screen flickered and went dark.

Three days later, Mr. Magatti made the last of a series of phone calls. "Yes, you heard me, clear as day!" he forcefully instructed. "Transfer our half to Mr. Bronentgen's widow. I am aware of the consequences! And while you're at it—" he briefly pondered an adequate gesture for the situation "arrange for a bouquet of flowers and a card with our condolences. Tell her our thoughts are with her, and tell her we will always be here for any support — any help at all that she may need."

Chapter 9

A year later in the following summer, Mr. Magatti, Robert and Maurice sat in the wild garden outside the giant, newly extended cabin sprawled in one corner of the small, secluded island. Three generous, self contained extensions had been completed, all with separate, underground bunkers and independent power sources. The main central cabin remained the largest part of the structure with a separate concealed bunker, extra recreation facilities and a sports room, with screens, loungers, snooker and pool tables.

The distant burbling roar of a powerful boat engine grew louder, approaching the far side of the island. They listened as it lowered to a gurgling grunt as the boat slowed to glide into a mooring berth. The engine revved up throatily, twice in succession, and then gave a hearty sputter before going silent.

"Marko's here!" Mr. Magatti unnecessarily announced.

"I should have got that same boat!" Maurice grumbled light heartedly. "She's just a beast!"

Mr. Magatti vigorously shook his head. "Too fast and little comfort! Too much focus on speed! Yours has the right balance and it's no slouch either."

"I agree." Robert added.

Maurice shrugged his shoulders. "I know!" he accepted. "Still sucks when he beats me every time we race!"

Marko eventually appeared from the untamed shrubbery, dressed in a crisp, well pressed, hand-tailored suit.

"The man of the hour!" Mr. Magatti called out. He glanced round at the other two, then down at his own suit and then back again at Marko. "Look at us! Why do we dress like we're going on a date?"

Marko walked up and Mr. Magatti reached over to pour him a double shot of scotch on ice.

"Everything go well?" Mr. Magatti enquired.

"Like a daydream." Marko replied while adjusting a wooden chair to sit among his new family. "It's going all over the news when they eventually find him. They'll think it was his dealer; I made certain of that."

He went ahead to describe subtle ways he had set the scene.

Mr. Magatti reached to the table and scooped a small handful of fresh purple berries from a crafted, bamboo bowl. Three vanished into his mouth, bathing it with tangy sweetness and after another sip from his glass, he looked up and smiled.

"Isn't it better this way? Gives a real tingling feeling when it's a worthy take-down!"

They all nodded in agreement.

"When news of his death breaks, we'll send out packages to the families of the missing men and to the parents of that girl."

The three men nodded again. Mr. Magatti was right; it felt odd but warm and tingly doing things a little different. Even the tentacles Maurice saw twirled in approval. He saw them on most days but he kept it all to himself — he was not quite ready to share, even though for the very first time in his life, he felt strangely calm and settled in the presence of other beings. In time, each assassin would share when ready.

"How is Mrs Mayward?" Mr. Magatti had acquired an interest in her welfare.

"Doing very well!" Maurice replied with appreciation. "I looked them up last week — they didn't know I was there."

To all four men, the alarming statement sounded entirely logical. Maurice regularly sneaked up to the Mayward's home to watch the family for a while and listen in on conversations. They were happy, healthy, and as far as he was able to tell from everything he observed, were enduring no vexations. As he had done with the car salesman and their bullying, drunken neighbour, he was keen to visit anybody who caused them any trouble.

"You all know Butterfly Pin?" Mr. Magatti asked after some silence.

"That the Chinese girl?" Maurice asked after a short pause. "Mei Hwa Li or something? The one who killed two uncles and a rogue, nasty-piece... was it a cousin or a neighbour?"

"It wasn't just an ordinary neighbour." Robert chimed in. "It was a family friend — *and* she also killed her dad. And this was about... she snuffed her dad... I think only two hours right after the neighbour." He tried recalling the precise name he was informed about. "Is it Min Hao Lin—?"

"It's Mei Huan Liu, I think." Marko interjected. "And she's one of the best in Asia!"

Mr. Magatti nodded. Mei Huan was rumoured to be one of the top assassins. From what little he could gather, she apparently killed two uncles, her father and his friend using nothing but a beloved, hand-crafted hair ornament.

"She killed them with a hair pin." Mr. Magatti was impressed. "A seven inch long, sharpened piece of animal bone with a large pink and black decorative butterfly attached to it. That's where from she plucked her name. I'll be a deep sea octopus if it doesn't have a nice sound to it!"

Mr. Magatti had attempted to uncover her full story but with sparse details, and nobody with direct connections, he was hoping to meet her to get more information.

"From what I've learned so far, her master wants her eliminated!" Mr. Magatti continued. "She's a top Wu-Shong fighter and he wasn't at all pleased when he found out she used all the skills he was teaching her to work as an assassin." He shook his head in sympathy. "He's hunting her all over the place. It's only a matter of time. I looked him up, he's real hardcore! A several level, high master. He wants honour restored to his craft — and to his school. Hundreds of students and Mei Huan was the only one to go astray."

They all turned to look at him. The words and his tone revealed a yet unspoken suggestion.

"She may be coming over to join us within the next few days," he confessed. "She sent someone to ask and how could I say no. Nowhere in Asia is safe now her master is on her trail. She has to get away and I figured, well, the more the merrier."

He took another sip from his glass.

"Of course she knows nothing of our unique situation. She's aware that I work with Robert, or Jingle for that matter, and she's heard that I might have links with Hedgerow Pixie. She asked for my protection and I agreed to only meet with her. We'll fill her in on all the rest once everything checks out." He lifted up both open palms. "But of course all this only goes ahead with your agreement."

All three nodded.

"Fake her death!" Maurice pitched in. "Solves both problems. Help her to disappear, and help her master fully restore the honour of his school!"

"My thinking exactly!" Mr. Magatti quickly responded. "Add a change of identity and everybody's happy!"

A long silence followed, punctuated by the occasional raising of a glass, and the bottle found the aged scotch rapidly being replaced by air.

"She's not having my room!" Maurice suddenly called out.

"Or mine!" Robert added.

Laughter from all four rang out across the wild garden.

Mr. Magatti finally nodded. "We will make arrangements for an extension of the cabin."

"She's not sharing my boat either!" Robert humorously declared.

"Or mine!" Marko added.

All four once again bellowed with laughter.

"I will arrange for another berth and another boat for the newcomer." Mr. Magatti announced. He shook his head and frowned comically. "Kids nowadays are just impossible: so spoiled!" He let out an exaggerated sigh.

Hearty laughter momentarily drowned out all other sounds.

When silence returned, each man slowly sipped their drink while staring at the grey ocean just visible through the wild growth. The island was everything Mr. Magatti had promised; remote, secluded, open rocky beach on one side and buried in wild vegetation over most of the land mass. With barely a twenty minute walk from one end to the other, there was a distinct impression of luxuriating on a growth covered, floating rock.

Maurice eventually broke the silence. "I'm glad Robert turned up on the day at the fountain."

"Abso-raggin-lutely!" Robert heartily remarked.

"Hallelujah!" Marko added.

"And I'm glad he aimed to shoot only at your hand!" Mr. Magatti chimed in. "When we initially expected you would turn up to do the job, his intention was to kill. I was absolutely insistent that we keep you alive! Robert thought it was too risky. I am very glad we did!"

"I'll drink to that!" Robert acknowledged.

They all raised their glasses.

With the gentle sloshing of waves lapping on to the rocks a short distance away, the four men, father and three adopted sons — men with strange code names that if heard by most ears would conjure images of race horses — sipped their drinks and casually enjoyed each others company.

"Carbon Chisel!" Marko broke out in a humorous tone. "That's dorky!"

"Oh is it, really!" Mr. Magatti spiritedly countered. "That from Hedgerow Pixie! Hey, where's your tutu?"

All four once again loosened up with laughter.

"Do pixies wear tutus?" Robert asked in mock curiosity once silence had descended.

Mr. Magatti leaned and pretended to scrutinize Marko's clothing.

"Apparently not!" he responded.

Marko sprayed out scotch, as a belly laugh exploded mid-way through a generous sip. Coughing, and with face twisted in a genuine wince, he pulled out his handkerchief to catch the stray liquor that had trickled out through his nose.

All four men found it exceedingly amusing. The second bottle of whisky was overly lightening the mood.

"At least I didn't ruin Christmas for everyone who knows my name!" Marko jibbed, while gesturing vigorously towards Robert.

Loud laughter rang out across the small island. Liquor infused jesting was infinitely humorous.

When all had gone quiet again, Marko glanced at Mr. Magatti. "You have the coolest code name I have heard in a long while!"

Mr. Magatti took another sip and then nodded slowly.

"I know," he mumbled softly. "I know."

The End

Printed in Great Britain
by Amazon

36252769R00215